SECRETS

Why had handsome, sophisticated Fergus Lynskey come from Ireland to Butte, Montana, to sweep Sky Macpherson off her feet and force her to break up with the man who thought she loved him?

Why had lovely, fragile Midge Treacy, wife of the city's most powerful man, died so suspiciously from what the law was too eager to call an accident?

Why did Sky's own mother stay so silent about her family's Irish past and its legacy of shame and danger that only now was making itself fearfully felt?

Why were there so many lies everywhere Sky turned—and where could she find the truth?

SKY

The unforgettabl
stunning novel t
currents

DEIRDRE PURCELL

Sky

A SIGNET BOOK

SIGNET
Published by the Penguin Group
Penguin Books U.S.A Inc., 375 Hudson Street,
New York, New York 10014, U.S.A.
Penguin Books Ltd, 27 Wrights Lane,
London W8 5TZ, England
Penguin Books Australia Ltd, Ringwood,
Victoria, Australia
Penguin Books Canada Ltd, 10 Alcorn Avenue,
Toronto, Ontario, Canada M4V 3B2
Penguin Books (N.Z.) Ltd, 182–190 Wairau Road,
Auckland 10, New Zealand

Penguin Books Ltd, Registered Offices:
Harmondsworth, Middlesex, England

Published by Signet, an imprint of Dutton Signet,
a division of Penguin Books U.S.A Inc.
Previously published in Great Britain
by Macmillan General Books.

First Signet Printing, March, 1997
10 9 8 7 6 5 4 3 2 1

 REGISTERED TRADEMARK—MARCA REGISTRADA

Printed in the United States of America

PUBLISHER'S NOTE
This is a work of fiction. Names, characters, places, and incidents either are the product
of the author's imagination or are used fictitiously, and any resemblance to actual
persons, living or dead, events, or locales is entirely coincidental.

For Pat Brennan with gratitude.

Prologue

February 1972, Dublin
Trinity burns. The old cobblestones of Front Square are alight with passion as students and ordinary Dublin citizens gather to listen to a powerful denunciation of Bloody Sunday.

Thirteen civilians shot dead by British soldiers in Derry— Londonderry to the Brits.

Speaker after speaker, breath spuming in the foggy, frosty air, parade on to the platform: boys newly become men in the aftermath of shock, girls with women's faces. The smallest and the last is a girl who had been there that day. Who had seen purple dye, then the bullets.

In the center of the crowd, Rupert de Burgh, a young man with curiously light-colored eyes, face waxen in the makeshift lighting, is transported with the fire of this young woman's rhetoric. His friend jammed beside him is so spellbound he cannot even cheer—Rupert can feel him trembling.

Someone at the front lights a rolled newspaper, tossing it in the air. Many hands, black stars against the flame and sparks, reach for it until it splits and sputters out. "They're killing our brothers up there." Rupert's companion turns to him. "Rupert, they're murdering our brothers."

"Come on, Rupert! Come on." He turns and pushes through the press of bodies behind.

"Where? Where are we going?" Rupert pushed on behind him. "She's not finished—where are we going, for God's sake?" His accent is not Irish. Rather, it is upper-crust English. Home Counties' Blue.

"To burn the bastards, burn them out—"

"Burn who?" But Rupert finds he is trembling too. He is panicked—and yet threaded through the fear are strands of joy.

The young woman's rhetoric reaches new heights; all

around, students raise clenched fists, wave their scarves, punch each other's biceps. Rupert's friend is joining in the chant now, louder, louder. "Burn the bastards . . ."

It is taken up by stragglers at the back. *"Burn the bastards."* They turn and run toward the covered archway, which leads toward the street outside. *"Burn the bastards."* It spreads toward the front. *"Burn the bastards . . . Burn the bastards,"* splitting and rippling in a widening V until row after ragged row wheels and runs.

The stewards appointed to marshal the event jump on to the stage in horror. One grabs the microphone: "Come back, come back," he shouts. "Order, please, *order . . .*" Too late. "BURN THE BASTARDS, BURN THE BASTARDS." The crowd has become a mob.

Fergus Lynskey, tall and rangy with floppy hair and a profile like a falcon's, is passing as the crowd pours through the archway through the gate and into College Green. He presses against the railings as the run begins toward Nassau Street, sweeping all in its path. "What's happening? What's happening?" he calls to one after another.

In response, one boy, his face transfigured with joy, waves both fists in the air: "BURN THE BASTARDS!" before running on.

"What's happening?" Lynskey asks a breathless girl with stringy, waist-length hair, who squeezes in beside him to remove her platform shoes.

"I can't run in these," she explains, wrenching at the buckles which hold them round her ankles.

"No," he shakes her arm, "what's happening—why is everyone running?"

"We're going to burn the bastards!" The girl kicks off the first shoe and begins to struggle with the second. Across the road, someone throws a brick or a stone through the front of Cook's travel agency. The shattering of plate glass is lost in the uproar.

"Burn who?" Lynskey, whose Kerry accent is as thick as cream, has to shout to be heard above the roars and screams, the noise of pounding feet.

Another crash as someone throws another brick, this one through the window of Barnardo's, the furriers. "Tell me," he wants to shake this girl, shake someone, "where are ye all going? Burn *who?*"

"The Brits, of course." Breathlessly, the girl kicks off the second shoe and is away, rejoining the stream.

Lynskey, who wants to join the Gárdaí and, confident of getting through the recruitment process, is waiting for the advertisements to appear, hesitates then dodges through the stragglers at the back of the crowd. He heads for the telephone box on the other side of the street, dials 999, passes on the information, then dials again—Store Street Gárda station this time. He asks for a sergeant, a friend to his family. "To the British embassy? They're too late, son." The sergeant is laconic. "The place is already on fire."

Rupert de Burgh, who has lost his friend somewhere along the way, arrives at the embassy, but instead of pushing through to the front hangs back. Watching. Exulting.

Sometime later, it could be ten minutes, it could be fifteen, the authorities are gradually taking control when Rupert becomes aware that a tall young man has materialized beside him. This boy, whose most prominent feature is a long, hooked nose, seems appalled at what is going on. "What do they think they're going to achieve?" He shakes his head and Rupert is glad to be standing in the shadow of a tree beyond the reach of the streetlight so the newcomer cannot see his expression.

A pair of youngsters start to rock a nearby car. "Stop it." The newcomer rushes over and grabs the nearest boy by the scruff of the neck. "Get away out of this—"

The youths, of an age when larger people can still frighten them, run away down the street. "I can't stand this," the hawk-like man comes back toward Rupert. "I wish I was already in Templemore."

"I beg your pardon?" Outside his parents' home, Rupert is always polite.

"Templemore," says the other man. "The training center. I'm going to be a gárda."

As sometimes happens in the most unlikely situations, Rupert de Burgh instantly sees his own future.

Mayville, Montana, June 1992
Sheriff Brian O'Connor, a heavyset man with thick black hair oiled straight back from a low forehead, replaces the telephone receiver and stares at it. Now and then, not more than once a year, maybe, the little hairs stand on the back of his neck. This is one such occasion.

His call had been from Joe Mason of Santa Barbara, California. A plumber by trade and no more than an acquaintance, what Mason had had to say made perfect sense. The time for pussyfooting with so-called "peaceful"—or even protest—solutions to Ireland's problems with England was past. And now Joe tells him that even the IRA, that last line of defense, might be going soft. Secret political talks, for God's sake, with the covert blessing of the yellow-livered, pandering Irish government. If this was true—and it seemed it was—it made a mockery of the reasons for which Pádraig Pearse and his fellow patriot martyrs had died in 1916. It made a mockery of the patience of people like himself, and other patriotic Irish-Americans and Irish-Canadians, who had waited all these years for justice.

The sheriff gets up from his desk and walks across to the window of his office. It is a perfectly ordinary Montana summer day and out there are ordinary automobiles parked in an ordinary lot but his life is about to change. He knows it like he knows his own name. Joe Mason is a member of a select new Irish-American-Canadian group, membership of which is restricted to ten people and is by invitation and personal recommendation only. And, as of one minute ago, Brian O'Connor is a member.

An odd common denominator among the ten is that not one has ever set foot in Ireland. So far.

Chapter One

At the time, the mutiny seemed such a little thing. If she had not flared up that day Sky would never have been switched to the shamrock assignment, might never have made the connections.

The early June day was hot. Hot for Butte, where 80 degrees is a heat wave. So hot that the weatherman on KLFM was forecasting storms. And maybe it was the wet patch on the back of her blouse that was the final straw, that made her jump up from her desk and march after Jim—or Jimbo—Larsen into his office, just seconds after he delivered the flyer.

Holding the piece of paper as though it were radioactive she pushed open his door before he had time to resume his seat. "I'm sorry but I told you last year was the end of it. That I wouldn't do it again." She smiled then, daring her boss to do something. Like fire her. Eight years was too long in the one job, particularly in a two bus town like Butte.

While she waited for him to say something, Sky, as tidy as a hurricane, sniffed with distaste at the disorganization of Jimbo's office, which offered barely space enough for one human, let alone two. The editor of the *Butte Courier* had never been seen to throw out a scrap of newsprint, his own or anyone else's, and he peered out at her from a grotto carved into bluffs of yellowing paper. "We've got to cover it." He seemed caught in disbelief at this unexpected revolt and settled into his chair to argue. "What do you suggest?"

"Send the kid."

This was mean: Lindy, the junior in question, was a beautiful, vague creature whose employment by the newspaper owed more to Jimbo Larsen's long-standing friendship with her father than to her skills, or even ambitions. Sky nurtured a suspicion that, far from paying her, Jimbo was actually accepting money from the girl's father to keep her off the streets. The kid showed flair for dress, however, and for the first time in its sixty-year history, the *Courier* sported an occasional fashion page. "Be good for her." Sky hardened her heart. "She could do with a solo ride."

"Come on!" Jim changed tack, pressed Save on his keyboard in case this proved a long haul. "This isn't like you," he wheedled. "Just once more? I'll do it myself next year—or maybe by that time the kid'll be OK on her own. Where is she, by the way?"

"I'm not her mother—" Sky stopped, noticed the way a spray of sunlight from the window glinted on the bald patch in Jimbo's sandy-colored hair and remembered how long they had soldiered together. She softened a little and studied the press release again as if reconsidering. She knew how important the upcoming rodeo was to the paper: the owner of the *Courier* was also the proprietor of the rodeo ground, and some of the cowboys from his ranch were expected to do well. It was the same every year: the purses were small, but a win, in a state as underpopulated as Montana, translated into prestige because everyone got to hear about it.

Sky had hated rodeos since, as a child, she had attended her first one in Augusta and had egged on the four-legged participants rather than the humans, no matter how skilled. "If I do it, let me ask you for the last time—*if* I do it—will you change your mind and send me to the nationals?" The Montana primaries were imminent and Sky, convinced that nationally this was the Democrats' year and that November would see the end of George Bush, had been campaigning for months to be allowed to join the big boys at the national conventions.

"Get real, Sky, you know there's a squeeze on." Circulation of the weekly had been trickling away. Competition was steep, with titles from other towns and states muscling in, and with the decline in newspaper reading. In some ways, the *Courier* was a victim of its own high editorial standards; Montanans, like the rest of the United States citizenry, tended now to prefer their news and information predigested and in seven-second sound bites.

"No conventions, no rodeo." She widened her smile. The task of the rodeo reporter was to record everyone and everything which moved that day within a five-mile radius of the ground, every breeder, dancer, wrangler, roper, their sons and daughters, mother and fathers, if possible their high school teachers. Each name printed translated into at least one newspaper sale, many more if the named one had relatives and friends out of state.

"That's blackmail!" But Sky could see Jimbo's heart wasn't in it. He hated carrying the dreary lists of names as much as she hated collecting them. "Call it graymail." She dangled the press release between her index finger and thumb. "You know as well as I do that you could do with some good national politics. This state has a stake in this election, you know, and Perot has more support than some around here'd like to think."

The editor glared for a second, then seemed to think better of what he had been about to say. "I'm not hopeful," his long Finnish face, always lugubrious, settled deeper into itself, "but I'll see what I can do."

"Good." Without giving him any further opportunity to slide under her defenses, Sky turned and left the office, making sure the half-glassed door clicked behind her. She knew the chances of her going to the conventions, either in Houston or in New York, were about as good as Dan Quayle's prospects of winning the presidency but she had gone too far now to backtrack. She balled the release and aimed it at the empty trash can across the room. The metal rang satisfactorily. "Good one." She patted herself metaphorically on the back as she slid behind her desk and peered to locate the cursor she had left to flicker in mid-sentence on her screen.

She was writing up her notes on a routine piece about the city's annual water shortage but, after a minute or so, she got up again and crossed to the coffee machine. The row with Jimbo was symptomatic of a deeper discontent. Somewhere, over the course of this spring, impatience with her doe-like existence, which had rumbled under the surface for so long, had erupted to demand action. "R. Sky MacPherson, you're bored, bored, bored, I'm *bored*."

"Hi!" Behind her, she heard the door open. The kid was back.

"How'd it go?" Sky turned around: she had to admit that, given the heat, the girl looked pretty good in cropped T-shirt and tiny skirt, which exposed her long brown legs to sensational advantage.

"All right, I guess." The kid had been sent to interview Butte's newly appointed public librarian. "Look what the cat dragged in." She held up a piece of brown paper, tightly folded to the shape of a small rectangle on which were scrawled in vivid purple the words *Edditor. Urjent.* "Some guy gave it to me on the way into the building. Should I trash it?" She held it over the garbage can.

"No." Sky resumed typing. "Bring it in to him. It's addressed to him, isn't it?" *Nice one, kiddo,* she thought with satisfaction, thinking of the editor's reaction. Served him right.

The junior, carrying the paper as though it was on a silver salver, crossed to Larsen's door and knocked, while Sky, sighing, sat back at her keyboard. Ten seconds later, while she was paging through her notebook, she heard the kid come back into the room. "What was it?" She looked up.

"Haven't a clue, he said just to leave it on his desk." The kid sashayed to the coffee machine. "Hot today, isn't it, Sky?"

"Sure is." Sky cut off the follow-up complaint with a burst of furious typing. "Must be at least eighty." She knew the sarcasm was wasted; never having been outside the borders of her home state, this dipstick had no idea what heat was.

Immediately after graduation, in an effort to get away from Montana but most particularly from her mother, Sky herself had spent three years, including three sweltering, sweaty summers, in Chicago as a junior on the *Sun Times.* By contrast to the humidity and discomfort there, Montana heat waves were short-lived, flares of light and balm that were supremely welcome after the long, blue-nosed winters.

The telephone bleated but before she could say "hello," she heard the familiar sound of daytime TV in the earpiece, then, "Is that you, Sky?" Her mother's voice plummeted like lead to the pit of her stomach.

"Yes, Mom?" She grabbed a strand of her hair and tugged until it hurt.

"If you're not too busy this evening, would you take me to Franklin's?" Shopping for gewgaws was one of Johanna's vices. The Ben Franklin chain, with its enormous range of goods ranging across hair ornaments, dried flower baskets, hideous sweats, dinky stationery and sports equipment, called to her like a siren. "Aren't you meeting the girls tonight, Mom?" Sky was falsely gay. The "girls," in their fifties, were the relicts of her mother's past, two divorced matrons who, like Johanna herself, persisted with incense, dirndls and long hair.

"Buffy can't make it, her son's coming in from Wisconsin." Johanna's voice was charming, low-pitched and retained its Irish lilt, and it drove Sky through the roof.

She pulled the hair tighter, stretching the skin on her forehead until it felt as though it was going to tear. "What about Hermana?"

"She's menopausal today. So will you drive me?"

"I wish you'd learn to drive, Mom."

"You know I can't master machines, Sky. Some people are just not meant to know about machines."

Sky gritted her teeth. "What do you need from Franklin's?" In her present mood she dreaded gliding down those wide, somnolent aisles in the wake of her mother, who always fell into a sort of trance the moment she pushed through the store's offer-clad doors. "You know there's a perfectly good store within walking distance of the house. Anyway, Mom," she improvised, "as it turns out, I may have to work."

"Well, golly, why didn't you say? If you have to work, that's all right. I'll keep a nice salad."

"See you later." Sky replaced the receiver and took out her frustration on her keyboard.

All her friends thought her mother delightful. What drove Johanna's daughter to distraction, however, was the assumption that everyone was on the same airy wavelength as she was. The pronoun most frequently used by Sky's mother was "we." Yin, yang, Jung's collective unconscious, mysterious herbs and teas, ginseng, strange powders and remedies recommended by Johanna's friends on the Blackfoot reservation—"we" all subscribed. It was just that "we" had all covered our real selves with phony selves piled on by the false brain-god of Thought. Johanna always turned off the news and *Sixty Minutes* on TV, watched only movies and her daytime soaps.

Knowing she was being perverse Sky's response was to insist on engaging her mother in conversation about every disaster and treachery consuming the world, on eating packet cereals and processed meats packed with E numbers. Yet even these ostentatious and childish ploys did not succeed in raising so much as a pained expression to her mother's unlined face. Johanna listened patiently without interrupting, constructed nourishing and tasty health food concoctions and removed them without complaint if her daughter left them untouched. "We"—including Sky—all knew Sky was in denial. It was just a matter of time before she came to her senses.

Sky read back what she had poured on to her screen and found it was garbage. "A-aaagh!" She swept both hands across the surface of the desk and paper clips, cutting, and Xeroxed press releases cascaded on to the floor.

The junior, surprised at the ferocity of the yell, turned round from her contemplation of the alley outside. "Do you have nothing to do?" Sky picked up the telephone and shot her a venomous glance while punching at the numbers. "Turn down the damned TV, will you?" she hissed into the sound of television glop before her mother could get a word in, then, "It turns out I'm not working, after all."

A storm hit Butte just as Sky and her mother pulled up at the curb near Franklin's, and rocked the little car with a barrage of pebble-sized raindrops. "We can't get out in this, Mom." She switched off the useless wipers. "It's forty yards to the door and it would be like swimming up a waterfall. This is no shower either—we'll have to go home."

"Wait just a little." Johanna inclined her head like a child determined on winning over an adult.

"Don't *do* that, Mom. You'll drive me crazy" Sky, who could think of a million better places to be than here, had to restrain herself from knocking her own head on the glass of her window. Her mother fixed her with a cornflower gaze as penetrating as a paring knife. This look was by far Johanna's most effective weapon, simply because it was not a weapon. "And don't do that either." This time Sky did crack the side of her head on the window. "What is it with you! I'm thirty-four years old and a divorcée and you make me feel as though I'm ten and caught with my hand in the cookie jar."

"I'm listening." The older woman's eyes did not blink or waver. "Only you know how you feel, Sky, or why you react like this. We'll go home if you want to."

Sky groaned and lowered her head to the rim of the steering wheel. The storm vibrated through her forehead, wormed a tunnel into her brain. "Mom, I'm going to have to leave again. This place—living at home—it's killing me." She looked over. "It's not you, personally, don't be hurt."

Then, finding herself still held in Johanna's gaze, "All right, it's partly you. It's a personality thing between us but you mustn't take it as an insult or that I don't love you," she heard herself getting worked up, "but you know what I mean—thirty-four-year-olds shouldn't be living with their mothers. No other species on the planet does it. It's the whole thing, Mom, you, Butte, that deadbeat paper. I've got to go somewhere else, be on my own."

Still her mother said nothing. In the livid light within the car, Johanna's dark halo of hair was imprinted against the window, which streamed red and blue from the blurred Special Offer posters on the storefront outside. She was too close, too blameless and, in the end, her silence proved unbearable. Before she knew it Sky had the door open and was outside in the fierce warm rain, blinded, her boyish haircut melding to her scalp. "All right, all right, forget it," she was having to yell above the bucketing, "we'll go inside. Who cares that this is a hundred dollar sweater?" She struggled with the folding umbrella she had picked up on the last Franklin excursion but by the time she managed to raise it it was no longer of any use and she threw it into the Nissan's backseat.

Johanna did not emerge from the car until her polka-dotted foldaway plastic raincoat was fully buttoned and the matching scarf tied under her chin. "Alrighty," she closed the car door with careful attention to the handle, "I'm ready," and smiled with neither recrimination nor triumph.

"Great." Sky took her arm and bundled her ahead toward the store.

They had the cavernous spaces inside almost to themselves. The staff moved through the aisles at a leisurely pace, reticketing and repositioning sale items and taking advantage of their unexpected leisure by calling to one another, their voices taking on a peculiar disembodied quality in the soft whoosh of the air-conditioning.

Sky left her mother and headed back into the rain and then into a nearby coffee shop where she stacked paper napkins into the seat of her moldy plastic chair to absorb the damp from her clothes. Unlike Franklin's, the air here was still and humid and before long she was steaming gently. Determined to suffer, she gulped decaffeinated coffee as flavorful as boiled tractor oil and chewed her synthetic jelly doughnut. She was the only customer and, ignoring the glances from the waitress behind the counter who tried to stare her into hurrying, she forced herself to quieten down and think.

How had she allowed herself to become trapped like this? But, of course, she knew the answer to that. Sky thought of her ex-husband, so loving, attentive, naturally witty—and an alcoholic.

He had been dry when she met him, and stayed dry for the first three months after their marriage, but it did not take long after that for her to learn that the normality was a veneer and that he was severely messed up, not only with drink but with drugs. At the time he had loved her so much, promised her so much, including the carrot—crucial to a girl who had trailed around the western states for so long in the wake of her mother—of living with her in the same place for the rest of their lives.

In many ways, she knew that her ex had done her a great favor. If he had not plunged so low and so quickly, she might still be trying to make the best of things with him, clinging to the hope that things might improve. Unlike the way in which she conducted her professional life, Sky had always shirked confrontation in matters of a personal or emotional nature; no matter how firm her resolve, at the first sight of someone else's hurt or confusion she caved in.

Her misjudgment of her husband's character and behavior had been a severe lesson and it meant that, while she continued to date and was never short of boyfriends, no one since Randy had succeeded in gaining her confidence. Sky considered that she had had a lucky escape and was determined she would never get caught like that again. For almost a year now she had sometimes enjoyed, sometimes endured the on-again-off-again relationship with her present boyfriend. Greg Landos was handsome, big into fishing, hunting, flying his dad's plane any time he could borrow it, and riding in his pickup—on the surface a typical Montanan who thought that only fruity Easterners removed their hats while eating. If conversation was not about one or another of his hobbies he floundered. She was on one of her downslides with Greg, and in her heart, knowing she was being unfair to him, was casting around for some gentle way to move on. It was certainly time. How to do it without devastating him was the problem.

Sky surveyed the dispiriting dregs in the bottom of her Styrofoam cup, as flat and uninteresting as her life: stuck in

Butte, in a job with no possibility of promotion, with a boyfriend who did not interest her. And in a mother-daughter scenario she knew was classic: she could live neither with Johanna nor without her. The only child chains were too strong. If only Johanna had an ugly, brutal, or even parsimonious temperament; if she drank, or was vulgar or had cheap affairs, like other women's mothers, it might have made things easier. But, deep down, Sky knew she took perverse pride in her mother's quirky individuality. She was doomed.

That evening, 350 miles upstate from Butte in the town of Mayville, Sheriff Brian O'Connor was stretched comfortably in the recliner in front of the TV in his untidy living room. The Cubs were slaughtering the Dodgers: Cubs at the plate in the ninth, bases loaded, pitcher winding up.

The telephone shrilled beside him. "Hot *damn!*" The sheriff put down his beer and, keeping his eye on the screen, lifted the receiver. "Yes?"

The Cubs' man at the plate hit one and the home crowd went wild, but something his caller said made the sheriff search wildly for the TV's remote control to kill the cheering. He sat upright to concentrate on what the other was saying. "I see." He frowned after about two minutes, then said, "May I ask who gave you my name?" He listened again, then: "I see. You know I've never done nothing on this scale before—"

The caller obviously interrupted because the color drained slowly from the sheriff's florid face. "*How* much? Could you repeat that? . . . Give me a day or two to consider," he said hoarsely after the other had complied. "I'll see what I can do."

He hung up slowly. This was unbelievable, the opportunity of a lifetime.

He had been worrying about how he was going to raise the five thousand dollars he would need as his contribution to the scheme being cooked up by his new *ad hoc* group of patriotic friends. The budget for what they were planning was modest and was being met largely by one of the Canadian members, a millionaire sexagenarian by the name of Jerry Flynn. However, in the interests of democracy, and on the basis that each member of the group would have more at stake if he contributed financially to the endeavor, everyone was expected to chip in. So far, any time Sheriff O'Connor needed to raise extra cash, all he had ever had to do was to identify and target individuals in his own catchment area for simple blackmail. Nothing moved in his jurisdiction without his knowing so he always had a readily available list of possible victims and an armory with which to ensnare them. He had, however, used his ammunition only when it was necessary to subsidize his meager salary—when he had to buy a new automobile, for instance. It had always proved successful because he had kept the scam small and was not greedy. Five grand was way out of the league in which he had played.

But, out of the blue, here was an invitation to take part in a deal that would not only allow him to pay his dues in one fell swoop but would net him a lot more besides. His telephone caller had been from the state capital, Helena, and although not connected with the group—the deal he was offering was a commercial one—he had given as his introduction someone from that city whom the sheriff recognized as a fellow traveler. It seemed so fitting, somehow, and although he felt a little daunted by the scale of what he was being asked to do, the sheriff liked the clean, quick sound of the operation.

If he accepted the commission, he was to speak only to his contact in Helena who would telephone him from time to time. Otherwise, provided he adhered to a time scale, he had a free hand in how he set things in motion. The job itself, a one-shot lucrative deal, was to find a method of shipping to Ireland a certain body-sized and weighted consignment in a genuine casket, with paperwork. That done, he would be paid immediately.

The sheriff knew that procuring the casket shouldn't be too difficult, given that he was a lackadaisical member of the St. Patrick's Brigade in Butte, an outfit that saw itself as one of those keeping the flame, but which fired up only on St. Patrick's Day. The present incumbent of the presidency was a funeral director, Bill Collins.

He reached for the telephone; he had been given two weeks to get going.

As he waited to be answered, he reflected that the stiff would be more problematic: what he had to find was a corpse with no relatives. Come on, he thought, surprised that a funeral home would not answer more quickly. It was a pity they couldn't just send off one of those famine coffins—

reusable boxes with hinged bases through which the corpse was dropped into the grave. If they were discovered they could always pretend the stiff had fallen out.

The telephone was at last picked up. "Hello, Bill." The sheriff forced warmth into his voice. "When's the next meeting of the old Brigade?" He listened, then: "I know, I know, but I'm busy and Butte's a long ways away. Why don't you all meet up here sometimes?"

A little later on that night, in Ottawa, Canada, investigators with a search warrant were letting themselves into the luxury home of a former government member. The ex-minister, who was in his sixties and now very rich, was vacationing in Europe with his wife.

In a matter of seconds, they had disabled the alarm system with a sophisticated scanner and easily gained access through the front door by inserting what appeared to be a thin, credit card–sized piece of flexible plastic into the door jamb.

Once in, as if they knew exactly where they were going, the four men walked quickly through the sunken living room, their feet making no sound on the thick pile carpet.

Efficiently, they searched a room fitted out as a study, opening every drawer, rifling the neat desk. It took them some time to unlock a large filing cabinet, but one of the dozens of needle-like devices on a key chain yielded results and the cabinet gave up its secrets.

One of these secrets was to have far-reaching effects on both Sky MacPherson and the sheriff of Mayville.

Chapter Two

Almost a week later, on the other side of the world, in Co. Kerry at the southwest corner of Ireland, two walkers were crouched low over the fluttering, struggling body of a small bird. They had come upon it while taking a walk across a remote headland near a beach. The pair, who were on vacation from Dublin city, had no idea what type of bird it was. Long-legged, it was about a foot long from the tip of its thin, curved beak to the end of its tail; its plumage, through which the wind browsed, was dark brown and buff. "Is it some kind of a seagull?" the woman offered.

"I don't think so." The man touched the bird with an index finger. It responded with a pathetic effort to get away, managing to put less than two feet between it and its human knights errant before flopping down again into the boggy grass. "Seagulls are much bigger and stronger looking. And don't they have webbed feet?"

"I dunno. Let's leave it." The woman stood up and tugged at his arm.

"Ah, no, we couldn't do that." The man reached out to stroke the bird, which reacted with a frenzy of wing flapping, producing no forward progress. "I think we should bring it to a vet. The poor thing, it looks all in."

"Suppose it dies in the car?" The woman stepped back as though the very mention of death might contaminate her.

"We'll wrap it up warm and put it in the trunk." Gently, the man scooped up the creature, which offered little resistance. "Take the sandwiches out of my pocket. We'll wrap him in the tinfoil. I've seen the ambulancemen on the telly do that with people who've been in accidents. It'll keep him warm at least and we'll leave a little space so he can breathe."

Gingerly, avoiding the long beak, the woman did as she was bid. As they swaddled the bird, it was so exhausted that it seemed to give up and lay still. "Is it dead?" The woman stepped back again.

"No, I can feel its little heart. Come on, we have to get to Tralee as quick as we can." They walked fast back to the car, trying not to joggle their patient, the man holding it as though it were made of eggshell porcelain.

When they got to the surgery, however, they were too late: the vet opened the little parcel to find the bird dead.

"What is it, Doctor?" The man, who seemed unwilling to leave, stroked the mottled feathers. The woman had waited outside in the car.

"Don't know." The vet, more used to dealing with mange, hoose and foot-rot, looked doubtfully at the pathetic little heap on his table. "Could be a whimbrel or something, but I doubt it. There's a fella up the town, a Dutchman, wouldn't you know, who knows a lot about birds. I'll ask him if you like—after all, you've gone to a lot of trouble."

"You done good. No, don't stay, but thanks for the call, I'll take care of the ambulance and all of that. You go home now to your wife and kiddies. But stay in touch, won't you?" *Yes!* The sheriff of Mayville, who had been moping around his empty house while waiting for his TV dinner to heat up, slammed down the receiver and scrambled to belt on his gun. One week into the two weeks he'd been given and he had still been shy of his corpse. This one looked like a prospect.

The call had come from the cab of a truck that belonged to a bonehead logger of his acquaintance named O'Shaughnessy on whom he kept a file of unprosecuted violations, reasoning that either he or his truck might, some day, come in useful: the man himself as a target for a few extra dollars, his truck for the haulage of something the sheriff might want moved.

While traveling north along 506, O'Shaughnessy had apparently come on a dead hobo half on, half off the road. And a woman, who smelled strongly of booze, maybe dead or maybe nearly dead at the steering wheel of a nearby Volvo.

Right away, Sheriff O'Connor had known who that woman was. She had to be Midge Treacy, lush, wife of Daniel Treacy, one of Butte's most respected and successful citizens. The sheriff had particular reason to know her because, only three weeks ago, the same woman, driving a different Volvo, had almost totaled him and his own newish Buick on the same stretch of highway. Her blood-alcohol count that first night had been over 500. She was—or had been, depending on whether or not she was dead—out on bail for that little package of charges and the case was due to be heard within a few days.

As he raced out to his car, getting soaked in the process, the sheriff could almost feel those little cogs and wheels whizzing round in his brain. And, as he gunned the automobile out of the driveway, he saw an even better prospect than the gods' gift of a hobo's funeral uncomplicated by mourners.

He had not heretofore included Treacy as a possible target for blackmail. Sure, after the Buick incident, he had toyed with the idea of stinging the guy for a few bucks over and above the replacement value but, it being the wife's first offense and no one having been injured in the crash, he knew she would probably get off with a slap on the wrist. As a blackmail possibility Treacy had seemed pretty weak, not least because, in his business dealings, as far as the sheriff had ever heard, the man was clean.

This was the good thing about staying in a small burg like Mayville, one of the reasons he never sought higher office in Helena or Missoula or Butte. Here, he was king. Here, everyone could owe him favors, even a judge and a medical examiner. And those who owed him nothing right now knew that to do a good deed for the sheriff was a sort of investment in the future.

The location O'Shaughnessy had given was less than two miles outside the city boundary. Not wanting to draw attention to himself, O'Connor put on neither siren nor roof lights and, although the temptation to drive fast was strong, tried to keep within the speed limit. Because of the storm there were fewer people about, which was lucky. The sheriff going anywhere was always a matter of speculation in Mayville. If there was trouble, he thought, if there was a big traffic jam, for instance—although at the best of times 506 was not a busy place—he could forget Treacy as a hot prospect for a few bucks and revert to Plan B, by which he would just use the hobo as a convenience to get the use of a casket.

His luck held. He got there so promptly that the traffic jam in attendance consisted of one auto and a pickup, both from out of state. Wipers still swishing uselessly, the Volvo's nose was buried in the metal crash barrier, which had served its purpose by preventing the car from going over into a ravine.

A little way in front of it, the hobo was as dead as last Christmas, his ragged clothes so wet now that they blended seamlessly with the runnels made by the rain on the surface of the highway. "There's nothing we could do for the poor man but the woman's still alive." The long-haired driver of the pickup, who could not have been more than seventeen, was overcome with the drama of the situation as, pushing his streaming hair out of his eyes, he crowded in behind the sheriff as he crouched over the body.

"We didn't want to move the woman, Officer." The woman from the automobile was also pretty shook. "She's in bad shape, she needs to get to the hospital quickly."

"Thanks, lady, I've already called for an ambulance." The sheriff straightened and walked across to the Volvo, stuck his head through the open door.

Midge Treacy was breathing slowly and heavily. Her head lolled sideways on her neck. Blood trickled from her nose and from a cut along her hairline, but otherwise she was as clean as a baby. The stink of booze, however, would knock a person down. "Show's over, folks, clear the highway now." The sheriff withdrew his head. "This is a dangerous spot here and in this storm we don't want to be causing any more accidents."

"Shouldn't you take our names and addresses, Officer? Won't you need us as witnesses?" The woman, who was sheltering under a golf umbrella, looked from the corpse to the sheriff and back again.

"Looks like both you guys are from out of state. You really want to have to come all the way back up here, give evidence, all that expense and trouble? Ain't nothing no one can do for that poor old tramp now. I know the guy, no relatives, no home. He's better off."

"Well, if you're sure . . ." The woman still did not look convinced.

"Of course I'm sure." The sheriff was geniality itself. "Poor old guy," he shook his head sympathetically, "he had no life. And don't worry about the lady, we'll get her squared away." Relieved, the woman went back to her vehicle to be followed by the kid to his. After a last lingering look, both of them drove off.

After their taillights vanished around the bend, the sheriff listened hard, waiting until the sound of both vehicles died away. The accident had happened less than half a mile from where Midge Treacy had almost driven himself and his Buick off the road. Although the blacktop was good, 506, which was narrow and had only two lanes, swooped and twisted treacherously right through the Purcell Range from Libby to Yaak; clusters of little white crosses, Montana's quirky highway markers to denote scenes of fatal accidents, grew along it like spinneys of little ghost trees.

Rain pattered on the sheriff's hat and on the hood of the Volvo. He turned up his collar and, confident no one was around, opened the trunk of the police car, packing the tools and office supplies in it toward the back. Then he walked swiftly to the dead hobo and picked him up. He was skin and bone and weighed as little as a fawn. Water streamed off the dangling arms and legs as the sheriff carried the body to the vehicle and stuffed him in, tidying the hands and feet until he was all nice and neat. He closed the trunk then walked around to the front. It was only then that he radioed for the ambulance.

It arrived within minutes and he acted real friendly. "Terrible thing, terrible . . ." After Treacy's wife had been lifted out and placed in the ambulance, he brought the driver round to the front of the Volvo. "Look at that," pointing to the streaming traces of the hobo's blood on the fender, "that's what musta happened. She musta hit a deer. Easy to do, this weather."

Then it was a simple matter to "discover" old Leon's body in the early hours of the morning while on a routine patrol further up the highway. By that time the sheriff had cleaned him up a little.

The following morning, Sheriff O'Connor put a call through to the offices of Treacy Resources Inc. in Butte. Her boss, said the man's snooty secretary, was naturally at his wife's bedside at the hospital.

"Naturally," the sheriff agreed. Very connubial. He pursed his lips as he called the hospital number. Hobo, shmobo. He had thought about it overnight and the prospect of a little cream from Treacy was just too rich to resist. After all, she'd had two accidents within three weeks: the woman was clearly a menace to herself and society.

Called to the hospital phone, the guy was chilly at first, as might have been expected, but when he heard what the sheriff was proposing, he agreed to meet.

National Headquarters of the Gárdaí in Dublin stands inside a set of gates to one of the biggest and most unspoiled city parks in Europe. A long, straggling building in gray stone, it looks like the barracks it is.

Inside, in one of the meeting rooms, a balding, ruddy-faced chief superintendent was wrapping up his conference. He looked around at the force assembled from various specialist units within the ranks. "That's as much as we can do for tonight, kiddies. I've got to get home." He yawned. Although he was inclined to speak in clichés more suited to the Hollywood movies for which he had a passion than to the sober circles of the force, everyone knew that the verbal style masked a mind as incisive as a scalpel. "I'm in the doghouse already," he continued. "I'd promised the missus I'd take her to the pictures tonight."

As the others started to gather their notes together and pack them away, no one dared offer the truth that the same missus would, no doubt, welcome a night off from the pictures. "We're all agreed now, are we?" the chief superintendent asked one more time. "Lynskey should go to the States."

Everyone in the group, twenty-seven men and two women, returned his gaze and indicated assent. Whatever they thought personally about Fergus Lynskey, none disputed that he was a good policeman. They were an oddly assorted bunch: with the possible exception of the chief super himself and Lynskey, not one would have chosen to socialize with any of the others. Drawn from Special Branch, the Emergency Response Unit, the Anti-terrorist Squad and the Drugs Squad, each member had been hand picked. The group's size reflected the scale of the impending investigation. The chief, whose surname was Daly and who therefore attracted the nickname Joxer, screwed the cover back on to his fountain pen. "How about you, Rupert?" He eyeballed the man directly facing him at the opposite end of the table. "Do you think he should go? As usual you're not saying much."

"No problem." Rupert de Burgh had eyes that seemed to absorb the colors of his surroundings, like camouflage. "We definitely need our own man there." The chief super nodded. He had never liked Rupert de Burgh but no one would have known it. Although the detective was technically an Irishman, having been born here because his mother had been on holiday in one of the crumbling great houses where her relatives still eked out an existence, in the chief super's book he was essentially English. He had lived in England until his late teens. He betrayed little vestiges of his origins now, however: his accent was indistinguishable from that of the educated Dubliner.

Bill Daly was familiar with the contents of his man's personnel file and knew he had come over from London to attend Trinity College in 1971 but had dropped out of academia after only a few months, applying to join the Gárdaí during a recruiting drive early in 1972. He had been promoted rapidly and had proved a good detective, conscientious, punctual, with a better than average record of detections and arrests, which was why he was on this special task force. He was also a bit of a whizz at computers and other electronics, skills which were in high demand. Unlike many members of the Gárdaí, his marriage seemed stable too, which would indicate a fairly well-balanced individual.

So what was it about him? Daly could not identify exactly what made him uneasy about the man: perhaps it was the watchfulness in his peculiar eyes. As the last of the stragglers made for the door, the chief super told himself, not for the first time, that there was no law which said policemen had to be nice guys. There were a few others on the force who could give Rupert de Burgh a run for his money in the lack-of-personality department. "Stay a minute, Fergus, will you?" he asked, as Lynskey followed the group to the door.

Despite Lynskey's easy manner, he was not much more popular with his colleagues than de Burgh. Many of them felt, rightly, that he bucked the rules and got away with it; that he had it both ways, respect and a long rein from the brass while continuing to get all the most active assignments. Whereas the others were frequently assigned to drudge work, Lynskey sailed past the paperwork and was always attached to any group put together to crack something big. He spoke French and German fluently so had traveled widely. His expenses claims were legendary.

Now he sat down again in the chair he had just vacated. Daly and he had met during training in the Gárda depot at Templemore but while one had opted to climb the promotions ladder, the other, who hated more than anything else on earth to be confined to a desk, no matter how prestigious, had resisted all urgings—of his superiors, of his former wife, even of his mother—to go the pen-pushing route, preferring to continue work in the field. Bill Daly was perhaps the only man on the force who knew that lurking under Lynskey's cynicism lay an unquenchable idealism, an unusual trait in an experienced detective. Apart from their friendship, it was why the chief superintendent played favorites with him.

When the door had closed behind the last of the group, Daly looked across his desk at his old friend. "What do you think? What are we dealing with here? I can't see a clear line through this. Is the intelligence accurate?"

"It's a bit murky, all right, but if you ask me," Lynskey stretched and yawned, "with the two situations we're looking at I think one could well be feeding off the other."

The chief superintendent sighed. "Nothing's ever simple, is it?"

"What I don't understand is how, if this guy the Canadians raided is so high up, they could have kept it quiet. I haven't seen anything in the papers about it."

"They chose their time. Apparently he's on vacation. And, as for the second part of what we're interested in, the FBI is pretty good about identifying subversives. If they say there's a new group in town, I'd believe them. And, as you know, they've been watching a few of their own guys for a while now." The chief superintendent paused. "I wish we had the latitude they have when it comes to tapping telephones . . ."

"What worries me, though," Lynskey studied the ceiling, "is who's feeding information from here. It's their timing that bothers me. Seems a bit neat that Ireland is flavor of the month for everyone all of a sudden, especially with—ahem—Operation Omega pending!" He delighted in teasing Daly about the fanciful names he dreamed up for problematic operations.

Daly did not rise to the bait but mulled over what Lynskey had said. "There's no proof there's anyone feeding from here."

"Doesn't it seem a little convenient that this group—if we're on the right track and if it *is* a group, of course—suddenly springs into action just when our friend across the water takes a vagary to come here"—Lynskey watched his boss. "And that they seem to be piggybacking on traffickers—which *is* known here."

"I hate royalty, do you know that?" The chief superintendent spoke with genuine passion.

"Oh, come now." Lynskey, who had been blessed with a long, hooked nose, raised his eyebrows so that he looked a little like a surprised eagle. "You can't blame poor old Big Ears for considering an honest invitation. And go on, admit it. Your so-called Operation Omega will be a lovely test of your security skills."

"I hope that's all it'll be, a test." Daly tugged at his ear, a habit when he was thinking dark thoughts.

"Come on, Joxer, cheer up. You know very well why our political masters are so anxious to facilitate our friend. Photo opportunities, a few nice snaps of firm handshakes and history being made and all the rest of it. Do wonders for our Taoiseach's ailing image. Not to speak of our own dear Minister."

"Why are you so sure there's a leak from here? I've kept it absolutely tight."

"I have what your screen detectives call a hunch." Lynskey grinned.

"All right, you and Kojak!" At last Daly smiled and reached for his jacket, thrown carelessly across the back of a chair. "You'll start with this fella, Treacy in the States. He's been getting a few interesting calls lately. There isn't much time, you know, and I'd feel a lot better if I knew exactly what they were planning. Given what we've been told about their backgrounds, it has to be something to do with bombs and bullets."

"Maybe . . ." Lynskey was thoughtful. "But that's why you're upping the national debt by sending me to America, surely? So I can find out?" He stood up.

"Do you need a lift?" Daly shrugged himself into the jacket.

Lynskey walked beside his friend toward the door. "I'll walk."

"Of all the weekends for that royal so-and-so to decide he wants to come over here." The chief superintendent stopped with his hand on the door handle. "As if we didn't have enough complications with the Association picking that weekend to implement its bloody overtime ban. You know Bodenstown's on as well?"

"Forgot that. I must say Bodenstown doesn't impinge all that much on my consciousness." The cemetery around

Bodenstown church in Co. Kildare, not far from Dublin, is the burial place of the Irish patriot Wolfe Tone. It is the site of an annual June commemoration march at which nationalist convictions and sentiments are reiterated, not only by thirty-two committed county republicans, such as Sinn Féin, but in latter years by some government members. To nationalists, the march to Bodenstown is an important aspirational symbol and, in the more fervid past, from time to time had been banned. "But sure it's not much of a headache these days." Lynskey was fidgeting—he wanted to be off.

"Maybe it's no headache to you," Daly pulled at his ear, "but it is to me. The force still has to be there. So that's even more of us missing from the streets on a weekend when there are three business conventions and the World Irish Dancing championships in the city. Did you know that? The place'll be swarming with pickpockets, our own and uninvited guests. We might as well throw our hats at it."

"I heard," Lynskey's tone was blithe, "but you'll come up with something. That's why you get paid your enormous salary, Joxer, and I'm just a humble foot-slogger!"

At just about that time, a Dutchman in the town of Tralee in Co. Kerry identified the little bird found by the two Dublin vacationers on the grassy headland.

In high excitement the Dutchman, who had access to a worldwide library of bird lore, broadcast the news that they had on their hands a *Numenius borealis*, an Eskimo curlew. A migrant that bred in Arctic tundra, probably in Alaska—although a nest had not been found for more than a hundred years—the species had been hunted mercilessly in the middle of the last century, to extinction, most experts thought, until one or two showed up at the beginning of this century. Since ornithological records began, only six had appeared in the geographical British Isles. And this, the seventh, was the first to be seen for a hundred and fifteen years.

Chapter Three

Obituaries! Sky glanced back at her computer screen with contempt as she poured her coffee. As if she had not written enough of them to last several lifetimes. And this one was turning out to be as interesting as watching paint dry.

It was now just over two weeks since her little mutiny about the rodeo began. As the date for it came closer her defiance rumbled on, under the surface, but as yet she was no nearer getting the go-ahead to travel to the conventions.

The door opened and the kid came in, carrying a high school yearbook. She dropped it on their communal desk. "The stuff you want is about in the middle. Maybe page thirty, forty, something like that—but I wouldn't hold my breath, Sky. There's not much there. If you ask me she was pretty mousy."

Of course there was nothing there, Sky thought. Why would anything go right?

She took the coffee to her desk and stared once again at the dispiriting words in front of her. She was trying to write about Midge Treacy, wife of one of Butte's finest, the powerful Daniel Treacy, who was benefactor to every good cause in the city.

Mrs. Treacy's life, by contrast to that lived by her husband, had been so private as to be almost invisible. According to the paltry few paragraphs Sky had managed to dredge from the newspaper's cuttings library, Mrs. Treacy had been sweet and gentle. But that was about it. For the past fifteen years or so, it appeared she had retired to the couple's hunting lodge in the northwest of the state, and was seen in public only rarely. To fill the space allocated for her piece, Sky had been forced to telephone around for anything she could find.

She found little—certainly nothing that might have been helpful as background for an obituary writer. The only drama in the woman's life had arisen a few weeks back when she had been charged with drunk driving. But the charge had never been heard because of her unfortunate death. Other than that, it seemed that she had led an invisible, perfectly blameless little life.

As drinking habits were hardly an appropriate slant to take in a woman's obituary, and as it seemed to be universally accepted by everyone she contacted that Mrs. Treacy had preferred the silent company of the Rockies to that of so-called Butte society, as a last resort Sky had had to plunder the office thesaurus, regurgitating "charming," "lovely" and "generous" in as many ways as possible. Sighing, she reached again for the despised but well-thumbed volume. Definitely time to move on, she thought again as, on her screen, she deleted "hideaway" and replaced it with "retreat,"

In the early years of her marriage to one of Butte's most prominent citizens, Daniel Treacy and, before she retired to seclusion in her beloved Rocky Mountain retreat, his wife, Midge's hospitality was, if low-key, always generous. As one of Butte's most charming [Sky backtracked and overwrote this with "stylish"] stylish if elusive society hostesses, in those early years she made her husband's guests to their remote but lovely [Never having been in the house and therefore ignorant of what it was like, she highlighted "lovely" and substituted "turn-of-the century"] turn-of-the-century home feel not only welcome but as if

"Even if you're not available for the rodeo, I can assume you're available for this?" Jimbo was beside her, holding out a piece of paper on which was scribbled the time and location of the monthly meeting of the St. Patrick's Brigade. Although the meeting itself was always private and this marking required only the briefest attendance to collect the secretary's notes and handouts, it was one he always assigned to himself. The Brigade took itself seriously, would not take kindly to anyone but the editor. Especially a woman whipper-snapper. "Look, Sky," he dropped the press release on her desk, "I know—we *both* know—you're too good for this rag but there's only the two of us"—he took no notice of the junior's gasp—"and while you're here you'll have to do the best you can. Just like me."

He went back to his office, leaving her to ponder the unfairness of her fate.

Before she went home later that afternoon, Sky took a detour to call into the funeral home where Mrs. Treacy's remains reposed. The piece did not have to be filed until next morning and, if she could not get details about the woman's life to fill the required page, she might as well pad it with descriptions of how serene she looked in death. And maybe she could glean a few apposite sentences from the relatives.

The shingled building stood in a wide alleyway between Porphyry and Silver and not far from Interstate 90, easily found by out-of-towners by virtue of the neon cross permanently lit over its front door. Owned by the Collins brothers, third-generation Irish whose grandfather had coughed his life away underground in the Orphan Girl mine, it was not the biggest parlor in town but quite impressive. Its stained-glass windows and brass door furniture gleamed and Sky, her reporter's eye desperate for detail, noticed that today even the veins of mica and quartz scattered through the freshly raked gravel in the parking bays sparkled as though it had been passed through a polisher.

On the streets outside, the rush hour—or what passed for rush hour in Butte—was betrayed only by the muffled toot of an automobile horn and the alley was quiet, just a handful of vehicles in the bays. She had obviously chosen a valley period in the respect-paying business and, before going in, took advantage of the lull, leaning against her little Nissan to catch a few moments of quietness.

The smell in the alleyway remained impregnated with heat, a soft stew of buttery tar and warm stone, engine oil and the indefinable spice that means city, no matter how big or small the population. For to be strictly accurate, although its residents always referred to it as a city, Butte was barely town-sized. From where she stood Sky could see a narrow vista of its loose folds falling from the end of the alley to the flats below the plateau.

Today there was no breeze, an unusual phenomenon at this altitude, and she pulled at the front of her white cotton blouse to peel the fabric from the damp skin under her breasts. She pushed up her sleeves and, taking off her sunglasses, raised her face to what was left of the sun, hazy and whitish now, as though already capitulating to the yellow thunderclouds piling up to the west.

"Sky! How ya doin'?" She opened her eyes to find Teddy Morzsansky, a school contemporary with whom she shared a desultory interest in photography and who, with his wife, worked in the parlor. "Fine, just fine, Teddy, gathering forces for the next onslaught, you know."

"Sure," he sympathized. "You look sensational, as usual, the tan suits you. So does the length of that skirt. Always loved those legs—sure you won't change your mind and marry me?"

"Tried it, didn't like it!" Sky, unselfconscious, smiled. It was an old joke between them, its familiarity pleasant. It had been a long time since the nine days' wonder of her spectacularly disastrous marriage had cast any shadows. "Anyway," Teddy was a head shorter than she and she rumpled his hair, "I believe Melinda might have something to say." The Morzsansky marriage was reputed to be happy.

"I've always said that guy was out of his tree—what was his name again?"

"You know what his name was. Randy."

"Yeah, Randy." Teddy loosened his tie. "You're here for Treacy, I suppose?" Without waiting for her affirmation, he turned back toward the door. "I'm going off, but I'll come in back with you. Not that there's much to see."

"What do you mean?" Sky unrolled the sleeves of her blouse and rebuttoned the cuffs.

"Casket's already closed . . ." He scanned the sky. "Looks like another storm's about due."

"It couldn't be closed. Isn't there some sort of wake?" Sky was annoyed. Not much she could write about a lidded casket.

"Sealed all right." He ran his fingers through his mussed hair. "It's being shipped back to Ireland, you know."

Sky removed her keys from the ignition. "Was she badly cut up? Is that it?" According to the local reporters' accounts in Libby, Daniel Treacy's wife had been killed when her car tangled with a logging truck on the plunging road between the Treacys' hunting lodge and Libby itself.

"Don't rightly know how bad she looked." Teddy walked ahead of her and pushed at the parlor's front door, then stood aside to let her through. "Did you hear the local news this morning? Truck driver's not to be charged—apparently he didn't have a chance, she was on the wrong side or something. You heard he had a phone in the cab and it was him called for help."

Teddy would never change, Sky thought, as she waited for him to lead her toward the chapel. He had always been a chatterbox—perhaps his cheerful nature helped him through the more dismal parts of his profession.

The inside of the parlor was as well kept as the outside and their feet made no sound on the thick red carpeting of the lobby. "Melinda must've gone to the powder room." Teddy surveyed the vacant reception desk. "She won't be long. Anyway, as I said, I didn't see her, the boss insisted on working on her himself. Stands to reason, I suppose, she being who she is an' all. Looks like your visit's wasted, Sky."

"I'll go on in anyway, now that I'm here." Such was the hush that both had instinctively lowered their voices while he led her into the short corridor that opened to the left of the reception desk. They stopped outside the farthest of four doors and he tapped briefly on it before looking inside. "No one at home except the sti—" Recollecting that, friend or not, he was talking to a reporter, Teddy amended himself. "You're safe. She was driving a Volvo too, you know." He nodded sagely. "So much for those commercials. But you've seen how big those loggers are. Must have been a doozy."

"The casket's very big." Sky searched her memory. Nowhere had she seen anything about Mrs. Treacy's unusual height for a woman.

"It's because it's being shipped. There's an inner and an outer one. There are a lot of regulations about it." They spent a further minute or so chatting about a forthcoming camera circle meeting and then Teddy moved away. "I'll leave you to it—anything you need, you just ask Melinda."

"Thanks." Sky pushed open the door and was immediately struck by the bare look of the place. Given the prominence of Midge Treacy's husband, she had been expecting a vulgarity of floral tributes, but instead, the heavy casket, made of dull metal in battleship gray, was adorned only with one pink rose, placed on the crucifix fixed to the lid. The vases, urns and wreath stands that usually swarmed in these chapels had been removed, as though someone was being either tactful or unwelcoming.

She pulled a miniature tape recorder from a pocket of her

purse. When working on features, as opposed to interviews, she rarely took notes, reasoning that anything worth remembering would stick. She was in such trouble on this one, though, and had such an amount of space to fill that she felt she needed every tiny detail, however unimportant. She listened for a second or two at the door and then, sure she would be alone for a while, took up a position at the foot of the casket, flicked on the recorder and, using verbal shorthand, described to it everything she saw and sensed: "Feeling of being isolated but not alone . . . subdued, pinkish lighting . . . profound hush . . . as if the room—no—it's not the room . . . as if *all* physical matter is sort of on tiptoe . . . waiting . . . For what? . . . Tall twin flicker of candles pooling yellow on smooth gray curve of metal . . . clean lines of the brass—gold?—handles—casket so still, solid . . . density . . .

"Moving closer now . . . One of the pink rose petals on the lid is wider, looser than its sisters, wilting in the stagnant air . . . Inscription on silver plate . . . 'Mary Dorothy Treacy, née Shelton, born 6 April 1943 died 18 June 1992 . . .' " She pressed the pause button to calculate how old the woman had been and was shocked to discover that Midge Treacy had been only forty-nine at the time of her death.

For some reason, the yearbook vintage had not registered and in the single adult photograph she had been able to find Mrs. Treacy had worn an ageless, classic suit and her blond hair had been pulled back from her pretty face in a severe French pleat. Sky was in the habit, when in difficulty with a piece, of not writing the opening paragraph until the rest of the article showed some shape and this was probably how she had managed to overlook her subject's age.

At least now she had a slant—"Killed at a tragically young age . . ."

Now, for the first time, she felt a twinge of interest in the subject of her obituary. This woman had been far, far younger than her husband and that single fact seemed to give her independent life. It suggested wooing and courting and flying in the face of convention—no hint of which Sky had unearthed so far in her research. Could it suggest love out of the ordinary?

Too late now to be speculating. She shrugged and reactivated the recorder. "Moving on again, thick oak—mahogany? teak?—paneling of the room . . . tall wooden crucifix carved in angular, modern manner on its own brass stand in its own corner . . . The absence of flowers is a puzzle . . ." Her back to the chapel entrance as she continued to murmur into the microphone, her concentration was such that over the machine's tiny whir she did not hear the door open.

"May I ask what you are doing, Miss MacPherson?"

Her tape still revolving, Sky turned and was staring up into the eyes of Daniel Treacy. She extended her right hand. "Please accept my sympathy on your loss, Mr. Treacy."

"Thank you." He shook her hand briefly. "Would you mind?" He indicated the tape recorder. In the restricted acoustic of the chapel, his voice was surprisingly strong and resonant for a man thought to be only two years away from seventy. She had seen him before but had never until now noticed, despite the authority he wore like a crown, quite how gaunt he was.

"I'm sorry." Startled but not intimidated, Sky turned off the machine. "I'm writing your wife's obituary and I came to pay my respects."

"I see." He stared hard at her. "Do you usually use a tape recorder to pay your respects?" Sky had noticed before that brown eyes fade less with age than blue, and it was those deep, impregnable circlets of dark brown that were undoubtedly Daniel Treacy's most arresting feature.

"How do you know my name?" she countered, holding his gaze, aware nonetheless of the incongruity of the occasion. "I mean, we've met only a few times, always in company and for very brief periods." She heard her official, reporter's voice.

"I know your work," curt now, "but I also know your family. Your father has a cabin not too far from our hunting lodge in the northwest. And many years ago in Ireland I knew your grandmother Elizabeth."

It was a shock—not only that he knew her father, whom Sky herself saw so seldom that she felt she hardly knew him, but that he had spoken of her mother's mother, whom Sky herself remembered, from her one visit to Ireland when she was a very young child, as a tall, gracious lady of about a hundred years old. That she had clearly not been a hundred years old was demonstrated subsequently in photographs and letters, yet it was still strange to have her referred to by her first name. Yet she knew that most of the Irish in Butte were descended from family in the same small area somewhere in the south of Ireland so it stood to reason that the older generation would know one another. This man, however, unlike many others of Irish extraction in Butte, did not wear his nationality like a badge, a trait which she of all people should understand. Through the years, her own family connection with Ireland had become tenuous: her mother had chosen her friends in Montana from different ethnic minorities.

Unlike many of her classmates of Irish ancestry, Sky had strenuously resisted imprisonment in the tight grasp of what she regarded as the Irish ghetto mentality. Although she went to a Catholic school, she declined to learn Irish dancing and always refused to participate in the parade on St. Patrick's Day. And on the grounds that she supposed only what she understood, she did not contribute time or money to the many collections for the "fight-for-freedom" cause, still espoused by some of the more radical Irish in Butte.

Her memories of that one, far-off visit had faded until they were simply little flashes, like a slowly turning magic lantern: a big feather bed in her grandmother's house in Cork city, a fluffy white hen in a farmyard to which she had been taken on a long, long drive, the smell of a peculiar soda they called red lemonade. Dreadful rainstorms. She had been taken to Ireland to visit her grandmother by her Aunt Goretti, now also just a distant voice on the telephone, albeit only from New York. "We're not a close family." She had spoken without thinking.

"I beg your pardon?" He was startled in his turn.

"Sorry, it appears that I've acquired the habit of voicing my thoughts." Her smile, intended to be rueful, died as she stared into those inscrutable brown eyes.

He was not afraid of silence, waiting for her to form the bridge. "Perhaps we could meet for coffee or something so we could talk?" She had to make an effort not to gabble. "I mean when—after—" gesturing toward the casket, "perhaps it's inappropriate at the moment."

"Perhaps." She could hear no trace of irony or sarcasm. "I'll get in touch. Now, if you'll excuse me?"

Wishing fervently that he had not caught her in the crass activity with the tape recorder, Sky reiterated her sympathies and eased herself out of the chapel.

Outside, the gun-metal sky had overcome the sun, and when she got back into the Nissan she rolled up the windows in expectation of rain. She sat in the cocoon of hot, unmoving air for a few moments, staring at the dash and unable to shake off the impression that she had been in some sort of fight. In the habit of placing every thought and feeling in neat boxes, she tried to analyze this disquiet but could find no label for it.

One thing she did know: she was aggrieved that her mother had not mentioned family acquaintanceship with Treacy. Sure, Sky had given her no opening: her own encounters with the businessman had been so transient as to merit no discussion at home. Yet she felt now that Johanna, who talked a blue streak about all her other friends and acquaintances, might have at least mentioned him. To annoy her mother, Sky picked up a giant-sized pizza on her way home that evening. Larded with pepperoni, anchovies and E numbers, she planned to eat every single piece of it.

She never got to, however, because when she opened the door, Johanna was standing just inside, the telephone to her ear. "Oh, here she is, sorry, hold on a minute, will you?" Johanna was never at ease with the telephone. She liked to see the expression in people's eyes when she spoke to them. "Here she is now," she repeated, holding out the receiver.

"Who is it?" Sky mouthed, as, juggling the pizza, the keys, her laptop and her purse, she struggled to take it. "I don't know," Johanna mouthed back.

"Hello?"

In her surprise, Sky almost dropped everything. The caller was Daniel Treacy and he wanted to meet her for dinner that night.

Chapter Four

"This is strange." Sky's mother watched her daughter's preparations to go out again. "His wife is not cold in her grave."

Since she and her mother had moved into the duplex, Sky had been meaning to do something about the décor in her bedroom: the landlord's taste ran to wallpaper covered in pink rosebuds, matching pink drapes and a green carpet, but every time she came to the point of action, something more important intervened. "His wife is not *in* her grave, Mom," it was typical of Johanna to have no sense of time, "she's still at the parlor. I told you." Sky was less impatient now than defensive but if she had learned anything in her career as a journalist, it was to remain open-minded. So Daniel Treacy's behavior was not normal for a widower so recently bereaved? Not necessarily: the words "normal behavior" applied differently to different human beings. And she could hardly complain since she was the one who had suggested a meeting.

"Mmmm." Johanna picked up a hairbrush and began smoothing her daughter's cap of fine blond hair—an inheritance from her father—and, despite everything, Sky, who had been going to tackle her about Treacy, felt immediately stilled. She suspended her operation with a mascara wand and luxuriated in the sensuous feel, the way her hair rose a little off her scalp in response to the strokes of the brush.

The squalls outside continued to buffet the double-glazing, but within the room she could hear not only the rhythmic shushing of the bristles against her hair but the purring of her mother's two cats, which habitually followed their mistress from room to room, and which had now nestled among the tumbled bedclothes.

Sky still fit an early description of one of her highschool friends: she was a "clean slob." Everything about her person and her surroundings sparkled with cleanliness, but no matter how many good intentions she had, she could never seem to keep her bedroom tidy. Right now, however, because of the premature darkness the lights had been switched on and, bathed as it was in yellowish light, even the clutter all around seemed to have assumed its own surreal beauty.

"Maybe he wants to offer you a job?" Her mother's voice was low as if she, too, was responding to her ministrations with the brush. "I'd be careful, if I were you."

"Why? I'm a big girl now." Sky closed her eyes the better to enjoy the sensations.

"Well—" Her mother stopped brushing for a few seconds as though thinking out what she was going to say next. When she resumed, her voice was a little higher. "We know him a little, dear. Hermana and Buffy and I met him at a St. Mary's fund-raiser and we were a little worried about his aura. So if he's thinking of offering you a job—"

"What job, Mom?" The spell was broken. Sky jerked her head away and worked again at putting on her mascara. "With all due respect, he couldn't be offering me a job, he doesn't own a newspaper. And how come you never said before now that you knew him?" Then she was sorry for snapping. "Thanks for doing my hair."

"Well"—Johanna examined the bristles,—"I still think it's a bit strange. A few hairs here, Sky, maybe a little selenium . . ." It wasn't worth another argument, Sky thought, she would take up the matter of Daniel Treacy and her mother some other time.

She bit her lip as her mother picked her way over heaps of discarded clothes, books and piles of newspapers, and went toward the kitchen; she would also shut up and swallow the supplement. The stuff might even do some good—who knew?

She stood up from her dressing table and kicked a path through the mess to stand in front of the cheval mirror. Not normally vain or self-regarding, she took the opportunity for a critical, full-length look at herself. She had to admit that her skin was still excellent and, even at the age she was, her eyes sported only marginal circles. Maybe her mother's pills and potions did counter all the black coffee and other pollutants she put into her system. She was wearing the best outfit in her closet, a straight-skirted silk suit of dove gray, a color

that highlighted her wheaten hair. Her father had also
donated his rangy physique, long arms and legs, wide shoulders, narrow waist and flat belly, while her mother's contribution had been the cornflower eyes, wide mouth and
prominent cheekbones. But there was that ski jump of a
nose. The lamp on the dressing table cast an oblique light
against it, throwing the bump into relief. That nose belonged
to neither of her parents and, in Sky's opinion, was the
physical cross she had to bear. All through high school and
college, she fought with anyone who could not see the nose
through her eyes, got into the habit of using it to bat compliments away.

"You're so beautiful, Sky."

*"For Chrissakes how could anyone with a nose this
crooked be beautiful? Don't make fun of me!"* At the same
time she could not have borne to have it fixed. Something
about her Catholic education had stuck. *Don't tamper with
God's handiwork . . .*

"Here," her mother was back with a glass of water and two
pills, "in case we forget in the morning. You look lovely,
Sky, you really do. But be careful when you meet him. Dark
thoughts are catching."

Sky covered a retort by swallowing the tablets as her
mother excavated her purse from the mess on the floor.
"Thanks, Mom," she checked that her little tape recorder was
ready, "for everything." She gave Johanna a perfunctory hug
and hurried out.

It would be too much to expect that Daniel Treacy was
responding to her invitation to talk about her own relatives,
she thought, as she gunned the Nissan into the evening
traffic. It was far more likely he wanted to influence her
obituary piece.

Her hunch proved accurate.

He had asked to meet her in the restaurant of the Copper
King Mansion on Granite. She arrived a little early and,
while she waited for him, perused the menu and chatted with
the hostess—younger sister of another schoolmate—
revealing casually whose guest she was. In response to the
girl's barely concealed astonishment, she let it be known
exactly why she was here. The last thing she needed was
gossip about herself.

The mansion, a three-story brick building, which had been
the home of William Clark, the billionaire mining boss, had

been restored to its former glory in the sixties, and its heavy furniture, old silver, crystal and china pieces gleamed with care. The Copper King Mansion represented the height of fine dining in Butte but it was a Monday night and during a brief scan of the dining room, Sky saw to her relief that her fellow diners were all strangers, tourists mainly, most looking uncomfortable in what was, no doubt, the one dressy outfit they had brought with them on vacation.

Through a window, she saw Treacy pull up and park his imported Saab convertible across the street and had to stifle her instinctive reporter's reaction that this was hardly a suitable vehicle for someone that old. She was already building a scaffold of impressions around this man which had nothing to do with the matter under review.

"Good evening." She was now waiting for him inside the door. "I was surprised to get your call."

"Shall we go through?" He seemed unwilling to participate in social niceties and, aware once again of the chilling depths of those eyes, she nodded meek assent.

Their corner table was discreet, with the buffer of an empty one between them and the nearest couple. As they were given their menus, a bus boy hurried over to clear the vacant table of cutlery and glassware.

"I booked both tables." Daniel Treacy had noticed Sky's look of surprise at the boys' action.

"I see." She busied herself shaking out her napkin. Whatever he had to talk about was well planned. "Is this how you always eat? At two tables?"

"Do you eat meat?" He looked up from the menu. "May I order for you?"

"Sometimes." Sky felt she was being bullied but, given the circumstances, decided to allow him to run the agenda. "Yes and yes." She folded her copy of the menu and placed it on the table in front of her. "Please do."

He beckoned for service and ordered lamb for both of them with a bottle of French Châteauneuf du Pape. "I'm assuming this is acceptable?"

"Please, Mr. Treacy." Where was the spousal grief? "I must say at the outset that this is a very unorthodox occasion. I think you must know how unorthodox." Then Sky, who frequently saw the funny side of the most inopportune scenario, felt the treacherous clutch at her chest in response to the question that had shot to the tip of her tongue. She had nearly asked at what time tomorrow was Midge Treacy's flight.

She stifled both the question and the laugh by pretending to cough. "Sorry," she gasped, pouring iced water into one of the glasses in front of her, "I got very wet today, think I must be getting a summer cold."

He watched her in silence while she drank the entire glassful and poured herself a refill. Then, "Yes, it is unorthodox. But I thought I could help you with some of your research. I don't want half-assed speculation about Midge masquerading as fact in the newspapers. Since you seem bent on writing the stuff, I would prefer to talk to you and get it over with and for you to get it right." It was the longest speech she had ever heard from him—he tended to leave public speechmaking to underlings—and she heard echoes of her mother's lilt. He spoke much faster than Johanna, however, with a sense of urgency.

As she had felt earlier at the funeral home, Sky sensed peculiar disquiet in this man. She tried not to think of her mother's warning about auras and about dark thoughts being catching. "Please forgive me, Mr. Treacy," she was not afraid of him and had to show it early, "but I can't help thinking that you are very composed for a man so recently bereaved."

She braced herself for an explosion but none came. Instead, he stared at her for several seconds and, knowing it was important not to flinch, she held his gaze.

The tension broke when the wine waiter held out a bottle for his inspection. "Thank you." Treacy reached into the breast pocket of his jacket and took out a pair of half-moon spectacles to look at the label. "That's fine. Please pour." Then, putting the glasses back in his pocket, "I'm not sure what business my composure or otherwise is of yours, Miss MacPherson, but since you ask, I do not wear my heart on my sleeve. My feelings don't concern your piece about my wife, surely." He was addressing her as though the waiter was not there.

Sky should have felt rebuked but, for some reason, did not. Instead, she continued to wonder why he had asked her here. This whole occasion was so out of kilter as to be bizarre. Of course it was: the man's wife was lying dead less than a mile away covered in lead or steel or whatever that had been used to seal up the poor woman

Yet she felt something deeper going on. If she was to recognize it when it arose, she must suspend ordinary disbelief.
Johanna, she thought wryly, would be delighted with her.

As it stood, she knew hardly anything of any value about
her host, other than what everyone in Butte knew: that
Daniel Treacy had arrived from Ireland nearly fifty years ago
and had never gone back, even for a visit, that he became
rich out of his original mining company, Treacy Resources
Inc., had diversified into lumber and other commodities, had
worked hard, married late—in his mid-forties—had led a private personal life, had supported nearly every charity in
Butte and lent his name to the letterheads of a few of the
health and arts organizations. Up to now, Sky had never been
all that interested in businessmen, preferring to profile or
interview people in other professions or the arts. In her experience, people who were successful at making money
became so because they were single-minded and tended to
cut out everything else, even in some cases, personal relationships. It made for short and boring copy.

The wine waiter was yet another of Sky's acquaintances,
this time from grade school. As he retreated, he raised an
eyebrow behind Treacy's back at the company she was
keeping. She shot him a quick smile. That Butte seemed
more like a large village than a fully grown city frequently
caused her to grind her teeth, but there were times, such as
now, when it was pleasant to have complicitous company.
She redirected her attention across the table. "Was your wife
from the same part of Ireland as yourself?"

"From the other end of the country," he shook his head,
"from north Mayo. Being of Irish extraction yourself, I'm
sure you're as aware as I am that most of the Butte Irish are
from West Cork. Midge felt quite isolated. Mayo people are
as different from Cork people as"—he hesitated, searching
the depths of his wine for an analogy she would understand—"as New Englanders are from Texans or Califor-
nians—or even Montanans."

"I see." But Sky did not. As she well knew, Ireland was
only three hundred miles end to end. How anyone could pos-
tulate that such a tiny geographical distance could make any
ᵇ⁻ᵃble difference was odd. "You never went back? Do you
ᵃNoᵗ old country?"
ment of thatᵗhook his head in a way that precluded develop-
ᵗⁱⁿᵍ ᵒf inquiry. "How is your mother?"

"You did mention my grandmother and my father, but you know my mother too?"

"Only in so far as I know who she is." Treacy let Johanna off the hook.

Their meal arrived and, as she watched it being served, she thought she had better continue with the inquiries about his wife although, if the truth be told, Daniel Treacy himself was turning out to be a far more interesting subject. "While we talk about your wife, would you mind if I recorded our conversation?" She hesitated before taking up her knife and fork. "My deadline is tomorrow morning and I won't have time to recheck anything." For the first time he looked unsure. "It's standard practice, I promise you," she reached into her purse for the machine before he could object, "but if it worries you that the tape is lying around afterward, although I usually reuse them over and over, I'll send it to you or destroy it."

"That won't be necessary. I trust you." He was a man who made quick decisions.

In spite of Sky's best efforts over the fifteen minutes that followed, however, the picture of Mary Dorothy Treacy painted by her widower proved so sketchy that it served merely to arouse curiosity. For instance, how could a man be married to a woman for twenty-four years and not be able to give any plausible reason for her lack of interest in going back to visit her home place and people? Sky's own family might have been cited in evidence but hers was most peculiar. She had always believed that the reason for Johanna's lack of interest in going back home was a symptom of her general come-day go-day attitude to life. Even taking Treacy's word for it that Midge had felt isolated from her fellow Mayo people, as he had maintained, would that not have meant she would have desired even more to go home at least once a year? After all, it was almost a cultural imperative among the Butte Irish, most of whom had far less money and opportunity. In Sky's experience, most of these expatriates managed to scrape together the wherewithal for annual or bi-annual trips to the "old country," and even those of the second and third generation frequently nurtured pipe dreams of settling back there some day. But now, if Daniel Treacy was to be believed, here was equal apathy from himself and his late wife. It seemed that at different times both had shaken the soil of Ireland off their heels for good.

And yet Midge Treacy had felt "isolated."

The story did not gell somehow. Sky concentrated on the staccato answers she was getting to her questions. According to Midge's husband, her life at the hunting lodge seemed to consist mostly of working on watercolors of the surrounding mountains or reading. She got up late every morning, never went shopping and, if she drove at all, it was never farther than the forty miles or so to Libby. The owner of an art supply store there supplied her with materials, and also obliged her by keeping some of the supplements from his own Sunday editions of the *New York Times* so that she could select books and order them from New York and Toronto.

"I'm sorry, there's not much more . . ." The conversation petered out and Treacy speared a small potato. Sky noted that just as her own food reposed virtually intact on her plate, a standard hazard of interviewing someone over a meal, he had not eaten much more than she. Perhaps, given the circumstances, it was understandable. As though conscious of her incipient sympathy, he glanced at her, and she saw an expression in his eyes that might, just might, have indicated a thaw.

Feeling he was giving her a cue, she searched for what she should say or ask. "I heard rumors that you were thinking of running for public office?" Although she had heard no such thing, asking a question from left field was a technique that sometimes freed up a conversation.

Not on this occasion. "Never in a million years. You were misinformed," Treacy closed up again. "And, to get back to the matter in hand, as I'm sure must now be evident to you, Miss MacPherson, Midge lived—*liked* to live—a very, very quiet life and to keep herself to herself."

If the woman was that fond of the quiet life, what was she doing driving alone along a dangerous highway that evening? Something was definitely not kosher here. It was not the time and the place to behave like a public prosecutor, however. "What did she like to read?" Sky put in her mouth a sliver of her meat, virtually cold now, and chewed.

"Popular fiction, mostly, women's novels, that kind of thing." He waved a dismissive hand.

She flushed with indignation but again controlled her tongue. So what if feminism was not his strong suit: the guy was nearly seventy. She swallowed her mouthful, then said, "Where was your wife bound for that night, Mr. Treacy?"

"God alone knows." He sighed. "She was heading south but it was unlikely she meant to get to Butte that night. The accident happened near Mayville, just north of Libby, as you know—maybe she was going there although, as far as I know, she had no friends or acquaintances there. If only I'd been at home at the time. Never mind," he took the first sip of his wine, "life is full of 'if onlys,' isn't it?"

There was no answer to that. "What about your wife's schoolfriends or their relatives?" she asked. "Has—sorry, had Mrs. Treacy kept in touch with anyone anywhere else in the States?"

Again he shook his head. "She went to boarding school in Ireland until she came out here for senior year in high school and, as far as I could see, lost touch with all her classmates soon after graduation. This is why we're bringing her back there. She will be buried in a small village called Crossmolina. All her people are there, and her friends, those who remember her, of course, will have the opportunity to attend. We put the death notice in the Irish newspaper."

"So how do you feel about going back after all this time?" Sky thought she had little to lose by moving the goalposts a fraction. "Of course, it will be a sad occasion—"

"Very." He found something interesting on his plate. "I'll not be staying for very long. I'll be coming back immediately after the funeral—there's some urgent business I need to attend to."

"You won't take advantage of the opportunity to go to your own home, visit with your own folks?"

"I'm afraid there will not be time." He looked up at her at last, his eyes in shadow. "But to forestall your next question, Miss MacPherson, some of my own relatives will no doubt come north for the funeral and I shall visit with them then. Please, could we stop talking about me?"

Sky accepted the reprimand and toyed for a while with her food. She waited for a decent interval while the tape beside her bread plate wound on, recording nothing but the useless clatter in the dining room. "You never had children?" she asked abruptly, as if it had just occurred to her.

"No."

She saw she had touched a nerve but was not to be put off. "Was this a source of sadness to your wife? To Midge?"

"It was her decision. I'm sure you must have enough by now, Miss MacPherson." He looked pointedly at the little tape recorder.

"Nearly finished." Sky was not going to be instructed as to how to conduct her business, no matter how sensitive this situation. "If you don't mind my saying so, sir, I couldn't help noticing that there were no flowers at the funeral parlor—"

"By my request," he interrupted her. "They would have to be left behind. I can't see any purpose being served by transporting wreaths across the Atlantic, can you? And before you ask, that was indeed my rose on the coffin."

She responded to the challenge and went fishing. "How was your wife's health, Mr. Treacy?" She kept her voice level. "We didn't see much of her in town and, as you've outlined, she did prefer her own company in latter years, could it have been because she was, well . . . delicate?"

"Who told you that?" His outrage was genuine and Sky recognized she had crossed the border of what was seemly. "I'm sorry, Mr. Treacy, I meant nothing by it. I realize how painful this must be for you—but there was that drunk-driving charge—"

"I really must insist now that the interview part of this meeting is over." He spoke across her apologies, then recollected himself. "Since you ask, my wife's health was good for a woman in her forties. Yes, there was that one charge. But search if you like, you won't find any other. She did not like crowds or the pollution of the city and chose her own lifestyle, with my full cooperation and enthusiastic support. Now, please turn off that machine."

Sky complied. The woman was at rest now and what had gone on within her marriage was none of a reporter's business . . . yet if the truth be told, her initial astonishment at the extent of this man's cooperation had yielded to the suspicion that he might be clouding the issues surrounding his wife's death. But consideration of that would hold. "I'm truly sorry if I upset you." She put the machine into her purse. "I guess I'm just naturally nosy. Like all reporters, I never have enough."

He stared hard at her, but then placed his cutlery on his plate over the half-eaten meal and sat back in his seat. "I'm sorry I was gruff," he said, "but these past few days, I've been under a lot of personal strain. I'm sure you understand."

"Of course." She smiled into those cold brown eyes. "Sometime in the future, when you feel comfortable about it, I should like very much to do a profile on you, Mr. Treacy."

"Out of the question."

Sky did not argue. There was a story to be told here and some day she would be the one to tell it. "Then would it be possible that I could talk to you some more on a personal basis?" She was undeterred by his grim expression. "I'd find your memories of my grandmother fascinating. My mother has told me a lot, and we do get letters—my grandmother lives in Cork city now, did you know?"

"I did not." He shook his head, took out his spectacles and polished them.

"So would you?" Sky took advantage. "Sometimes it's nice to get another perspective."

"No tape recorder?" He held up the spectacles to the light.

"Definitely not notes, Mr. Treacy. This would be a personal favor you would be doing for me."

"Then perhaps some time in the future—must keep in with the press." He gave her a wintry smile but before she could respond he looked at her half-cleared plate, and went on, "I don't wish to be rude, but I have some friends waiting for me at home, and tomorrow, as you might imagine, is going to be a difficult day. I wonder if you would mind if we skipped dessert?"

"I hate to waste this delicious food but like you, as it happens," Sky indicated his own unfinished meal, "I'm not very hungry. Must be this summer cold." She folded her napkin.

Was content she had scored an opening.

Chapter Five

The air in the small kitchen was cloudy with incense when Sky got home: the Bliss Sisters were in session. This was the name she had given to her mother's trinity of like-minded friends. And, to judge by the number of mugs, used teabags and scented candle stubs in evidence, the group had been in residence for a couple of hours.

"Greg called while you were out." Sky's mother was sitting behind Buffy, massaging her friend's neck. "He says to tell you everything's all set for Friday." He and Sky were going to his parents' cabin on Flathead Lake for the weekend and, while she loved the place, she wished she could go there alone. Buffy, who was holding the two cats on her lap, sniffled and blew her nose but Sky did not feel up to listening to a recital of her woes or of the Bliss Sisters' interpretation of them. "I thought you weren't meeting tonight, Mom?" It was after nine thirty, and since her own room was so untidy, she had been hoping for vacant possession of the dinette table to transcribe her notes and finish her piece.

"We weren't, but it's a crisis. Buffy's son was supposed to come in from Wisconsin," Johanna continued kneading, "but he called an hour before she was leaving for the airport to pick him up. Buffy hasn't seen that kid for fourteen months, Sky. How was your dinner?"

"Young people! Anyone like more chamomile?" Hermana got up from her chair and lumbered to the stove, saving Sky the necessity of reply. In every sense of the word Hermana was the heavyweight of the Sisters: a two-hundred-pound six-footer with chopped hair and a face like a scrubbed dinner plate, her bluff manner hid a huge, marshmallow heart. She was not the brightest of the group: she had looked blank when Sky once asked her if she had adopted her name, the Spanish for "sister," as a homage to feminism. "Chuhheez . . . ! Is that what it means?" Her face had pinkened with pleasure and astonishment. "That's not it, though, Sky. You see Mom and Dad wanted a boy—Herman, you know?" In the moments when she was not being driven crazy by all three members of the Bliss Sisters, Sky adored her. She declined the offer of chamomile tea and turned to leave. "I have to write an article, I'll do it in my room. Take care now."

"You bet." Hermana tore the outside wrapper off a store-bought box of sunflower seed cookies and flung it on the table.

The single-story duplex Sky shared with her mother stood in its own circular lot; the other apartment had been vacant for more than six months, an arrangement which suited them fine because the party walls were paper thin and allowed neighbor-to-neighbor access to the most private activities. For many years, when she wasn't longing to escape altogether, Sky had wanted to move the two of them out but it was all a matter of money. Johanna was without means—her only income came from twelve hours of weekend work in the coffeeshop of a nearby hospital. Her unworldliness, so attractive to everyone else, was another source of irritation: she would wash used paper plates or use the same tea bag ten times over, but then would hand out whatever money was in her wallet to the first bum with an appeal bucket who knocked on her door.

The other members of the Bliss Sisters helped look after her: Buffy, who was a good cook, frequently brought over some food, and Hermana, whose guilt-ridden husband paid alimony way over the odds, now and then "lost" a few dollars somewhere in the duplex, to be found gladly by Johanna as money she herself must have put away some time and forgotten.

Sky's salary kept them in reasonable comfort, but rent increase would have meant serious curtailment of trips to Ben Franklin, and that Sky would not have been able to take her weekends away, with or without Greg. These breaks from her mother and her job were essential for the maintenance of her sanity.

She closed the door of her room, cleared a space on the folding card table she used as a desk and went to work, trying to blot out the murmur of the women's voices from the kitchen. She was ruthless with the piece, writing directly on to her laptop as she transcribed from the tape recorder.

Somewhere within the hour it took her to finish, she became aware that the therapy exercise in the kitchen had wound up, heard the goodbyes and the slamming of an automobile door. Both Johanna's soulmates lived on the Flats, a mile or so on the other side of town.

When the obituary was at last finished, Sky felt sluggish because of the wine she had drunk earlier, so she stood and performed a few stretching exercises, somewhat proscribed because of the lack of space on the floor, and then went down to the kitchen to brew a last cup of decaf.

Johanna was sitting staring dreamily at her own reflection in the dark glass of the window over the sink. Declining the offer of something to drink, she began to wind a strand of her curly hair around an index finger, a mannerism she usually affected when upset. "Tonight's weird, Sky. There's something really strange going on. I haven't thought about your father for ages and now, out of the blue, in he comes."

"In where? Sorry, Mom." Sky's retort had been automatic. "What were you thinking about Dad?"

"Oh, just . . ." her mother wound faster, "he's definitely around. I feel him very strong."

"Come on, Mom, don't be so aggravating." Then Sky noticed that, unusually for her, Johanna looked uncertain. "Want to talk about it?" She poured hot water over the brown powder in her mug and carried the drink over to the table.

"Not really." Her mother's voice was sad. She came and sat beside Sky: "I suppose what brought it on was Buffy and all she's going through. I suppose it's a young man's disease, being casual."

"Is this what you're feeling about my dad?" On her last visit to her father nearly eight years ago, and shortly after she had returned to Montana from Chicago, Sky had found Larry MacPherson alone and blissfully happy, making a living from guiding rich men through the hunting and fishing territory he adored.

Johanna and he, who were members of a commune when they met, had not married, preferring, as Sky's mother always maintained, to preserve untainted memories of their glorious time together. The split had been friendly: Larry, who had been only about eighteen, had hung around until after Sky was born then had drifted northward, first to Alaska, and, having worked his way through northern and western Canada, had come finally to settle near Yaak, Montana, in a corner made by the northern and western borders of Canada and Idaho. Over the years he had sent money—sporadically, but as much as he could afford—right up to Sky's twenty-first birthday. "Do you miss him tonight, is that it?" Sky grimaced at the bitter taste of the decaf and spooned sugar into it from the bowl on the table.

"I don't know how you keep that figure of yours, Sky." Her mother sighed. "No, it's nothing like that, if I had to do it over, nothing would change." Then she smiled. "Guess it's hormones, darling. I'm as menopausal as Hermana."

"Don't talk such nonsense, Mom, this isn't like you."

"I know." Johanna got up from the table and began clearing off the debris. "Must be that storm this evening. Something's about to break—I can feel it—ahh!" She gave herself a little shake. "Sure the apple will fall on the head that's under it, as the old people used to say."

"Less of your Irish blarney." Sky enjoyed these times of truce when, for short periods, her mother did not annoy her as much as she usually did. "Here, this is too hot anyway. Let me help with that." Leaving the coffee, she took the dishrag and used it to sweep cookie crumbs off the table into the palm of her cupped hand. "Listen, Mom . . ." Reluctant to break up the truce, she hesitated as to the best way to broach what was on her mind, then went for it anyway. "Daniel Treacy seems to know a lot about our family. Even Dad. How come you never told me?"

"I never knew he knew your dad." Something about her mother's voice caused Sky to cease operations with the dishrag. She peered at Johanna, who was turned away from her, again staring into the blackness of the lot. She was being unusually evasive. "Mother! What gives here?"

"You know as well as I do, Sky, that the Butte Irish all come from my part of the country. Of course we all know—knew—each other."

Sky sent dates and years flying through her head: if her mother had come here aged sixteen in 1954 and Treacy had arrived forty-eight years ago, in 1944, that would have made Johanna only five and him twenty or so when he had left their home parish. "Why the mystery? Why didn't you tell me this before? You led me to believe earlier this evening that you didn't know the guy—"

"I didn't!" Johanna's indignation was too strong. "You never asked me directly before. It never arose."

"Mom," Sky threw down the dishrag, "I'm sick hearing stories about Lahersheen and all the rest of it, about Grandma and my precious uncle Francey!" Johanna's brother, Francis Sullivan, was the only one of the clan who could have been said to have made good. He was a writer and a rich man, and his visit to his American relations had been long promised. "Look at me, Mom." Sky sank on to one of the chrome and plastic dinette chairs. "I know the names of your ex-neighbors, your horses, cows and dogs, even your goddamn farmyard chickens. How come the name of Butte's most prominent citizen never fell from your lips before?"

"Language, Sky! I told you before, you never asked." When Johanna turned round, Sky saw that her lips were set.

"Don't think it rests there, Mom." She accepted a good-night kiss.

"I'm tired, I'm going to bed." Her mother placed a finger over her own lips. "It's late now, we'll talk tomorrow. Stardust! Moondancer! Come on, you guys!" Followed by the two tail-high felines, she left the kitchen.

Having filed her piece early next morning, Sky informed Jimbo that she was going to the funeral parlor for the removal prayers.

"He was surprised. "All we need are the names of the guy who says the prayers and the chief mourners and we know them already. You don't need to go."

"I'll go anyway, I want to." Sky was annoyed she had mentioned it in the first place.

"Suit yourself." The editor shrugged and picked up his desk telephone.

As she had expected, the funeral parlor was crowded. Although she was in plenty of time for the ten o'clock ceremony, there was no space left in the chapel and she had to stand outside in the corridor, pressed against the wall in the crush. She exchanged pleasantries with other reporters and faces she recognized among the dark suits and chains of office, and wondered where poor Mary Dorothy Treacy was now and what would she think if she could see this parade of respect she had neither sought nor received in life.

Daniel Treacy arrived on the dot of ten, ushered through the throng in the corridor by the officious funeral director.

From her vantage point against the wall, Sky watched his bearing as though she was writing a color piece about him. Immediately she felt like an emotional voyeur. Whatever Treacy's state of mind or heart this morning, he did not want others to see it. His stare was fixed on a point somewhere ahead of him and above the crowd as Bill Collins cleared the way for him into the chapel. One or two of the suits tried to sympathize with him as he passed, but he moved on as though he had not noticed.

As the murmur of prayers began inside the chapel Sky wondered again why her mother had not come. Johanna, although not an official churchgoer, was a great one for the satellite societies and support groups which surrounded all of the Butte religious organizations. She and the Bliss Sisters were always ready to help out with collections and cake bakes, and were frequent attenders at the funerals of those whose relatives they knew only peripherally. "But you knew this man from your home place, Mom." Sky had assumed that her mother would come with her to the ceremony.

"Ah, no, I don't think I'll come today. No." Her mother had concentrated on her bowl of nuts and seeds. "I'll think about the poor creature. That'll be all that'll be necessary."

If proof were ever needed that she should pursue whatever story her mother had about Daniel Treacy and his wife, this was it, but Sky knew that, in her own sweet way, Johanna could be the most stubborn of people and she did not interrogate her any further.

As she heard the prayers in the chapel drone into the final decade of the rosary, she wondered if she should follow the cortége out to the airport. She would quite like to see for herself what procedure was followed—for instance, was the casket just loaded on to the plane as though it was a crate of fruit? Or was there some prescribed ceremonial such as there was with military bodies being returned? On balance, however, she decided not to go: she was now determined to keep Daniel Treacy to his promise of an interview after a suitable interval, and she might spook him if she appeared to be taking too personal an interest in him now.

The prayers ended and Collins, helped by Teddy Morzsansky, cleared the corridor outside the chapel so that the casket could be taken to the waiting hearse. Outside, the alleyway sparkled: chrome, wing mirrors and metallic automobile paint winked and flashed with prisms from watches and jewelry, gold glinted on wrists and in ears, the gravel glittered underfoot. A quick morning storm had lifted the weight from the air and the day now promised perfect Montana summer.

What awaited Midge Treacy in her native County Mayo? From everything Sky knew about Ireland, the cold, wet clay of that country would close over her like a suffocating blanket. Poor woman—Sky turned to watch as the casket was loaded into the back of the hearse—is this what she would have wanted?

She sensed that Daniel Treacy was impatient now to get going, although his features remained frozen as he shook hands briefly, or nodded in acknowledgment of the condolences of his peers, colleagues, employees and their well-groomed wives. As soon as the hatch door of the hearse was closed, he walked briskly to the following limousine and got in. To the super-alert Sky, this haste, too, seemed inappropriate. It was not as though the flight was a scheduled one and they had to catch it: she knew the casket was being carried on Treacy Resources' private plane. It was as though Daniel Treacy had already washed his hands of his wife and wanted to get on with next business.

Like a dark, ragged guard of honor, the crowd parted to line both sides of the alleyway as the hearse and limousine moved slowly away from the front of the funeral parlor. It would be a small, sad procession to the airport and Sky wondered, not for the first time, about the lack of correlation between money and happiness.

She found herself standing beside Teddy and Melinda Morzsansky, the three of them making a subgroup a little apart from those on either side. As the limousine passed, Sky, who somehow continued to harbor the absurd notion that her profession afforded her some sort of invisibility, stared hard into the vehicle to gain a last glimpse of Daniel Treacy. The window glass was slightly tinted but she could make out his face. Just as his eyes met hers.

The small hairs on her forearms rose a little and she knew, without doubt, that her presence disturbed him. So much so that she failed to notice that two of the mourners, appropriately dressed and with neat haircuts, had detached from the crowd and were walking purposefully down the alleyway toward a plain, beige-colored sedan.

* * *

BUY DAD A SIX-PAK!! ONLY $23.95!! The sign shrieked at them from the canopy of a gas station as Sky and Greg drove into Polson, the town which stood at the southern tip of Flathead Lake. The six-pack in question comprised six car washes, some bright spark's idea of a novel gift for Father's Day. "You getting your dad anything for the twenty-third?" She looked across at her boyfriend, whose driving style was casual to say the least. One booted foot on the dash beside the steering wheel, which he held with just one pinkie.

"What?" He removed his hat and, with his arm, mopped his forehead along the line of the sweatband, then replaced it. "You gotta be kidding! Support Hallmark?"

"Relax, relax, I only asked." Sky was not in the mood for discussion or argument. As it happened, she had been thinking of her father even before she saw the sign; the open road—more open, perhaps, in Montana than in any other state—always reminded her of his free spirit. Although not in the habit of contacting Larry on Father's Day, she had been thinking it was time she wrote him a letter. Their last exchange of correspondence had been at Christmas.

"You grumpy or sump'n?" Greg swung the pickup into the parking lot of a grocery store. "This place OK?"

"It's where we always stop, isn't it?" Sky surveyed the store frontage, the piles of watermelon inside the glass, without enthusiasm. "And no, I'm not grumpy."

"Coulda fooled me!" He turned off the engine. "Now move that cute little butt and get me ma vittles, woman!"

"I wish—" Sky stopped. "Never mind." She hopped down from the cab of the vehicle and slammed the door. "Come on, pick yourself a cart and follow me." It would have been too easy to puncture him: Greg's posturing always swelled in direct proportion to his insecurity. Women's silence made him uneasy and she knew she had been unusually quiet on the trip.

Although he had not worked up the courage to ask her, Sky knew only too well that Greg wanted badly to be married. He had had dozens of ultimately unsuccessful relationships with women. She also knew that his apparent inability over the long haul to sustain a woman's interest—despite his physical attractions—bewildered him. The main reason that she always returned to him after trying to walk away was that she could not stand to remember the hurt look in his eyes. He would never be Iron John, but he was straight and kindhearted and to leave him seemed tantamount to branding a puppy with a hot iron. "Maybe you're right, I am a bit crabby. Forgive me?" She took his arm and felt a renewed stab of guilt as she saw the look of relief that crossed his handsome face. Then he had to wreck it. "Course I forgive you, babe!"

"Just do me a favor, please, Greg?" She pulled him around to face her.

"Name it!"

"This weekend, just for once, would you cut out the western shit? And before you ask, you know what I mean, the babe, woman, macho crap. I'm feeling a bit sensitive and it would make things so much easier."

He looked sheepish. Then, after a small hesitation, "Sure. Sorry, Sky, didn't realize it was that bad."

"It's not." Sky did not want to get into it. "Not yet. Just heading it off at the pass, so to speak, OK?" She turned away and walked into the store ahead of him so as not to give him any further opportunity to show how vulnerable he was and make her feel guiltier still.

They stocked up: beer, deli meats and salads, chips, barbecue sauces and charcoal, steaks, sausage, bread, cookies and packs of their secret vice, Snickers bars. As they emerged into the sunlight they carried enough food to provision a small weekend army.

The cabin was eight miles from the town, at the end of a wooded private road. Sometimes, when contemplating the length of time it took to get here from Butte, Sky thought she and Greg must be out of their minds. And yet, no matter how endless the journey to get here or how early the start, on arriving at the house again Sky always marveled at her good fortune in being given access to this magical spot. And there was some comfort in knowing that they were not the only ones who behaved in such an irrational manner, spending almost as much of the precious weekend on the road as at the cabin. A great number of their fellow cottagers were in exactly the same situation. It was the American way.

Greg backed the pickup into a little clearing and they carried the groceries into the house, which was right at the water's edge. The first thing Sky always did on arrival was to open all the waterside windows and doors and walk out on to the sundeck, built on stilts so that to stand at its rail felt like riding the prow of a little ship at anchor. Although Flat-head's shore was full, all lots taken, there was no sense of crowding: zoning was tight here and the house sites were large and heavily wooded. They had been late starting from Butte this morning and already it was getting on for dusk. Barbecue smoke curled through the trees from several fires along the shore. "OK, ba—? Sorry—OK, Sky?" From behind, Greg put his arms around her waist. "Want a Snickers?"

"Sure." She accepted the candy and leaned back into his embrace, hoping he wouldn't ruin the peace by making sexual overtures to her right away. "It's a beautiful evening, isn't it?"

"Hungry?" He squeezed her waist.

"Mmmm." She did not respond physically. "Not yet, this'll tide me over." She unwrapped the chocolate bar. "Let's just stand awhile and enjoy this, it's so lovely."

"Sure." Accepting the reflectiveness of her mood, he stood back a little.

Slowly, savoring its nutty sweetness, Sky munched the Snickers and let the peace of the place infiltrate her soul. As the sun sank below the rim of the hill behind the house, the snowcaps on the Mission range to the southeast glowed pink and a little breeze sprang up to riffle the weeds that came through the boards of the deck on which they stood.

Far out on the rapidly darkening water, engine note no louder than a mosquito's whine, a lone speedboat pulled a skier. Abruptly, the skier somersaulted, a flash of bright blue swimsuit against the dark of the treeline and then was gone. Instantly, the boat slowed and came round in a wide, slow arc, gentle as a moorhen rounding up her chick, then motored quietly to her berth about a quarter of a mile along their own side. As she came near, a dog gambolled into the shallows to greet her, and Sky heard laughter, thinned by distance, as the craft's occupants tied her up and then, raced by the dog, ran up the foreshore. In front of where Greg and she stood, the leaves on a young birch whose roots were in the water shivered silver in the belated wash that had been sent toward it.

Then, one by one, the lights on the docks and in the houses on the shore opposite came on so that the dark collar of trees which fringed their bay was pierced with points of gold. "Happy?"

Greg's breath was warm on her neck. As she turned to kiss him she managed to subdue the niggle. She was definitely happy. For now.

That weekend, like all weekends at Flathead, passed more quickly than any single day in the city. They arrived Friday evening, it was lunchtime Sunday and they were going back. "I wish your hours were more flexible." Greg, who worked for his father's liquor store, had leverage.

"Tell that to the *Courier.*" In spite of her ambivalence about Greg, Sky was as reluctant to leave as he was. "Maybe they could change publication from Wednesday to Thursday to suit us."

"Aw, shucks!" He grabbed for her and she kissed him but then pulled away.

"We'd better get rolling, huh? Won't be home until after midnight even if we leave now, this minute."

"Sure." He turned away to buckle the straps on his backpack and she could have cried on seeing the set of his shoulders. All weekend long he had been on his best behavior, considerate in bed, more gentle than she had come to expect, and she could have nothing to complain about. But pacing around every conversation, like a hungry wolf, was the knowledge that sooner or later the question of their future together would have to be addressed seriously. The animal was there now, yellow eyes glinting with greed, waiting for one of them to let down the fence. They both knew it and each recognized the knowledge in the other. It was breaking Sky's heart—not for herself, but for him.

She was exhausted when she let herself into the duplex at about one o'clock on Monday morning. Johanna had left a light burning over the kitchen stove, signal that there was an urgent message.

Thinking that it had to be from Jimbo, she almost did not bother to go pick it up but then, in case it was an unexpected early marking, walked wearily over to the bulletin board.

Mr. Daniel Treacy called about the interview. You're to call him at his office Monday A.M. See you breakfast, Johanna, XXX.

Her mother had never, ever signed herself "Mom," even when Sky was in grade school and begging that she try to be as like other mothers as possible.

Before she went to sleep, Sky summarized what she knew to date about Daniel Treacy into her tape recorder, a habit she had developed which always ensured that, no matter how fast her brain was racing on the night before a challenging day, she got some sleep. If what she needed to remember was written down or in the recorder, her brain could let go.

"Here goes." She switched on the little machine and dictated to it what she already knew, where to find the other references, who to contact for background.

But then, willy-nilly, she found herself enumerating facts that had been nagging at her about the death of Treacy's wife. "Like, for instance, the newspaper stories say she was driving south, probably to Butte. And that she'd told no one she was coming. But the accident happened in the middle of the night and she couldn't have made Butte without stopping. Where was she going to spend the night?"

She pressed the pause button and decided to summarize what she knew about Midge Treacy. She set the machine in motion again. "One, the woman was very young, much younger than her husband. How did she get here to Montana—to the States, even? What did she work at before she met him?" While the little tape rotated, Sky tried to remember if the late Mrs. Treacy's profession had been mentioned in any of the material she had been able to find. If it had, it had escaped her notice—but, then, she had not been looking for it. She had assumed, like everyone else, that the life of Mary Dorothy Treacy, née Shelton, had been of interest to the general community as "just" a professional man's life.

"Two," she murmured, "when did she get here? He says she did senior year in high school here. So she had to have come as a child. And yet Treacy had said all his wife's relatives were in Ireland and that she went to boarding school over there. Why did she switch schools? Could she have been an orphan? Sent out here? Sponsored?" Again she strained for answers, any hints she might have missed in the obituary research material, but came up with nothing. "Three, only a small detail, why a *pink* rose? It's worth asking. Four—" Sky pressed the pause button. After a few seconds, she clicked the machine off altogether and lay staring at the ceiling. This was supposed to be a personal interview she was doing with Treacy, not an interrogation about his wife. And yet her brain was prompting that his relationship with his wife in life and in death was proving to be what was most interesting about him. The fourth question she had been about to dictate to her machine related to the possible existence of a third party in all this. Could the shy Mrs. Treacy have had a lover? Perhaps she wasn't heading for Butte that night, as it had been put about, but going to meet him? Or her?

And was this the reason that the rose was pink and not red? Treacy knew of his wife's affair? Anyone among those at the funeral chapel who had hung back or seemed particularly grief-stricken? None that she could recall. Sky put her tape recorder on her night-table, turned over and stared through the window at the trees outside. She was letting her imagination run away with her. And now that the woman was dead, was it any of R. Sky MacPherson's business if Mrs. Treacy did walk a little on the wild side?

But as she drifted off to sleep, her brain continued to worry at the question that underpinned all others. Why was Daniel Treacy, the reluctant subject, suddenly so eager to talk?

Chapter Six

"May I take that for you, sir?" The palace official, in full dinner regalia, held out his hand to take the newspaper cutting from the Prince of Wales, who had just finished perusing it. The two men were being driven home from a public dinner engagement at the Guildhall.

The cutting had been given to the Prince after a discussion on ornithology with one of his table companions. Well known as a watercolorist and for his love of the countryside, it was not as widely known that the heir to the British throne was also a closet twitcher, one of that band who will go anywhere in the world at a minute's notice to see a rare species of bird.

Before folding the cutting and putting it away, the official glanced at it: apparently the Irish Natural History Museum in Merrion Street was mounting an exhibition centered around a new acquisition. An Eskimo curlew.

FANCIERS EXPECTED TO FLOCK TO MUSEUM
. . . harassed museum staff are already under siege as fanciers from around the world seek details of when the bird can be seen. "We are very short staffed at the moment," said a museum spokesperson last night, citing cutbacks in the general public service, "and the fact that right now is a holiday period does not help."

Like everyone else, the palace official knew that the Prince was attracted to the holistic, more mystical side of existence and reckoned he would think it not a coincidence that he had been given this information just as he was considering an invitation to go to Dublin for the first time.

The Dublin branch of Amnesty International was hosting a huge international conference. The centerpiece was to be the first European appearance of Naboom Kebele, the Nelson

Mandela of the central African state of Kaman, a country which, after gaining independence from Britain, had just emerged from a period of devastating tribal and civil war. Kebele had been imprisoned for even longer than Mandela and, like the South African, the longer he had been incarcerated the more his cult status had grown. Against immense odds, he had orchestrated a peace movement which culminated, after forty years of unrest, in the signing of an agreement to hold nationwide elections.

The palace official, who was dead set against the visit for security reasons, knew that the Prince held the African leader in such high esteem, despite Kebele's well reported anti-British rhetoric, that he was longing to meet him. He had also expressed the desire many times to visit the Irish republic. But no heir to the British throne had visited Éire— even in a private capacity—since the setting up of the state in 1922, and the official guessed that the Amnesty invitation had been sent as a stunt, that its issuers had not entertained much real hope of it being accepted. The main caveat, as the seemingly endless campaign of violence continued to rage on in Northern Ireland, was whether or not the Irish felt they could guarantee the Prince's safety.

The official sighed as he folded the newspaper cutting and put it away. This would strengthen the Prince's desire to get to Dublin.

The answer to why Daniel Treacy had called Sky was not long in coming.

Next morning, while she waited to be put through to his office, she tried, as she always did, to visualize the scene at the other end of the line. She had been to the corporate headquarters of Treacy Resources before—a modest glass and steel structure at Prospect and Park near the Montana College of Mineral Science and Technology—but always as part of a hack pack, when the company's PR machine wanted the press there for some reason of its own. She had never seen beyond the public spaces. Somehow, she imagined Daniel Treacy's office would be Spartan yet affluent, no-nonsense furniture and technology combined with corporate good taste.

"Thank you for calling, Miss MacPherson." He was on the line.

In the normal course of such a conversation, Sky would

have injected enough warmth into her response to melt the permasnow on the Rockies, but instinct warned her that Treacy could probably detect bullshit at a hundred paces. "You're welcome," she said, in a neutral tone. "I'm delighted you called so soon. I hope everything went well in Ireland."

"Everything went according to plan. It was a sad occasion but life must go on."

"Of course." They were already fencing, she could feel it. "I'm so sorry—did you get back this weekend?"

"Last night." She heard the shutters come down. "Now, about this damned interview."

She wrestled for control. "When would be convenient for you?"

"We could have lunch today. Here, if it would suit you. I could have our people rustle up something."

Sky thought fast. She liked to meet people in their own environment yet, in Treacy's case, she thought the invitation too pat. He was attempting to haze her through the arena, like a cowboy running one of Jimbo's damned rodeo steers. In her hesitation the skirmish was lost and she heard herself agreeing to be at his building at a quarter of twelve the following day. Since she had not much to do this morning, she could easily have acceded to his first suggestion, that she come over right away, but she was not going to yield everything. "The paper goes to bed at noon Wednesday and," she decided to stretch the truth, "I already have some stuff lined up to do for it today so tomorrow would be better."

"Fine. I'll have you collected from reception. Looking forward to it, Miss MacPherson."

She was left with a humming receiver in her hand. "Missing you already ..." she murmured, in a nasty singsong tone, and then had to explain herself to the kid.

By the time she was shown into Daniel Treacy's office, Sky was as prepared as she could ever be about her subject. The depressing result of research conducted through the entire Monday was a slim folder containing PR handouts about Treacy's companies, a few puff pieces from the local press over the years and a sprinkling of three-paragraph cuttings from those few nationals and business organs that had been enticed into Butte by the efforts of the Butte-Silver Bow chamber of commerce. For instance, in 1989 *U.S. News and*

World Report had included a thumbnail sketch of Treacy in its half-page on the "resurgence" of business in the city. The writer had profiled him as "taciturn but effective" and had tagged him and his companies among those to be watched.

Johanna might have been able to help, but all that had greeted Sky when she came into the kitchen before going to work on the Monday morning was another note: her mother had apparently taken it into her head to go visit one of her Blackfoot friends, who had moved in from the reservation and now lived near Helena. She had taken an early bus and asked Sky to make sure to feed the cats in case she was delayed. Which almost certainly meant she was not coming home that night. Sky caught herself being as indignant as though she was the mom.

She had even sought help from the Butte-Silver Bow Public Archives, a well organized source that had proved invaluable to her in the past. By the end of the day, however, she had had to conclude that there was precious little of personal interest available on Daniel J. Treacy who, for the forty-eight years he had lived in Montana, seemed to have been able to exercise remarkable control over everything written about him. Apart from mentions of his birthplace as County Cork, there was nothing of his childhood, education and early life. In other states, this might have appeared more peculiar than it was, but in Montana everyone, or almost everyone over a certain age, had come to the state from somewhere else. The native Montanan of over thirty-five sometimes seemed to Sky as rare as a genuine gold nugget in Hellroarin' Gulch, the mecca for Butte's tourists at the World Mining Camp and Museum.

As she was ushered into his office, she was pleased to see that her guess at his taste in office décor had not been wide of the mark. Except for a framed photograph of his wife— the same one used by the *Courier* over its obituary—Daniel Treacy's office might have been furnished from an upscale office-supply catalog: pale wood and steel, parquet flooring, a large abstract oil in a metal frame. His desk was immaculate. The floor-to-ceiling windows, which ran all along one wall, showed a fairly standard view of Butte—defunct pit-head machinery towering like skeletal dinosaurs over the rows of shingled roofs, the mile-wide slash of the Berkeley Pit beyond, and beyond that again the white-tipped snaggle teeth of the Rockies. "Are you Catholic, Miss MacPherson?"

The question startled her as he came from behind his desk with hand outstretched.

"I'm sure you must know from my pedigree that I am, or at least that I was born that way." She took his hand and he shook hers formally before shepherding her toward the window where a small, white-clothed luncheon table had been set up.

"It's just that from this office, as you can see, I have a fine view of our statue." He smiled widely at her—his smile took years off his face, she saw—which unbalanced her to the extent that she could not decide whether or not he was making fun of her. The 90-foot-high statue of Our Lady of the Rockies, its steel sections helicoptered to the peak that shadowed the city from the northeast, although supposed to be a non-denominational tribute to motherhood, was Catholic Butte's pride and joy, its Rushmore, its Christ of the Andes, visible for miles around and illuminated at night. But hardly what she would have expected as an object of veneration for Daniel Treacy.

"So you have," she murmured, pretending to gaze up at the white figure while waiting for him to make the next move.

"Yes." He held out a chair for her. "Treacy Resources helped out a little with the funding and labor."

The first course, smoked salmon and crayfish, was already laid out, wine cooled in a bucket to one side of the table and, as Sky took her seat, a waiter materialized through a doorway into an annex room without any visible signal from her host. The weather had held and, despite the central air-conditioning, the heat radiating on to her right shoulder and neck from the sunlight that shafted obliquely through the window felt familiar and comforting. She declined wine when it was offered. Her glass was immediately taken away and a tumbler filled with Perrier. This was a class act, she thought, watching Treacy through her lashes. "Shall we begin?" he looked expectantly at her.

"Thank you." Sky chose deliberately to misunderstand him, shaking out her napkin and taking a dainty piece of the smoked salmon. Not wishing to irritate him, however, she made small talk, asking him general questions about the way his companies operated and meshed, the answers to which she already knew from the research in her briefcase.

"Let's cut to the chase, shall we?" After a few minutes of this, he signaled to the waiter to clear away their plates. "All of this is in the public domain, Miss MacPherson, as I'm sure you know. I was under the impression that you had a different sort of profile in mind."

"I have indeed." Sky took her recorder out of her purse. He frowned but said nothing. "I know I promised no taping," she kept her tone casual while activating the machine, "but I'm sure you can appreciate that writing notes while eating is virtually impossible and holds up the proceedings. And since you're such a busy man . . ."

"Go ahead." He stared into his consommé.

Although she was burning to know why he was coming out of the woodwork now, of all times, she hoped this would become clear in the course of the conversation and began with his childhood. After a few minutes this seemed to have been the usual stuff of the Irish immigrant, shoeless, four-in-a-bed large family, small farm, tiny fishing village, education truncated by lack of funds and opportunity. It was textbook *Quiet Man* or that other bible of the Butte Irish, *Man of Aran,* and she became impatient. She moved him as quickly as she could through the reminiscences about his hard-working mother and father, his boyhood excursions to catch salmon or shoot rabbits, wishing he would get to the part where he decided to emigrate.

"You seem bored. How much of this do you know already, Miss MacPherson?" he asked suddenly, startling her out of her own train of thought.

"None of it, I assure you." If he saw through her that easily she was losing her touch.

"Not from your mother?" Those merciless eyes missed nothing.

"She never spoke about you."

"I find that hard to believe. Her family and mine lived in adjoining townlands. Treacy Resources has not been hiding its light under a bushel—there have been photographs of me in the newspapers from time to time."

Always the same ones and carefully controlled, Sky thought. "My mother and I moved to Butte only eight years ago," she said aloud, "and, forgive me for saying it, the difference in your ages meant that she was only five or six when you moved to the U.S. Anyway, she is a very unworldly woman. The names of businessmen, however prominent, do not feature much in her conversation."

He continued to stare at her and Sky knew that he did not

believe her. What she had said was entirely true—she and her mother had lived in various small towns in the western half of the state before Sky had gone east, and part of the deal between them, if Sky was to come back to Montana after the breakup of her marriage, had been that they live in a city. Butte had been the result. "You don't know my mother," she repeated, "and she never mentioned you until we spoke about you in connection with your wife's death."

"And what did she say about Midge's death?" He was very still, as tense as a length of steel cable, and Sky knew that she must pick her words carefully. She would postpone consideration of this until later.

"She said she would be thinking about your wife."

"Thinking about her?"

"It's how she is. She believes in the Oneness of thought, that sort of thing. That we can all connect somehow. That, in many ways, concentrated thinking about someone is as beneficial to communication as actually being in that person's presence."

"I see." He raised an eyebrow and Sky felt absurdly that she should defend her mother. It was one thing for her to criticize and be skeptical, quite another for an outsider to disparage Johanna's beliefs. "I'm sorry, I'm not expressing it very well. It's not *Star Trek,* but with my own eyes I have seen evidence that extrasensory perception does exist. The telephone ringing a second after you think of someone you haven't seen for ages, that sort of thing . . ."

His expression remained quizzical. "And do you believe something similar, Miss MacPherson?"

This was it. He was on a fishing expedition too. He was afraid she—or her mother—might be psychic. He definitely had something to hide about his wife's death. "I believe anything is possible, Mr. Treacy," she said coolly, "but no, I do not subscribe to my mother's wilder notions."

She had passed the test. He relaxed visibly. "I'm sorry if I appear somewhat on edge." He resumed spooning his consommé. "I'm quite tired, as I'm sure you will understand."

"Of course I do." Sky studied him covertly while she let him rest and the main course was served. His appetite had not improved, she noticed: he had eaten only half of the starter and a third of the consommé. He was good-looking, in an ascetic, Gary Cooper way, with one of those lean faces, peculiar mostly to males, which improve with age. Judging that he would not be the type to indulge in vanity, she did not bother to search for traces of transplants or expensive hairpieces in his springy, iron-gray hair, which would probably have been curly had he not worn it severely cropped.

"Will I do?" He did not raise his eyes from his plate and she had the grace to be embarrassed.

"I'm sorry." She shrugged. "Guess I'm not as good as I think."

"On the contrary, I've long been an admirer of your style. Wasted in this town, if I may say so." Then, before she could respond, "May I ask *you* a question, Miss MacPherson?" He sat back to let the waiter serve small boiled potatoes and broccoli.

"Sky, please. 'Miss MacPherson' makes me sound like a Scottish schoolteacher in *Little House on the Prairie*." She was rewarded with a grin, the first sign of genuine spontaneity since she had become interested in him as a subject. "Very well, Sky, my question is about your name—your byline. You sign your pieces 'R. Sky MacPherson.' I've wondered, now and then, what the R signifies."

Sky, who hated the flower child name with which she had been afflicted by her hippie parents, always told strangers the R stood for Roberta. She felt she had little to lose by revealing it to this man. "I'll tell you if you won't laugh." She raised her chin.

"I promise I won't laugh—shall we eat?" He picked up his knife and fork.

"It's Rainbow." She braced herself for ridicule but none came.

"If you hate it, why not change it? This is America, after all, land of the free and so forth."

"It would hurt my mother too much." She did not accept the bait. "She raised me mostly on her own and I thought I owed her. I used R.S. back east but then I discovered that R.J.s and D.J.s and S.J.s are ten a penny in Montana. At least 'R. Sky' is distinctive. And people here don't seem to worry about it too much."

"Rainbow Sky," he said, without a trace of irony. "That's even more distinctive."

"I think we'd better get back to the interview." She was uncomfortable at the turn this was taking. "I did some research on you."

He inclined his head to indicate he would have expected

as much and Sky, noticing that the tape had run out, reached to turn it over. "Excuse me."

"Look, I asked you here for a reason."

She looked up. His voice had changed completely and his eyes were no longer like agates. "I thought you had." She held his gaze, while flipping over the tape.

"Without that, if you don't mind." He put a hand over hers on the machine.

"On the record, however?" They were coming to the nub of it. His hand was warm and strong but the skin had the papery feel of age.

He hesitated, then: "Is there any median way between on and off the record?" He let go her hand and pointed at the machine. "Such as mutual trust?"

Sky decided to go with it. "You can trust me."

"Very well." He became still again. "Look—this may seem odd to you—"

"I'm thirty-four years old, Mr. Treacy. I'm a Catholic-educated divorcée, who had more than twenty communes and squats throughout Oregon and Montana on my housing list before I was ten. I have a mother who talks to trees and a dropout father who says he loves animals but who shows people where and how to kill moose and bear. I've an alcoholic ex, who lives in his parents' basement. My boyfriend thinks only fairies drink wine and, for good measure, my name is Rainbow Sky. Nothing seems odd to me."

The corners of Treacy's mouth twitched. "When you put it that way . . ."

Sky knew she could not help him further, and waited while he made up his mind. He regarded her gravely for a few moments. "You have your grandmother's hair. Your byline photograph does not do it justice."

Sky, astounded at this turn of events, involuntarily touched her bangs. "I was always under the impression I got this color from my father."

"Your father has ordinary blond hair, American hair. Yours—your grandmother's—is very distinctive. It's called strawberry blond where I come from. As far as I remember, your uncle Francey has it too. How is Francey, by the way?"

"He's fine, as far as I know. We hear from him now and again." Knowing she had to bide her time until he felt able to say what he really wanted to say, Sky had recovered some of her poise. "He struck it lucky, inherited money and married well. He is happy and quite rich." As she spoke, she saw that Daniel Treacy, so sure of himself, so powerful and successful, was now swallowing so hard that his Adam's apple jumped in his throat.

Finally he came out with it. "Actually this is about your— your grandmother. I'm very anxious for news of her. She will be seventy-five years old on the eighteenth of August next, as I'm sure you're aware."

He swallowed again and she had to struggle not to show how astonished she was at his precision. The man had been—perhaps still was—in love with her grandmother. Where did that leave poor Midge? "H-have you continued corresponding with her?" Her stammer annoyed her.

"We have never been in correspondence. And before that stinging intelligence of yours inspires you with your next question," his stare intensified, "I do, did, love my wife." He stopped to let it sink in. Then: "Your grandmother and I were friends of old. I continue to have the Cork newspapers flown to me. I don't want to see Elizabeth's name in the death columns of the *Examiner* without meeting her again." He looked down at his unfinished meal. "However, for reasons I hope presently to make clear, I don't want to go back to Cork. Miss MacPherson—Sky—" He leaned forward, and for a moment she thought he was going to catch her arm so she kept absolutely quiet, afraid to encourage him by moving a single muscle.

"I wonder if you could influence your mother, or perhaps your aunt in Chicago, to invite your grandmother to come to Montana as a treat for her seventy-fifth birthday?" His expression had changed so suddenly that she was taken aback: far from being forbidding and powerful, he looked like a child. "I'll pay all expenses. She need not know this. If you think it would not upset her, I'll send a plane. You could say the whole family saved up."

He saw then he had gone too far too fast. The light in his eyes died and he folded his napkin. "Very well." Now he might have been offering a business deal. "I can see you believe that the private plane is out. It's just that to get to Butte from Cork by scheduled transport is such hard work and she is not in the first flush of youth. Of course, she would have to have someone travel with her. I'd take care of that, too."

"I've no aunt in Chicago." Sky at last found her voice.

"Perhaps you mean Goretti. She moved to New York a number of years ago."

He held up his hand to stop her. "No matter. I can understand quite well what a shock this is to you. And, having disturbed you to the extent I have, I hope you don't mind if I make things even worse. You see, Sky," he picked at a crumb on the white tablecloth, "I can save you a lot of digging around in dusty old files nearly fifty years old. Maybe even a trip to Ireland. All I ask is that you keep an open mind and remember that, although it is a cliché, there really are two sides to every story." His face carved itself into fierce lines. "Are we still in a state of mutual trust?"

Not a muscle, she said to herself, don't move a muscle . . .

"The reason I came to America and have never been back is that, as you have no doubt guessed, I was in love with your grandmother but it couldn't work out."

"I see." Sky recognized his choice of syntax. There was more to come.

"I'm going to tell you something which has not ever been made public in this country, something I have dreaded being made public ever since I came here, although I am quite sure your mother and many of the other Irish with antecedents on the Béara Peninsula—particularly the older ones—well know. You are not the only one with name problems. I changed my name when I got here. My real name is McCarthy."

She frowned in bewilderment. "Is that all?"

"No, that's not all. It didn't work out between your grandmother and me," the tan on Treacy's face was turning yellow as the blood drained from underneath it, "because I killed your grandfather."

She half rose from her seat but this time he put a hand across the narrow table to restrain her. "Ask your mother or any of your aunts, Sky. It was an accident, I swear to you. An accident."

Chapter Seven

Hoping that her mother would have returned, Sky drove straight home, only to find the house still empty. She resisted the urge to call Greyhound and Intermountain for the bus times and instead, reasoning that she had every right to find out what had been kept from her all these years, gave herself permission to go into her mother's room to look through the letters she knew Johanna kept in the bottom drawer of her lowboy.

The drawer, which was deep, was so full it was difficult to open fully and as she tugged impatiently it jerked on its runners, spilling its top layer all over the floor. As well as the personal letters there were old bills and receipts, snapshots, empty envelopes, flyers, junk mail, shopping lists and sheaves of yellowing newspaper clippings. A few of these had been taken from Irish newspapers but most had been carefully culled from Sky's own work and were right up to date. The last piece was her obituary on Midge Treacy.

Never having pegged her mother as a sentimentalist, the unexpected sight of this chronicle of love and pride was unsettling and moving; it was a reminder that no matter how old or confident or successful the child becomes, the mother continues to hold out her arms to assist the first steps of the little baby.

Worse was to come: as she picked a few of the pieces off the floor she revealed underneath a series of snapshots of herself on her First Communion day, all serious smiles and blond ringlets tied up under her white veil. Naturally Johanna had never got around to putting them into an album: "I must sort out my paperwork one of these days," was a constant refrain and yet she always found something far more interesting to do. "Oh, Mom," Sky's throat closed over, "I'll help you with your paperwork—and I'm sorry for all I said to you . . ." although she knew this soft resolve was unlikely to last. She cleared her throat and began the systematic search for clues.

It was not long before her softness dissipated. Although tidiness was foreign to her nature, Sky's work practices were methodical, and half an hour after she started she had several orderly piles all around her on the patchwork quilt which covered the big bed, all the Irish relatives' letters put to one side for sub-sorting. "Grandma, Uncle Francey, Aunt Goretti, Aunt Margaret, Grandma again, Aunt Abbie, Aunt Constance, Uncle Francey, Uncle Francey again . . ." Her lips moved in litany as she went about her task. It emerged that her mother's most prolific correspondent by far was Sky's grandmother. None of these letters covered more than two pages, however, and could hardly be called profound, consisting as they did of straightforward news of the doings of the aunts and of Francey. Not one mention of anything to do with her husband's violent end, and no mention anywhere of Daniel Treacy/McCarthy.

Although it was difficult to have any genuine attachment to someone she had never seen, of all her Irish relatives Sky imagined herself closest to her grandmother, despite the pedestrian nature of the correspondence and occasional telephone calls between them. Like her mother's scattiness, her grandmother's straight, strong script had always been a given in her life, giving her as real a presence in grade and high school conversations as other kids' grandmas. Sky had always thought she had plenty of time in which to make the long-promised adult trip to Ireland. Now, confronted with the fact that the old lady was now seventy-five, she saw that maybe she had not.

Her uncle Francey's letters gave her a shock of a different nature. Quite a few of the envelopes contained personal checks, some for hundreds of English pounds. All, except the two most recent—for two hundred pounds apiece—were hopelessly out of date.

Sky stared at them in disbelief. There had been weeks when she had had to borrow money from Greg to pay utilities and here was this small fortune—she totted up the amount, which came to £3,450, maybe as much as six thousand dollars—lying here all the time. Her recent upsurge of tenderness forgotten, she folded the two good checks and put them in the pocket of her skirt. Her mother would try the patience of a saint.

Francey's letters proved no more helpful than her grandmother's and contained no reminiscences of past lives in Ireland, although they did report on the writer's sporadic trips back to Cork to see his mother. If Francey had noticed that his checks to Johanna had not been cashed, he did not mention it. Too rich, Sky supposed sourly.

Constance's letters, from her sheep station in Australia, were the longest, describing the strangeness of life out there, begging for photographs of the Rocky Mountains to counteract the flatness of where she lived. The other aunts' letters, gossipy but rushed, and which appeared to owe more to duty than the pleasure of corresponding, were no more helpful. It must be difficult, Sky thought, looking at her mother's family relationships spread all around her on the bed, to maintain contact purely through the good offices of the U.S. postal service. Joanna always fell on these letters with pleasure yet never seemed to feel the need to meet in person any of the senders.

It struck Sky then that her mother was not alone in this. That not one of these people seemed to have any need to see the others. She picked up one of her aunt Goretti's letters again: here was Johanna's sister, just down the road, relatively speaking, in New York, not married, no family ties and yet even she had never yet managed to make the long-promised trip West. She had preferred, as she admitted guiltily in her letters, to spend her annual two weeks' vacation soaking up the sun in Florida.

Sky looked again at the outdated checks she had arranged in a fan shape to one side of her uncle Francey's stack; if she had known about all this money she would certainly have insisted that her mother go east. It was not as though Johanna was tied to the house and, working only on weekends, she was free all week. She was not slow in going walkabout on the reservations.

Here was something else that had not occurred to Sky since grade school, when everyone in the class compared family circumstances with everyone else: of her grandmother's six living children—there had originally been eight but one girl had died in an accident and another was missing, presumed dead—Sky was the only grandchild. Margaret, Goretti and Abigail were spinsters, and neither Francey nor Constance, the only two who had married, had had children. Unusual for an Irish Catholic family.

This was a weird bunch she had inherited, although, she thought grimly, her mother would fight her on that one. One of Joanna's more treasured ideas was that birth was not a random accident of genetics; if she was to be believed, we choose to come into existence from some other, ethereal plane we have inhabited since our last earthly outing and, what was more, we choose not only where we will be born but to whom. She had no answer to the question as to where that left the abused and the starving.

So what did that say about Sky herself? Supposing, just supposing, there was an inkling of truth in Johanna's theory, what baby in her right mind, having decided to be born in America, would "choose" to be born to Johanna and Larry and to be lumbered with a name like Rainbow Sky? As she gathered the sub-files of letters into one neat stack, Sky thought it was no wonder she had rushed to stand in front of a justice of the peace with the first man who had appeared halfway normal.

Greg. She looked at her watch. It was still only midafternoon, and it was unlikely her mother would be home before nightfall—it was conceivable that Johanna might even stay away a second night. Sky felt she would go out of her mind if she had to stay in the house and wait.

She bundled all the letters and papers back into the drawer of the lowboy and then called Greg at the liquor store. He was surprised and delighted to hear from her, and yes, he could get off for a few hours. She changed out of her working clothes into jeans and a T-shirt and then, before picking him up, decided to check in at the office, although she knew she had no markings.

Tuesday afternoon, after the paper went to press, was always the slowest of the working week. "Oh, hi, Sky!" The kid was pecking at a keyboard with two fingers; in trawling to find something useful for her to do, Jimbo had hit on making her Letters Editor. Her job was to select some of the most controversial pieces of mail for publication and to type them. Not a very taxing occupation. "Mr. Larsen was looking for you—oh, phooey!" The junior sighed as she examined a broken nail.

Sky checked the board, saw she had no messages and crossed to Jimbo's door. She put her head around it: "You wanted me?"

"Don't forget the shamrock lot. It's tonight."

As it happened, Sky had completely forgotten that she was
to cover the St. Patrick's Brigade meeting and was too keyed
up about her personal affairs to engage the editor in another
argument. Anyhow, the job would take less than ten minutes
if she timed it right. "If that's all, I'll see you tomorrow," she
said as sweetly as she could.

"How was the interview with Treacy?" he called after her
as she left his office.

Daniel Treacy's momentous revelation had put the profile
of him on the back burner as far as Sky was concerned but at
this point she was not anxious to engage the editor. "Fine,
fine," she called over her shoulder, "I'll talk to you about it
tomorrow."

"Please do."

"You bet!" Sky, detecting Jimbo's unusual interest in this
one, registered it, filed it at the back of her mind but did
not stop.

A few miles away, at Mooney airport, the little Horizon Air
plane disgorged its passengers, who had traveled from
Billings. Most were Butte residents, but one or two, like
Lynskey, were coming to the city for the first time.

Most airports at which he had landed exuded a sort of anxious calm: in Butte, he saw, people strolled around the
tarmac, even coming right to the steps of the plane to greet
those arriving. The chief would have loved it: although it
lacked the urgency of wartime, the layout of the airport, the
low scale of the buildings, the little planes would have
reminded him of the closing scenes of *Casablanca*.

He took a cab to his hotel, which rejoiced in the name of
the War Bonnet Inn, and along the way asked the driver to
stop at a drugstore, where he bought a bottle of mineral
water and all the current newspapers they had in stock.

The War Bonnet proved as unexotic as all the other tourist
hotels in which he had stayed in the course of his career, but
it was comfortable and clean and, having unpacked—a
matter of a minute or so since he believed in traveling
light—he lay on the bed and scanned his papers.

One of them, the *Butte Courier,* had what he was looking
for: a long piece on Daniel Treacy's wife. It was written by
someone called R. Sky MacPherson, whose thumbnail picture byline showed her to be as wan and big-eyed as all the

others who posed for these publicity shots. The piece told him very little he did not know already.

Lynskey was tired but refused to sleep just yet. New places always excited him—it was one of the perks of the job. He decided to take a walk.

After Greg dropped her back to the Nissan, which she had parked in the yard behind the liquor store, Sky drove immediately to a telephone. At the other end of the line only her own voice answered her from the duplex.

She debated whether to go home—perhaps her mother would come back in the meantime—before she went to dance attendance on the St. Patrick's Brigade. She felt sticky and disheveled, and could have done with a long shower and clean clothes but decided that, since the job required little more than being a courier, she would not bother. Who cared what the Luddites of the St. Patrick's Brigade thought of her appearance? The only reason Jimbo continued to carry their stuff was because they were advertisers, sponsoring three premium-priced color supplements for Christmas, at Easter and for St. Patrick's Day. He subtly disassociated the *Courier* from the wilder anti-British sentiments behind most of the articles he had to carry in those supplements but the newspaper needed the Brigade's money.

Could she confide her indefinable unease about Treacy to Jimbo? The thought occurred to Sky as she drove slowly across town. The *Courier*'s editor had a finer mind and wider experience than his present job might indicate to an outsider. It had taken Sky the best part of a year after joining the *Courier* to recognize that this man, with permanently furrowed forehead and tired eyes, had once been a whizzkid. Originally from Missoula, with a good degree from the University of Montana and a postgraduate qualification from the Columbia School of Journalism in New York, had worked both for the *News* and the *Post* in Washington—which had led to a healthy contacts book—and had been marked out as a rising star in the profession. But at the age of thirty or so, he had chucked in the rat race, for no good reason that Sky could see except that he had a beautiful wife who was a native of Butte and who could never settle anywhere else. His sons were both at Harvard Medical School.

Jimbo could be irascible and vengeful, as in his marking her to cover the St. Patrick's Brigade, but she had deep

respect for his journalistic instincts. She also liked him—
except for the rare occasions, usually about once a year,
when he went on a monumental bender lasting two or three
days, during which everyone knew to steer clear of him. On
those occasions he would stay in the office and not go home,
rambling on about projects he would do if it wasn't for the
f——ing rest of the world, becoming by turns aggressive and
self-pitying until shortage of sleep and lack of physical
capacity to take in any more booze rendered him unconscious. He would sleep among his paper towers for about
twelve hours and wake up remorseful and ashamed. The rest
of the year he worried over his computer and his calculator
and performed to less than a third of his journalistic talent. In
Sky's view, he had just given up.

Having examined the pros and cons of telling him what
was on her mind, she rejected the idea. Her imagination was
probably running away with her—after all, Treacy had
insisted that the killing in Ireland was an accident—and it
had been almost half a century ago. It was stretching it a
little to connect it with what everyone else accepted was a
tragic auto wreck in understandable circumstances; after
Mayville, the road to the northwest was a narrow, tortuous
nightmare and those logging trucks were monsters. No, she
decided, she would not speak to Jimbo, at least until after
she'd heard her mothers' version of the story and maybe had
done a little more digging into the car wreck that had killed
Midge Treacy.

The meeting of the shamrock lot, as the editor so inele-
gantly termed the group, was being held as usual in a private
room in the War Bonnet Inn on Cornell. Much of what went
on socially in Butte happened either in the Plaza or the War
Bonnet, both run by Best Western.

Sky pulled in in front of the hotel and, because it was not
eight o'clock, sat listening to a country station on the radio
until it was time to go in. She had covered this event a few
times before, when Jimbo had been unavailable, and the trick
was to be sitting outside the room a few minutes before the
end of the meeting to let them think you had been there all
the time.

She had parked in a spot fairly close to the inn's front
entrance and, having killed fifteen minutes or so, was just
about to go in when she spotted the funeral director, Bill
Collins, who was king of the shamrocks for this year,

coming through the entrance door. She shrank down in her seat so he would not see her.

She needed not have worried, Collins looked neither right nor left as he hurried to his automobile. Assuming he had been called away from the meeting to the parlor, Sky, watching through her wing mirror, waited for him to drive away before she got out but was surprised to see that he continued to sit in the driver's seat as though expecting someone to join him.

The minutes ticked by. Then Sky, whose hearing was acute, heard the faint buzz of a mobile phone. She saw Collins pick up the receiver, hold it to his ear for a few moments and replace it. His windows were closed and he had his back to her so she was unable to tell whether he had spoken or not.

She leaned over the passenger seat as though searching for something under it as he hurried past her again and—still without looking around—toward the doorway of the hotel. Just before he went inside, another man, whom Sky did not know, heavyset and with powerful shoulders, came out on the steps and then performed an about-turn to accompany Collins through the doors, as though he had been sent to fetch him back to the meeting.

The call had been by arrangement. Sky laughed aloud: could Bill Collins, good ole daily-communicant Bill with his pious face, conservative suits and lace-up Oxfords, be involved with someone other than his wife? Although it was none of her business, she was charmed: maybe she should run it up the flagpole with Teddy—he'd know.

One way and another, she thought, as she got out of the car, this was certainly turning out to be an interesting day. She was still smiling as she walked toward the front door and did not see the man coming obliquely at her from the side. "Having fun?"

"Oh." She was startled. He was tall and thin with a curved nose that would not have disgraced one of Johanna's friends on the reservation, and fell into step beside her. "You looked as though you were having a great time."

"Are you Irish?" It was a rhetorical question: his voice ran and rilled and could only have been from that country.

"Bingo." He did not offer his name. By that time they were at the door and he opened it for her.

"Thank you." She smiled at him as she passed through. "This your first time in Butte?"

"First time anywhere near the Rockies, actually."

"Well, have a great vacation."

"It's getting better by the minute." His frank stare would have made her blush, had she been the blushing type.

"Thanks again. Goodbye." She walked off toward the room where the meeting was being held but, as she went, was conscious that the man watched her every step of the way.

She got there only seconds before the secretary, an old bat with the thin, pursed lips of the self-righteous, came out with her xeroxed notes. As she handed them to Sky, who was the only reporter there that evening, she looked around as though disappointed. "Anything you'd like me to highlight here?"

Sky scanned the two pages but could see nothing she had not expected: badly phrased calls on President Bush to use his influence with the United Nations and/or on the EC to mount an inquiry into the torture perpetrated by a biased police force on unfairly arrested Catholics, a reiteration of the standard motion condemning the British army of occupation in Northern Ireland, announcements of forthcoming benefits for the families of prisoners-of-war. "Would you like to interview anyone?" The woman sniffed. "Our President, Mr. Collins? Mr. Larsen usually does."

"Yes, that'd be good." For no reason other than she was fed up with this old biddy, Sky decided to ruin King Shamrock's day. If, indeed, he did have an assignation, the assignation would have to cool her heels.

The interview lasted all of five minutes. Bill Collins, although tense enough—Sky was not well enough acquainted with him to know whether or not this was his natural state—seemed delighted to see her. He complimented her on her work and behaved as though he was perfectly happy to settle in all night with her to lead her through the labyrinthine history of the conflict in Northern Ireland.

"I've told Jim Larsen all of this already," he cracked his knuckles, making Sky wince, "but nothing ever appears. I guess I'm just not persuasive enough, but then he's not Irish, not like us."

"This is really wonderful background, Mr. Collins," Sky saw the danger of being cast as a co-conspirator and rushed to cut him short, "but, as you know, the space for the community notes is quite tight. We are a commercial operation, after all—"

"But this is *news*. Why can I never get that across to anyone?"

"I agree it's news, of course it's news, Mr. Collins, but, given everything else I have on my plate, I would not be able to do this story justice."

"Another time, perhaps? I don't think the general run of the American population fully understands what's happening over there in occupied Ireland, Miss MacPherson. They're killing our people, yours and mine. Day after day," he grabbed her arm but such was his intensity that Sky knew he had not noticed he had done so, "it's just terrible. The British propaganda machine is given such a free rein over here. It's all this stuff about 'special relationships', especially since Reagan and Maggie Thatcher hit it off so good!" Gently, Sky extricated her arm and he looked down at his hand with surprise. "I'm sorry, Miss MacPherson, I do get carried away. I know that." He tried to smile. "But as a person of Irish extraction yourself, I'm sure you'll appreciate how frustrating it is for us. We find it very hard to get our message across and we're blocked at every hand's turn. We're not lunatics or fanatics, you know"—he cracked his knuckles again—"but if we got an opportunity from a fine writer like yourself, we could start getting our message into the mainstream of Montana politics. In our own way we're as important out here, you know, as they are in New York or Boston. Every cog turns the wheel."

"It certainly is fascinating and you're right, I don't know half enough about it." Then, fatally, "Maybe we'll get together sometime."

"When?" He caught her arm again.

"I'll call you." Annoyed at herself for giving the opening, she added, "How's Mrs. Collins?" watching for him to blink.

To her sneaky admiration, his eyes gave no more than a surprised flicker. "She's fine, fine—do call me, won't you? Larsen is always promising coverage and never delivers."

"I'll call you," she promised.

And pigs will fly, she thought as she walked back to the Nissan.

Back in the duplex, she took a long, long shower and

then, snuggled up in a toweling robe, emptied her mind of everything to do with work and settled down to read. Greg had given her a present of E. Annie Proulx's *The Shipping News*.

Chapter Eight

The north Mayo rain was colder and wetter in the predawn blackness than at any other time of day. Although it was only half past three in the morning, during mid-June west of Ireland skies lightened around four o'clock this far from Greenwich.

The first part of the job now accomplished and the phone call having been made, bang on time, from the public box in Crossmolina, the Hiace van, white because this was the most common color in Ireland, was nearing the town of Ballina. It wore 1990 registration plates, neither new nor old enough to excite comment, and was being driven at a steady pace just below the speed limit in case there was a nosy Gárda not tucked up in his bed. The van's three donkey-jacketed occupants were jammed close into one another along the front bench seat. They were burly men. Three workers, maybe in construction, going out on an extra early start because of the long daylight. Or fishermen traveling north to Killybegs to catch the tide.

The van's engine was well tuned and the regular swishing of the wipers was the predominant sound in the cab. No one spoke. Perhaps, being Irish, they were not all that keen on grave robbing, after all.

"At last!" Sky threw aside her novel and ran toward the door at the sound of her mother's key.

"Hi, sweetie." Johanna struggled through the door, her arms filled with an enormous package wrapped in brown paper. "How was your day? Come on in, Hermana."

The questions died on Sky's tongue as she saw her mother's friend.

"You sure it's not too late?" Hermana seemed uncharacteristically reluctant as she eased herself through the narrow frame.

"Not at all." Johanna was already in the kitchen and

lowering her burden on to a chair. "Come on in, take the weight off your feet—ooh, sorry, Hermana! You know I didn't mean anything odious by that, darling." Sky's mother giggled then turned to her daughter. "Hermana picked me up from the bus, Sky. I didn't want to call you, thought you might be busy or with Greg or something."

"I was worried, Mom, it's after ten o'clock, you could have called." Sky closed the door and followed them.

"Now, Sky, I'm an old middle-aged lady. Who's going to mug me, for heaven's sake?" Johanna's laugh, as false as a two-dollar bill, echoed from the cubbyhole under the sink where she was foraging for cans of cat food. "The very idea. Here we are, my little ones," cooing at the cats which slalomed around her moccasins, "poor mites, did you miss me? Like some tea, Hermana? Put some water on, Sky."

Sky bided her time, making the tea and bringing it over to the table while her mother's verbal torrent continued to spew all over the can opener and the catfood she was dispensing. Hermana's presence was not serendipitous: Johanna was ducking an interrogation about Daniel Treacy. It was why she had gone away so early, stayed overnight.

Eventually, she wound down and sat at the table with them, still avoiding Sky's eye.

"There's something I want to ask you, Mom." Sky spoke quietly.

"Yes, dear?" Johanna darted a look at Hermana.

"What's in the package?" Annoyed at the confirmation of her suspicion, she decided to keep her mother in suspense.

"It's a rush basket Freda Little Calf gave me." Johanna's relief was almost comical. "Her sister's making thousands of 'em for the tourists. I thought I'd let the cats sleep in it—put in that little blanket Buffy made for me for last Christmas? She wouldn't mind, I'm sure—"

"Mom," Sky was through being subtle, "that's not what I want to know and we all know it. What gives with Daniel Treacy and Grandma? And how come you never told me that was not his real name?"

"Is it not?" Her mother tried her best to sound ingenuous as she busied herself squeezing the last drop of liquid out of her tea bag with the back of her spoon. "My, my! How about that!"

"No, it's not. His name's McCarthy. And you know it as

well as I do. Don't bother to deny it, Mom! So tell me what happened."

"Gracious!"

The fluttering about was getting under Sky's skin but she let her mother be for the time being. "Yes?" She bit her lip.

"It was all a long time ago, dear, and I was so young at the time—let me see, what age would I have been . . ."

"Let me help you, Mom, he's already told me his name is McCarthy. He's already told me he killed my grandfather. But he said it was an accident and he said you'd be able to tell me what happened. Does that jog your memory?"

"It's not *my* fault, Sky, don't talk to me like that!" Johanna found refuge in maternal indignation.

"This is very upsetting for your poor mom, honey." Hermana, whose bulk dwarfed the cheap chair on which she was sitting, almost overbalanced in her eagerness to rescue her friend. "It's something she doesn't like talking about." She steadied herself by catching on to the sides of the table. "Dark things are better left buried, don't you think?"

Sky kept her eyes on her mother's face. From behind came the sounds of the cats' fastidious chomping at their food. "There was a court case," Johanna said at last, "but he was set free, Sky. It was all a storm in a tea cup. Here, kitty, kitty, kitty," she bent to pick up both cats, "good girls, you finished, then?"

Sky counted mentally to three. "Mom?"

"Yes, dear?"

"Please tell me the truth. He says it was an accident. Was it?"

"I think so." Johanna raised the cats' bodies until she was holding them like a furry shield across her chest. "Why don't you write to your aunt Margaret? Or even Goretti? They're much older than I am, they'd remember better. The whole truth is that all I can recall is a great drama in the house one night and then a funeral. My father's funeral. I didn't *know* Daniel Treacy, Sky, I've told you—"

"But you did know, you *do* know, that he was in love with Grandma. And that he killed my grandfather. And then he ran off to the States."

"It wasn't like that—I told you, the judge wouldn't have let him go. "Oh—" Johanna looked to Hermana for support. "It was an *accident,* I'm sure of it. Yes," she nodded vigorously, "it was definitely an accident."

"I think you should write to your aunts, Sky." Hermana patted her friend's hand. "Or, better yet, why don't you call them?"

"I'll have to call them anyway." Sky got up from the table and went to the sink to rinse her cup.

She might have known. Her mother could not face even the tiniest measure of unpleasantness. She let the silence behind her develop, then turned around and said, casually, "By the way, he wants to invite Grandma over here for her seventy-fifth birthday."

"Wow!" Johanna's gasp of excitement was audible. "I was afraid I'd never see her again—it's so expensive to go over to Ireland."

That's your own stupid fault, Mom. Sky thought of all the out of date checks in the drawer. She had had enough: she needed to think things through before she delved into the minutiae of the story or made concrete plans for her grandmother's visit, which was so clearly in the cards now. "I'm very tired, Mom. We'll talk again in the morning."

"Of course, Sky." Her mother looked like a teenager. Sky kissed her cheek, Hermana's too, and left them to it.

It might have been an accident and it might not, she thought, as she closed her bedroom door. Either way, she was going to make a few discreet inquiries about the death of Mary Dorothy Treacy, conveniently out of the way just before her grandmother's birthday. It was a little too tidy to be coincidental.

Long after she turned out her light, she heard the buzz of talk from the kitchen, Johanna's light, excited lilt, Hermana's baritone rumble.

She extracted the story bit by bit from her mother over breakfast the next morning. Johanna was reluctant to resurrect her own mother's colorful past but the bones of the story proved quite simple. Sky's grandparents had had a row late one night, something to do with her grandmother flirting with Daniel McCarthy at a local dance. Things had gotten heavy and out of control, her grandfather had gone out for a walk to cool down, had met McCarthy, who was out shooting rabbits, they'd had words, there'd been a struggle and McCarthy's shotgun had gone off. McCarthy was charged but had been let go.

"That's not too bad." Sky looked at her mother with compassion. "Why the secrecy? You could have told me all this long before now. As a matter of fact, I think it's quite romantic."

Johanna stared at her then. "Well, it was your grandfather, but I suppose since you didn't know any of the people involved . . . For us at the time, though, it wasn't at all romantic, we were marked people in the parish. Not everyone believed Daniel McCarthy was as innocent as he seemed." Johanna looked at her lap. "Or my mother." This last was so faint Sky barely caught it

"What about Grandma?"

"Well, I was a child, I keep telling you. No one in the family ever talked about that time, Sky, maybe now . . ." She looked bravely at her daughter. "Why don't you write to your aunts, like we suggested last night?"

"I will, Mom, but I want to hear it from you."

Her mother looked away. "I do think she loved him, yes." Her voice was small as a child's. "But she got married to my stepfather not too long after."

"He died too."

This brought Johanna's head whipping around. "Much, much later. Mossie Sheehan just fell off a roof. It was an *ordinary* fall—wash out your mouth with *soap,* Rainbow Sky MacPherson!" Her indignation would have been amusing if the subject was not so serious. "Lord save us from journalists, you're all such Dramatic Annies." Johanna took too large a mouthful from her cup and hiccuped. "Sorry—" she hiccuped again, then: "You all see complicated stories in the simplest things! I can assure you, Daniel McCarthy had nothing whatsoever to do with our stepfather's death. He had already been over here for years. I was long gone myself by that time—I didn't even make it home for the funeral."

"Aha!" Sky pounced. "So you've known all along that Treacy and McCarthy were one and the same."

"So what?" Johanna had recovered and the cornflower gaze was much in evidence.

"So, I want to know when did you figure out Treacy and McCarthy were the same. And how come it was never mentioned at this breakfast table?"

"He was at a funeral I attended," Johanna was on her dignity now, "and I recognized him from a photograph my mother kept in a drawer in her bureau at home on the farm.

As far as I know, you never asked me anything about him, Sky, so how was I to know you might be interested?"

Helplessly, Sky looked at her. For a woman who seemed so gentle, her mother always managed to do her own sweet thing.

"He hasn't changed all that much, you know." Johanna settled herself more comfortably—as far as she was concerned, the difficult part of the conversation was over. "And he's quite handsome, isn't he? My, my! After all these years, to think that he still loves her . . ." Her nose crinkled over a sentimental grin.

"Don't change the subject."

"Oh, isn't it sweet!" Like the guileless smile of a child, Johanna's lit her face and was always irresistible. Now she clutched both hands to her kaftaned bosom. "Wouldn't it be wonderful if she still loved him too and they could live happily ever after?"

"It's obvious we're going to have to agree to Mr. Treacy's—Mr. McCarthy's generous offer and have her over here in August." Sky found herself willy-nilly caught up in this geriatric love story. She got up from the table to pour herself another cup of coffee. "Why don't you be the one to make the first move and call her? Don't get too wound up in advance, though, Mom. She's an old lady. She might not want to come, you know."

"A call to Ireland? Oh, Sky, you know we can't afford it."

Slowly, drawing attention to the action as though she were a stage magician, Sky reached for her purse on the kitchen counter and pulled out the small wad of checks. She separated the two that could still be negotiated. "Sign those, Mom," she said softly, "and write on them the following words: "Pay to R. Sky MacPherson.' "

Openmouthed, her mother took the checks and the pen offered with them and did as she was bid.

"I'm not going to say anything about this at the moment," Sky took the two checks back, "but if you don't write this very day to your brother and ask him to replace that lot," she indicated the pile of useless paper on the table, "I will." Then Sky, to whom the telephone was as essential to life as strong coffee, finished the thick brew in her mug. "And make the goddamn call to your mother, Mom. We have four hundred dollars here," she waved the two good checks under her mother's nose, "and, anyhow, it's Treacy's invite. We'll bill him for expenses."

Throughout that day, she was so busy with routine work that she had no opportunity to pursue her private agenda with Daniel Treacy. She typed up the shamrock report and a couple of quotes from Bill Collins, and set up the stories which would pass for news in the next edition, including the hated rodeo. Not that she would cover it, a principle was a principle, but efficient work habits were ingrained. At least the kid or the freelancer or whatever sucker eventually got to report on it would not want for the preliminary research.

She was due to interview one of the planners at City Hall about zoning violations and was immersed in the stack of paperwork on the relevant regulations, when she realized Jimbo was standing at the desk. "Got a minute?"

"Sure." She rose and followed him into his office.

"Tell me about the interview with Treacy." The editor leaned back in his chair and put his feet on the only clear space on his desk.

"It went fine, he's an interesting guy—well, I'm sure you know that." Sky was cautious. Although the story was a scoop of sorts, Jimbo's persistent interest in it alerted her that something out of the ordinary was going on. He usually let her get on with her stuff and made his comments when he saw the copy. Could he know about her personal angle? Or even about Treacy's past?

She dug a little: "I haven't transcribed it yet, Jim, and you know I can't ever judge these things until I've done that. Any particular hurry on this one? I may have to see him again, so if there's anything special you'd want me to ask him . . ."

"Hmmm," he looked through his window, "nothing at this stage. You're talking to him again? That's good. Just stay alert."

"What about?" Then Sky wished she had not asked. Given her family involvement, she would have preferred to have done her own investigations outside the ambit of the newspaper.

"It may be nothing." He looked speculatively at her and, removing his feet from the desk, seemed to come to a decision. "Anyhow," he continued, as though the conversation was already over, "I don't want to say anything which might influence you in the wrong direction. Best to approach these things open-minded. But after you've talked to him again and transcribed your notes, come in and we'll discuss it. Before you write up your piece."

Sky was almost through the doorway when his voice stopped her again. "Did he talk much about his wife?"

"Not a great deal, no." She searched his face for clues. "Look, Jim, have you heard anything I should know?"

His expression was bland. "Just thought I'd ask. We'll talk again."

Sky did not know as she closed the door behind her whether she was glad or sorry they had had the conversation. On the one hand Jimbo had confirmed her own unease. On the other she had her mother and grandmother to consider.

"Shit," she muttered under her breath, picking up the telephone on her desk and punching out her home number. "Did you call Ireland yet?" she asked her mother, without bothering with preliminaries.

"No, darling." Johanna sounded surprised. "It's still far too early over there. At least I think it is . . ." Her voice trailed away.

Sky had no time to go into the ins and outs of time zones. "Good," she said, "hold off for a little while, until tomorrow, will you? Something's come up."

"Oh, Sky! Have we got our hopes up for nothing?"

"Of course not. All I'm asking, Mom, is to give it just twenty-four hours. I have to talk to Treacy again and I don't want to present him with a *fait accompli*. I just want to make sure he really meant what he said, OK?"

"Oh, I'm sure he did, Sky. Don't worry." Johanna's voice cleared happily. "There's plenty of time. Do you think we should maybe paint the living room before she comes, Sky? It's a bit dingy, you know."

Assuring her mother that they could discuss it that evening, Sky got rid of her and then for a long time sat staring at the silent telephone.

"Everything all right at home, Sky?" The kid looked over from the cabinet where she was replenishing the files from a small stack of new reports and publicity material.

"Everything's fine." Sky snapped to attention and checked her watch. She was due at City Hall within five minutes.

The dreary interviews at the planning office took much longer than she had expected and it was after five when she got back to the office. The kid had left a Post-it note stuck to the telephone: *Mr. Daniel Treacy called. Wants you to call him urgently.* Loath to let him set her agenda, Sky stared at the little yellow sticker. Then curiosity won the battle and she flipped open her contacts book.

She was put straight through, but all Treacy wanted, it seemed, was to ask her if she had mentioned his invitation to her mother. Although his language was formal, even brusque, his tone was breathless and apprehensive.

She filled him in, fibbed that they had not yet been able to get in touch with the house in County Cork, and said she would pass on any developments. Then she asked for a further interview for her profile, assuring him that it would not take long and that all she needed was to flesh out a few details. After a brief pause he agreed, and they made an appointment. At her suggestion it was for the following Monday. That would give her a little time.

She hung up and, on impulse, crossed to Jimbo's office. Before she went careering off on what might well turn out to be a non-story and one that might embarrass the *Courier,* she decided to come clean. "Busy?"

"Accountants!" Jimbo pushed the concertina of computer printouts away from him. "You're working late for a Wednesday. What can I do for you?"

"It's Treacy, and this is confidential. I have a personal interest in it, too, so can I trust you?"

"Jesus! You've fallen for the guy!"

She looked at him in amazement: the thought was so incongruous and so far from the truth that it threw her completely. "Of course not!"

"Sorry!" Jimbo waved her to a seat. "It's all these numbers. Putrefy the brain."

Sky took a deep breath. She told him about the long-ago love story and Treacy's invitation to her grandmother, the name change after the death of her grandfather, letting the editor believe that Daniel Treacy had fled to the United States not only because of her grandfather's death but also because of a broken heart.

Then, as she moved on to the next phase and recounted the reasons for her unease about Midge Treacy's death, she saw the skeptical expression in Jimbo's eyes switch to one she could not interpret and began to realize how ridiculous her theory sounded: other than linking the two deaths through

Treacy, she had no basis for thinking that the automobile wreck was anything other than a tragic accident. "Sorry," she said limply at the end. "Butte's finally got to me, I guess . . . I know, I know, keep taking the pills, it's laughable. Sorry I've wasted your time."

"Do you see me laughing?" Jimbo's face was impassive.

"You mean to say you think I might be right?" Sky was astounded.

"Not necessarily, but it's worth thinking about. I wasn't going to show you this until I saw your piece—you know how it's good to keep puzzle pieces separate until we've enough of 'em to put together in some sort of order—but take a look at this. Now, it's not exactly along the same lines as what you were just telling me, but what do you think?" From a drawer in his desk he took out a garish piece of paper and passed it over.

Across a set of four discount coupons for Folger's coffee, which had been torn from a magazine or weekend supplement, someone had scrawled, in lurid purple marker:

Ask Daniel Treacy about his precious darling wifey and the hobo she murdered. What kind of a funeral did HE get? One Law four the Poor and one four the Hog Muck Rich.

Signed,
Someone Only Interested in Justice.
(One Of The Few.)

"How long have you had this?" Sky turned over the coupons to see if there was anything further on the back. There was not. "A few days." He was watching her closely. "It came the day after the Treacy funeral."

"How was it delivered?"

"By hand, in this." Jimbo drew out a brown paper bottle bag addressed, in the same purple marker, with: *Editor. Urgent.* Ironically, it bore the name of the liquor store owned by Greg's father. Sky recognized it not for this, however, but because it was the same bag that the junior had held over the trash can and that she had diverted into Jimbo's office.

Over the years, the *Courier,* like every newspaper in the world, had received its share of anonymous so-called tip-offs, which invariably proved to be the products of insane or revenge-filled minds. Sky figured this was one of those;

even way out in the boonies, where Treacy's wife spent her time, a murder was unlikely to go unreported. "Anyone remember who delivered it?" She passed the coupons back across the desk.

"Apparently the guy was black." Jimbo put them and the makeshift envelope back into the drawer. "Or, to be more accurate, that air-head out there thinks he *might* have been black but, knowing her, he might have been dirty." He shrugged in resignation.

"Oh, come on," Sky felt she had to defend the kid out of female solidarity, "she's not that bad. If he is black, he shouldn't be too difficult to track down." African Americans were generally thin on the ground in Montana. She peered at her boss. "You're taking this one seriously, aren't you? What have you heard?"

"I'm not sure." He closed his drawer as gently as if it were made of Sèvres china. "And I haven't heard anything, honest. Normally I wouldn't read something like this twice, as you know, but—"

"But what?"

"You sure you hadn't heard anything about the wife before now?" Jimbo was wearing his faraway look, which always meant his brain was trawling at high speed.

"Look," she was getting impatient, "the woman never registered with me until she died. Why should she? All right, she was a recluse—to each her own—but the only thing that could possibly go against Midge Treacy's unblemished character was that she apparently took a few drinks now and then."

"I see."

"Jim, I'm due home, I'm going into overtime now."

"It was more than a few drinks."

Instantly, Sky remembered Daniel Treacy's reaction when she had asked about his dead wife's health. "So what?" she countered. "I gathered from people I spoke to when I was writing the piece that that was all in the past."

"I'm not so sure." Jimbo stared at her. "I heard the woman was a lush. Big time. By all accounts we're not talking amateur here but world-class. And not in the far distant past either but right up to her death."

"But that message on the coupons talks about murder," Sky argued. "Drunks rarely commit murder. They're too interested in getting tanked, Jim. And, more especially still, drunks with as much money as Mrs. Daniel Treacy don't need to kill to get their hands on a hobo's bottle of wine."

The editor's expression did not change. "Keep your eyes and ears open—and a call to the Mayville cops might not be a bad idea. Why don't you fly up there tomorrow? Maybe call in on Libby too. Check it out. I've got to finish this for the accountants by six o'clock tomorrow evening," he waved a disparaging hand at the printouts, "or I'd go up there myself. I have my own theory as to what happened but I'd like to see what you come up with."

Sky sighed. "For God's sake, Jim, the woman's dead—" Then she stopped, her reporter's instincts sparking up. If Daniel Treacy's wife had killed someone during her lifetime, the bagatelle of her death was no bar to a great story. "What's your theory?"

"Not yet."

She tried for five minutes but Jim refused to yield another iota of information or even guesswork. "Better you get if for yourself. As I said before, I don't want to influence you." She had to settle for this.

Back at her desk, she tried to see the potential story from as many angles as she could. If Midge Treacy had been involved in something illegal, that was big news for a newspaper like the *Courier*. But if Treacy himself knew and had used his money to hush it up, that would be sensational. Sky was punching the number for Libby Information when she remembered that her mother and her grandmother were personally involved in this. But she did not hang up.

Chapter Nine

Surrounded by thick forest, Libby is a pleasant little city, its low-slung buildings and wide parkways typical of most conurbations in Montana where space is a commodity always in plentiful supply. It is also a Godfearing place, with gaggles of sparkling clapboard churches and chapels setting out their wares on discreet noticeboards. As she came in from the little airfield in the rental car, Sky noted the billboards and banners advertising the city's centenary year and took a note that it might be worth a feature sometime.

As she had passed through a few times before on her way to visit her father, she knew the layout of the city and found the county sheriff's office with little difficulty. The young deputy at the front desk was casual but friendly. He did a cursory check on the computer files, and told Sky that as far as he knew, no hobo had been found dead in Libby in the past few months. "You say it could even be a murder? You'd need to check with the troopers and the feds." He let his gaze fall to the white linen V over her cleavage.

"That's our information." Sky willed her hands not to fly to her blouse buttons. "And I thought I could short circuit a little. You know how the feds are . . ." but as she went on to tell him that the tip-off had been anonymous, she could see he was far more interested in her body than in her story. She took a breath. "I'd appreciate it, officer, if you'd listen rather than look."

His neck suffused with color as he turned again to the keyboard in front of him. When next he spoke his voice was prim: "I can assure you, ma'am, that as far as Libby is concerned you're wasting your time. We have investigated no murders of homeless persons this year."

She asked him then about the accident at Mayville that had killed Midge Treacy.

"I'm not sure we handled that. Are the two events

connected, ma'am?" He forgot his embarrassment and was instantly alert.

"No, not as far as I know at present," she became conciliatory, "but they might be. Our informant seemed to hint that they were. I'd sure appreciate some help on this one—my editor will not be amused if I arrived back with zilch." She saw that he was still smarting and smiled brilliantly at him. "*Quid pro quo*—could I buy you lunch? Where's the best place in town?"

After some cajoling, he thawed and, although he refused lunch, agreed to drive her out to the scene of the accident when he went off duty an hour later.

She filled in the time by having a cup of coffee in a motel and then taking a stroll through the park-cum-graveyard behind it. After the break in the weather, the heat was building up again and, conserving her energy, she sat on a bench to watch the comings and goings at a block of apartments nearby—obviously custom built for senior citizens since zimmer frames were much in evidence and no one she saw seemed a day under seventy.

Sky hoped death would take her quickly and not let her linger on until parts of her fell irreparably into dysfunction like pieces of old mosaic peeling off the façade of a building. She thought about Midge Treacy. Had alcohol made her unsteady and feeble? Had she been drunk that night? After the postmortem nothing had been said in the papers about the alcohol content of her blood.

Autopsy. Try as she might, Sky could recall nothing about it; she reached for her tape recorder and made a note to check into the medical examiner's report.

Mayville was about twelve miles from Libby. The deputy found a safe place to pull off and park when they were still quarter of a mile away from the place where the Volvo had plunged off the highway. Montana Power was stringing wires along the route and while the road crew slung the cable across the road ahead, traffic was temporarily halted in both directions.

Sky and her escort got out of the car and climbed the steep gradient along the line of stalled vehicles, many of whose drivers were shooting the breeze while they waited for the delay to clear. The two-lane road had been cut into the side of a wooded mountain; the trees towered from the bluff to the left but on the sheer drop to the right, the ferny tips were well below them.

A knot of people stood at the accident site, which was the apogee of a sharp bend, just ahead of where the utility workers had pitched their cherry pickers.

Volvo or no, Treacy's wife had not stood a chance.

Sky and the deputy joined the group, exchanged good-natured banter about the inefficiency of utility companies, and then Sky moved a little away. The quick growth of summer had not yet healed the scars of Midge Treacy's death. Hundreds of feet below where Sky now stood, a wide, irregular brown stain marred the dense symmetry of green. No wonder the casket had been closed, she thought. The Volvo had evidently burst into flames when it hit. She examined the highway: no tire tracks or skid marks, no twisted metal or even a single glint from the smallest shard of glass.

"Seen enough?" The deputy came over to her.

"Something strange here. If she hit the logging truck, surely it's odd that, even after a clean-up, there isn't even the tiniest piece of debris around—"

"Who said she hit the truck?"

"I assumed—"

"As far as I know, she just cut in front of him and off." He made airplane gestures with his hands. "He pulled up and called for help. He got a fright but there was no contact between them."

Sky searched her memory for the precise wording of the newspaper reports. The deputy was right: none had mentioned collision. Now the conclusion seemed obvious: Midge Treacy had driven straight across the bend and off. It was so dangerous she need not even have been drunk.

She felt sympathy for the unfortunate logger. "How about the truck driver?" she asked. "You say he got a fright—I'd say it was more like cardiac arrest. He was on the side of the drop, after all—a split second more and he would have gone over too."

"Yeah." The deputy was looking at his watch. "These guys are good though. They might seem to be reckless but they're always on the watch for renegades. Now if there's nothing more?"

Sky thought rapidly. It looked as though her journey was wasted. She was not ready to relinquish the story just yet, however. "Whatever about debris? There're not even any skid or tire marks." She peered again at the road. "Don't you think that's a bit strange?"

"Lady, this is a bad bend—a *bad* bend."

"But it looks as though she didn't even try to stop." Sky paused. Could the Volvo's brakes have been tampered with?

"She'd had two previous accidents, miss."

"Who came up to this one?" Sky saw he was becoming impatient.

"State troopers, I guess."

"Who in the state troopers? Could you give me a name?"

"Don't rightly know. I was on vacation. It was probably some of the brass. The Treacy name is big in Montana and brass attracts brass."

"Don't I know it. Did they bring the ambulance crew? Did she go to the local hospital or straight to Butte?"

"I can check when we get back. Look, Miss MacPherson, I really better get goin'. My wife don't like if it I'm not home afternoons. She sees little enough of me as it is."

"Sure. Sorry. Just one more thing, where's the wreck?"

"They're usually brought in to Deke 'n' Skippy's Auto. If you like, I'll show you where it is when we go back through Mayville."

"Okay." Sky let it rest for the moment, then, "Thanks. But maybe you should let me off in Mayville? I'll call into the auto shop but I'd also like to make a few inquiries of the police there."

The Mayville cop shop was similar to many Sky had seen before, not dingy, not smart. Utilitarian—that was the word, she thought, as she waited for a subordinate to fetch Sheriff Brian O'Connor who, she was told, had come to the scene of Mrs. Treacy's accident. On one of the desks by the window, the base of an electric fan was in contact with a metal filing tray and was making a tremendous racket; she moved it slightly, then stood in front of the cooling draft.

"May I help you?"

Wheeling round, Sky instantly hated the man she saw standing a few feet away in front of the door into an inner office. It was chemical hatred, the type that flares for no reason. She judged him to be in his mid to late fifties and, despite his name, he seemed almost Latin in appearance, with over-full lips, eyes of a nondescript hazel, and black, oiled hair groomed without a parting. His belly strained the flimsy material of his shirt but, for all that, his forearms and shoulders were well muscled and he moved as though he worked out. Slung prominently low on the pants of his uniform, his gun rode his fleshy hip like a monstrous excrescence and, overall, the sheriff gave the impression that he would be a person with whom it would be unwise to tangle.

"I sure hope you can help me, sheriff." She introduced herself and smiled with what she hoped was disarming sweetness.

But he interrupted: "Is there a problem?"

"I'm not sure." Sky was not going to let him take over: it was time for a little dissembling. "You see, my newspaper is running a series of articles on road fatalities—"

Again he interrupted, "To what purpose?"

She attempted to stare him down, with no success. Then: "It's a newspaper, sheriff. We run stories we believe will interest our readers."

He did not react to her sarcasm. "You the one that wrote the obituary on Mrs. Treacy?" Despite his name his accent bore no trace of Ireland, rather the flattened vowels of the Midwest; he had to be second or third generation. He sat behind his desk, shuffled up a handful of pistachio nuts from a dish beside his telephone and started to crack them open with a thumbnail.

"Yes, that was me," She decided, after all, that it would be in her interest to let him run the show.

But if she was expecting a comment on her literary style, or even on the factual content of the obit, she was disappointed. He said nothing, just loosened his belt a notch and opened a drawer in his desk, searching through the papers inside. "What's your interest in the dead lady?" He looked up as though the question had only now occurred to him.

"I told you—"

"Yeah, yeah! You told me—road fatalities. But how come it's *this* wreck you find so fascinating?"

Sky had been expecting either cooperation or stonewalling, not an interrogation. "I've been working on a profile of Mrs. Treacy's husband, as it happens. It's to be a major piece—"

"What happened to the road fatalities?"

"If you would let me finish a sentence, sheriff, I was going to say that the two pieces are connected only by coincidence.

Reporters work on more than one story at a time, as I'm sure you're aware."

"Treacy's cooperating with your story?" His eyes were now as immobile as a basking lizard's, and he seemed to have forgotten whatever it was he had sought in the drawer. Sky could not figure out what he was at. She nodded assent to his question, then, in an attempt to win him over, smiled again. "It's quite a scoop for my paper, but I wouldn't say, sheriff, that he's cooperating exactly. It's more like he's putting up with me. He has spoken to me. Do you know him?"

His features relaxed slowly. "Who doesn't?" he muttered, resuming his search.

Sky waited, unwilling to antagonize him further. As she watched him leaf through the papers, the suspicion niggled at her that she had seen this man somewhere else. Before she could work it out, he snapped the drawer shut and locked it. "It's not here."

"Were you looking for something in connection with the accident?"

"My report from that night."

"It's not in the computer?" Sky flicked a glance toward the purring monitor on the man's desk.

"Not yet."

She did not bother to ask why not. She was tired of this guy. "Here's my telephone number." She fished in her purse and gave him the standard-issue business card with its blue-and-white *Courier* logo. "I would appreciate it if you would give me a call as soon as you find your report."

He took the card without comment and she knew that dinosaurs would lay eggs again in Montana before he would call her. But she wanted to cut her losses now, to get out of this man's office. Perhaps the truck driver would be more help.

It was only when she was outside that Sky remembered that she had not asked him about the hobo.

She had even less luck with the logging company, drawing a blank when she called the human resources manager in the firm's Helena headquarters. After what seemed like an interminable delay she was told that the driver in question was off duty and it was not company policy to give out home addresses or telephone numbers. "When will he be back at work?" She was finding it difficult to continue to sound sweet: this whole exercise was turning out to be a bummer.

"One moment, please." The line went dead and she had to insert four more quarters into the coin slot. Jimbo was going to hear about this: budget constraints or not this was the last time she went out of town without a mobile telephone—she had been campaigning for one for months.

The manager came back on the line with news that did not improve her temper. The truck driver had taken some vacation and was not expected to return for a week.

After another fruitless hour spent in the mortuary of the local newspaper, where she found only mirror-images of the *Courier*'s own coverage of the story and obits, Sky found she had a headache and decided she needed a coffee top-up. A bell jangled as she pulled open the glass door of the nearest coffee shop, a wood-and-checkered emporium with café curtains and smily faces painted on the windows. Immediately, she saw she had company. A high school couple held hands across a table in a booth on one side of the room, but in a corner, Sheriff Brian O'Connor and another officer in a deputy's uniform were hunched over glasses of iced tea. At the sound of the doorbell, both turned round. O'Connor returned Sky's glance with a look that could have felled a moose. Then he twisted toward the lunch counter where the waitress—big hair, violet eyeshadow and a bosom that defied the attempts of her pink gingham uniform to subdue it—was filling sugar dispensers. "Hey, Velma," he called loudly, "you layin' those eggs?"

"Keep your britches on, they're comin'." The waitress continued serenely about her task.

Sky slid into a seat on the unoccupied side of the shop and outside the sheriff's line of vision.

"What's your pleasure, honey?" The waitress came out from behind the counter and plonked a glass of iced water in front of her on the "rustic" wooden table.

"Just coffee, please, black."

While she waited for her order, Sky reviewed her single page of notes. Until the police report from that night showed up, the only thing new she had learned from this sorry expedition was that Midge Treacy's Volvo had gone over the cliff all by itself.

"Here y'are, honey, black as the heart of Satan!" The waitress was back with the coffee jug. Her spectacular cleavage trembling, only a few inches from Sky's nose, she flipped over a cup and filled it. "You on vacation?"

"No, just passing through."

"Shame," the waitress cleared off the rest of the place setting, "it's pretty around here."

"Velma!" O'Connor glared across at her.

"You're on my patch now, sheriff." She smiled complicitously at Sky and threw her eyes to heaven. "Men and their stomachs!" White nurse's shoes squelching on the floor, she walked off toward the serving hatch between the lunch counter and the kitchen, calling, "You want another soda there, kids?" as she passed the lovestruck teenagers.

As Sky watched her hold sway in her small domain, it struck her that if anyone knew of a murdered hobo anywhere around Mayville or Libby it would be Velma. She waited it out until the sheriff and his sidekick, ignoring her, got up and left the shop. She noticed they left without paying.

Chapter Ten

Sky called the waitress, who had sat in the booth with the teenagers.

"Sure thing, ma'am, more coffee?" Velma collected the coffee jug and brought it over.

"Thank you." Sky introduced herself.

"A reporter, huh? I thought so." Velma indicated the spiral-bound notebook, which did not appear to impress her. "What can I do for you, honey?"

Sky came straight to the point. "I was wondering, Velma—you don't mind if I call you Velma?"

"Don't answer to nothin' else!"

"I was wondering if you'd heard anything about any unusual death around here recently. Probably a hobo. Has any stranger died lately in suspicious circumstances up this part of the state?"

The waitress used her free hand to puff out her hair to even bigger proportions as she thought. "Suspicious circum-stances? You mean murder, suicide, that kind of thing?"

"That's right."

"Not that I can think of," Velma said at last, "unless you mean Old Leon."

"Old Leon?"

"Yeah, we're not even sure that's his real name. He was found dead up on the side of the highway, poor old guy, but that certainly weren't no murder or suicide. That was, let me see—" Velma raised her voice and called to the teenagers, "You kids hear anything about Old Leon being murdered? Anything like that?"

"Not me," the girl piped up. "My dad said he musta froze to death."

"Drank himself to death, more like." The boy sniggered.

Sky knew that once she had a name it would help in getting the other information. "This man, Leon, he was homeless, was he?" She flipped over a page in her notebook and included the teenagers in the question. "How did you know him?"

"But I told you," Velma objected, "that weren't no murder or suicide—sure the guy drank a bit—"

"That doesn't matter for now." Sky sat with pen poised over the virgin page. "Did he used to come in here?"

"Yeah, we never knew when to expect him. He'd no teeth, and Vern back there," she indicated the invisible chef behind the hatch, "used to make him special meals he didn't have to chew, eggs sunny side with mashed potato, corned beef hash, stuff like that, y'know?"

"Tell me about his death."

"Well, I don't know too much." The waitress sat in the seat opposite Sky. "All I heard is he was found by the highway. By the sheriff, as a matter of fact, it was him brought the poor old guy in. I think the kids are right. He probably froze. You know, a few drinks, lie down for a little sleep . . ."

"But if it was spring . . ."

Velma considered this. "Yeah, but spring nights up this far north can be cold sometimes. You never heard of eupathermia?"

Sky forbore to correct her. "If he was found beside the highway, could he have been hit by an automobile?"

"Weren't a mark on him. So the sheriff said anyhow. That right, kids?" Velma hollered at the pair. "You two hear anything different?"

"Uh-huh." The teenagers left their own seats and came to sit at the table opposite Sky's booth. "My dad knows the sheriff, says the sheriff told him several of Old Leon's toes were almost fallen off." The girl was pretty, in a cheerleader way, until she opened her mouth and showed severe overbite. "Is this going to be on TV?"

"I'm only a newspaper reporter, I'm afraid." Sky fished out three business cards and handed them around. "You sure the sheriff was the one found him?"

"Sure thing! Not much pie around here Brian O'Connor don't have a finger in." Velma put the card in the pocket of her uniform and hitched up her cleavage until it rested more comfortably on the tabletop.

Since Sheriff O'Connor had also found himself at the scene of Midge Treacy's death, Sky's conviction was beginning to grow that she was glimpsing some of Jimbo Larsen's so-far-disconnected puzzle pieces. "Tell me a bit more about this Leon." She sipped her coffee. "I know he was a hobo and he had no teeth, but how old was he? How did you all know him? And can any of you remember where he was found?"

They all knew to within a few hundred yards where on the highway the body had been found but, for the rest of it, old Leon's personal details proved sketchy. None of the three knew how old he was—he was just known around town as Old Leon and could have been anything from forty-five to seventy-five. He was a long-haired tramp of inoffensive temperament and relatively discreet drinking habits, who had been coming through Libby at no particular time of year and at no regular interval for years. "Spring, summer, fall, any time," the boy volunteered. "My mom used to give him my old sneakers." From what they could remember, old Leon, who never stayed around more than a couple of days, could have stood anything from five feet six to six feet. "He was sorta hunched over," this from the girl.

He walked with a shuffle and had blue eyes or maybe gray or maybe light brown. "Couldn't tell, but then no one looked overmuch." Velma eased herself out of the booth and went to fetch more coffee.

"Where is he buried?" Sky thought she might find another puzzle piece if she could establish the tramp's last name.

"Don't even know if the poor guy had a funeral. Maybe Vern could help—HEY, VERN!" Sky fancied she saw cups rattle with the ferocity of the yell. Too late, she realized the hobo was unlikely to have a headstone.

Vern, thin as a rod and a perfect foil to Velma's opulence, knew little more than the others and, figuring she had gleaned all pickings in the coffee shop, Sky declined a further refill and got up to leave.

"This going to be on TV?" It was Vern's turn to ask.

"I've told you all I know." Sheriff O'Connor's thick brows now all but concealed his eyes.

Sky would have put her last dollar on a bet that he was concealing something important. "And thank you for that, sheriff, but could I ask you something else, please, that I meant to ask you when I was in before. It was you found Old Leon, wasn't it?"

If she had not been watching so closely, she would have

missed the brief flicker through the dark eyes. "If you're back to your road fatalities, Mizz MacPherson," he brushed something from the surface of the desk into the palm of his hand, "you're on the wrong track." With care, he deposited the contents of his palm into the trash can beside his desk and looked back at her. "That vagrant died of drink and exposure."

Sky saw that somehow she had rattled him. She pressed her advantage: "It's just that . . ." Then intuition kicked in again. With this man she had to be cautious. "Oh, never mind, it's not important."

"Oh, but it is, Mizz MacPherson. You have a theory, perhaps? Were you about to tell me that you thought Old Leon's demise was in some way connected with Mrs. Treacy's accident?"

"Just something else flashed through my mind. Nothing at all to do with this story. I've been very busy lately."

He scribbled a telephone number on a message pad, tore it off and handed it across the desk. "I'd like to be kept informed, Mizz MacPherson. It's in all our interests that the number of—ah—road fatalities be brought down."

"Of course, sheriff." As she took the piece of paper, she saw that flicker again. "My newspaper is always anxious to help the law. Catch you later."

He nodded and picked up the handset on his desk.

Outside, Sky paused outside the sheriff's office and shook her head as though to dislodge something unpleasant from her hair. She saw the pair of teenagers from the coffee-shop walking slowly along the opposite side of the street— the boy slouching self-consciously, the girl animated and graceful—and was jealous: those kids could write whatever they liked on the blank page of their lives. They had it all ahead of them.

"You wired, Mizz MacPherson?"

Sky jumped. She had not realized she had spoken aloud— she had been followed outside, until she heard the sheriff's voice at her shoulder. "No, I'm not, and I'd thank you not to sneak up on me like that. You startled me."

"You sure you're not wearing a wire?"

"You want to search me?" She faced down his stare until he turned on his heel and went back inside.

* * *

Deke 'n' Skippy's Auto (*You Bend'm We Mend'm*) spread itself over a littered half acre behind a chain-link fence on the outskirts of Mayville.

Deke was absent but Skippy proved tall and rangy—and about as talkative as basenji. On seeing Sky's press ID, he scratched his freckled scalp as he considered her request to view the Volvo wreck. "I dunno," he said at last.

"Why not?"

Another eternity of indecision as he looked at the ground, then at the clouds. "Sheriff say it's OK?" he asked eventually.

"I didn't ask him. What's the harm in just looking? Would you like me to go to his office and ask him if it'd be OK? I'm sure he wouldn't mind—but I'm on a tight schedule . . ." Sky, who saw no reason to reveal that she had already encountered the man who seemed to run everything in Mayville, smiled and touched his arm. The gentlest, most "trust-me" of touches.

"I dunno." This time, however, Skippy dared to meet her eyes. "Maybe."

"Thanks a bunch." Sky did not wait for him to make up his mind. "I won't be a moment. If you'd just point it out?"

Silently, he pointed a bony finger in the direction of the far corner of the compound. Then: "She's silver. Or was. Pity. She weren't more'n two weeks old." Skippy pursed his lips, as though he had said too much. Sky might have suspected he was hiding something if she had not already categorized him as one of Mayville's least voluble citizens. She turned her attention to the car.

The snub-nosed frame that sat on its four wheel-pods although bent was still recognizably a Volvo but the fire-blackened frame was no longer silver and it was missing any shred of glass, cloth or rubber; Sky touched it and flakes of black snow fell on to the ground. She peered inside: all that was left were twists of iron, a few bolts and a stalk that had once been a steering column.

Realizing she had been expecting some revelation or clue from looking at the wreck, she was disappointed. Nothing could be deduced from this sad black hulk, drowsing in the sunny ordinariness of the Montana summer afternoon.

A plane droned overhead as she walked round the wreck, trying to determine if she was overlooking anything. She glanced up at the plane and, out of the corner of her eye, caught a flash. She looked toward it and saw Skippy: he was facing in her direction while talking into a mobile telephone. She had no idea what had caused the flash, perhaps his watch. And although she had no proof that he was talking about her, the goosebumps rose on her forearms.

Skippy knew more than he pretended.

"Hi, Skippy!" She went over to him, waving and smiling brightly. Seeing her come, he terminated the call and put the telephone in his pocket. Too quickly. He looked uncomfortable when she reached him. "Thanks a lot." Sky maintained her breezy façade. "You were right, Skip, not much to see, I'm afraid."

"Sure."

"Well, any time you're in Butte," she pulled out one of her cards, "you just give me a call. As it happens, I'm in the market for a good secondhand compact."

"Is that so?" The mechanic's relief was comical.

"Nothing too fancy, a VW or a Hyundai or another little Japanese, maybe? They don't pay me too good down there in Butte. You got anything right now?"

"I don't do the sellin'. That there's Deke's department."

"Deke your boss?"

"We're partners." Skippy's face gleamed with pride.

"Well, now you and I are acquainted, Skip," Sky felt that in all compassion she could not put him through much more, "you be sure and tell Deke I'm interested, OK?"

"You bet."

As he took the card, putting it into the breast pocket of his coverall without reading it, Sky scribbled Deke's name into her notebook. "Just a couple more things, Skip." She beamed brighter than a lighthouse. "Is there any way of knowing what the condition of the brakes of this thing were like before she took off on her sailing trip?"

Skippy looked desperately from the wreck to Sky and back again. "Nope," he said uncertainly. "Leastways, I don't rightly think so. I gotta go."

"Yeah. Sorry to take up so much of your time. I suppose that was the law you were on to there on the telephone? To say there was a pesky woman reporter looking at the wreck. Were you told to report in if someone showed an interest?"

Skippy's expression was now of pure terror. "I gotta go," he repeated, almost breaking into a run as he hurried away from her.

* * *

Back in Butte, Fergus Lynskey was sauntering toward the registered office of the *Courier*. Mizz R. Sky MacPherson had been a revelation to him: he had recognized her on the instant he had seen her emerging from her car outside the hotel. Despite the fey picture in the paper he had expected a termagant—these women reporters always were. Yet R. Sky MacPherson was so beautiful she stopped his heart. As disheveled as though she had been pulled backward through a bush, she nevertheless exuded sexuality: even her carelessly combed tomboyish hair had glowed with it. He refused to think about it.

To say that Fergus's love life was no great shakes was an understatement. He took full blame for the shambles of his marriage. He had loved his wife, a flight attendant with Aer Lingus, to distraction. But the pull of their jobs, both involving long periods away from home, had stretched their love so thinly it had snapped. Their separation had not been angry—rather, it had been puzzled, as though neither quite knew what was happening or why. But for him the result had been catastrophic.

For a short period after they parted he had played games with himself, kidding himself that it was wonderful to be free again. He became a regular patron of Dublin's subterranean late-night dance clubs and wine bars along Leeson Street, dancing, inhaling cigarette smoke, drinking indigestible and overpriced wine, even having the odd joint or two. Getting off occasionally with long-legged, blond-haired girls with angels' faces.

Once, however, just before the four o'clock dawn of high summer, he had tottered out as usual to chase after a taxi, of which there were never enough. An hour later, he was still waiting, his back sore from leaning against a set of railings. The street glowed with gentle light, dimming the blue of the quietly revolving roof lights of the Gárda car on watch. It was not the first time he had been here at dawn but he saw, as though it was the first time, the empty chip bags that eddied around his feet, the pools of vomit that stained the footpaths; and although frantic inebriation was part of the scene, he was now repelled by the sight of a drunken girl, barefoot, kohl streaming down her cheeks like a pair of sooty rivers, being helped along the street by two equally drunken youths.

He sobered up. For the first time, he saw the seediness of

the subterranean existence he had led, where he had been feeding chat-up lines not only to women of his own age— some still defiantly wearing their wedding rings—but to girls young enough still to be at school. Now he saw not fun but an entire street glittering with suppressed unhappiness. Relieved, he gave up going there.

This was not to say he was entirely celibate. Dublin was overflowing with available women, lonely civil servants and bank clerks from the country, girls attending nighttime carpentry and mechanics' courses in the techs in hope of meeting men—only to find a preponderance of women like themselves. In pubs and rugby clubs and hotel bars, women everywhere were on the prowl and, now and then, Lynskey, hating himself, went home with one, usually to some bedsitter or flat as dingy as his own. He always tried to sew silk purses from these encounters, arranging to meet the girl again, hoping against hope that this one might be different. It never was.

Then he heard his wife was pregnant and the thought of her having a baby without him sliced him open. Less than six months after he had split up with her she had taken up with an accountant, with whom she now lived happily in a Dublin suburb. Her new life of tennis clubs and coffee mornings was far removed from her modest existence with Lynskey. Although he wished her well, he could not bear to think about her having a child that should have been his.

While growing up, he had always imagined himself settling down in a ramshackle house like his own in Kerry, a house rattling with hordes of children. He was the youngest of ten siblings, six boys, four girls, whose father had died when the eldest in the family was just fourteen. His mother, now retired, had been a national school teacher, and she had had to struggle hard to bring them up on her own.

It had been a struggle with a successful outcome now they were spread all over the world: London, Canada, Germany, Saudi Arabia, Tanzania, the Philippines. Six were married— seven if Lynskey was to be counted—three, a priest and two nuns, were celibate by choice. His mother had eighteen grandchildren and four great-grandchildren.

Lynskey had married in high hopes of adding to this number but his ex-wife's pregnancy seemed to seal off forever his own chances for the life he had always assumed he would have and he shut down his heart. He became a good policeman, always the first to volunteer for night work or the messiest assignments. And although he did not give up women, he gave up hopes of love and family. Ever since, he had projected the cynical self-confidence that the world admires yet does not like. Except in the minds of the only two intimates in his life—his mother and his friend, Bill Daly—who both knew the truth about him, to his co-workers and acquaintances he was a clever, smart-assed git.

The office of the *Butte Courier* was located in a nondescript, flat-topped building of only one story, indistinguishable from its neighbors except for the lettering on its glass front door.

"Can I help you?"

Lynskey's eyes widened as a gorgeous creature, with legs so spectacular she could have modeled tights, looked up from the open drawer of a filing cabinet and spoke to him. Did this place breed these women? "I'm looking for R. Sky MacPherson." He kept his eyes firmly on the girl's face.

"I'm sorry," her voice was breathy, "but Sky is not available right now. Could I take a message?" This was delivered singsong, as though learned by rote.

"No message, I'll catch up with her." He leaned confidentially on the front desk. "I'm an old friend from Ireland. Do you know where she'd be?"

"Ireland, huh?" The girl looked doubtful. "Well, I'm not sure I should be telling you this, but she did say she had to go to a barbecue tonight. This one." She picked a leaflet from an in-tray on the top of the filing cabinet and gave it to him. Crudely printed, it advertised a fund-raising event for a sick little girl in a local high school.

Chapter Eleven

On her return from Libby, Sky, who had promised to accompany her mother to a benefit to raise money for a child who needed liver treatment in the Mayo Clinic, was so tired after the events of the day that she asked to be excused. But she perished as usual on the twin spears of Johanna's cornflower eyes.

"Okay, okay." She threw up her hands in capitulation. "But I'm not staying long, okay? Hermana or Buffy can give you a ride home."

The event was being held in the parking lot of the local Catholic school and, while it was relatively well attended, the lot was so vast that by huddling within range of the heat emanating from the row of home barbecues commandeered for the occasion, the crowd made itself look smaller than it was and the atmosphere felt flat.

Sky hated small-town small talk and hung back, happy enough to stand alone in the shadows by the wall of the school building. She was peering without enthusiasm at the blackened hamburger and wilted shreds of coleslaw on her paper plate, and wondering how soon she could decently leave, when she was joined by a very tall, very skinny man.

"It's the soot I like."

"I beg your pardon?" Sky was taken aback. If this was a joke, the man's expression showed no sign of humor as he bit into his own burger. Then she recognized the eagle's-beak nose. This was the Irishman who had held open the door for her at the War Bonnet.

"Soot. I like it." He held the hamburger up to the nearest light—a security fitment on to which some optimist had taped a colored gel. "What about yourself?"

"You're not following me, I hope?" She could not remember what he had been wearing on their first encounter, but tonight, as though his accent were not enough, he was advertising his nationality on a faded sweatshirt that declared his love of Guinness. "Yep. You got it in one. I'm not following you. This is a public event, isn't it?" He juggled plate and plastic fork and stuck out his right hand. "Fergus Lynskey."

Sky shook it. "Sky MacPherson."

"That's quite a moniker." He whistled as they shook hands. "And I know who you are now. You're that famous reporter. I'm pleased to meet you." He popped the last of the hamburger into his mouth. "Nice state you have here, Miss MacPherson. I've always loved the Rocky Mountains. You're from around here yourself?"

"Sort of." Sky was unused to a man with such breezy self-confidence. The effect she usually had on men was to render them shy. "Do you know them well? The Rockies?"

"From books." He pronounced it "bewks" and, despite herself, Sky had to suppress a delighted smile. "This your first time in Montana?"

"Or anywhere west of Manhattan."

"I'm Irish—" Then Sky, annoyed with herself, moved quickly to correct any erroneous impression he might have that she wore shamrocks in her hair on St. Patrick's Day. "At least, my mother and her family are Irish. I was born over here. But I'm not at all famous, I'm afraid."

"It's not a crime to be Irish, you know," he grinned, "and you are famous. I've been reading your stuff in the local rag. And you've got your picture over your byline. In my book that's famous. Tell us about the name, why don't you? What does the R stand for?"

Once again, Sky found herself confessing her real name. And, once again, the revelation prompted not ridicule merely another whistle. "No wonder." Lynskey dumped his paper plate into a nearby container. "I can see why you wouldn't want to go through life with *that* hanging around your neck."

This was such a refreshing change from the customary reaction—people usually tried to come up with something jocose or, even, words of comfort—that Sky found herself taking to him. "Glad you think so." She trashed her own plate and its untouched load. "What do you do?"

"Secondary teacher—you'd call it high school. I do it solely because of the holidays. In Ireland we get three and a half whole months off in the summer. If that's not a solecism." His long face lightened up as he grinned, showing good, if uneven, teeth. "Now if only we had the weather."

"Solecism, eh? You're a teacher, all right. Yeah, I hear the weather can be a bit capricious over there." Sky grinned back.

" 'Capricious'? *Touché,* R. Sky MacPherson. Must write that down."

"That's enough, Mr. Lynskey. What do you teach?"

"A shower of reprobates! Actually, I teach Irish and religion. Irish teachers usually get landed with religion. They seem to go together at home. Like Mutt and Jeff."

Sky was charmed. "Lynskey. *That's* not an Irish name if I'm not mistaken."

"You are indeed. It is very much an Irish name. And I'm from a very Irish county. Kerry."

"You and my mother are—were—neighbors, then. She's from the western part of Cork." She pointed to where the Bliss Sisters were presiding over the coffee urns. "That's near Kerry, isn't it?"

"In a manner of speaking. In many ways, there are no two counties which are further apart." He held up his hand. "Don't ask. It would take centuries to explain that. Suffice it to say that the inter-county rivalry in that part of the world can sometimes make the Trojan wars seem like a bunfight. Which one's your mother?"

"The one with all the colors."

"What a marvelous woman!" He sounded sincere and for once Sky did not feel the need to explain Johanna's odd attire. Tonight, she was wearing one of Freda Little Calf's deerskin outfits, complete with headband, neck thongs and cross-gartering. It was decorated with beading and fringes and little silver bells and over it she had thrown a cotton shawl in vivid reds and blues, which she had kept from her days of psychedelia.

"Marvelous might be a bit strong . . ." But Sky found herself looking at her mother and the other Bliss Sisters through this stranger's eyes. She was so used to apologizing for them—to herself and to others—that she was surprised to find that this man could be right. She outlined a brief history of the Sisters and her mother's relationship with them.

Lynskey listened easily, making no effort to sound those approving "mmm"s and "really!"s, which bedevil getting-to-know-you conversations, and Sky was suddenly enjoying herself. Apart from Jimbo, this was the first man she had met for years whose conversation might offer more than sport, the price of wheat, automobiles, cattle or real estate.

"Would you care for some coffee?" She heard the first tentative tunings of the Catholic school band, always a signal that the meal was over and that the entertainment was about to begin. She wanted very much to continue talking to this man.

"Never drink the stuff. Rots the stomach lining. Any tea, by any chance?" Fergus Lynskey settled himself comfortably against the wall as if he had lived in this parking lot all his life and was accustomed to being waited on by women he had known for ten minutes.

Sky was so used to men reacting sexually to her—or at least to her minor celebrity—that his self-possession and confidence were exhilarating. She hurried off and practically tore a paper cup of hot water and a tea bag out of her mother's hands. "What's the rush?" Under the colored lights strung around the barbecue area, Johanna's eyes were sparkling. She was always at her best at these charity functions.

"No rush." Sky's own good humor was bubbling to the surface and made her reckless. "It's not for me. See that man over there?"

Johanna turned around and looked to where Lynskey lounged against the wall. "Which one?"

"Don't stare, Mom. The tall one—the one with the long legs and the faded sweatshirt."

"He's new." Her mother put a finger to her lips, considering. "I wonder, now, who would have brought him? What's his name, dear?"

"Fergus Lynskey. He's a teacher from Ireland. And guess what, Mom? He already thinks you're marvelous, just by looking at you. How about that for a first, huh?" Before the astonished Johanna could react, Sky had kissed her cheek, taken the tea and was walking away with it.

"Thanks. Is there sugar in it?" Fergus Lynskey pushed himself off the wall and looked askance at the watery liquid with its appurtenances of string and label. "Sorry, I forgot—"

Sky was about to go and get it when he stopped her. "No matter. When in Rome . . ." He dunked his finger in the cup, pressing the tea bag against the side.

The band was forming up and the child for whom the benefit was being held, a swollen-faced little girl of about four, was being carried on in the arms of her father. "Listen," Sky turned impulsively to Lynskey, "I know where you can get better tea. Or even a real drink. Do you like pasta?"

He raised an eyebrow. "I've heard about you American women. And do you kiss on the first date?"

"Come on, don't be snide."

"I'm being no such thing. It was a perfectly serious question."

The proprietor of Pirelli's restaurant and bar, a Finn who was distantly related to Jimbo Larsen, had gone all the way with his Italianate theme. He had commissioned a mural of an erupting Vesuvius for the wall behind the bar, the candles on the red checkered tablecloths were held by wax-encrusted Chianti bottles and the Muzak looped itself endlessly through selections of Neapolitan songs. "At least the decibel level is tolerable," Sky apologized, after they had ordered their meal.

"It's nice. I like it." Lynskey looked around. "People don't eat late in Montana, I see." The threesome at the only other occupied table were already arguing over who was going to pay for what.

"Not during the week." Sky discovered she was hungry and broke off a piece of breadstick. "Tell me about yourself. I forgot to ask you if you're married."

"Something you probably should have asked me before you brought me here."

"All right. But are you?"

His face clouded and, for a split second, Sky was shocked at the depth of her disappointment. "Don't worry about it," she said quietly. "I had no designs on you anyway. Let's just enjoy the meal."

"Have you ever heard of the Irish solution to the Irish problem?" His expression remained serious.

"You mean the IRA?"

Lynskey's shout of laughter was so unexpected and startling that even the busboy looked up from his apathetic laying of tables for the following day. "No, you goose." Lynskey chuckled. "God, you Americans!"

Sky stared at him, not because of her blunder, whatever it had been, but because, despite the beaky nose, he was so attractive when he laughed. *Stop it!* she warned herself. *Stop it . . .* One of the principles by which she had always conducted her love life was that other women's men were out of bounds. "I always thought the IRA was the main Irish problem."

"It is, it is, of course it is!" He chuckled again. "But that's not 'the Irish solution to the Irish problem.' " Again he became serious. "I'm separated from my wife. There's no divorce in holy Ireland, as I'm sure you're aware, so what we do is separate officially through the courts. Hugely expensive and that way everyone gets to be equally miserable and stay miserable. Except the lawyers and bishops, of course."

"I'm sorry." But Sky was not. She sipped some wine. Then: "Don't talk about it if you don't want to, but was it recent? Have you any children?"

"No, to both questions—do you mind if I dig into this garlic bread?" She took this as a signal not to probe any further and changed the subject, asking him why he chose Montana as a vacation spot. Apparently, it had been a spur-of-the-moment decision. "Normally I spend my summers washing trains."

"What?"

"Part-time job. My wife's maintenance payments are rather a drain." This was a lie as Lynskey's wife had eschewed maintenance payments from the day she had moved in with her new partner. Yet the penniless teacher cover story was the one he habitually used.

"So why aren't you doing that this summer?" The mental picture of him sloshing buckets of soapy water over locomotives was irresistible.

"Because I'm forty next birthday," he took a deep slug from his glass, "and I've seen nothing of the world."

Over the next hour or so, they chatted easily about Kerry and Cork, about Montana, about films they had each seen and liked, and discovered their tastes were similar. Sky wondered how best to slip in the facts about her own marital situation but the natural time would have been after his own semi-confession and the moment had passed. To bring it up now might look too forward.

The conversation flowed easily over the coming presidential elections, about which Lynskey was well informed, and then moved to the situation in Northern Ireland, about which he was reluctant to talk: "It's just that there is no way to explain it in one conversation, or even two or three or a dozen. It would take years, especially—saving your presence—

to explain it to an outsider. Almost as long as it's been going on."

Sky did not push him but was intrigued to learn that he had already encountered Irish patriotism, Butte-style. In the War Bonnet's bar, he had encountered some of the shamrock lot after their meeting there.

"That's why I was there. I was covering that meeting."

"Well, if I'd know *that* . . ." He grinned.

"*I'd* have run a mile in the other direction!" She took up the joust.

"You and what army?" It was an expression new to her but the gist was clear and, faced with such a speedy onset of intimacy, Sky felt shy. Lynskey seemed to suffer no such qualms, however, and took her hand. "I'm glad I came to that barbecue tonight. Will we have one more for the road?"

She hesitated, aware that the proprietor of Pirelli's was sitting stone-faced behind the cash register at the door. They had already had two post-prandial Sambucas, their waiter and the busboy were long gone. She looked at her watch. "It's after eleven fifteen, I had no idea it was so late. We'd better not—but can I drive you to your hotel?"

He cocked his head to one side. "Only if you let me kiss you goodnight, R. Sky MacPherson."

Sky knew she should have been offended. In the past she would have been offended. Now, looking into this man's eyes, she experienced something she thought she had long ago outgrown: an adolescent thrill somewhere deep in the pit of her stomach. "You'll be lucky, Lynskey."

They drove the short distance to the War Bonnet in silence and she was glad to find that this Irishman apparently saw as little need for small talk as she did.

She saw no activity in the parking lot and, feeling somewhat silly, she pulled up the Nissan a little way from the front door of the hotel, outside the circle of light cast from within the lobby. Lynskey squeezed her hand. "I'm definitely glad we met." Then he leaned over and kissed her briefly on the lips. "I'll ring you tomorrow." He was gone before Sky could register the anticlimactic nature of the kiss.

As she drove home she thought of a thousand questions she should have asked him, a million things she should have said. Like, how dare he assume so much? Like, how did he know she'd be at work? Like, how come he never bothered to ask her if *she* was married—if she had a boyfriend . . . ?

Like, how long was he staying? Like, when would she see him again?

Johanna was already in bed when Sky let herself into the duplex. As she tiptoed down the hall to her bedroom, she thought of another. How come Fergus Lynskey was at the benefit in the first place? It was an unlikely attraction for a lone tourist.

For his part, getting ready for bed in his anonymous hotel room, Lynskey was giving himself a severe talking-to. He had been out with beautiful women, had been to bed with them, for God's sake. Why should one chaste kiss, a few hand squeezes, reverberate like thunder through his body? He had been afraid to kiss her properly, although she had seemed ready for it.

Lynskey's world was threatened by this woman. She had shaken his usual composure to the extent that he feared he would not be able to keep intact the breezy, bright façade, which camouflaged his loneliness. Up to now he had managed quite well, thank you, and his colleagues, and many of the women he had met and superficially loved, believed him to be quite a ladies' man.

He went to his briefcase, undid the combination locks and took out a cumbersome satellite telephone.

The chief superintendent, who was shaving before going to work, was peremptory. "Any developments?"

"Nothing significant. I've made contact with a local reporter here, R. Sky MacPherson. She wrote a pretty good obituary on Treacy's wife but, as far as I can see, knows nothing." He was testing himself: testing his ability to use her name without betraying interest. It seemed to have worked because his boss did not react. "Anything else?"

"The St. Patrick's Brigade seems innocuous, I had a good look at some of them last night. Didn't get to talk to the president, the one who runs the funeral home where the coffin came from. I'm going to do that first thing tomorrow."

"Do that." Daly was impatient to get off. "Next time, have something to tell me. The meter is ticking."

Lynskey pressed the "end" button and returned the phone to the briefcase. He got into bed and lay with his hands behind his head. He wished he still smoked.

Chapter Twelve

"You're not trying to convince me that your turning up like that out of the blue last night was a coincidence?" Sky fiddled with the digital tuning on the Nissan's radio. She had been delighted when Lynskey had telephoned that morning. She usually worked Saturdays, but she had raced through a few catch-up calls in the morning and decided to take the afternoon off. Now, with Lynskey in the passenger seat, she was driving them on a picnic. She had turned off the interstate at Three Forks, and they were heading toward Madison Buffalo Jump.

"Do you want it to be a coincidence?" He was staring straight ahead. "It can be anything you want."

"I want a straight answer." She gave up on the radio.

"I was out for a walk and I smelled the burning." Lynskey paused. "Will that do? Remember, I told you I like soot." When she glanced over at him his expression was deadpan and she could not help but laugh.

He was wearing the faded sweatshirt again today but instead of last night's jeans had donned a pair of cotton shorts, which looked as though he had borrowed them from a much smaller man. On his bare feet he wore old-fashioned buckled sandals and Sky thought that his prehensile toes and long, muscular legs had to be as white as the day he had been born. What she had heard about the Irish climate had clearly not been exaggerated. "You still haven't given me a satisfactory answer," she prompted. "Did you not worry about integrating with a pack of total strangers? Or that you might not be welcome?"

"Listen, love," he pulled playfully at a strand of hair sticking through the back of her baseball cap, "what are you bothered about? It was a good cause, wasn't it? Where there's a good cause going, I'm your man. And when you think of it, MacPee, wouldn't you say I'm still getting quite good value for my few dollars' donation?" He made an expansive gesture that embraced her, the car, and half of Montana.

"Anyway," he looked away from her through his window, "you'll discover that teachers have no finer feelings. They get thumped out of us in training school. Blushing violets don't survive for long in front of classfuls of sixteen-year-old brats stuffed to bursting with hormones. Now, let's stop talking about me. I'm bored with me. What are you working on at the moment?"

Sky looked across at him. "Oh, this and that. The usual."

"Sounds riveting."

"It's a job, you know."

"Seriously," he smiled, "anything interesting?"

"I don't think you'd find it interesting. Well, maybe. Can I trust you with something I've just started? It's pretty confidential—at least at this early stage. And I'm a bit out of my league. I've no training as an investigative reporter—oh, I know we're *all* supposed to be interested in turning up rocks and seeing what's underneath, but somehow those kinds of stories don't come my way." She hesitated. "Until now, I think."

"Now you've really got me curious. Of course you can trust me, my lips are sealed." He made the gesture, both index fingers crossed over his clamped mouth. Then, when he saw she was still dubious about telling him, "Sure what's it to me, R. Sky MacPherson? I'm only an Irish teacher and all that bothers me is the *tuiseal giniúnach*. Anyhow, I'll be gone in a few days, won't I?"

Before she had thought about it, she had stretched out her hand and touched his hair, "What's that—those words?" Its softness under her fingers surprised her. It was curly, longish, already flecked with gray, and although there was a lot of it, it felt fine and silky. Warm, fine and silky. She was already fantasizing as to how it would feel in her hands when—*if*—he were to kiss her breasts . . .

"Are you sure you want to know? It's grammar, the Irish genitive." He responded to the invitation, leaned over and kissed the skin under her jaw. "You're gorgeous," he whispered, "do you know that? You're temptation incarnate." Then he pulled away. "I'm sure this is against some very, *very* severe code of the American highway."

"I'm sure it is." Sky was glad for the rush of the wind through the open windows of the automobile.

Luckily he did not seem to notice her confusion. "Hey, MacPee, spill the beans to your uncle Fergus. What is it about this work that's so secret? Is it an undercover job?"

"Don't think that I'm fooled for a second by your clever impersonation of a dweeb. Undercover job, indeed!"

"All right." His grin was broad and unabashed. "So, anyway, what are you working on?"

"You're really interested?"

"Really, *really*."

Tentatively at first, she began to tell him about the previous day's trip to Libby and points north. As she had suspected, he proved an attentive listener and, within minutes, she found she was using him as a sounding board. She was still talking when she turned off the engine and let the Nissan freewheel to a stop on the flat ribbon of highway near their destination. "You see, the thing is," she leaned into the back seat for the picnic basket Johanna had packed that morning, "I've nothing at all to go on. But every instinct in my body says something's wrong. And that this Sheriff Brian O'Connor's in it up to his neck. But what 'it' is I don't know. It's very frustrating."

She trailed off and looked toward the buffalo jump, an extraordinary cliff that erupted from the floor of the prairie like a carbuncle and was the only height for miles around. Through the open window, the shush of the breeze through the grasses was like a cool waterfall. "I'm missing something, I know it."

"This Skippy fella," Lynskey's voice was slow and considering, "you're sure he was talking about you into that cellular phone?"

"As sure as I can be. But he's not bright enough to have much to do with anything. No, it's that sheriff. And I just know Skippy was on to him about me."

"Now who's being melodramatic?" Lynskey pushed open the passenger door and unfolded his long legs on to the grass. "Come on, maybe the fresh air'll clear our brains. Over here, is it?" He took the basket from her and, without waiting for her acquiescence, set out for the buffalo jump.

Sky registered his use of the word "our" and as she got out to follow him realized that he was making partners of them. She let him get way ahead of her while watching with pleasure the easy way his long legs covered the ground. Over the past summers, Montana had suffered from drought; the recent storms were not enough to prevent the yellowing of the knee-high vegetation and she tried to find an analogy for the image Lynskey presented as he strode through it. All that came to mind was a picture from one of the nature books she had loved as a child, and it was hardly flattering: what she saw was a giraffe at full stretch through the African veldt. With his beaky nose, long, thin frame and pale skin, Fergus Lynskey should not have been attractive. Yet somehow he was not only attractive but devastatingly so to R. Sky MacPherson. "Take it easy," she cautioned, "the guy's just passing through."

He was waiting for her at the peak of the buffalo jump, seated in the scrub, a gleam of triumph in his eyes. "You're not all that fit, are you, MacPee?"

"I'm not about to win a medal at the Olympic Games, if that's what you mean." She smiled down at him, noticing for the first time that although she had originally thought his eyes to be gray, in the brightness of this light they were, in fact, dark green.

"Too much skulking around in smoky bars in search of scoops, I'll betcha!" He reached up and pulled her down to sit beside him. "Can we eat straight away?" Eager as a child, "I'm starved."

When Sky's mother packed a picnic, she went all out. They unwrapped chicken breasts, a Thermos of chilled cucumber soup, individual packets of Saltines and two types of cheese, a salad of peppers, carrot sticks, raw cauliflower, broccoli and mushrooms. For dessert, Johanna had put in two small pots of Jell-O and to drink, a second Thermos of iced tea. "Terrific!" Lynskey surveyed the feast. "But I'll have to teach you Americans the art of trotting mice on tea. *This*," he sniffed disparagingly at the insipid yellow liquid Sky was pouring into two paper cups, "doesn't even smell like tea. I hope you're not insulted?"

"On behalf of the American nation, I apologize."

Catching her off guard, he leaned forward and smacked a quick kiss on her lips.

"What was that for?" Instinctively, Sky's hand went to her mouth.

"Do I need a reason?" He was staring at her in a way that made the hair on her forearms rise. Then he grinned and was the cheeky self she was coming to know. "Because it's a gorgeous day? Because this little breeze blowing through your hair is the freshest and warmest little breeze I've ever felt? Because I'm now feeling sorry for all them poor buffalo that were driven off the edge of this cliff just so we could have such a perfect picnic here?"

"It was the most efficient way to slaughter them." Sky found refuge from the effect of his proximity—and the kiss—in adopting tour-guide mode. "The Native Americans were very ecologically minded."

"Were they, indeed?" He sank his teeth into a chicken breast.

"Stop it, Fergus!"

"Stop what?" He was innocence personified.

"Stop looking at me like that."

"Right. Done." He dropped his eyes. "But hold on there, a second, willya?" He chewed swallowed and carefully placed the chicken breast on the paper napkin beside him. "Now, is this look better?" He crossed his eyes.

"Fergus!" Sky was laughing now.

She stopped abruptly as he reached out and took her in his arms. "This is the second date, MacPee," his voice was husky, "so I think a proper kiss could be in order, don't you?" This time, there was no playfulness. With his free hand, he brushed her hair away from her face and looked into it for what seemed like an hour. Sky met his gaze and then dropped her own eyes to watch his wide mouth, the depth of the channel above the upper lip, the fullness in the center of the lower one. The sounds around became louder. She could hear the grass bend to the wind, the peeping of a bird she could not identify. On and on it went, that eternal moment as she waited for him to kiss her. She knew that when he did, everything would be different between them.

"Everything will be different if you kiss me." As usual, the words popped out as quickly as she thought them.

"I know." He did not change his position. "I think maybe we shouldn't. Maybe it's better keep things as they are for the time being. What do you think?" She felt as though she were made of fragile plaster. That if she were to be the one to make a move, she would shatter. "I think so too." She tried to say it without moving her lips.

"We'll kiss again. We'll do more than kiss. That's a promise, R. Sky MacPherson." He stroked her forehead and then, gently, he raised her face. "Here's a little taste to be going on with," brushing her cheek lightly with his fingertips.

It took a little time to get back to the way things had been. At first, they ate in silence, not the companionable silence Sky had so quickly got used to, but one filled with darts.

"Come here, Sky." When they were almost done eating, he took her and settled her with her back to him and both arms around her, facing both of them across the lip of the jump. "Settle down. Just look at that."

Sky looked. The jump was four, maybe five hundred feet high, in the sweep of prairie that spread like a great golden plate as far as the horizon on three sides, rising on the fourth to meld with the blue and purple Rockies. In all this honey-colored space, Butte was just an irregular, brownish stain. The few visible farms were little clusters of red-roofed insignificance climbing out of folds in the grasslands; the highway they had left was visible only because of three puffs of brown dust, miles and miles apart, which appeared in line with one another.

The soft west wind was warm on Sky's face and she closed her eyes, revelling in it, in the feeling of Lynskey's arms closed around her. "How could anyone go back to Ireland after seeing this?" The whisper in her ear was low.

"*Don't go, then . . .*" This time, to her relief, the words remained unsaid. "Now, let's demolish everything that's left." Quietly, he kissed the nape of her neck and loosed his hold on her. "I'm still starving."

They polished off the remnants but then, as she was repacking Johanna's picnic basket, Sky remembered Greg. "Oh, my God!"

"What's wrong?" Lynskey turned from where he was framing a picture through the viewfinder of his pocket camera.

"Greg. I forgot."

"Who's Greg, when he's at home?"

"He's my boyfriend." Squarely, Sky faced him. "I was supposed to meet him today and it went clear out of my head."

"I see. We'd better get you to a telephone, then." Sky had to admire this man. She found it difficult to believe they had known one another for less than twenty-four hours. It occurred to her then that not only had she forgotten the

appointment with Greg but that he had not entered her head
since she had met Lynskey. She had to end it with him: it
would be grossly unfair not to. "What are your plans for
tonight?"

"Nothing much. I thought I'd see if there was a film I
haven't seen yet. But what about this Greg?"

"Leave Greg to me. Would you like to have dinner? Look,
Lynskey—" Sky stopped walking. She took a deep breath.
"You'll probably think I'm being too forward—too
American—but if what is going on between us is what I
think it is, well, actually—even if it's *not*—then Greg and I
are no longer—well—Greg and I . . ."

She hated pussyfooting and here she was, behaving like
the queen of the pussyfooters. "What I mean is," she
amended, "that even if I hadn't met you last night, Greg and
I were finished. I was planning it anyway. I just haven't had
the guts to do it."

He let out that whistle she was beginning to know. "Poor
guy. Come on, Sky, get a move on. You've got to ring him."
He strode on ahead of her and unexpectedly Sky felt let
down. He had not responded to what had been almost a declaration of undying love. Was she being as foolish as always?

All right, she thought, hurrying to catch him up—he was
now fifty yards ahead—maybe she was reading too much
into it. From now on, she would play it cool. Whichever way
Lynskey's wind blew, she'd blow with it. "You always walk
so fast?" She was out of breath when she finally reached him
and they were getting into the Nissan.

"I always walk when I'm thinking," he held open the
driver's door for her, "and I was thinking about your
dilemma. Tell us a bit more about this Daniel Treacy." He
closed her door, walked round to his own side and got in.
"You seem to think he's a bit of a mystery man."

Sky engaged the gear shift and moved out on to the
highway. "I've told you all I know."

"Oh, sure." He changed the subject and in the hour and a
half it took to get back to within sight of Butte, told her
about his home town of Tralee, its history, the annual festival that brought girls from all over the world in search of a
title commemorating some local heroine called Mary who
was known for her beauty and virtue.

"A beauty pageant?" Her good humor restored, Sky was
lulled by the rise and fall of his rapid-fire English.

"You could call it that," Lynskey chuckled, "but it's hard to explain. It's not swimsuits, and the girls don't have to have the body beautiful. Not even the face beautiful. It's more goodness, personality, that sort of stuff. They do party pieces—"

"Forget it. You're right, it is hard to explain. It's too Irish for me."

"It's a pity your mother wasn't born two miles north of where she was or you'd be eligible."

"Give us a break! I'm a bit elderly for beauty pageants—hey!" she looked across at him. "How come you know the exact spot where my mother was born?"

"You told me yourself last night."

"I said the name of the place, but no one, not even anyone from Ireland, has ever heard of it."

"I have," he said quickly. "I used to play football. There's a couple of lads on the Cork team from around there."

"You've done everything, haven't you? And you certainly seem to know a lot about me."

"You talk a lot, MacPee. You told me a lot last night."

"And just why *were* you at the benefit?"

"I wanted to meet you," he said slowly, after the briefest of pauses. "I saw your photograph in your newspaper. I went into your office," he had the grace to sound embarrassed, "and a young lady said you were probably going to be there. I'm sorry, Sky. Do you forgive me for the deception?"

The city was now ahead of them, far below. "All right, I forgive you, I suppose I should be flattered. Now, Mr. Schoolteacher, have a look at that. There's my city." She had always loved the surreal look of Butte from up here, the way the derelict pithead machinery towered like giant insects over and among the house roofs. As they descended, she offered to take him on a tour of the city, "That's if you're staying, of course—if you don't see a photograph of someone you like better in the *Great Falls Tribune* or the *Bozeman Daily Chronicle*."

"I said I'm sorry. And you did say you forgave me. Of course I'm staying. I told you I have three and a half months' holidays."

"Teaching must pay better in Ireland than it does in Montana."

"I'll be a shadow of my former self by the end." He smiled

mischievously. "The War Bonnet is my little treat for the
beginning. To stoke me up, like . . ."

The white Hiace was again being brought into use. Just
before dawn it had been driven into the garage of a semi-
detached house on the outskirts of Sligo, where it had
remained during the hours of daylight. The house belonged
to a national schoolteacher, married with five children, who
lent his garage from time to time. Not too often. Maybe once
every two years.

Now, just after midnight, the van, with its complement of
three men, was being driven out as quietly as it had come
in. "I wish it was over." The driver was younger than the
other two.

"Shut up. Just drive—you're being paid well enough." The
man beside him spoke with the authority of long leadership.

Meanwhile, in the Dublin suburb of Churchtown, the dawn
chorus, more disturbing than melodious, had reached full
pitch, blackbirds, song thrushes and sparrows, starlings and
robins swamped by the chuckering of magpies, as raucous as
adolescent boys.

Rupert de Burgh was oblivious to them as he walked
quickly to the telephone booth at the corner of his road,
which was lined with solid, semi-detached houses. He had to
make the call and get back into his house and bed before his
wife woke and noticed he had left.

He inserted two fifty-pence coins and waited. "Toby?" He
never bothered with the preliminaries. "You got the cutting?" He listened, then: "I do trust you. Just be sure to
choose the right moment and watch his eyes. Good luck." He
replaced the receiver and hurried home.

When he had first arrived at Trinity College in the early
seventies, Rupert, who was the son of a well-to-do Tory MP,
had been like any other expatriate middle-class English student. But, on his first day, while sitting quietly in the buttery,
a pint of beer in his hand, he had been befriended by the boy
sitting on the next stool. Perhaps it was the attraction of
opposites, perhaps his charismatic new friend recognized
fertile, virgin ground when he saw it but Rupert's true education began that day.

He had been aghast to find, over the weeks and months
which followed, that what little he had thought and been
taught about the Irish had been filtered through the self-

satisfied sieve of English Tory revisionism. Within a short time, he had performed a *volte-face* from his upbringing and had become estranged from all his former friends in England, even from his parents.

Christmas that year had not been a success: Rupert's quiet public persona had never been mirrored at home, but this time his behavior was exceptional. He found fault with everything, not only with his parents' views but with their wealth, their house, their staid way of life. Even their singing of English carols at the traditional Christmas service in the local Anglican church.

During that Christmas break he had gone to work on his brother. Toby, who hoped to go up to Oxford, had always been in awe of his more energetic elder sibling and would have done anything Rupert asked of him. Rupert tutored him about Cromwell, about the Penal Laws where the English treated Catholics as less than vermin, about the devastating famine in Ireland that halved the population while England continued to extract its corn taxes, about gerrymandering in the North, about systematic discrimination against nationalists. About Pádraic Pearse and the other heroes of the Easter Rising. And when the IRA was blamed for the killing of fifteen people in the bombing of McGurk's bar that Christmas, Rupert was able to show Toby how it wasn't the IRA who did it: it was British intelligence agents who wanted to up the ante.

His poor bewildered parents, who had sent off a superficially compliant, well-mannered boy to read English at a long-established university, albeit a provincial one, found themselves playing host to a raging, angry radical. The conflict had come to a head on Boxing Day, when Rupert refused to accompany them for the traditional visit to an elderly bachelor uncle, a retired Guards' colonel who babbled away harmlessly about Winston Churchill and the war. As his mother wept, Rupert ranted on about colonialism and the oppression of Irish civil rights. Finally his normally placid father had had enough. He issued an ultimatum: either Rupert came with them to visit their relative or he was out. Rupert was delighted. His Trinity fees were paid for the year so he went back to Dublin. When term resumed, however, he went to no more lectures or tutorials but hung around the bars or used the library for his own purposes.

And then, after Bloody Sunday, he had run with the rest to

set fire to the British embassy where he had stood in the shadows and had been inspired to join the police by the young and unwitting Fergus Lynskey. Who had been too caught up in his own passion to have noted anything distinctive about Rupert de Burgh.

Chapter Thirteen

To take advantage of the spectacular vista of the Continental Divide, for which the site of Daniel Treacy's house had been chosen, the south side was virtually all glass, with floor-to-ceiling windows curving along it like petrified waves. Expensively but simply furnished, the large living room had a parquet floor, which shone in the dazzling light, three white sofas placed in a U shape in front of a marble fireplace on the fourth wall, a couple of easy chairs, also in white, and occasional tables in glass and dull gray steel. Even the lamps were shaded in white and there was only one picture: hanging over the fireplace was a large, steel-framed abstract in pale grays and white. The sparse simplicity was deliberate. Nothing was to detract from the scene outside.

The house was twelve miles northeast of the city, tucked away at the end of a private road near Elk Park Pass at almost six thousand feet. In front of the windows at which Treacy stood, the yard surrounding the house fell away in a series of terraced lawns, lush as Oriental paddy-fields, toward the edge of a bluff. Beyond this was a wide green ocean of fir and pine and beyond that again were the mountains, jagging the intense blue hem of the sky.

Treacy knew that in the bars and restaurants of the invisible summer Saturday evening city only a few miles from his house, everyone was gearing up to have a good time. Down there, people were having conversations and spats; they were laughing and being silly and eating cheap food, drinking convivial glasses of beer and wine, making plans to meet for Sunday brunch, to go to local fishing holes or to have barbecues or picnics.

It was a scene on which he did not care to dwell. King of the Castle, he thought sadly, remembering the game he had played as a child in Ireland. Sometimes vicious, always rambunctious, it involved pushing and shoving and clawing your way to the top of whatever elevation—rock, a mound of earth—was designated for the day. As a child Daniel had never achieved the status of king, always having been over-come by bigger, heavier and more determined boys. "Well, you've made it now," he said, to his empty, elegant room and stupendous view.

Damn that girl. It had been at least six hours since he had first called and he was not accustomed to having to leave three messages for anyone.

At least her mother had had good news for him.

Almost furtively, although no one could be observing him, he took a slim silver case out of the inner pocket of his jacket. Opening it, he looked at the photograph it contained, an old black-and-white snapshot of Elizabeth Sullivan. It was one of those old-fashioned group shots, taken by ama-teur box Brownie owners the world over in the thirties and forties, and she was surrounded by her large family. Sky's mother, who was tiny, perhaps five years old, was standing at the front.

It had taken all of Daniel Treacy's ingenuity and a lot of his money to secure that photograph, which was more than forty years old. He had had it enlarged and enhanced, but even American technology was unable to obliterate the fact that the unseen photographer's hand had shaken a little as the shutter snapped.

Nevertheless, to Treacy, Elizabeth Sullivan's luminous beauty shone from it as clearly as though her image had been painted by Titian. She was holding the youngest of her eight children, whom he knew to be Constance, who was now on a sheep farm in Australia.

There was little he did not know about Elizabeth's family.

What marred the photograph for him was that she was standing beside Mossie Sheehan, her second husband, long since dead, but the memory of whom could nevertheless inspire him with hatred. Elizabeth's first husband had been a mean fool, but Mossie had been the one who had deprived Daniel of the woman he had loved for more than forty-eight years. He had rejoiced savagely on learning of Mossie's death but by then, cruelly, he himself was married. But now that Midge was out of the way . . . His heart jumped as the image of his wife's waxen face rose before his eyes.

He closed the case and replaced the snapshot in his inside pocket, then crossed the perfect room, the clicking of his shoes on the parquet emphasizing how alone he was. He sat on one of the sofas, picked up a book and attempted to concentrate. Having read a paragraph, however, he had to begin it a second time. When it still made no impression on his brain, he threw the book from him. Nothing, he thought, could be worse than this emptiness.

Instantly, he rejected this idea: he must not feel sorry for himself, self-pity was the most ignoble of human failings. He picked up the remote control and pressed a button. Smoothly, doors in a console slid open and the television came on. He spent a minute or so flicking around the channels but could find nothing he wanted to watch. He switched it off again.

He looked at his watch: Elizabeth's granddaughter was turning out to be good at her job; he could see she was not to be put off. Where was she? Why was she not returning his calls? He wanted to impress his own version of his story on her before she discovered too much. Monday, when they were due to meet, might be too late. And he doubted if he could wait that long to find out if Elizabeth was coming. He wondered if he could risk calling Sky's home yet again. Time was getting shorter and shorter. He reached for the telephone but decided against it. Even reporters probably took Saturday nights off.

Daniel Treacy left his beautiful room and walked toward the cantilevered staircase that curved to the second floor and the bedroom suites. His shoes felt like concrete blocks.

On the roadway outside the house, a man in a plain beige sedan noted the lights going on in the upper story.

As Sky pulled in, the parking lot of the War Bonnet Inn was teeming with conspicuously ID'd conventioneers who, in high spirits, were being disgorged from the taxis that had taken them in from the airport. "Oh, great!" Lynskey groaned, as they stopped behind one of the vehicles. "This is all I need. I've read about these conventions. I probably won't get a wink of sleep."

"You'll survive." Sky left the engine running and looked across at him. Now that she had decided to finish with Greg, Lynskey's presence made it imperative that she did so tonight. She said, "Look, after I've talked to Greg, would you like to eat dinner? What kind of food do you like?"

"Home cooking. I want to eat at your house."

"But my mother's there." Sky was thunderstruck.

"That's just it. I want to meet that wonderful woman. Thank her in person for that picnic. Would she mind?"

"I'll have to call her." This was definitely a first. No man with whom she had ever been involved had wanted to meet her mother. "Why don't you give her a shout from the telephone in my room while I have a quick shower and put on some real trousers? You can call your Greg too, see if he's in. If he is, you go off and meet him, I don't mind waiting, however long it takes. But if you can't reach him we could go straight to your house. And if that look in your eyes means you're worried about the proprieties, I promise I won't jump you—honest!"

"What look?" But as Sky turned off the ignition, she felt a little like Pinocchio, or any puppet she had known in her childhood. It was still less than twenty-four hours since they had met and Lynskey was running her life. "Anything else you'd like to organize for me?" she asked, as he opened the door and unrolled himself from the passenger seat.

"Not for the moment. Come on." Then he bent down and grinned at her. "Unless, of course, you'd like me to help you buy a bigger car. Me legs are crucified!"

His room was as Sky had expected, inoffensive, beigey décor, two beds, a TV, a mirrored dressing table, which doubled as a desk, a coffee table flanked with two chairs and windows framed with thick, swagged drapes. She sat on the side of the one of the beds, staring at the telephone. What was she to say to Greg? From behind the closed bathroom door, over the rushing of the shower, she could hear Lynskey's baritone warble. Quickly, before she lost her nerve, she picked up the receiver and punched out the number of the liquor store.

Greg had already left. She called his home. Busy.

Guiltily relieved, she called her mother. Johanna was bubbling with delight. She had finally got through to Ireland and Sky's grandmother was seriously considering the invitation. And of course she would be thrilled to have Sky's young man to dinner. "There were a few calls for you." Sky heard the rustling of paper and the scrape against the receiver as her mother put on her glasses. "One from Bill Collins— and—Greg and oh! Yes—guess what? Daniel Treacy called *twice* for you. We had a nice chat the second time. I told him about my mother. He's lovely, really, when you get to know him, isn't he, Sky?"

"Sure, Mom, lovely. I've got to run. See you soon." She tried Greg's home number again and, when it was still busy, checked in at the office. Her voice mail repeated the messages she had taken already from her mother. Bill Collins. Treacy. And Greg. Collins could wait until Monday but Treacy? Twice?

She copied the number he had left into her contacts book and was punching it out when she heard the shower being shut off. She hung up. But the singing started again and the sound of running water. Lynskey must be shaving, she thought, and decided that Treacy could wait. She was on time off and she deserved it.

Before her nerve failed, she tried Greg for the third time. This time the phone rang but the receiver was picked up by his father. Greg was out, and no, he had not said when he would be back. Sky asked him to say she had called and, hating herself for feeling so pleased at a further postponement of what she had to do, looked around the room to try to discern what type of person Lynskey was.

He certainly seemed tidy. His suitcase was nowhere in sight and, through the slightly open door of the closet, she could see a jacket and pants hanging. Apart from the edition of the *Butte Courier* on the dressing table—the one that held the Treacy obituary—and a little travel alarm clock by the bed, the only sign that the room was occupied was a briefcase on the coffee table.

What type of man traveled on an extended vacation through the Western states of the U.S. of A. lumbered with a briefcase? Sky smiled affectionately. This guy was fascinating but a definite oddball. Did she dare? She glanced at the bathroom door: the water was still running. Quickly, she crossed to the coffee table. The briefcase was locked.

The singing stopped and the water was shut off again. Sky had barely time to get back to her original seat on the bed before the bathroom door was opened a crack: "You finished? Is it safe to come out?"

She nodded, trying to keep her conscience from shrieking aloud about her snooping. The sight of him wearing nothing but a towel around his waist compounded her agitation; his torso was hard and muscular, if a little on the skinny side. He noticed her scrutiny. "I know," he said cheerfully. "I'm no

Chippendale. But you should see the rest of my family. I'm the fat one. What's the matter? You look like a guilty child. Was it very bad?" he asked gently, coming to sit beside her. "Was Greg upset?" He bent and kissed her softly on the lips.

Sky, who was losing count of these chaste kisses, managed not to grab him. "He wasn't in. I feel dreadful about this. I was never very good at tough love or whatever it's called."

"You've done it before, surely?" He pulled back, his expression skeptical.

"Only once, when I left my husband." Sky knew she sounded like a weakling. "I suppose I do things obliquely, show by my behavior that it's time for a break. They usually get the message." She looked down at his hands, square on his lap, and noticed that he bit his nails. "That sounds appalling, as though I'm whatever the female equivalent of a womanizer is . . . I'm not, you know, I don't think I could flirt to save my life."

"You don't have to."

When she glanced up, his eyes seemed to be emitting light. She was uncomfortable in its blaze and also with the tenor of the conversation but felt that she should carry through to the end. "Greg's different, somehow, I've tried to tell him, I mean to show him . . ." Miserably she trailed away.

"There's only one way to tell him, you know, and that's to tell him." He made it sound easy.

"I know." She looked directly at him. "It's my problem, not yours. Now, about dinner, my mom says it's okay for you to come over."

He reacted with the shout of laughter that had so startled her the night before in Pirelli's. "Thanks a million." He got up and padded to the closet, "I can't wait. I'm starved."

"You always seem to be starved."

"I'm a big fella, MacPee. Now turn your back like a good girl so I can get dressed." She complied and then asked why he had a briefcase on holiday. "Oh, that!" His voice was airy. "You wouldn't want to know what's in that."

"Why not? Is it a secret? I've told you all my secrets—"

"All right, all right, you win. But you're not to laugh."

"I won't."

"I'm writing a book." No matter how she begged, he refused to tell her anymore. "It's just a book, Sky," he said at last. "Every teacher—no more than every journalist, I dare say—thinks he has at least one book in him."

"I want us to kiss properly." Sky could have torn out her unruly tongue. Nevertheless she turned around to face him. He was still barechested but he had donned his pants and she had surprised him in the act of putting on his second sock.

He dropped it. "Only if it's skin to skin."

Watching his eyes, she unbuttoned her cotton blouse, then felt behind her and unhooked her bra. She shed the garments and sat, head high, to wait for him. He continued to hesitate, however, face working as though he did not want to touch her—and for a few awful seconds she thought she had made a fool of herself. Then, in two strides, he was beside her and had pushed her back on the bed.

His hands felt cool and surprisingly delicate on her breasts, like the wing feathers of a bird. She arched her back and he held both nipples gently between finger and thumb, rolling them so they swelled and hardened to bursting point. He kissed them, fluttering his tongue over first one, then the other, and the skin over her entire body seemed to contract until it felt as tight as a drum.

He moved to her mouth and this time his kiss was anything but chaste. Sky tightened her arms around his neck and pulled, tumbling them over until they were entangled. His lips were all that she had fantasized, full, warm and demanding.

Then he stopped, as suddenly as a guillotine. Holding himself still above her, he looked into her eyes. "You wait, MacPee. You just wait."

Sky could not read his face. "Why not now?" She was breathing hard.

"Now is not right." For a brief instant, she almost thought she detected fear in him.

One thing was certain, though: this was not the cocksure Paddy she had taken with her to Madison Buffalo Jump. Although her body pulsed, she managed a smile. "Whatever you say, Lynskey. I can wait."

The silence between them as they both got dressed and drove to the duplex was of such complexity she did not dare begin to analyze it. She began to worry how Johanna would react to him. As she took him in, however, she heard laughter from the kitchen and realized the Bliss Sisters were in session. "Sorry about this," she whispered, "I didn't know."

Before her eyes, Lynskey reinvented himself, wading in with all verbal guns firing, even moving his accent up a notch so that all three women were instantly snowed.

During his enthusiastic demolition of Johanna's meatless meatloaf, he blarneyed and flattered the three outrageously, telling yarns, even flirting. Within half an hour of his arrival, they were behaving like teenagers, Sky's mother most of all: Johanna's eyes sparkled the brightest and her voice took on the lightest timbre.

"Woodstock?" The meal over, Lynskey pushed aside his tea and gaped theatrically. "You don't mean to say I'm actually in the presence of three people who were at Woodstock? Ladies, I'm lost with awe, not to speak of envy."

This sent Johanna rushing into her bedroom to find the photograph album, which contained the proof. As she returned with it and all three crowded around to show themselves off to Lynskey as girls, he winked at Sky, who was sitting, chin in her hands, wishing she could begin to understand this man.

It might be a help if she could be alone with him. The memory of their half complete encounter was still raw and she wanted him so badly she felt it must be written on her forehead. Far from seeming to wish the same thing, she thought wryly, as far as Lynskey was concerned she might as well be one of the cats who were snoozing in their basket at her mother's feet.

Chapter Fourteen

At Hermana's prompting, Sky's mother finally agreed to sing for their guest, but only if someone would help her. "How about you, Sky?"

Then Johanna turned to Lynskey. "She has a beautiful voice, Fergus, beautiful, but she won't use it."

Embarrassed, Sky batted away the chance to make a show of herself in front of the Irishman. She knew she had an unusually rich speaking voice—she had always been chosen in grade school to read the finale in the Christmas pageant—but she felt her singing voice left a lot to be desired.

After much discussion, during which dusk stealthily withdrew light from the kitchen to gild the sky outside, Buffy agreed to sing and the two women launched into "Blowin' in the Wind," Buffy's breathy mezzo making a perfect blend with Johanna's sweet soprano. Throughout the song, Sky's mother plucked shyly at her hair so that by the time they were embarked on the song's penultimate verse, the braid was undone and her hair had fallen around her face and shoulders in a soft dark cloud.

In normal circumstances, Sky would have been so mortified she could not have borne to watch the display but she saw it through Lynskey's eyes and was glad he had afforded her an opportunity to see her mother as the unique individual she undoubtedly was. An endangered species. She resolved to be less impatient with Johanna but knew immediately that her resolution was a waste of brain cells.

The telephone shrilled in the hallway just as the last notes of the song died away and, as she went to answer it, Sky looked back to see a tableau she reckoned she would remember for a long time: her mother and Buffy locked in sentimental embrace, Hermana surreptitiously blowing her nose and Lynskey's beaky face wreathed in benevolent smiles.

"Hello?" Sky's voice sang as she answered the phone.

"I've been trying you all evening. Did you forget we had a date?"

"Oh, God." The sound of poor Greg's aggrieved voice was like a blow. "To tell you the truth, Greg, I did."

"Where the hell were you? They said at the office—"

"Don't take that tone with me. You don't own me, you know." Sky took refuge in moral outrage from her guilt. During the pause that followed, she could almost see his huff: thick, gray and dense as iron, it crushed the air between them so she felt claustrophobic and flat. "I'm sorry," she offered, "I didn't mean to yell."

"I never pretended to own you." He was stiff. "I just thought—"

"Look, Greg—" She got stuck. Use of a blind telephone was the cowardly way to break up a relationship.

"What?" His belligerence made it easier for her.

"We have to meet." She forced herself to be crisp, "I'm real sorry about this evening but we have to talk."

"Please, Sky, please!" His pain shocked her.

"We have to talk," she forced herself to repeat.

"You want to break up with me."

Visualizing his ravaged eyes, she wavered but then went through with it. "I want to *talk* to you about it."

The panicked silence crackled. Behind her, she heard the scrape of chairs from the kitchen, heard Hermana and Buffy talk over one another in their eagerness to impress their fond goodbyes on their new friend, Lynskey. "Greg, are you there?" She could still hear him breathing at the other end of the line. "Greg?"

"I'm here. If you've decided on this, Sky, there's nothing to talk about, is there? But standing me up is a helluva way to let me know."

"I told you that was a genuine mistake. Honest."

"Yeah, well—"

To her horror his voice broke and she rushed in again, "Greg, I want to be your friend—"

"*Don't!*" he cried. "Don't patronize me, whatever else."

"I won't patronize you." She was feeling his grief for him now, "I'm sorry—I really am."

"Yeah, sure. Goodbye, Sky. See ya around. Have a nice life." He clicked off.

She stood for a few moments with the receiver still

jammed against her ear. This was not as she would have planned to do it but now that it was done, through the surge of shame and regret, trickled the threads of something lighter, brighter: a sense of infinite relief, akin to the feel-good sensation of childhood after she'd unloaded all those misdemeanors in the confession box. As she replaced the receiver, Sky was infused with a need to fill her room, the house—the world—with daffodils. "Going already?" She turned to Buffy, who, with Hermana at her shoulder, was coming through the doorway from the kitchen into the hall.

Buffy leaned over and mouthed into Sky's ear, "He's peachy. I'd hang on to that one if I were you!" In a normal tone, she continued, "Look after your Mom, now, Sky, you hear?"

"Thanks, Buffy. And thanks for the song. It was lovely."

"What a guy!" Hermana enfolded Sky in a bear hug and then held her off. "What a guy!" she repeated. "I might even take him myself if you don't want him." Then, furtively: "Take my advice, honey, and you think about that Greg. He's not up to your intellectual level."

Around Hermana's bulk, Sky saw Lynskey twinkling up at Johanna, who was refilling his tea cup. "I think I have competition, Hermana." She nodded in the direction of the kitchen.

"Oh, *you*!" Hermana chuckled and took Buffy's arm. "We'll see ourselves out, dear. Now remember what I said?"

"Who was that, darling?" Johanna picked up one of the cats as Sky came back into the kitchen.

"It was just Greg." Sky did not trust herself to look in Lynskey's direction.

"Your mother was telling me all about Daniel Treacy and her own mother, Sky. What a wonderful story."

"You don't mind?" Johanna planted a kiss between the ears of the cat she held. "Fergus knew a lot of it anyway, dear. He says you told him earlier."

"I did." Sky wondered briefly at Lynskey's persistent interest in Daniel Treacy but dismissed it.

"In all the time I lived in Ireland, you're the first Fergus I ever met!" Johanna beamed from Lynskey to Sky and back again.

"Don't encourage him, Mom." Sky plonked herself at the table. "He's insufferable enough."

"Do you miss the old country?" Lynskey drained the

herbal tea and held out his mug for a refill. He seemed to be settling in for the duration.

"I can't say I do." Johanna's voice was now as full of rills and runs as his own. "My family, of course, I miss them. Although I can't say in all honesty that we have been close. Odd that . . ." She trailed away, a faraway look in her eyes. "My mother and my brother, Francey, in England . . . I was very close to him growing up. But we've all scattered now."

"I hear your mother's maybe coming over for a visit?"

Johanna looked at Sky, unsure of how much she should divulge. "I've told him, Mom." Sky sighed. "And he knows it was Daniel Treacy's idea." She yawned. "Speaking of Treacy, he's left several messages for me and I suspect he'll try to see me tomorrow, rather than Monday. I'm really tired. I think, if you guys don't mind, I'll drive Lynskey home now."

Lynskey took the cue and got to his feet. "Sorry. I've overstayed my welcome as it is—and I want to walk. I really do. It's early morning on my time clock."

"Don't go yet, we were just getting started." Johanna's disappointment was genuine.

"I'll be back, Johanna, don't worry. One of the advantages of having such super-attenuated holidays is that you can travel with few plans. And having met you and your daughter," he straightened and looked directly at Sky, "I've already changed mine. You'll be seeing a lot of me," his eyes gleamed with wicked *double entendre*, "I guarantee it.

"The dirty deed done?" he murmured, as Sky accompanied him along the little corridor to the front door of the duplex.

"Mmmm." Sky was wondering if he would kiss her.

"Thank God for that." He was enigmatic.

"That's a bit much, isn't it?" Although she found his honesty exhilarating Sky's guilt prompted a spurt of loyalty to her former boyfriend. "You might at least *pretend* you're sorry for poor Greg."

"Oh, I am, I am," his smile belied it, "but I'm happy for me. C'mere to me." He enfolded her in his arms and kissed her strongly, but again broke off before she could respond. "There. That'll hold us for a while."

"Christ, you're something else, you know that? Are you sure you want to walk?"

"Sure. Tomorrow's Sunday. But if you don't want to see

me, I'm a resourceful fella. I'll find something to do."
Before Sky could remonstrate he held a finger to her lips.
"There's always the king-sized bed in the War Bonnet Inn.
Grand place, the War Bonnet."

As she closed the door behind him she wondered if this
on-again off-again stuff, which was driving her crazy, was a
deliberate technique. But that fleeting look of fear on his
face back in his hotel room had been real.

Before she turned in for the night, Sky called Daniel
Treacy. Her suspicions had been correct. Something had
come up for him on Monday and he wondered if they could
meet in the morning instead.

In Killybegs in Co. Donegal, the omens were favorable. The
weather was perfect: although it was not yet raining, the livid
clouds, so low that the hilly landscape beyond the town was
obliterated, were about to burst. Out to sea, a gale whipped
long sheets of white foam from the crests of huge Atlantic
rollers. Cold as winter and blowing sharply from the northwest, it might have been December rather than June.

The big inner harbor was sheltered from the worst of it,
and although the timbers of the trawler fleet, lashed tightly
together, creaked and screeched as they ground against each
other, they were safe.

Even had the weather been fine it would have been
unusual to see commercial activity in Killybegs so early on a
Sunday morning, yet it was not unknown and the few people
out and about paid little attention as fish boxes were loaded
from the small lock-up garage at the end of the main street
into the white Hiace van backed up against it. An elderly
man, walking his fat, arthritic spaniel past it, did not even
glance at what was going on.

The men worked efficiently and in silence. Loading completed, one climbed into the driver's seat, one secured the
vehicle's back doors, the third scanned the lock-up's interior, making sure that nothing untoward would show to the
prying eye. He went back inside and twitched at a pile of old
nets and canvas sheeting in one of the back corners. Satisfied, he came out into the overcast day and secured the door
with a rusty chain and padlock. Then he joined his colleagues in the van and they moved off.

As the Hiace traveled out of the town and toward the coast
road, behind it, at the pier, one of the smaller trawlers, the

Agnes Monica, slipped her moorings and nosed carefully out from between the companions tied on either side of her. As the captain took her forward, the hands on deck made sure that the vessels they were leaving exposed were tied up again. Then, as the trawler came clear and chugged slowly across the harbor toward the open sea, the men busied themselves with ropes and boxes and a general tidy up. All the activities preparatory to a day's or a week's fishing.

The captain knew they would attract little attention, even putting to sea in such filthy weather. Those who fished from Killybegs were not fainthearted but, in any event, unlike the supertrawlers which tracked the shoals across the open Atlantic, the *Agnes Monica* was a coaster, plying the inshore waters along the heavily indented shoreline and augmenting its usual catch of mixed fish with the contents of a few lobster pots. Everyone in the town would know that although she might be in for a bit of bumping, it would be nothing she had not encountered before.

They had spread the word that they might head around and over toward Rathlin and that they would be gone for a few days. That should cover them with their colleagues; as for the law—the captain grinned to himself as he chugged toward the harbor entrance—the Gárdaí were as transparent as children. They entrusted most of their so-called undercover activities to the night hours and were all snugly tucked up by now. The day shift was still turning over under its duvets and resisting its wives' exhortations to get up and get ready for early Mass.

The transfer of the fish boxes on to the *Agnes Monica* was effected in a tiny cove, invisible from the road above, about eleven miles west-northwest of Killybegs. Swirling sheets of rain obscured all but the nearest of the stony fields, which sloped steeply toward the cliff. The three men in the Hiace could not have asked for better conditions.

The trawler was hove to just outside an inlet, and if there had been anyone around to see, he would have assumed that the yellow-jacketed deck hands were priming the lobster pots stacked neatly along the rails, prior to throwing them over. What he would not have seen, unless he was right on the shore, was the Hiace. Having bumped down a tortuous little track, no wider than the span of its axles, the van was now tucked into a rocky indentation eroded into the cliff face. The three men jammed into the seat spoke little but it was clear that one was in charge. As the rain and wind pounded against the vehicle, and the other two swore at the discomfort, this man, gloved hands folded in his lap, sat as patiently as a sphinx, while the dinghy from the *Agnes Monica* was driven before the wind through the entrance to the cove. Although the distance to the beach was less than eighty yards, the craft was traveling so fast it was virtually surfing on the breakers. As it beached heavily, the two men jumped clear and dragged it up on to the packed wet sand.

This cove was shaped like a horseshoe; on either side, a pair of rocky promontories extended like protective arms into the sea, almost touching each other at the entrance, which was less than ten feet wide. The narrow mouth acted like a funnel for the wind, concentrating its ferocity so that the whirling spray and spume rebounded off the streaming cliffs, black and shiny as onyx.

The trip back to the top of the cliff was even more difficult than the descent. At one point the Hiace got stuck on the track, tyres spinning and spitting pebbles in all directions. Cursing, the men got out and wedged small boulders under the back wheels and pushed—no small task against the hill—until it lurched free.

But they still had to rejoin the road, which ran along the clifftop, where the risk of exposure was greatest, and they halted in a little hollow about thirty yards away. As one of the men got out and climbed the slope to check that their exit was clear, the young driver was on edge and sweating. He pulled at the collar of his oilskin after less than a minute. "Where the fuck is he gone?"

"Shaddap. You and your nerves—you've been gettin' on *my* nerves all morning." The accent of the sphinx-like man, although obviously cultivated in Donegal, was overlaid with transatlantic vowels.

The driver shot him a venomous glance. "It's all right for you. When this is over you're safely back in America. And I know where *your* money's going and it's not to feed kids like mine is."

"I said, shut up." The man in charge reached into the pocket of his oilskin and took out a gun: small, black and snub-nosed. Almost casually, he leveled it at the head of the driver, who was struck speechless with horror.

Seconds passed. Steam rose from their wet clothes and obscured the windscreen. Still holding the gun, the commander leaned forward and cleared a patch, the sleeve of his jacket squeaking against the glass. "Are you going to be quiet?"

Still speechless, the driver nodded.

"Good." His companion lowered the gun and put it away.

Just then the third man reappeared and jumped in. "All clear. Come on, get the fuck on with it!" He, too, was showing strain.

Still badly shaken, the driver swallowed with relief as he felt the bite of potholed tarmacadam under his tires. "I'm not doing this again, d'ye hear me?" He felt safer now that the third man had rejoined them. "This is the last time. I promised Marie. There's too many fuckin' eyes in this fuckin' country." When neither of the others responded, he threw the Hiace into top gear and put the boot down.

The road they were on was not the main route back to Killybegs: narrow and twisting, it wound along the top of the cliff and joined the main road a few miles outside the town. "You're going too fuckin' fast," the third man yelled, as the tires squealed on a bad bend, "you'll attract every fuckin' policeman from here to Letterkenny."

The driver did not reply, concentrating on the few yards of roadway ahead of the speeding vehicle. The rain was now so heavy that the wipers were useless, and as for the light—it was less half past eight in the morning than nightfall. The driver flicked on his headlights but they were of little help, illuminating spears of rain and drifts of mist. "Slow—fuckin'—*down*!" the third man yelled again.

"Jesus!" The driver swore. A white Gárda car, blue roof lights revolving slowly, was parked against the verge about fifty yards ahead. Standing beside it, in yellow slicker and Sam Brown, which glowed in the headlights of the oncoming Hiace, the officer was flagging them down with a torch.

"Don't stop. Run it!" snapped the commander.

Instinctively, the driver obeyed, flooring the accelerator so that the Hiace leaped. The Gárda jumped backward, crashing heavily against the hood of his vehicle as the van sped past.

"Jesus, now they're on to us, Jesus, Jesus—" Having screeched around the first past of a corkscrew at the end of the short straight, the driver barely made the second, spinning the tires in the soft mud on the verge. "Why did I agree to this?" His voice was high and thin. "We were doin' rightly as we were, Marie'll kill me—"

"Shaddap and slow down. You'll kill us all." By this time

they were almost at the T-junction on to the main road and the commander's voice cut through the driver's panic so he again obeyed, moving his boot from the accelerator to the brake. But the rubber was slippery from the wet and his foot slipped. The van shot through the junction and on to the main road, squealed into a skid, its rear swinging wide and ricocheting off a telegraph pole sending it across the crown of the road and on to the wrong side.

The elderly driver of a Toyota Starlet coming toward them had no chance to get out of the way before the Hiace hit him head on.

Back on the secondary road above the sea, the Gárda, still badly shaken after his own near miss, was calling into Head-quarters. He did not hear the crash above the crackling of his radio and the continuing roar of the storm.

The only survivor was the Starlet driver's greyhound.

The news reached the chief superintendent in Dublin later that morning. "Who's the fucking independent operator who decided to do a Dan Dare?" He glared around the table at his task force. Some members, still at Mass maybe, had not yet come in but he had not wanted to wait.

"He's new in Killybegs." The only woman present spoke quietly. He was just starting to drive in to work, along the main road," she leaned forward and pointed to an Ordnance Survey map spread over the table, "this one here—"

"I know where the fucking road is."

"Sorry." The woman was not put out. "He was coming out of his gateway on to this road and he had stopped for a second. He thought he caught a glimpse of a vehicle driving too fast on the coast road that runs below the main one—"

"I see." Daly's tone was larded with heavy sarcasm. "Well, him and his fucking great ocular appendages can get themselves to hell on some offshore island. It took a lot of resources to set up this operation." Again he scowled around the table. "Where's de Burgh?"

"He's on his way in, sir," the woman officer ventured. Then, knowing better than to say anything more, they all sat waiting.

The chief got up and went across to a little side table. He poured coffee from a Thermos flask into a cup, added three spoonfuls of sugar and brought it back to the table. "No one can find that bloody trawler," he said quietly. "It seems to have evaporated into thin air."

"Does Lynskey know what's happened?"

"I've left a message for him to ring in—*shit!*" The chief threw his plastic spoon across the room.

Chapter Fifteen

Toby de Burgh was of average height and build, and although his face was passably handsome, he was one of those men who could, with ease, fade into the background of any gathering. His only memorable feature was his light-colored eyes. Unlike Rupert, who was still estranged from their parents, he had taken full advantage of his family's money to set himself up, and was now wealthy on his own right from his activities in the City. He was a bachelor but not one who featured in the society columns, and his flat, furnished with massive Queen Anne and heavy Victorian furniture, showed no sign of a designer's hand. He was bidding farewell to his guests, the Prince of Wales and his detective.

He closed the door and sat at the table to review the course of the conversation. It had not gone too badly. Toby had no illusions that his illustrious guest had come because of his charming personality: he knew that the Prince was hoping he would donate a substantial sum to one of the organizations which received his royal patronage. Pleading another engagement, His Royal Highness had stayed less than forty minutes and had refused even a glass of wine.

It was not as though Toby himself was enamored of a prince who held the honorary post of Colonel-in-Chief of the Paratroop Regiment, the very regiment responsible for Derry's Bloody Sunday.

He poured himself a glass of Calvados and gathered his thoughts for the telephone call to his brother. The tabloid clipping Rupert had sent him, TWITCHERS EXPECTED TO FLOCK TO MUSEUM, still lay on the table. Sipping his drink, Toby reread it then carried it to his desk, where he picked up the telephone.

When the call was answered, he did not identify himself. "Nothing much," he said softly, "but I could tell by his reaction. I'd bet strongly, more than strongly, that the venue is go. He pretended not to be interested. So much so that I could see he knew too much about it." Without waiting for an answer, he hung up.

Alone in the sitting room of his house in Churchtown, Rupert put down his own telephone and went to the door to listen: the bass thump-thump of the stereo unit in his sons' room continued unabated while, from the kitchen, he could hear his wife in heated argument with his daughter. Family as normal.

Quickly, he made a call to Sheriff O'Connor in Mayville, Montana: "It's go. The venue is as we discussed. And there's one other thing, there's a man called Fergus Lynskey," quickly, he spelled it, "L-Y-N-S-K-E-Y, out there to Butte. Be careful, he's posing as a teacher. I don't know where he's staying, some hotel in the town, but try the biggest. He's one of ours, on the lookout." Like Toby, he did not wait for a reply and, after he had hung up, turned to look at himself in the mirror over the fireplace in the sitting room. He had never liked it, a wedding present from his wife's sister: it had too many curlicues and cherubs in its thick gilt frame. But he liked the look of himself. In that mirror he was a man of substance.

From these two telephone calls grew a daisy chain of further calls. Within ten minutes, plans for the operation had moved into high gear.

"Hire a car if you have to. Just get a move on your end, Lynskey—hold on—" The chief superintendent broke off in response to a knock on the door. "Yes?"

It was ten minutes after the meeting at Gárda headquarters had broken up and, seeing his boss was on the phone, Rupert de Burgh reversed out of his office. "I'll come back."

"What is it, de Burgh? Tell me now, or I'll be gone. I'm on my way to Killybegs."

"It was that I wanted to talk to you about." De Burgh was apologetic. "I'm sorry I missed the meeting—I couldn't get here on time. But I've done a bit of work up in Donegal before, I know the lie of the land and I'm sure I could spot a few faces for you. Could I be useful to you if I came along?"

"Hang on a mo'," Daly said into the phone, then, to de Burgh again, "Come back when I'm finished this and we'll discuss it." He waited ostentatiously until the detective had left the room, then: "You still there, Fergus? Right, I've got a new name for you. Again, the feds got it from the Mounties in Ottawa—they seem to be really on the ball up there. This is a fella called Jerry Flynn." He listened, then, "I know, it's the first we've ever heard of him but until a few days ago we'd never heard of this Sheriff Brian O'Connor either. Apparently this Flynn character is flying down to a rodeo somewhere in Montana today—he has horses as well as everything else. And guess who his guest is going to be?" He listened, then: "Bingo. But no, I don't know where the effin' thing is. That's what you're out there for. Just do it yesterday. Our friend across the water is getting itchy for an answer about the famous visit. So's the Taoiseach—another two points down in the polls today."

Out in the corridor, de Burgh, who had been chewing gum, popped a new piece into his mouth as he leaned against the wall. "Waiting to see the headmaster, are we?" another detective chided as he walked past.

"Yeah." De Burgh did not smile. The walls and doors were thick and largely soundproof, and although he strained his ears, he could hear nothing but a faint murmur, and then the dim percussion of the telephone being slammed down.

He eased himself off the wall and had his hand on the door handle when it was wrenched away from him. "Oh," the chief stood inside, "I was just coming out to get you. We'll be leaving in about ten minutes."

"There's another couple of things. Could I have a moment, chief?" De Burgh's face was serious.

The chief sighed, walked back into the room and behind his desk. "Grab a pew." He indicated the chair in front of it.

"Thank you." De Burgh put his notes on the table in front of him. "Oh, sorry," he seemed only then to remember the gum in his mouth, "where's your can?"

"Here." The chief gestured toward the side of the desk. "What's on your mind?"

"It's nothing much, chief." De Burgh went around and pulled the can toward him so the desk was between himself and the chief. He sat down. "I just wanted to tell you that, sometime soon, I'll need a few days off. My sister-in-law's having a baby and my wife is going over to England to help." As he was speaking he had leaned forward to deposit the wad of gum. "I'll have to hold the fort with the kids."

What the chief superintendent did not see was that de Burgh had transferred the gum from his right to his left hand, sticking it to something already palmed. And while he made a movement toward the can as though discarding it, he was sticking the gum under the lip of the desk, as far back as he could manage. "Filthy habit," he apologized again, "but it keeps me off the cigs."

The chief superintendent made no difficulties about the time off but instead of standing up to go de Burgh sat on. "The other thing I thought I might mention, but it may be a hoax . . ."

"I'm all ears."

"I got an anonymous telephone call at home just before I left. The guy was trying to disguise his voice but he might have had a Cork accent." The chief tilted his chair so far back it was in danger of falling. De Burgh hesitated. "He seemed to be saying that what we're looking for is buried in the grounds of a hotel in Glengarriff."

"That's at the opposite end of the country from Killybegs. You're sure he said Glengarriff?" And when de Burgh nodded assent, "Did he say which hotel?" The chief superintendent had gone very quiet.

"No."

"Do you realize how many hotels there are in Glengarriff?"

"I did say that maybe it was another hoax." De Burgh shrugged. He knew that Glengarriff, one of the most beautiful places in the southwest of Ireland, was a tourist Mecca. Just now it was coming up to the height of its season.

"Leave it with me." The chief pursed his lips.

A few minutes later, de Burgh was speaking to his brother from a telephone booth outside the gates of the Phoenix Park, less than a half a mile from Gárda headquarters. "Done." He listened, then: "That won't happen, Toby, you don't know our cleaners. Anyway, there're cutbacks in overtime among them too, it's unlikely they're going to be that thorough. In any case, it won't be there for long. Talk to you tonight from Killybegs."

He hung up and walked fast back through the park toward his office. It suited him that the Gárdaí were at sixes and sevens.

The previous year, at his wife's insistence, he had increased his mortgage so that he and his family could take a once-in-a-lifetime holiday. They had chosen California. On the last night, in a hotel bar in San Francisco, the Irish detective had, unusually for him, struck up a desultory conversation with a plumber from Santa Barbara whose name was Joe Mason. The two had stayed up talking long into the night. They had exchanged telephone numbers and addresses, as one does on holidays, and de Burgh had largely forgotten about his new friend.

But then Mason's call had come, with a careful, obliquely worded request. It did not take de Burgh long, however, to realize that he was being asked to collaborate in a plot to infiltrate the annual republican commemoration of the patriot Wolfe Tone at Bodenstown in Co. Dublin. The plan was to take the Taoiseach hostage just before he read his speech and then to read their own proclamation of nationalistic defiance.

Initially Rupert had thought the plan crazy but even as Joe Mason continued to speak he had seen the glimmer of possibility that these people could be useful.

He had flown to London to confer with his brother, and the more they discussed it, the more they saw how they could use these misguided and outdated idealists for their own purposes—or, rather, de Burgh had seen it and had managed to persuade Toby.

Up to now, the de Burghs had remained independent of any of the recognized subversive groups. Yet they constituted a two-man oragnization which had bided its time and watched for an opportunity to make its contribution. Rupert was content to wait, for decades if need be, as he wormed his way closer and closer to the heart of the Irish security service. This quisling service which now doffed its cap to the English.

The beauty of Joe Mason's call was that it had dovetailed nicely with the chance for which the brothers had waited so long.

It arose because of Toby's lifestyle. He was gay and one of his lovers, who had not come out, was a senior official in the Foreign Office in London. It was for this reason alone that his urbane and wealthy City friend had cultivated him. The arrangement, in which Toby and his friend met only at parties and at the houses of people with equal need for anonymity, suited the de Burghs' purposes very well, although until recently, the gossip and inside Foreign Office information had been of such little significance that Toby had begun to think he was wasting his time. Until he had hit the jackpot.

He and his friend had been enjoying a cognac in their palatial bedroom during a weekend houseparty in Surrey when the civil servant had gossiped about a possible trip to Éire for the Prince of Wales.

Within hours of receiving this nugget, Rupert was in touch with Joe Mason: he would help with Joe's group effort and would let them know the timing. But, of course, he did not tell him what he and Toby really intended. He was not sure if the Americans would have the guts for it.

Unknown to Bill Daly or Fergus Lynskey or anyone else, another thread had been added to the skein of mayhem.

After a restless night, haunted by erotic fantasies wherein she was being pleasurably engulfed by the huge soft lips and sinuous limbs of a fabulous creature resembling a benign praying mantis, Sky woke just after dawn. Reluctant to let the dream dissolve, she kept her eyes closed and tried to maintain it while her body reveled in the warm hollow of her mattress. Then, with a sensation like walking under a cold waterfall, she remembered Greg.

Her eyes flew open on the salmon pink day. Dammit. Why did every silver lining come with a cloud? She would not be able to live with herself unless she spoke with him face to face.

She tumbled out of bed and not bothering to cover her nakedness—Johanna would not be up for hours yet—padded toward the shower. Inside, she kept both hands on the controls, letting the water pour over her, alternately hot and cold. Johanna insisted that showers were essential for cleansing the aura and, for once, her daughter did not disagree. She concentrated on directing her mind toward the first task of the day. Daniel Treacy.

She rehearsed the headlines of the story: the mysteries surrounding Midge's life, the opportune crash that had killed her, the closed coffin, the sheriff's attitude, the scrawled note on the coffee coupons, the feeling that Skippy was part of an upstate conspiracy, Treacy's odd rush away from the funeral home, his long-time obsession with her own grandmother. His questionable past. By the time she stepped out of the shower and was toweling herself dry, Treacy occupied every corner of her mind.

She arrived at the offices of Treacy Resources exactly on time. "I'm sorry to call you in on a Sunday," Treacy was sitting across from her behind his desk—no hospitality today—"but, as I told you last night, I'm afraid I have meetings all day tomorrow and the coming week is busy. I will be out of town for most of it. What are these one or two details you wish to know?" He began to drum the fingers of one hand on the desk-top. This from a man who had called her three times and who was, in a sense, bent on infiltrating her family.

Sky decided once again she would not be intimidated. "Do you never take time off, Mr. Treacy."

He stared at her, then, slowly: "As you are aware, my wife is not cold in her grave. However, as it happens, Miss MacPherson, I have acceded to well-meaning pressure from a business acquaintance and I am going on an—ah—outing this afternoon. Not that it is any of your concern."

"It transpires that some of the details I need to ask you about concern the death of your wife."

"Indeed?" His tone was icy. "I would think that as my wife is so recently dead and buried, the *Courier* would have the decency to desist from prying into such a painful and personal area of my life."

"May I ask what you were calling me about, Mr. Treacy? I got one message at the office and two at home."

The fingers stilled. "I am a tidy man, Miss MacPherson, with a tidy mind. I do not like loose ends. And, since you ask, I do know that you have been digging around about my wife's death in the north of the state."

"Sheriff O'Connor?"

"Never mind how I know. Why are you poking around?" His composure slipped a fraction.

"Because it's my job." She kept her voice cool. "You could save us both a great deal of trouble, even grief, if you would talk to me and tell me the truth about what happened to your wife."

"The truth, Miss MacPherson," he locked his eyes with hers, "is that I genuinely do not know. I was not there that night. I do not know in what state poor Midge was when she drove to her death."

"Wasn't there a postmortem?"

"There was very little for the medical examiner."

Suddenly, Sky felt dirty, with little entitlement to the high moral ground she had claimed earlier for herself and the *Courier*. "I'm sorry," she said.

"Are you? Sorry enough to desist from pursuing this non-story?"

"There is just one thing." Nettled again, Sky took a deep breath. "Had your wife anything to do with the death of a hobo on the highway somewhere north of Libby?"

Treacy got up and turned to gaze through the window toward the statue of Our Lady of the Rockies. He clasped his hands behind his back. Seeing traces of white on the knuckles, she let him be. If he was ever going to tell her, now was the time.

As she waited, Sky committed this room and everything in it to memory. On her last visit she had noted its austerity, but now she went further: unusual for an executive in his position, there was no clock, no memento, no award, framed certificate or executive toy. Except for the single photograph of his dead wife, it was as though Daniel Treacy had had the place scoured so that no clue to his own personality or interests could possibly be divined.

Around them, in the unnaturally quiet building, the internal workings of the structure—the humming of the air-conditioning, the odd creak—which highlighted his silence might have been unnerving, had she not been so concentrated on the man at the window. "I knew it would come out eventually." He spoke so quietly she almost missed it.

He turned to face her and, with the blaze of light at his back, his features were in shadow. "Midge did kill that hobo," he said, "but it was a genuine accident. She was drunk at the time. Too drunk to do the right thing."

Sky held her nerve. If she said anything now, she might ruin what was next to come.

Treacy walked slowly back to his desk and sat down again. "It's been a terrible burden on me. Now you know. What are you going to do about it?"

"That depends on what your wife did not do. Do you mean it was a hit-and-run?" Treacy nodded and, such was the pallor of his face, she felt almost sorry for him. But she hardened her heart. This man was rich—rich enough for others, including the police, to do dirty work for him. "And there was a cover-up."

"Yes." He folded his hands in his lap and looked down at them, an uncharacteristically humble posture that puzzled Sky. He was also avoiding her eye.

"Was the sheriff involved in the cover-up?"

"He's an old friend of Bill Collins. Bill Collins is an old friend of others. That's the way it works, apparently. And that man she hit was drunk."

Sky, ignoring the implicit appeal, remembered she had had calls from Collins, had assumed that the funeral director wanted to talk to her about the shamrock lot and had been in no hurry to return them. "Look," she had no wish to torture the man in front of her, "I'll be honest with you, Mr. Treacy, I don't know yet to what use I'm going to put this story. I have to think about it. But we have a bit of time, there's no rush. Your wife is dead, after all. In a way," she softened her voice, aware that the man's bereavement was so recent, "she already paid a terrible price. I'll talk to my editor. We're not in the business of persecuting people."

"Thank you." Still Treacy did not look up.

"We'll talk again. Anyway," she tried to sound cheerful, "we have to talk about my grandmother's visit . . ."

He looked up at last. "Do you think she'll come? She certainly won't come if she thinks I've—"

"Try not to worry." Behind the awful weariness of his eyes, she could see hope and heard herself tell him that her mother was going to call Ireland again that night. "They're eight hours ahead and she imagines it will be less expensive and they can talk longer if it's late night here and early morning there."

"But it's Sunday, and, anyway, there's no need—" he began, but Sky held up her hand.

"You can't control everything, Mr. Treacy."

Chapter Sixteen

An hour after Sky left Treacy's house, although it was only ten thirty in the morning, heat already shimmered inches above the tarmacadam and baked the paintwork of the vehicles in the McDonald's parking lot. Inside, however, the patrons, clad mainly in T-shirts and cutoffs, felt the chill of the super efficient air-conditioning and rubbed at their goose-bumped flesh.

"It was an amazing change." She and Lynskey were eating Sunday brunch, although for Sky the meal began and finished with strong coffee. "In retrospect, I have the impression that he was sort of waiting for the bad news, you know?" She looked around, irritated at the level of chatter in the echoing room. "It's terribly noisy in here."

"Reminds me of Dublin Zoo." Lynskey bit into the second of his Egg McMuffins. "But to get back to your man, I wouldn't blame the poor chap. You certainly ruined his day. You're pretty sure that note's the real thing?"

"It appears so now." Sky watched in fascination as he poured two packets of salt over his second carton of french fries, then said, hearing echoes of her mother, "That stuff'll kill you, you know."

"What?" Lynskey paused a fraction. "All these fries?"

"All that salt."

"Listen, my mother's eighty-two and she likes a bit of mashed potato with her salt. We like salt in our family. So your man was poleaxed, what happened then?" With his left hand, he scooped up a fistful of the fries and put them in his mouth.

"Are you left-handed?" Sky tended sneakily to subscribe to the unproven notion that left-handed people are more intelligent than their more numerous right-handed brethren. She had always been attracted to intrinsic intelligence the way some women are attracted to power.

"Ambidextrous," he chewed with evident enjoyment, "comes in handy, no pun intended." He grinned, then: "So go on, did you get the feeling there was more to tell?"

Considering her answer, Sky looked away. They were seated beside the wall of plate glass facing the parking lot and, as she watched, a big Lincoln, springs bouncing under the exuberance of what seemed to be dozens of children, was turning slowly through the entrance. Multicolored balloons streamed from every open window and even through the thickness of the double glazing she could hear the high-pitched excitement from within the vehicle. "I wish I was that age again," she said.

"A birthday, obviously." Lynskey paused long enough to look affectionately at the festive Lincoln then went back to his meal. "Can't say it makes me homesick, though. Thank God I won't have to deal with kids for another three months at least. So did you? Feel that McCarthy had more to tell?"

Startled, Sky looked back at him. "How do you know his real name's McCarthy?"

"You told me, silly. That first day, on the way to the Buffalo Jump."

Had she? Sky could not pinpoint any conversation in which she had mentioned it. "You keep bringing us back to this subject," she said suddenly.

"Do I?" Lynskey tore open another packet of salt. "It's a fascinating story, you've got to agree. It has everything, money, sex—albeit over a long distance—death in mysterious circumstances. Yeah. Even the possibility of a happy ending."

As usual, Sky could not contain her suspicions. "You're not thinking of using this for your novel, are you?"

Lynskey's shout of laughter caused several of the restaurant patrons to look round. "Give us a break, love," he said, when he had managed to control himself. "I'm a schoolteacher. My novel, when it comes, will be small and perfect and full of serious *angst*. Stuff like money and love and death is too trivial for me."

Sky smiled and, as the birthday party erupted into the restaurant, began to go through what Treacy had said, how he had behaved. The more she talked, the more convinced she became that she was seeing only the tip of the story. Lynskey seemed to agree, nodding over his rapidly diminishing pile of fries, encouraging her with astute prompts.

"What do you want to do?" They were walking to the Nissan.

"I dunno." He shrugged. "What do people do in Montana on a Sunday in late June? What's on that I can boast about back home? Anything really special? I have my camera." He patted a bulge in the back pocket of his awful shorts. "I thought of asking you to take me out to the Little Big Horn battlefield but then I remembered it's Sunday and I'd prefer to do it when there weren't so many people about."

"I don't mind taking you out there, but it's quite a distance, you know—it's beyond Billings—"

"I know." His long face lit up. "I saw a newspaper ad for a rodeo somewhere around here this weekend. That has to be the most quintessentially American Western thing I could see. Would it still be on, do you think? Could we go?"

"It's on, all right." Sky hesitated. Briefly, she told Lynskey about the spat she had had with Jimbo the previous week.

"Well, of course, we don't have to go, I'm sure I can catch one somewhere else along the way." But he looked so crestfallen that Sky changed her mind. The wretched rodeo would be a way of entertaining him and would earn her a few Brownie points.

"Are you sure you don't mind?" His pleasure was infectious when she told him they would go.

"Everyone has to go to a rodeo at least once in his life—I think." She laughed as he kissed her cheek.

Jimbo was delighted too, once he had gotten over his astonishment. "I'll contact the photographer—he can meet you there. And I'll pull off the kid, give her something else to do next weekend." Even from home, Jimbo's telephone voice was different from the one he used for face-to-face encounters. Flat and snappy, it gave the correct impression that the instrument was not his favorite medium of communication. "Bye." He hung up abruptly.

"All set." Sky joined Lynskey in the Nissan. "I'll just wheel by the office to collect the paperwork I need and we'll go right away. It's not all that far, just over ninety miles."

"I'll never get used to the distances here. You say ninety miles like we say three. That Little Big Horn must really be far away."

"Welcome to Montana, buddy." As they pulled out of the lot, heading toward the newspaper office, Sky looked doubtfully at the pale freckled skin of his upper arms; Lynskey had at last dumped the sweatshirt and, in honor of the heat, now wore a T-shirt in bright green emblazoned with legends supporting the Irish national soccer team, which had evidently taken part in some festival or competition called Italia 90. "You'll need a hat in this sun," she pulled her sunglasses from the glove compartment, "but we can buy one at the grounds. You're already looking a bit pink."

"I'm grand. Sure I can't go home without a suntan, can I?"

"You never heard of melanoma?" But Sky grinned. His enthusiasm was impossible to resist. She might even enjoy the rodeo for once.

The man from Helena, the state capital, who had engaged Sheriff O'Connor in the matter of the casket, was speaking on a secure cellular phone to a woman in Vancouver.

This woman, slight of form and with Oriental features, lived frugally in an expensive apartment, which had a view across the water toward Vancouver Island. Her furniture was of carved or lacquered wood and brass, her wall coverings and soft furnishings in shades of gold and red. She had bought her home ten years previously, paying cash and finding little difficulty in passing scrutiny by the building's interviewing committee. She had no family ties, no pets and, being new to their city, no local friends. The committee members expressed a doubt among themselves that her aura of self-sufficiency might border on eccentricity but they approved her anyway.

They were not disappointed. She proved an exemplary tenant with perfect manners, paying her service and maintenance charges promptly. Although she had never agreed to serve on any of the subsequent committees, or to attend any meetings called to discuss affairs of mutual interest, she was exceptionally polite to her neighbors when she met them in the elevators or in the lobby. And, indeed, her lifestyle was so quiet and unobtrusive that if had not been for these fleeting encounters, she might not have been in the building at all.

What the interviewing committee had not known was that, before moving to their exclusive block in Vancouver, this woman had been the mistress of many politicians and scions of industry in Toronto, Ottawa and, being bilingual, in French-

speaking Montreal. Neither did they know that she was not
planning to stay among them for much longer but was *en
route* to her retirement destination, the house she had had built
on a tiny, so far uninhabited island she owned off the coast of
Brazil, which did not enjoy reciprocal extradition treaties with
Canada. They could not have known that although her tax
returns showed her to be a woman of substantial means,
whose income was derived from shrewd investments in stock,
they bore little relation to the true extent of her holdings.

Through diligent and imaginative use of her assets, this
woman's wealth, hardly any of which was held in Canada
but was spread over the Cayman Islands, Switzerland and the
Isle of Man, was more than enough to fuel the economy of a
European statelet for at least three months. Her turnover was
as big as that of a modest multinational corporation which, in
a sense, she had become. She was answerable to no board,
however. And none of the operations she masterminded took
place within the borders of her domicile. Instead, she controlled them through a network of five trusted deputies in
Anchorage, Los Angeles, Orlando, Mexico City and Helena,
chosen because it was so relatively obscure and crime-
free that it would attract little unwanted attention. These
deputies, her only full-time employees, were each paid a
salary higher than that of the President of the United States,
and provided the woman received the profits she expected in
a given endeavor, any excess they garnered, through favorable fluctuations in exchange rates, for instance, was their
own business.

The lieutenants also had a free hand in the recruitment of
underlings, provided that these minions adhered to the
pyramid structure the woman laid down in the blueprint for
her organization: temporary workers received and relayed
orders only from and to the layers directly above and below.
This precaution ensured that no one except the woman and
her five lieutenants had a full picture of any operation. And
not one of the five knew about the work of any of the other
four. The woman did not believe in consultation, democracy
or round table meetings. She did almost all of her business
by electronically secured telephone and her only face-to-face
engagements were in Ottawa with the pricy accountant who
had once been her lover.

She listened carefully as her man in Helena, who knew
that his boss always wanted the facts, no matter how

unpalatable, explained what had gone wrong with the operation in Ireland.

The crash of the Hiace—which could not have been foreseen—had served to redouble the attentions of the Irish police and government. The goods in the northwest of Ireland were safe, her man assured her, but it would be unwise to access them.

He then outlined the problems within the state of Montana, which could be contained: the newspaper was only a two-bit outfit with a cash-flow problem and would have to back off sooner rather than later. The FBI angle was well covered—he knew that the woman had a well-paid mole—and although the Irish cop's presence in Butte was a wild card, it was wound in with the work of the newspaper reporter and a method could be devised to deal with them both at once.

It was the first full briefing the woman had had. Normally, having set up an operation and provided the seed money, she let the others run it. Her genius lay in identifying niche markets: in knowing what product was most profitable in what part of the world. Her apartment was cabled and also sported a satellite dish and, as she spent a good proportion of her time watching television, she was well versed in foreign affairs. She made it her business to know which organizations might need funds for their own purposes. And exactly where.

Although she knew she was not the first to identify Ireland as an entrypoint into the lucrative European market, the present Irish operation was her first foray into that country. Cautious as always, she had instructed that this test operation be kept small. The follow-up, however—ready to be put in motion the moment she gave the go-ahead—was the biggest she had ever prepared.

Now, as she listened to the bad news pouring down the line from Helena, she was weighing up her options: whether she should cut her losses and shut the whole thing down, or whether she should order damage limitation and proceed with the test. She had a great deal at stake: the main business, which was to follow this exercise was not only the biggest of her career, it was to be her last, before the curtain fell on her retirement.

* * *

Sky and Lynskey held hands like high school sweethearts. Even for Montana, it was a gorgeous day and, as the miles unrolled under the Nissan's tires, she felt young and irresponsible, even happy. The steady wind through the open windows was warm on her cheek and neck; to the west, under the crystal sky, the amethyst of the mountains seemed further away than usual, while eastward, the recent storms, not enough to count as full-blown rains, had refreshed and softened the prairie, hazing its straw with pale and supple green.

After a bit, almost shyly at first, Lynskey began to tell her about his geographically far-flung but close-knit family.

After he had finished, Sky could not help but compare his mother's view of child-rearing to Johanna's laid-back and *laissez-faire* approach. "That's quite a group of achievers, she must be some woman. All those vocations and professions scattered all over the globe."

"And then there's yours truly."

"Teaching is an honorable profession."

He was silent and, for once, she did not leap to bridge the gap. She had to give herself a stern talking-to. Although she felt as though she and Lynskey had known one another for aeons, they had met less than forty-eight hours before. She had to slow herself, and it was obvious he wanted to take things easy. She shifted down a gear to negotiate a non-existent bump in the highway. "So, you're all away from Ireland except you?"

"Yeah. Us Lynskeys could field a modest international think tank. Between countries of residence and spouses, at last count we covered eleven nations."

"It's nice for your mother that she has one of her children left in Ireland. At her age she must rely on you a lot."

But this assumption, too, was misconceived. Apparently, Lynskey's mother was as spry as a forty-year-old and had filled her retirement years with twice as much activity as when she had been in harness. "Remember she's a Kerry-woman." Lynskey smiled affectionately as though this explained his mother's stamina. "She loves cards—she's a member of three different poker schools. She's in a creative-writing circle and last year she took up Italian because she intends to travel to Verona in August and wants to understand first-hand what the operas are about." He reached for

Sky's hand and squeezed it. "She reminds me a bit of your mother. Same spirit."

Sky thought of Johanna's willow-like attitude to whatever life threw at her and raised her eyebrows at the notion of there being the remotest similarity between her and Lynskey's redoubtable mother. "Maybe. But she sounds a lot more like my grandmother. At least, they're more of an age."

She told him then of what she knew about her grandmother's lifestyle in Cork, how, when she was sure her family was reared, she had moved back to the city from the fastnesses of West Cork. How, at the age of sixty-two, she went to college and graduated with a degree in music, how she was now one of the leading lights in local music circles. "Come to think of it, she does sound a lot like your mother."

"It's odd she's never been out here, isn't it?" he asked. "After all, three of her family are here, and crossing the Atlantic is only a matter of a few hours, these days."

"She just never got around to it, I suppose. As my mother told you last night, ours unlike yours, is not a close family."

The rodeo ground was buzzing. As they threaded their way through the horseboxes, steer trucks, feed and veterinary wagons, pickups containing harness and blacksmith equipment, she could hear the amplified voice of the announcer urging on the barrel-racers inside the arena.

The only thing Sky liked about rodeos was the smell of the air: horseflesh, fresh sweat and dung, earth, leather, barbecue smoke, the scent of canvas, warm metal and frying onions, fresh coffee and beer. In a way, she thought as she showed her press card and ID at the entrance, the cocktail epitomized Montana. "I have a guest," she told the man scrutinizing her passes.

"I can pay," Lynskey protested.

"Not when you're with me, you don't." Sky waved to a colleague from a Great Falls radio station as the man allowed them to pass through. "This is work."

"Nice work if you can get it. I can't believe I'm here." Lynskey snapped a couple of drovers leading one of the bulls toward the arena.

"Believe it," Sky waved at another acquaintance, "you'll be sick of cowboys before the day is over." She left him briefly to go and talk to a woman she recognized from Butte. To her exasperation, when she went back she found he had joined a line in front of a hot dog stand. "I don't know what it is about American food," he was unabashed at her obvious disapproval, "it just doesn't fill you up. Want something? Come on, it smells delicious."

Sky held firm and walked a little way off to wait for him and take color notes. She was leaning against the tailgate of a station wagon and trying to summon up enough enthusiasm to walk across to an old-timer for a quote, when all heads around her turned in response to a helicopter slowly descending at the far side of the showgrounds.

Choppers were not unusual in Montana but this one was big enough to transport a modest glee club and obviously heralded the arrival of a VIP. She hurried back to Lynskey, who had not yet reached the head of the hot dog line, and told him to meet her at the announcer's stand in fifteen minutes.

She arrived at the fringe of the landing site just as the pilot switched off the rotors. The reporter from the radio station in Great Falls was ahead of her, standing a little in front of the curious onlookers, recorder held protectively to his breast.

The buzz of the crowd stilled as she moved up to join him, and she was amused to see, as from the arena the amplified voice of a young girl sounded the first notes of the "Stars and Stripes," that he straightened his shoulders and laid his free hand under his recorder in the approved hand-over-heart position. Patriotism most alive and well in Great Falls. As for herself she concentrated on the throp-throp of the slowing rotors.

When the door of the aircraft opened, she recognized the elderly man who alighted first; she had seen him here in previous years and had even interviewed him briefly, but his name escaped her. "Remind me who that is?" she muttered out of the side of her mouth to the radio reporter.

"Name's Jerry Flynn." He was checking his tape. "He's a Canadian. Logging, minerals, that kind of thing. He also runs stock in Alberta on one of those million-acre spreads."

Flynn, whose hair was longish, was wearing full Western gear, a huge cream-colored Stetson, hide boots, check shirt under fringed jacket and a thong tie clasped with the silver and turquoise head of a bronco. "Talk about cheesy! He'd make a good Buffalo Bill, whaddya think?" the radio reporter gibed under his breath.

Sky did not altogether agree.

Although to judge by the wrinkled skin on his face, white

mustache and liver-spotted hands the guy must have been at least in his sixties, his body was in good shape and she thought that the outfit did not look anymore incongruous on him than it would have on Jimmy Stewart, who was one of her mother's favorite stars. Cheesy, though, was an apt description of his smile. The guy had two gold teeth on one side of his mouth.

The clothes of the much younger man who followed him out were similar but horribly inappropriate because of his weight. "He could eat for the Olympics." The radio man looked worried. "Never saw him before—you know him, Sky?"

"Uh uhhh." Sky was staring at the third passenger just now getting out. Conservatively dressed in dark jeans and plain shirt, and looking around the ground as he descended, was Daniel Treacy. She had barely time to register her surprise before she was walking alongside the radio reporter toward the chopper to do her job. "This is a first. Never saw Treacy here before either," the reporter hissed. "Let me talk to him first, OK?"

"Sure."

While Treacy and the fat man stood a little apart, Jerry Flynn continued to stand at the door of the helicopter, talking to the pilot who had remained inside. Of course, Sky thought, Flynn had to be the "colleague" of whom Treacy had spoken that morning. So far he had not seen either her or the radio reporter—or if he had, he was ignoring them. She had little time for further speculation because Treacy spotted her. "We meet again, Miss MacPherson," he said, as she and her colleague reached him.

"We do indeed." Sky introduced the radio man, who immediately asked for an interview.

"No thank you." As though willing Flynn to hurry, Treacy looked over his shoulder at his host, who was still talking to the pilot. Sky realized that, apart from the few seconds during which she had seen him walk from the door of the funeral parlor to his limousine, this was the first time she had seen him outdoors. In this bright sunlight, he looked tired: his complexion was gray and, standing so close to him, she could see deep, violet-shaded rings around his eyes.

"Nothing serious, sir," the reporter persisted. "Our listeners would just like to know how you're enjoying yourself today, that sort of thing . . ."

Treacy glanced at Sky then, not waiting for the reporter's cue or question, raised his voice to a commanding monotone and spoke into the microphone, congratulating the American Legion on another successfully organized event and assuring everyone that this would prove to be the best ever. Then he turned to the fat man. "I'll go ahead, see you at the booth." He smiled his cold smile at Sky. "Perhaps we shall run into one another again during the course of the afternoon." He walked off toward the arena.

"How about you, sir, what do you hope for today? I'm sorry, may I have your name?" The radio reporter immediately switched the microphone to the other man but Sky watched Treacy's retreating back.

The fat man was also a Canadian but had nothing to do with farms and stock. "Unless I'm foreclosing!" His belly heaved over a bronchial laugh. "I'm Mr. Flynn's banker, just along for the ride. Rodeo's the only place I see creatures bigger than myself." Again he laughed as Sky half listened, scribbling as fast as she could.

While she wrote, she continued to watch Treacy's progress and saw him pause once or twice to speak to people before he was swallowed up in the crowd. Then her eye was caught by Lynskey. Her companion for the afternoon was standing not in front of the announcer's booth, as they had arranged, but at a corner of the stand. She was too far away to discern his expression but, as she watched, she saw him take his little camera out of his back pocket and take a one-handed photograph of Daniel Treacy. She almost dropped her notebook. Then, as the fat man beside her was joined by Jerry Flynn, and the radio reporter switched the interview to him, she saw Lynskey turn, point the camera at the stand behind him and snap again, then turn back toward Treacy.

She had not imagined it. Fergus Lynskey was deliberately photographing Daniel Treacy.

Or was he? With the camera still to his eye he was now aiming at her, waving his other arm over his head to attract her attention as he did so.

Slowly, she waved back and, half listening as Flynn answered the radio reporter's questions, continued to watch Lynskey's activities. He was photographing all round him, the perfect tourist.

Sky forced herself to pay attention to her job. Although Daniel Treacy and Jerry Flynn were probably the same age, their appearances were entirely different. Whereas Treacy's closely cropped hair, lean face and thin, slightly stooped body lent him an autocratic, tired, somewhat ascetic air, Flynn's more flamboyant presentation sparkled with energy and vigor. This was an elderly man, sure, but one with drive. And unlike Treacy who did not flaunt his money, Flynn had no objection to flashing his: on his pinky he sported a ring, the diamond in which had to be, to Sky's inexperienced eye, at least two or three carats. And when he smiled, which was often, one of his canine teeth flashed gold.

She decided that she had plenty of material, and thanked the two Canadians, told the radio reporter she would see him around, and walked toward the stand. Lynskey saw her coming and, as she watched him surge toward her, long legs covering the ground so they would meet half-way, Sky remembered that it had been his idea to come here.

"Isn't this great?" He beamed as he reached her, the little camera now dangling from a wrist strap.

Chapter Seventeen

The meeting at Gárda Headquarters was coming to a close. It was taking place with much reduced numbers: the chief superintendent and Rupert de Burgh were in Killybegs and a detective inspector was temporarily in charge. The meeting had taken longer than planned—it was almost midnight— and the blond wood table was littered with coffee-stained Styrofoam cups and with the balled-up cellophane wrappers and Sunday-stale crusts from bought-in sandwiches.

Word had been issued to the press office that the accident at Killybegs was to be downplayed, except for the normal expressions of regret about the tragic loss of life of the retired chemist, so popular in the area, and of the three fishermen, all of whom had left young families. Gárda presence at the funerals was to be minimal. It was agreed that not a word of admonishment was to be spoken to the young officer who had inadvertently precipitated the crisis in case he began to make the wrong noises.

There was still no word on the whereabouts of the missing *Agnes Monica*.

Sky stared at Lynskey's camera. Then, looking directly at him and giving him no time to dissemble: "Why are you photographing Daniel Treacy?"

"What? Where?" Lynskey wheeled around and scanned the crowd in the stand. "Is he here?"

"Gimme a break. I saw you, Lynskey."

"Saw me what?" He looked down at her, his long face creased and frowning.

"Saw you deliberately taking photographs of Daniel Treacy." Sky searched his expression and could see nothing but genuine puzzlement. "You took two photographs of him."

"I'm glad I did—if I did—but how would I know what he

looked like? Not that it matters a damn, Sky, I swear to God I was just taking everything in. But if he's here, I'd love to see him. Will you point him out to me? Better still, will you introduce me?"

"He's vanished into a hospitality booth." Sky was still not convinced. "You sure you didn't recognize him coming out of that helicopter?"

"Why would I?" He chuckled. "For God's sake, MacPee, would you ever lighten up? What's the big deal, anyway?"

Sky had no answer to that. She was unsure what concerned her. In the brief pause, Lynskey's eyes grew mocking. "Look at us," he flapped a limp wrist and flounced a hip, "we're having our first row. Shall I storm away and insist on getting a taxi home? Blow all my traveler's checks but keep my dignity at all costs?"

Despite herself, Sky laughed. "That's better." Lynskey hugged her shoulders. "We're not going to let old mystery man come between us, now, are we? I'd still like to see him, though."

Sky, telling herself she was a suspicious bitch, promised she would point him out.

She was so busy during the next hour or so, however, that she almost forgot about Treacy. And, intent on her story, she also failed to notice anything unusual about the two men in Stetsons, who sat munching Fritos high in the stand toward the back row. These two, although they consulted their programs and seemed to be enjoying themselves as much as anyone else, did not seem to be talking to one another. Another odd factor in their behavior: instead of watching the action, they spent most of their time scanning the crowd.

Sky could not be blamed for failing to register the jarring presence of the two men. Her hands were full: the name of every human and animal competitor in the rodeo was listed in the official program so, although she had no difficulty with that part of her assignment, she also had to direct her photographer and engage in tedious gathering of the names of every spectator of note, along with homey little anecdotes about them:

The Willard F. Keyneses barely made it on time for the barrel-racing, nearly missing the fine showing by their daughter, Sara, who turned in her best ever time and came fourth. They told this reporter that their pedigree

Jerseys are producing record numbers of calves on
their spread up by Opportunity . . .

In the stands, Maynard and Peggy Olsen from
Wisdom showed off their first grandchild, Otley, to
their friends and rivals the Chuck Fenweigs, who are
busy rebuilding since their barn burned down this
spring . . . The William Harringtons were expecting
great things of their Palomino, Misty. Misty's beaten
every cowboy so far this season . . .

Finally, she located the proprietor of the *Courier* and did
the obligatory interview. The old man, to whom the Butte
paper was just one more page in a balance sheet, gave the
same answers to her questions as he had the year before, and
the year before that again. "Yuck! I hate doing this . . ." The
bulk of her work done, she rejoined Lynskey in the stands: in
her absence he had been adopted by every family near him.
Long legs spread wide, he was surrounded by drink cans and
plastic bags and was chewing something. "You're just a
snob." He rummaged in one of the sacks. "You can't cover
Watergate every day."

"You can't cover Watergate *any* day in Montana."

"Rubbish. There are no small stories, only small reporters.
Here, cheer up and have one of Mrs. Krabb's homemade oat-
meal cookies, they're delicious." He beamed at a woman
behind him.

"No thank you." She turned her attention to the arena,
watching with gloomy satisfaction as one of the huge cross-
bred Brahmas strolled out of his chute and refused to buck
off his rider—or even to run—acknowledging the ribald
groans of the spectators with a surprised look on his jowly
face. "You wanted to see Treacy?" She dug Lynskey in the
ribs. "There he is."

"Where?" Instantly, he sat up straight.

"Down there, in front of the bull." Sky pointed to where,
backs to the stand, Treacy and the fat man were standing
near the recalcitrant animal, which continued to resist all
attempts of its rider and a raft of the drovers to prod him into
being a good sport.

"So that's him." Lynskey leaned forward to get a better
look. "I wish he'd turn around so we could see his face."

"I still can't work out why you want to meet him so
much."

"You've been talking about nothing else, MacPee. I told you, I love a good story." He had to raise his voice to be heard above the crowd, which was in full cry at the bull, which had now spread its legs like a dog balking at being dragged along on a lead.

The rider was furious. He raked the bull's sides with his spurs, but all in vain. The beast simply eyeballed the crowd, swinging its massive head in a slow arc from side to side.

Knowing she was probably in a minority of one, Sky was delighted with the performance. "Come on, bull," she encouraged it silently. "Don't give in now. Stand your ground." As though it had heard her, the bull slowly turned its head toward the stand as a sudden gust of wind whirled an empty popcorn bag a foot across its snout. Startled, the bull drew back a little and pawed the ground. Encouraged that this was some sort of progress, the rider once again dug in his spurs and the drovers redoubled their prodding.

The announcer's booming chuckles on the crackling PA system rose to a sudden shout as, without warning, the bull sprang four-legged into the air, twisting viciously to unseat its rider who tumbled to the ground. Then the animal charged the fence, scattering its tormentors and embedding one of its horns in the woods.

Sky and Lynskey sprang to their feet, along with everyone else in the stands, but for a few seconds, all that could be heard, besides the cracking of the fence, which seemed in imminent danger of collapse, was the shouting of the clown who was trying to draw away the maddened animal. Sky could see neither Daniel Treacy nor his fat companion, who had been standing directly where the bull had struck. "Are they all right?" she shouted to Lynskey, who had leaped up on to his seat for a better look. "Can you see them? Are they hurt?"

"Naw." He helped her up beside him. "From what I could see, Treacy pulled the fat fella back just in time."

Sky caught a glimpse of Treacy. He was helping his friend to his feet but seemed to be doing it one-handed; his left arm was hanging loosely from his shoulder. "He *is* hurt." Before Lynskey could answer, she was skipping down the steps of the stand to get to Treacy and the story.

By the time she got to the ground, the clown and the wranglers had detached the bull from the fence and were leading it, docile as a doe, back to the pens.

"Bad luck for young Tuff Wexler," the announcer opined from the safety of his box, "but that's rodeo, folks," and went on to call the name of the next rider.

A few spectators were crowding around Daniel Treacy when Sky got to him. "You've hurt your arm, Mr. Treacy? Were you frightened?"

He looked coldly into her eyes. "Of course I was frightened, Miss MacPherson, and you may quote me on that. Now, if you'll excuse me, I must have this shoulder seen to." He turned to his companion, who was puffing visibly and as pale as mist. "You're sure you're all right? Come with me to the medics, you've had a shock."

The incident was already yesterday's news, and in the chute the next rider was aboard his bull. The gate crashed open and animal and rider erupted into the arena. The man was off within five seconds and as the clown distracted the animal, the announcer cut in: "If Sky MacPherson from the *Butte Courier* is on the grounds would she come to the front of the announcer's booth please, R. Sky MacPherson."

The Oriental woman looked through one of the waterside windows of her Vancouver apartment. Outside it was drizzling and the stippled surface of the water between where she sat and Vancouver Island was as gray and lifeless as she felt.

No deal was ever snag-free, but this little trial run in Ireland was far more trouble than it was worth. She was as confident as anyone could ever be that she had not attracted the attention of the Mounties—her reclusivity and elaborate precautions with all communications saw to that—and, because of her FBI mole who was indebted to her in ways that he would never like his wife or his boss to find out, never worried about the Americans. However, the Irish police were an unknown quantity. She did not like dealing in the dark and the quality of the information her people were receiving from Ireland was not good; she was irritated that her money had been squandered. Perhaps she had become too greedy. Perhaps she was being given a sign.

Still at the window, she tapped out the numbers to call her man in Helena but, despite standing instructions to him and to all her lieutenants that while an operation was under way they should never be out of contact, she received only the automatic answering service and instantly pressed the "end" button. Her first reaction was of fury but it was followed instantly by worry. The Helena man was one of her most long-standing and trusted: something must be wrong.

In downtown Vancouver, a detective who specialized in staying one step ahead of the latest communications technology, readjusted the faders on his equipment. And in Helena, the FBI agent assigned to decode the scrambled signals on his target's telephone sat on patiently.

"I'll kill her. I'll kill her . . ." Sky, strapped into her seat, did not know she had spoken aloud.

"I beg your pardon?" Daniel Treacy, his face strained and even grayer than before—presumably, Sky thought, with pain from his injured shoulder—looked across the narrow aisle.

"Nothing." Sky glanced at him. "Are you in a lot of discomfort?"

"A little." They were having to shout over the din of the helicopter rotors. The message, relayed at the showgrounds to Sky via Jimbo Larsen, had been that her mother had had an accident and was in the hospital. Apparently, one of the cats, lying in wait on the duplex roof, had snatched a hummingbird from a feeder attached to the eaves. Johanna had fetched the kitchen step-stool but in climbing on to it, in an effort to rescure the bird, had overbalanced and fallen off. Jimbo had not known to what extent she had been injured; all he knew was that she had been conscious when taken to the hospital.

"Who's with your mother now?" Treacy yelled.

"A friend who found her." Sky thanked the fates that Hermana had called in unexpectedly that morning. She had called the ambulance and had had the presence of mind to contact the *Courier*'s editor at home. "She'll stay with her until I get there."

"I hope your Irish friend will find his way safely."

Sky had no doubt that Lynskey, who was driving the Nissan back to Butte, would have little difficulty. "He's meeting me at the hospital later."

"It'll be quite a gathering." Treacy's wan smile lightened his austere features.

"Yeah," Sky agreed, "lucky for me you had the use of the helicopter. Are you sure your friends don't mind you taking me with you?"

"They're not going back to Canada until tonight and they

don't need the aircraft until then. And to call them friends is a little overstated." He leaned forward to look through his window. "They're business acquaintances." Sky was so consumed with worry about her mother that she did not care a fig about the relationship between Treacy and his colleagues.

It had been Lynskey who had suggested she go back to Butte in the chopper with Treacy. He had taken charge, overseeing the telephone calls Sky had made to Jimbo and the hospital, liaising with the paramedics who were strapping up the businessman's shoulder. To give Treacy his due, Sky thought now, he had offered instant cooperation.

Through the window on her own side of the aircraft, she could already see Butte. The pilot was taking them low, skimming over the flat mountain-top ridge above the city where the Class of '92 had staked its claim to immortality in symmetrical rows of white-painted boulders, spelling out its identity. An image of Johanna's proud, tearful face at Sky's own graduation was almost too much to bear; she closed her eyes and, although she had not prayed since grade school, begged for mercy for her mother. *Please, God, please* . . . Then, hating this hypocrisy, she opened them and engaged her host. "Are you going to sue the rodeo, Mr. Treacy? You certainly have a case."

"If anyone should be sue,"—again a ghost of a smile—"it should be our fat friend. It wasn't the bull, it was him. He fell on me." If she had not been so concerned about her mother—and so careful about protecting the big story she was sure lay at the heart of this man's conduct—at that moment she might have liked him.

The hospital was quiet; even the gingham-clad volunteers with their wicker baskets full of books and goodies did not do their rounds on Sunday afternoons.

Sky's mother had been formally admitted from the emergency room. "She's comfortable." The youthful Asian intern scanned the clipboard in his hand. "We've given her something for the pain and we're waiting for the specialist to view her X-rays. But I think he will confirm what we already suspect, Mizz MacPherson, your mother has broken two vertebrae." Sky's heart lurched. A broken back could mean paralysis. She could not bring herself to ask but mumbled that she wanted to see her mother right away.

As she followed the intern toward the room, she tried to

prepare herself to deal with this unthinkable situation. In all of her thirty-four years, she could not recall Johanna's having to spend a single day in bed, even for a summer cold. Her mother's robust health, which she attributed to her holistic lifestyle, had always been a matter of pride to her. To think of her helpless—perhaps for ever—was inconceivable.

Johanna was conscious but her neck and head were so rigidly confined in a brace that she could not see her daughter until she was standing right over the bed. When she recognized her, her face brightened. "Hello, darling. Here's a nice pickle we've got ourselves into!" Her speech was a little slurred from the medication but otherwise she was as calm as though she was receiving Buffy and Hermana in her own kitchen for a cup of tea. Gently, Sky picked up one of the inert hands, noticing as she did so that the pins which held her mother's long hair had come loose; one was dangerously close to an eye. She removed it, careful not to jog the metal clamps which framed Johanna's head and neck. Then outrage, relief, anger, fear all conspired together. "What the hell were you doing, Mom? Where's Hermana?"

"Take it easy, Mizz MacPherson." The doctor placed a soothing hand on her arm. "Your mother's had quite a shock. There'll be plenty of time for explanations later. What we have to do now is rest." His face split in a dazzling, professional smile as he turned from Sky to his patient. "Isn't that right, Mom?"

"Moondancer had a little bird," Johanna had difficulty getting her tongue around the words, "a litt-le *bird* and I had to rescue it, Sky."

As quickly as it had arisen, Sky's anger died away. "Of course you did, Mom." She sat abruptly on a chair beside the bed.

"Hermana's gone to get me a few things from the house. I'll be here a few—a few days, I guess."

"I guess you will."

"It was good of you to come home from work, darling. Thank you."

"I told you I was at the ro—" Sky began the automatic correction then bit her lip. "You're welcome. Are you feeling much pain?"

"Nothing." Johanna's forehead creased with the effort to remember something. "There was a me—message for you, Sky—oh, darn it, I can't—I can't—"

"Hush, Mom, it doesn't matter. You rest. The surgeon will be here soon."

Johanna smiled beatifically at the intern. "This young man is my angel. And, of course, my own dear guardian angel saved me. It could've—I could've—" Here the words deserted her and, driftng away, she closed her eyes in sleep.

Bathed in a rush of love and recognizing that, guardian angel or no, she had a lot for which to be grateful, Sky leaned forward and kissed her mother's still, pale face. "Don't worry, I'll look after you." Then, remembering that the intern was still with her, she straightened up. "Tell me the worst. Will she walk again?"

"It's too early to say, Mizz MacPherson."

The doctor's expression closed in and she remembered she should have known better than to ask. So jumpy was the medical profession in the U.S. about malpractice suits, concealment of information, misleading information, that she knew that no one below the rank of a fully insured specialist would venture an opinion. "Thank you, doctor, we'll be fine here. Would you mind leaving the door open?" She dismissed the intern as politely as she could and settled down to await the specialist's arrival.

As the minutes ticked by, she heard, from other rooms along the corridor, the muffled sounds of visitors, TVs, doors opening and closing with small thuds. With none of her belongings lying about, no flowers or cards, Johanna's room, with its gray steel furniture, unnaturally tidy bed and plain sateen drapes in a nondescript shade somewhere between peach and pink, seemed too quiet and antiseptic. Like the anteroom to a morgue.

As she went to the window to distract herself, Sky heard the muffled throb of the helicopter propellors and wondered whether Treacy, too, would be admitted. When she knew more about her mother's injuries, and no matter what the outcome, she must remember to ask after him. The very least she could do would be to thank him.

Chapter Eighteen

Sky was able to thank Daniel Treacy sooner than she had imagined. A few minutes later, left arm secured across his chest in a sling, he arrived in Johanna's room a second or two in advance of the specialist, the young intern and a nurse. "Oh!" Sky, who had risen when he came in, hesitated on seeing the medical entourage behind him.

"Mizz MacPherson?" The specialist, whose jaw was as well manicured as his hair and who was still wearing his golf shoes, shook hands with her. Then, hand still outstretched, he turned to Treacy. "You're the patient's husband?"

When the confusion was cleared up he asked that both visitors step outside the room while he went about his work. "I'll wait with you." Daniel Treacy sat on the bench seat in the corridor and indicated that Sky should sit beside him. "A broken neck, is it?"

"Back."

"That can be bad but not necessarily so these days. No matter what this initial prognosis turns out to be, however, I give you my personal guarantee that everything possible will be done for your mother."

"Thank you, Mr. Treacy, but I'm sure we'll be able to manage. What about your shoulder? Is it broken?"

"No, it's just a dislocation. They've fixed it, more or less, and now it's just a matter of letting nature take its course. But to get back to your mother, I hope you don't think I'm stepping out of bounds but I insist you let me help. If you're not satisfied with what's going on here, you might consider the Mayo Clinic."

Sky was not sure if she welcomed this intervention, no matter how well-meaning. She demurred tactfully but he seemed not to hear her reservations and said he would make a few calls when he got home. "And, of course, your mother's

accident alters the complexion of your grandmother's proposed visit."

"I beg your pardon?" Sky could not comprehend what he
was saying.

"Elizabeth." He stared at the wall opposite where they sat.
"Your grandmother. Her visit."

"Well, obviously we can't look after her now. My mother
will be in no—"

"On the contrary. I'm sure that now that this has happened
she will want to come as soon as possible to see her
daughter. And, of course, your mother must be given time to
rest and recuperate without the added burden of worrying
about guests." At last he turned to look at her. "I'll see that
she's looked after, Miss MacPherson."

"But you can't—"

"It's the least I owe your family." His eyes were so intense
in his pale face they seemed almost black. "You said this
morning that your mother was going to call Ireland tonight.
If it would not be too much trouble, could you make that
telephone call? I know you'll want to give your grandmother
the distressing news, but could you let her know that I shall
be calling to issue an invitation to her? And, please assure
her that if she is worried about the propriety of staying in my
house, I shall be happy to arrange a suite for her in the hotel
of her own choice or yours."

In other circumstances the notion of a seventy-five-year-
old woman being worried about propriety might have struck
Sky as funny but now it did not seem so. "I'll do it and I'll
call you when it's done."

There was no sound from her mother's room. Sky hoped
hard that Johanna was not in any pain, as she tried to imagine
what was going on. She forced herself to remember her
mother not as she was now, trussed up like a torture-ready
victim, but as the mom who, when Sky was growing up, had
sat for hour after hour on the side of her bed reading aloud
from books thought unsuitable by other moms: Johanna had
included authors like H. G. Wells, Orwell and Kerouac as
well as Anna Sewell and Louisa M. Alcott. The downside of
Sky's childhood had been the endless, unsuccessful struggle
for ordinary friendships with her peers. In the places where
she and her mother had paused long enough to constitute a
home, other kids' mothers allowed visits to the MacPhersons
only as a last resort and sleepovers were never authorized.

They knew that Johanna was as likely to distribute tales of star-crossed lovers as sunflower seeds and popcorn.

Yet, in retrospect, Sky's eclectic early upbringing had been mainly beneficial: long before she hit second grade she had known where Saigon was and what it signified, could recognize not only Bob Dylan but Che Guevara and the Berrigans. For one glorious summer, she played unfamiliar games with hordes of ragged, dark-skinned children in the dust of California while her mother strove to help Cesar Chavez better the lot of immigrant Mexican fruit pickers.

"You're smiling."

Startled from her reverie, Sky muttered something about being lost in a daydream. "Look," she stood up, "I appreciate all your kindness, Mr. Treacy, but you should go home and rest that arm."

"It is a little uncomfortable, I guess those bloody pain-killers aren't all they're cracked up to be." He levered himself to his feet as Sky reiterated her promise to call him when she had spoken to her grandmother.

"Are you sure you'll be all right here?" He glanced at the closed door. "They're taking a helluva time . . ."

"That's probably a good sign." She felt if she said it firmly enough it would make it true.

Treacy had been gone a good ten minutes before the door opened and the specialist came out. Sky, who had fetched herself a soda from the Coke machine at the end of the corridor, was on her way back to her station but she stopped dead on seeing the gravity of the man's expression. "Sit down, Mizz MacPherson." The specialist subsided on the bench. "We need to talk."

Dumb with apprehension, Sky came to sit beside him.

"There's good and bad news," he began. "The bad news is that we'll have to operate on those vertebrae," seeing Sky's blanching face he put out a hand to comfort her, "but the good news is that I have every reason to believe that the operation will be successful and that, apart from a bit of arthritis, maybe, in later life, she can make a full recovery. She was lucky. We'll take her to theater in the morning. Have you got Blue Cross?"

Sky shook her head and, although she tried to control them by squeezing her eyes tightly shut, the tears burst forth. "Don't distress yourself." The specialist misconstrued her emotion. "It'll be expensive but I'm sure we'll find a way round it."

"It's not that—" Sky could not continue. Her tears were of relief. It was only now that she realized how convinced she had become that her mother had been destined for permanent paraplegia. "Can I see her?"

"Of course. But she's heavily sedated. We had to pull her around a little, I'm afraid. She won't know you're there."

Behind her, Sky heard a familiar heavy footfall and looked up to see Hermana trudging round the corner of the corridor. "Oh, Hermana, she's probably going to be all right." She ran down the corridor and, like a child, flung herself against the older woman's bulk.

"Of course she is." Hermana, laden down with paper bags, tried to return the hug with her forearms. "She's well protected, someone like your mother. We all know that."

Normally, Sky would have skirmished around this terminology but right now she could not have cared if the Bliss Sisters had carted in the entire staff of the Maharishi to pelt her mother with lotus blossoms. She disentangled herself and scrubbed at her eyes. "I'm being silly. I'm not going to help her if I go on behaving like this."

The specialist had come up behind: "I'll be on my way." He consulted his watch. "We'll need your mother's details, and you'll have to sign consent forms for tomorrow and so forth. Try not to worry." He patted Sky's arm. "It'll take a bit of time but I've dealt with a lot worse."

"It's going to cost a fortune, apparently." Sky took some of Hermana's load as the specialist went off, and the two walked into Johanna's room. "I suppose you know we don't have Blue Cross."

"We're well protected," Hermana repeated. "I've called Buffy and she should be here in the next half hour."

They unpacked the sacks and stowed the contents, most of which were superfluous as Johanna would be wearing nothing but hospital gowns for the next few days at least. She continued to sleep although Sky was sure that the frame in which she was confined must be uncomfortable.

She and Hermana were seated by the bedside, reminiscing in low tones about Johanna's eventful life, when the door opened again and a disheveled Lynskey appeared. "I drove like the clappers," he announced without introduction. "How is she?"

They filled him in and Hermana urged Sky to let him take her home for a break. "Buffy will be here in a few minutes and we can call you if there is the slightest development. Go on, Sky, you've had a terrible shock."

"I could do with a shower." To Sky, who felt she must have aged ten years in the past hour, the prospect of clean water and fresh clothes was all too appealing.

She allowed Lynskey to drive her back to the duplex. He said nothing during the short trip and she appreciated his tact. Except for a few young couples who strolled hand in hand along the deserted streets, and a gang of kids who had set up an impromptu baseball diamond at the top of a hill, they might have had Butte to themselves. She found it difficult to keep tabs on reality; so much had happened that it was weird to find that it was still daytime and that this was an ordinary Sunday.

She realized that she had a thumping headache—sure sign of caffeine deprivation. The Coke had helped but her only other fix that day had been with Lynskey in McDonald's, so long ago now that it felt like yesterday. No wonder she had made an exhibition of herself in the hospital corridor, that her moods had been bumping up and down as though riding a child's seesaw.

"Will you come in?" Even the duplex seemed unfamiliar when Lynskey let the Nissan coast to a halt in the driveway.

"Are you sure?" He did not immediately turn off the ignition. "I can easily wait out here."

"Don't be silly." Sky pushed open the door and got out.

He offered to make coffee while she had her shower, and she accepted with alacrity. Then, remembering his voracious appetite, "And there would be some homemade muffins in the freezer." On her way down the corridor toward her bedroom, Sky remembered she had had nothing to eat since getting out of bed that morning. Was it only this morning that she had gone to interview Daniel Treacy in his echoing office?

She peeled off her clothes and tied on her bathrobe. Towel in hand, she was going toward the bathroom when she heard the telephone and stopped, staring at the instrument on Johanna's little half-moon table beside the front door. It could be the hospital. She willed Lynskey to pick up the extension in the kitchen but the shrilling continued and she snatched up the receiver. "Hello?"

"Miss MacPherson? R. Sky MacPherson?"

She did not recognize the voice and her panic grew. "Yes, this is Sky MacPherson, who's this, please?"

"This is Bill Collins, the funeral director. We spoke before. I've left several messages for you, Miss MacPherson."

Sky collapsed against the door. "Yes, I'm sorry, Mr. Collins. I was going to return your calls tomorrow."

"I think it is very important that we speak."

She could have strangled him. "I'm sorry if you were dissatisfied with your coverage in the community notes, Mr. Collins, but—"

"It's on another matter entirely," he cut across her. "When would you be free? Now if you like?"

"I'm sorry, but that's out of the question. My mother—" To her annoyance, Sky's voice unexpectedly wobbled. She cleared her throat. "My mother's in the hospital. I've come home just for a few minutes to collect some of her things."

"Oh!" Instantly his voice changed, became professionally solicitous. "Nothing too serious, I hope?"

"Serious enough, Mr. Collins. My mother has broken her back. I'm very worried about her. Now I'm sure you'll understand . . ."

"Of course, Miss MacPherson. But I would still like to speak to you about something at your earliest convenience. Perhaps I could call again tomorrow. Depending on how your mother is getting on, of course."

"I'll call you. Goodbye, Mr. Collins."

Odious man. Knowing she was overreacting, she flung the receiver back into its cradle. How on earth could Teddy and Melinda Morzsansky continue to work for him?

"Everything all right?" Looking around, she saw Lynskey standing in the kitchen doorway.

"Goddamn shamrock lot!" She made a sweeping gesture with the back of her hand, swiping at the telephone.

"That's our lot, I take it?"

She saw his expression and was contrite. "Oh, Fergus, I'm sorry. I didn't mean you, of course it's not you." She moved toward him but stopped. "What is it? I said I'm sorry . . ."

"I'd close that dressing-gown if I were you." His voice was low and controlled.

Sky glanced down and saw that the belt had untied itself and her nakedness was exposed. "Sorry." Embarrassed, she reached for it but when she looked up again he was coming toward her.

"Don't close it, don't—" He grabbed her shoulders, his fingers biting so hard they hurt. "I know it's probably inappropriate now—"

"It's not." She was whispering.

"But your mother . . ."

"I know." *Forgive me, Mom . . .* Sky closed her eyes as he scooped her into his arms and carried her like a baby toward the open door of her bedroom.

As they tumbled together on to the bed, her fingers got in the way of Lynskey's as she helped him tear at his zippers and buttons. "I'm terribly afraid this won't take too long." Lynskey's breath was sounding hard in his throat.

"I know."

The parking lot beside Killybegs Gárda station doubles as a temporary morgue for written-off vehicles. Although the rain had moved off, the gale was, if anything, stronger than before and the sky remained overcast, permitting no moonlight to penetrate. Conditions were ideal for the man lurking across the street.

It was coming up to three in the morning, and although he knew he was pretty safe Rupert de Burgh listened intently. From where he stood the remains of the Hiace and the Starlet were illuminated only by an overspill from the two lit windows in the station.

As satisfied as he could be, above the howling of the wind and the banging of a loose slate on a house nearby, that no one but himself was around, he broke cover and ran across the empty road.

As he crept across the parking lot, he kept well away from the elongated rectangles of light cast from the station windows but the light sparked briefly from the metal can he was carrying. Out of the corner of his eye saw the flash and froze, caught like a discus thrower poised on one foot. He waited until he was certain he had not been seen, then moved in a tight circle behind the two crashed vehicles, keeping them between him and the station.

As he sprinkled the gasoline, taking care not to make any sudden movements that might attract attention, the fumes tickled his nostrils and he felt a sneeze coming on. Quickly he placed the can into the gaping hole where the Hiace's hood had been, balancing it on the engine block. The sneeze erupted as he lit the first match. Its force extinguished the flame.

Keeping his nerve, he lit a second and held the little flame to the muslin bag that contained the matches. When he was sure it had taken, he placed the bag at the start of the gasoline trail he had laid.

Then he ran. He was out of range, but only just, when the Hiace blew, taking with it the Starlet, a squad car and two of the Gárdaí's private vehicles.

Chapter Nineteen

In Sky's bedroom, she and Lynskey lay like spoons. With one finger, he traced the hollow between her right shoulder and earlobe. "I wanted you so much. From the first second I saw you getting out of your car. And then, when I saw you lurking in the shadows of that schoolyard—my God!" He pulled her round and kissed her gently, first one eye, then the other.

"Mmmm." Sky threw her arms around his neck and gripped hard. "Shut up, Lynskey. Stop talking for once. Don't say anything, not one thing more." He smelled of aftershave and sweat and sex, a potent intoxicating cocktail which had invaded her body. She now wanted him so badly it hurt. It *had* been too quick, she thought, but he had buried her in the strength of his own passion.

Belatedly she brought her mother back into the frame. "I should be getting back to the hospital."

"Of course." Lynskey nuzzled her cheek and then was still. "Your mother was right. Did anyone ever tell you you have the most beautiful voice on earth?"

"I'm not actually thinking of my voice just at the moment . . ."

Neither of them moved for several charged seconds. Then, quick as a flame, he crushed her lips under his. She felt him come alive again and moved to accommodate him but he stopped. "Will you trust us?" he whispered into her open mouth.

"Trust us? Trust us to do what?" Sky, so full of heat and desire she felt she could not wait another moment, would have agreed to anything.

"Let me take charge, Sky, just for five minutes. See if you like it. I promise you, you will."

"Yes, anything, just hurry—"

"That's exactly what I'm not going to do this time."

Lynskey stopped kissing her and looked down at her, his expression tender. "Trust me," he repeated.

He pulled himself up, straddling her pelvis. When she attempted to raise herself to kiss him, he pushed her gently back on the pillows and extended her arms wide, away from her body. "You said you'd trust me. Don't touch. Don't do anything at all, leave it to me."

Trembling, ultra-conscious of his weight on her hip bones, she tried to keep still as, slowly, he tightened his grip on her with his legs and then leaned forward to run the outside of his joined hands between her breasts. "Lie back, close your eyes, just *feel*, Sky . . ."

She surrendered as he opened his hands and spread them so he was massaging her stomach with the palms while the thumbs tickled the undersides of her breasts, releasing rivulets of sensation. "Come on, feel me, feel it, Sky." He tightened his thighs and, although she tried to resist, she could not avoid raising her own in response. Again he spread his hands over her abdomen, his thumbs continuing to caress her breasts. "Feel what your body is saying to you. You're gorgeous, gorgeous—"

He bent forward again and encircled one of her breasts with his lips. He did not bite, and the pressure was minimal, but whatever he was doing with his fluttering lips and the flat of his tongue against her nipple caused her to cry aloud.

He did the same to the other and, as his mouth connected with her, Sky seemed to split into two. Despite her best efforts to keep still, her top half writhed as he continued the rhythm of the titillating massage, using his hands, fingers, lips and tongue as before, while her lower half, clamped into immobility, seemed virtually weightless and not to belong to her at all.

He took her right to the edge until she was moaning and crying, begging for release then, abruptly, he eased off her pelvis. She grabbed for him, expecting him to enter her. "I told you I didn't want you to do anything," he insisted, fobbing off her hands then sliding his own smoothly under her. "Over now, come on, flip over for me."

"I hope I can last—" Sky did not think she was capable of making such a sound in her throat.

"Ssh." He pushed her head down into the pillow and again she surrendered as he began with joined hands at the top of

her spine, spreading them only when he got to the swell of
her hips.

She gasped. He was using his thumbs to tease the cleft
between her buttocks in the same way he had used them on
the tender skin under her breasts. Of their own accord, her
legs drew up as, deep within, the orgasm began to ripple.

"Not yet, not yet . . ." He pushed her straight again,
pulling her thighs apart a little. Then he repeated the action,
slowly, tantalizing her by not using his thumbs until the last
minute although she bucked and reared and begged. "You've
skin as white as the feathers of a swan . . ." he brushed his
fingers across her buttocks, "you're the most perfect, beautiful woman, you're an egret, a white dolphin—"

Sky knew it was the end. "I can't wait—"

Instantly, he pushed up her thighs and entered her from
behind, cradling her breasts and stomach in his big hands,
kissing the skin between her shoulder blades and at the back
of her waist as she shuddered and cried on a long, sustained
note, which seemed to come from someone else's throat.
From far away, she heard him join in.

He was the first to get his breath back. "Jesus! What a
racket. Just as well we didn't wait until the War Bonnet—
someone might have called the management."

Sky never wanted to open her eyes ever again in her whole
life. The pillow against her cheek was as soft as the water in
a warm swimming pool. "You're good at this, Lynskey," she
breathed. "You should patent yourself—the world would
beat a path to your door."

"Thank you," he rolled off her, "but somehow the world's
a bit shy, these days."

"Just one thing." Sky turned on her back. An insect
walked across the ceiling and, as she watched, it seemed to
pulse in conjunction with the blood behind her eyes, bigger
and smaller, bigger and smaller . . .

"What?" Tenderly, he stroked the hair out of his eyes.

"Egrets?" She looked across at him. "Swans—*dolphins*?"

He had the grace to look sheepish. "I didn't think you
were in any state to hear."

"Think again, Lynskey." Luxuriantly, Sky reached behind
her to the headboard and pulled so that her body tautened to
its full length. She felt she had been transported to another
medium, where human skin and bone could stretch like
elastic. Then the vision of her mother swam in and she sat

up. "My mother. We have to go back—at least *I* have to go back to the hospital. I'll drop you somewhere."

"You'll drop me nowhere. Of course I'm going back with you." Lynskey planted a lazy kiss on her nose and then tumbled off the bed. "Come on."

They took a shower together, and when they were drying off she noticed a little circular welt, about the size of a dime, just below his hip. "What's that?" she touched it. "It looks like a scar."

"It's a birthmark." His tone was offhand. "Great conversation starter, women love it."

She was about to give him a playful slap when, over the running of the shower, she heard the telephone. "Damn." Again fearful it was the hospital—and with a resurgence of guilt that she should already be there—she reached for a towel, wrapped it around herself, and plunged out. She got to it at the third ring.

"I'm glad I reached you." Jimbo's dry voice reassured her immediately. "I tried the hospital but they said you'd gone home for a spell."

"I'm on my way back, as it happens." Sky scrubbed at her shoulder with a corner of the towel. "I was just collecting a few things."

"How is your mother? They wouldn't tell me anything."

She filled him in as succinctly as she could. When she was finished, he cleared his throat. "Look, Sky, take as much time off as you like. Don't even think about the office. We'll manage—and I know you're probably worried about the expense but come and see me and we'll discuss it."

"Thank you." Sky was touched. Maybe Butte wasn't such a bad place, after all. Then she thought of all those checks in her mother's lowboy. She would contact her uncle Francey. "Thanks a million, Jim, but I hope that won't be necessary. What about the rodeo copy?"

"Could you drop in your notes sometime tomorrow? I'll get the kid to write them up."

"I hope she can decipher them." She pictured the hieroglyphics in her notebook.

"Time she learned, isn't it?" Jimbo dismissed this, then, with uncharacteristic hesitancy: "Er, there's one other thing." He cleared his throat again. "Is that Irish teacher with you?"

"No." The lie was instantaneous. "Why?"

"Now is not the time but I want to talk to you about him, Sky. Look, I know this is a bit delicate . . ." Conscious that the shower had been turned off and that Lynskey could probably hear her, Sky was silent. "Are you there?"

"Yes." She turned her back on the bathroom door.

"Don't get a fright," his voice became crisp, "and I hope you don't think I'm interfering, but there is something you should know about him."

"Not now." Behind her, Sky heard Lynskey emerge from the bathroom and pad quietly toward the bedroom.

"Of course." Jimbo's tone became even more impersonal. "Just call me any time you feel you can. In the meantime, take care of yourself. Give my regards to your mother. Sam sends her love too—she says I'm to invite you to dinner anytime or just to talk, okay? I won't badger you with calls, I'll leave it up to you to get in touch."

"Thanks. And tell Sam thanks too."

"You bet." He hung up before she could say goodbye.

Slowly, Sky replaced the receiver. The euphoria of just a few minutes before had drained away so completely that she felt as thin and as flat as a dollar bill. She knew Jimbo Larsen: he would never dream of indulging in petty gossip or interfere in someone's private life. There had to be some good reason for him to have said what he had. She glanced toward the bedroom. The corridor in which she stood benefited from no natural light and the sunlight flooding into it through the open door of her room seemed unusually bright. She could not hear anything from inside: Lynskey was a quiet dresser.

He sensed her behind him as she padded through the door. "Is there news?" Clad only in a towel, he looked around from the mirror at which he was using one of her hairbrushes. "I hope you don't mind?" He held it up questioningly.

"Mmmm." She shook her head. "That wasn't the hospital, it was just my editor enquiring about Mom. Look, I'm getting nervous, I've been away an awfully long time, could we hurry?" He looked hard at her and she was afraid she might have betrayed herself but he said nothing and they completed dressing in silence.

She tried to behave naturally with him in the car, even holding his hand. All the time, however, Jimbo's warning sounding like a siren in her ears: *There's something about him you should know.*

"Are you all right? You're very quiet?" He raised the back of her hand to his lips and kissed it as they neared the hospital.

"I'm fine." She shot him a quick smile. "I think it's just all hitting me now. I feel awful that we were—you know—with my poor mother lying there in that state . . ."

"Try not to worry, sweetheart. They can do great things now. Are you sure that's all that's on your mind? You're not regretting what we did, are you?"

When Sky responded to this by glancing across at him, she saw watchfulness. "Of course not." She gave his hand what could pass for a happy squeeze.

"Good." He seemed to relax as he squeezed back. "Because I sure aren't. I can't wait for a return match." Sky smiled back but knew, from those alert eyes, that he had not believed her.

Johanna, her two faithful companions in attendance at her bedside, was still sleeping when they got to her room. "At least she's in no pain." Buffy was stroking her friend's inert forearm. "You poor thing, Sky. You must have gotten a dreadful shock."

The guilt about her romp with Lynskey while her mother lay here like this smote Sky with such intensity that her stomach constricted. "She's not gone into a coma or anything?" she gazed down at her mother's caged white face.

"No." Hermana lumbered to her feet and stretched her big body. "The doc says she's in great shape. It's just all the painkillers and sedation. They want to keep her quiet until they do the operation in the morning—oh, hello again!" She had caught sight of Lynskey, hovering in the doorway.

For the next hour or so, the four of them came and went in and out of Sky's mother's room, conferring in low voices with the medical personnel, who were doing little except monitoring Johanna's vital signs. Lynskey organized coffee and sandwiches, fetched and carried, made himself indispensable, so much so that, gradually, he seemed to be taking charge. Even the intern began deferring to him, addressing him first when he had anything to say.

Sky began to feel ever more helpless and guilty and—because of her unease about Jimbo's warning—increasingly irritable. She tried not to let this show but when, for the second or third time, the intern, having rechecked her mother's blood pressure, turned his back on her to talk to

Lynskey, the room, which was spacious as hospital rooms go, suddenly felt claustrophobic and overcrowded. "I'm sorry, doctor," she did not care that she sounded petty, "but I'm the patient's relative. I'd appreciate it if you would consult with me." Both Lynskey and the doctor turned to her with surprise. "I'm the daughter," she repeated.

"I'll leave." Lynskey grasped what was going on. "No, it's all right," he brushed aside the Hermana's putative protest. "She's under a lot of pressure. I understand completely." Then he was gone, leaving Sky with a sense of anticlimax. This was not what she had wanted—or was it?

She was leaving the hospital a little later, acceding to the Bliss Sisters' urgings that she get some rest, when she just avoided bumping into a man carrying a bunch of flowers. "Greg!" she tried to sound matter-of-fact. "I was going to call your house to talk, I really was, but then—"

"I'm real sorry about your mom," he interrupted, holding out the flowers. "Is there anything I can do?"

"Thanks, but there's nothing anyone can do except wait." She did not bother to ask how he had found out. "But I sure appreciate the thought. Look," she added impulsively, "I *would* like us to talk."

After a pause, "When?" Then he became defensive. "But don't give me anymore shit about wanting us to be friends."

"You calling like this already tells me that we are."

Another pause. Then: "Could you use some company? Will I come home with you?" Sky could see no reason why she should refuse him. She owed him a lot and, despite the serious thinking she had to do about Lynskey, she was not all that sure she wanted to face whatever truth lay in wait for her. In any event, she knew the next few hours would pass like years in the empty house. "I'll tell you what." On impulse, she took his arm. "Why don't we go for a walk?" She looked at her watch. "It's such a warm evening and I could do with some air." Then, fearing Greg's propensity for hiking. "A *short* walk, maybe in the forest."

As they left the city behind and Montana's immense skies and open spaces unrolled above and round the pickup, Sky's spirits lifted. On such a lovely evening, the travel writers' excesses about the Rockies—snowy peaks now tinged with gold under the sinking sun—were justified; the antiquity of those jagged, thrusting contours dwarfed everything around them, including the concerns of R. Sky MacPherson.

They drove in silence until Greg turned off the highway on to a secondary route into the forest. "I know I said we'd talk," she turned to him, "but I don't really know what to say. All I can come up with at the moment is 'thanks.' "

He went to take her hand but stopped himself, tipping his hat back on his head as though this was what he had planned all along. He smiled at her. "Sorry it couldn't work out. Don't forget," he stared ahead again, "if you ever change your mind . . ."

Sky felt like a grub, but she knew that the unkindest response of all would have been to say anything that would give him even a smidgen of hope.

He wheeled on to one of the narrow forest trails, running through a tunnel of cool green between the trunks of lodge pole pine, quite bare at this level: there were so many that they had been forced to race upward in competition for available light.

As the pickup, its springs fashioned for this kind of road, bounced joyfully along, the temperature plunged. Sky held the sides of her seat, and watched the way random handfuls of light lanced off the hood in front of her. Despite her feelings of being taken for a patsy by Lynskey, of her dejection at an inability to bid graceful farewell to the man beside her, she could not help but be affected by her surroundings. The feeling was of exhilarating isolation and, although she had never scuba dived, she knew this was what it must be like to sink downward into a new world.

Greg pulled the vehicle into the side and they got out.

After the noise in the truck, the hush as they walked along under the high green canopy, seemed at first absolute. Then the forest asserted itself, a sort of folded silence in which myriad sounds—a faint twitter, a flutter, rustlings, a little crash, a hum, a few clicks—swarmed through the furrows. She felt eyes all around as she walked a little ahead of her companion, endeavoring to put everything out of her mind except the sharp scent of the pine and the thicker, slighty musty smells of bark and forest floor.

Progressively, however, her awareness of Greg's tacit presence padding behind her became overpowering. Just ahead, a pale butterfly fluttered upward from a black-eyed Susan and danced off along a boulevard of light between two trees; she followed its progress until it slipped off into the shadows and then became aware of how the light had diminished. The evening was shrinking. It was now or never. "Greg?" She stopped and turned round to face him.

He stopped too.

"Words are easy, I know, but I'm really sorry, more than I can say."

He looked so stricken that if she could have taken his suffering into her own heart she would have done so. She wanted to kiss him but that was impossible. "I know I said we'd talk, but there isn't much to say, really, is there?"

"Guess not." He shrugged. "I do—sorry—did love you, Sky."

"I know you did." Helplessly, she touched his hand.

He did not react.

Defeated—he was not going to help her out and she did not blame him—she stepped back a little. "Well . . ." she hesitated, "I guess I'd better be getting home."

"You bet." He turned, too quickly, and walked ahead of her back toward the pickup.

At least she had tried. Greg needed a cheerleader and she was not it. Yet the more Sky tried to convince herself she had done the right thing and every step she took after his straight, stiff body, the more guilty she felt.

On the trip back to the duplex he was stiff and formal, so much so that she was astonished when he accepted her invitation, issued as a semi-automatic reflex, to come inside. It was what she always said when he drove her home.

Yet she had so much to do that once inside, her brain fell into its busy mode and she was able to stall him in the kitchen while—with only limited success—she made the calls to her aunts and her uncle Francey to let them know what had happened. Francey was at a country show—he was heavily into Shire horses—and his wife was out too. Sky left a message with the valet or butler that he telephone her urgently. Constance's husband said she, too, was away, but Sky reached the two aunts in the States, and Margaret, who continued to live on the farm in West Cork.

There was no reply from her grandmother's telephone but she felt she could assume that now the bush telegraph had been set in motion, one of the others would reach her. Margaret had been of the opinion that Sky's grandmother would make the trip but that she would insist on paying for it herself. "We're not the poor relations, you know." Her tone had been acerbic.

Sky looked at her watch as she replaced the receiver and walked back in to Greg; she was regretting her invitation to him. Events were piling up so fast around her, she thought. She must try to stay calm, make a priority list. Her mother came first, before her grandmother, before Jimbo's puzzling call about Lynskey, before Greg, before the story she was pursuing on Treacy. Before anything. "Sorry about that." She plastered a smile on her face as he looked up.

She sat at the table opposite him. The doorbell rang. "Oh, God, it's like Grand Central Station." Heaving herself to her feet she went out to answer it.

It was Lynskey. Behind him, a cab was leaving the driveway.

"I kept trying to ring." The Irishman had changed his clothes and now looked relatively dapper in a sports jacket and slacks. He spread his hands in apology. "You were engaged all the time. I couldn't stay away. Look, before you say anything," he seemed almost shy, "I know I was too bossy back there at the hospital. Will you forgive me? I get carried away sometimes, comes of being a teacher, I suppose. I was only trying to help."

That treacherous giggle bubbled to the surface. "This is my worst nightmare . . ."

"What's wrong, will I go? Tell me what you want me to do, Sky. Stop laughing." He grabbed her wrist. "Are you hysterical? Sky, for God's sake, I don't want to make things any the worse for you—"

"Do you think you could?" Sky could not control the laughter now. "Come on in! Greg's inside—oh, my God!" She doubled over as tears of mirth rolled down her face. "Come on in, all of you."

He looked blankly at her. "Greg?"

"Come in." She pulled him in and closed the door behind him.

She had herself under some semblance of control as she ushered him into the kitchen. "This is Greg, this is Fergus. Coffee, Fergus? Oh, sorry, it's tea, isn't it?"

Silence burned between the two men, then Greg rose. "I'd better be gettin' going."

"Are you sure you won't have more coffee?" Sky still felt giddy.

"No, thank you." Greg pushed his Stetson to the back of his head. "You know where I am if you need me. Give my love to your mom. Don't bother seein' me out, I know the way." He left the kitchen. A second or two later, the slam of the front door reverberated through the house.

"Sorry about that. I didn't know . . ." Lynskey hung back, leaning against the door jamb.

Sky picked up Greg's mug and took it to the sink. She squeezed Lux from the squeegee bottle on to it, more than enough to wash the dinner dishes of the Sixth Fleet. As she ran water from the faucet and scrubbed with the dishmop, as though to remove without trace the mug's inoffensive pattern of daisies and sunflowers, he came over to stand beside her, staring at her with knitted brows. "What's the matter, Sky?" His voice was soft. "What have I done?"

"Nothing." She scrubbed harder then ran more water over the mug to rinse it.

"I know it's not nothing."

"Somebody told me that there was something about you I should know." She put down the mug and picked at the grease congealed in the crack where the formica on the counter joined with the metal surround of the sink.

"Who? What did they say?" Another man might have sounded indignant, or furious, or hurt. Lynskey did not even sound inquisitive.

She locked eyes with him. "That's all. That there's something about you I should know. What should I know about you, Lynskey?"

"Maybe it's that—" Whatever he had been about to say he bit back. "My life's an open book!" he substituted, attempting a smile.

"I don't believe you." She turned back to the sink and scrubbed again at the already squeaking mug.

Lynskey came behind her and put his arms around her. "You can trust me, R. Sky MacPherson." He hugged her close, a nonsexual embrace that was full of consolation.

"Don't patronize me. For Christ's sake, please don't patronize me." She felt very, very tired and no longer cared who was trustworthy and who was not. As Lynskey stroked her hair, she found she could not give two hoots even about stories or deadlines or the *Butte Courier.*

Or even if he was with someone else. If he was lying to her, so what? Now was what mattered, and right now she felt safe and comforted.

He took her chin in one of his hands and tilted back her

head. "I promise you," his voice deepened, "I promise you that you can trust me."

Over her head, however, Lynskey's eyes were dark and full of doubt. He had almost revealed the truth. That he had fallen in love.

Chapter Twenty

Sky was happy to accept Lynskey's offer to drive her back to the hospital. Left alone she might have fallen asleep at the wheel.

He had tried to dissuade her from going—there was little she could do. But her guilt was insistent and he gave in. "I have to call in at the hotel first, though," he said as he helped her into the passenger seat. "I'm expecting a message. A friend of one of my sisters lives in Seattle and she's half expecting me to show up sometime this week. I rang earlier to tell her my plans have changed—my plans *have* changed, haven't they?" He took her silence for assent. "She wasn't in. I'm expecting her to call me back."

Sky waited in the car when they got to the hotel. Her limbs felt like Jell-O and she wondered how she was going to get through the night, not to mention facing the world tomorrow. Apart from her concern for her mother, she did not want to hear Jimbo's bad news about the Irishman: although she was cagey about making too much of this new relationship—formed, after all, on the rebound from Greg—Lynskey's plea to trust him had found receptive ears. She wanted to trust him.

He had parked in the dropoff point in front of the hotel's entrance rather than in the lot, and each time the glass doors opened, she could see little clusters of conventioneers standing around in the lobby. Once, when she caught a glimpse of Lynskey, he was frowning, reading a note on white paper, holding something brown in his other hand. Next time the door opened, he was coming through. She wound down the passenger window as he bounded toward her. "Everything okay?"

"There was a message all right." He hunkered down to talk to her. "I'll have to go up to my room to make a call. Do you mind waiting? Or would you like to come in and have a drink in the bar?"

"I'll wait here." Sky could not have faced the hubbub she knew would attach to the conventioneering crowd.

"All right, so. I won't be long." He loped away and she could see that the brown object, now sticking out of the pocket of his jacket, was a small padded envelope. What kind of hotel left telephone messages for its guests in brown padded envelopes?

Lynskey walked straight up to the reception desk in the lobby and placed the envelope on the surface between himself and the young clerk. "Excuse me. Do you remember who left this in for me? If you didn't recognize him, a description would do."

"I don't know, sir." The boy went to pick it up but Lynskey was too quick for him, pulling it out of his reach with a fingernail. "Could it have been a courier?"

"I'm afraid I can't help you, I've just come on shift." The clerk plucked a clipboard from under the counter and scrutinized it. "I could try to find out for you, if you like, but I think my predecessor has already left."

"It's all right. It'll do tomorrow, but it's important to me to find out. What's the name of the clerk who was on duty earlier?" He took a courtesy note from the pad on the counter and scribbled the name the boy gave him. "You're sure there was only this envelope and the one telephone message?"

The clerk checked the pigeon hole again. "That's all sir, just two for you this evening." Lynskey thanked him and hurried to the elevator.

In his room, he tapped in the combination to unlock his briefcase. Before he made the call to the chief superintendent, however, he took a clear plastic bag from one of the pockets of the case and carefully placed the brown envelope inside. He fished out a second one and, holding it open with his left hand, turned a small object out of his jacket pocket so that it dropped straight into the bag. The object was a bullet.

He reached the chief at home. He was not perturbed by the warning in the brown padded envelope, had expected it sooner or later. In many ways it gave him satisfaction: it meant he was getting somewhere.

At first the chief superintendent was irritable at being woken but thawed after a bit and told him what had happened in Killybegs, including the demolition job on the vehicles. Lynskey listened in silence but, entirely concentrated on his own side of the operation, had few suggestions to offer. Daly was less sanguine about the bullet than his subordinate. "It's not only you, you clot, you've involved that reporter. I hope you haven't given her any idea of the scope of this thing?"

"Naw." Lynskey was glad his friend could not see the grin on his face, "She believes it's all to do with Treacy and his wife. But don't worry, she'll be all right. I'll make sure of that."

"Speaking of Treacy, is he involved or not?"

"So far I've no proof either way and the feds have got nothing, for all their watching. Could be he's just an unfortunate citizen. We'll see. Look, there's something else you should be exercised about. I think these beauties know where to find me a little too easily and I don't think the leak's over here, unless I'm being watched by people I can't see. I think you'd better step up the navel-gazing at home."

"We're running checks but so far everyone has come up clean. And as for Project Omega, no one knows except yourself, the Commissioner, meself and the three politicos about your man maybe coming over here. Unless those last three are blabbing. I doubt it."

"Yeah, well, nothing would surprise me. Keep trying." Conscious of Sky waiting in the parking lot, Lynskey looked at his watch. "I'll courier the two baggies and the film to the feds. You should have results by Tuesday at the latest. That camera'd better be as good as Technical Branch says it is. I was quite far away. You'll know our Irish friend"—even though he had been assured that his satellite phone was secure, and although he rarely took risks with names, he did now—"but the other two, the Canadians, should be new to you. Flynn's the one looks like Hopalong Cassidy."

"Speaking of the feds," the chief asked, "see them around?"

"Oh, here and there. They wouldn't last a minute in certain parts of Dublin, they stick out a mile—even when they try to blend into the landscape. And you should see the cars."

"Well, use them if necessary.

"Yeah, yeah—look, I have to go." He explained then where he was bound and about Johanna's accident.

"The mother too? Sounds like you're in over your head," his friend drawled laconically.

"Yeah, yeah."

"Be careful out there!"

Lynskey smiled as he punched the "end" button on the phone. Like a good proportion of their colleagues, they both adored *Hill Street Blues,* missing the reruns only when matters of life or death—or newer episodes of *L.A. Law*—intervened.

When Sky and Lynskey got to the hospital, Johanna was alone except for the nurse on duty, who was taking her pulse. "I sent the other ladies away, but they said be sure and call them if there was the slightest change. There's no need for you to be here either—she's going to sleep all night."

"I'd prefer to stay." Sky sank lower in the chair, testing its long term comfort.

"Feel free." The nurse checked the level of the drip running into Johanna's arm.

"What's in it?" Lynskey asked.

"Saline, mostly." The nurse wrapped a blood pressure cuff around Johanna's arm and pumped it up. "There's really no need to whisper. Her sedation and analgesic medication is in here too and you won't wake her. We don't want her to move around too much."

She checked the meter in her hand as she released the pressure, then, "That's fine." Making a note on the chart at the foot of the bed, she smiled across at Sky. "Try not to worry, your mom's doing fine. I'll be in and out during the night but you or your husband need me any time, Mizz MacPherson, you just holler. I'll be at the station just down the hall." She clipped the pen back into her breast pocket. "Love your work, by the way. My daughter's at the journalism school at Northwestern, Illinois."

"Great. Good luck to her—and thanks." Sky was still reacting to the connubial assumption about herself and Lynskey, and did not dare meet his eyes as the nurse left.

She dozed a little over the next few hours, hardly rousing during the night nurse's periodic visit. At some point in the early morning, she came to, to find herself covered in a light, woven blanket. For a few moments, she had no idea where she was. The only light in the room came from a green bulb recessed into the ceiling; under its dim wattage, the objects in her direct line of vision—the knobs at the end of her mother's bed, which were used to raise and lower it, the drip stand, even the slats of the closed venetian blinds between the sateen drapes—glowed outlandishly. Then she smelt the hospital smell and remembered.

Shaking her head to clear it, she struggled upright to see that Lynskey was sitting, Buddha-like, on the floor opposite the end of the bed, his back supported by the wall. "Do you want anything?" he whispered, not moving a muscle. "I can go for coffee, if you like."

"What time is it?" The inside of Sky's mouth felt like a brush. She glanced across at her mother. Johanna was sleeping as before. "Just after three." Lynskey uncoiled himself and stood up. "Coffee, then? Black?"

"Sure."

After he padded out, Sky rubbed her gritty eyes then did a few stretching exercises to restore her circulation. When it came, the coffee was watery and weak, tasting of plastic. "Yuck," she grimaced.

"I know." Lynskey used his fingers to unknot the tension in her shoulders. "If it tastes anything like the tea, it tastes like donkey's pi—I mean urine. Sorry." He grinned. "Don't finish it. Would you like me to get you a few pillows? You could lie down on the floor. I'm fine, not a bit sleepy. I'll keep watch."

"I think I'll call my grandmother. I promised Treacy I would and it's eleven o'clock in the morning over there."

She used the booth beside the drinks vending machine in the hall, charging the call to her home number. When the operator put her through, the line to Cork, for once, was as clear as though it stretched only between the duplex and the next door neighbors'. Not for the first time, Sky was struck by how young her grandmother sounded. She already knew about Johanna's accident, Sky's aunt Margaret had reached her in the interim. "Poor Johanna." Although she sounded concerned, she did not seem panicked by the news. "Of all the things to happen. Still, they can do wonderful things with surgery nowadays."

"Daniel Treacy—I mean, McCarthy—continues to insist on being involved." Sky took a deep breath. "He assumes that because of the accident you'll want to come over right away, like tomorrow. He's offered to put you up."

"Hmmm." Her grandmother was noncommittal.

"Look, Grandma," Sky did not feel up to pleading

Treacy's case, "he says he'll call you himself. I'm to break the ice, so to speak."

"I'm still in shock that he has surfaced after all these years. I knew he was in Montana, of course . . ." her grandmother hesitated, "but it is a bit silly, this, isn't it? At our age. I haven't seen Daniel for nearly half a century. I don't know how much you know, Sky."

"He's told me everything."

"Everything?" Her grandmother chuckled. "How indiscreet."

"Of course not everything. Look, Grandma, I'll leave it to the two of you to work things out. I'll call him now and tell him you're expecting to hear from him."

The old lady's voice grew firmer. "One way or another, I will come over to see Johanna. It's about time I went to the States anyway. It's a place we should all see at least once before we die. And I can't wait to see you again, Sky. I had hoped it would be here in Ireland, of course."

"Don't talk about dying, Grandma. You've years yet."

They arranged to speak again that night, when Johanna's operation was over and when the flight schedule was firm. Then Sky called Treacy, figuring meanly that since everyone else was awake he might as well be too.

"Is she very upset about your mother?" He did not appear to have been asleep.

"I think you'll be surprised at the way she sounds," she did not want to engage in this, "and she's quite philosophical about Mom. She's worried, of course—"

"That's only natural." The Irish traces in Treacy's accent had intensified.

"I'll leave you to it. I hope you didn't mind my calling at this hour but I figured you'd want me to."

"Of course."

She told him her grandmother was at home and expecting his call and, although he seemed inclined to ask more questions, cut him off as politely as she could.

For once Lynskey did not pound her with questions when she went back to the room. Instead, he settled her down in the chair, covering her tenderly with the blanket. It felt wonderful to have someone else taking charge. "I'm not usually such a wimp."

"It's three o'clock in the morning." He crouched down

before her to tuck in the ends of the blanket and his voice softened. "And, little girl, you've had a busy day. Now go back to sleep."

She woke again sometime later to find he was no longer there. Assuming that he had gone to the bathroom, she held up her watch to catch the green overhead light and, seeing it was now only five after four, although it felt as though she had been asleep for a lot longer, snuggled the blanket over her shoulders.

But, as sometimes happens at that time in the morning, even in the teeth of extreme fatigue—or perhaps because of it—her mind sharpened and began to race, skittering around and across the surface of her impressions of the last few days. So much had happened, both personally and professionally, that it was difficult to organize the mishmash into a coherent sequence. She began to make one of her mental lists, enumerating in order of priority what had to be done later that day.

Before anything, of course, came Johanna's operation, but Sky decided that while her mother was in the theater she would slip home to shower and change. She could call her grandmother and then, on her way back to the hospital, drop in the rodeo notes for the kid to decipher. And it was then that she could find out from Jimbo what it was he wanted her to know about Lynskey. Or did she want to know at all? Her gadfly mind shied away immediately.

Where was the man? She checked her watch again—he had been gone longer than ten minutes. Too restless now to sit and wait, she shook off the blanket and went to find out what was keeping him.

She saw him straight away: he was next to the corridor, using the public telephone. Sky wondered to whom he could be talking at this time in the morning—it was certainly not his sister's friend in Seattle.

Then, as she noted the set of his shoulders, the intense, almost covert way he held the mouthpiece close to his lips, a set of tumblers clicked into place in her brain. Everything fit. Everything that had puzzled her about him and his behavior, the locked briefcase, his persistent interest in Daniel Treacy—even taking photographs of him—Jimbo's warning.

This was no teacher.

Her sense of betrayal was balanced by chagrin at her own

stupidity. She had fallen for the oldest trick in the book: a tumble in the hay and the pillow talk was his.

Sky could have cheerfully slit her throat: she had handed him everything she knew. She had been too trusting, or besotted, to follow up on her suspicions.

Keeping her eyes on him, prepared to walk forward if he turned round, she backed carefully into her mother's room, sat in the chair, pulled up the blanket and closed her eyes. Her heart seemed to have enlarged with anger and she fought to control its beating, taking long, deep breaths.

When she heard him come back into the room, she stirred as though just waking up. "Mmmm, what time is it?"

"It's about quarter past four." He came over to stand beside her. "Anything I can get you?"

How about an AK-47 to shoot yourself? But Sky cuddled down under her blanket. "Nothing, Fergus." Her voice was dreamy. "Well, maybe a cup of that awful coffee. It's a very long night, isn't it?"

"Yeah, not too long now, though. If this hospital is anything like home, they'll be around in a couple of hours waking everyone up. Coffee it is."

When she knew she was alone, Sky, her temper barely contained, threw off the blanket and sat upright. The goddamned nerve of the guy. The knowledge that, just a few hours before, she had been rolling around in ecstasy under this traitor served only to double her fury. Dolphins and egrets, indeed. Her face burned. She'd show him egrets.

It took every iota of willpower and self-discipline to smile when he came back with the coffee. It helped a little that the night nurse came in with him to change Johanna's drip and catheter bag, and to monitor her blood pressure. This process took a few minutes, and by the time it was finished Sky had her anger somewhat in check. She could no longer sit in the chair, however, but paced the room like a hungry cat. "You're very agitated." Lynskey was leaning against the wall, arms folded across his chest. "It's awful but there's nothing we can do except wait. I don't want to sound like a broken record, but you know I think you shouldn't be here at all. You'd be much better off having a good sleep in your own bed."

"I wouldn't have been able to sleep."

"I suppose not." Lynskey was watching her carefully now,

nothing showing except the compassion of a lover, and she had to remind herself how smart he was.

She smiled at him, even managing to drop a light kiss on his cheek. "I can't tell you how much I appreciate all you're doing for us, Fergus. You're being marvelous."

"You're welcome." He went to hug her but she evaded his arms, pretending to be engrossed in thought.

"It's stifling in here." She went to the window and parted two of the slats in the venetian blinds. "It's a lovely night. Would you hold the fort while I go out for a bit?"

"Sure."

Out in the parking lot she searched for something distracting on the Nissan's radio but could find only Jesus slots, lonelyhearts, wailing country, hard rock, or sad souls pouring their hearts down the phone lines to the night time jocks. She killed them all, wound down the window and wallowed in the silence.

The bright security lights stained the empty lot with hard-edged shadows and, in front of where she sat, the hospital's bulk seemed unfriendly and alien. She felt lonely. Despite her mother's surface flakiness, and Sky's own attitude to her, Johanna, now lying pinioned and vulnerable only a hundred yards away, had always been a constant in her life and she knew she had been careless with this privilege. Suppose her mother were to die in the operating theater? "Oh, Mom," she whispered to the blank windows of the hospital, "you do know I love you, don't you?"

Unable to bear just sitting there, but unwilling to return to the room, she rummaged in the glove compartment and retrieved the notebook and pen she kept there. Turning on the map light, she made a list of every doubt about Lynskey and about Treacy.

She could come to only three possible conclusions about the former: the Irishman was either a private detective, an undercover cop, or, worst of all from her point of view, an investigative reporter.

The consolation was that at least the story itself was now in much sharper focus. She was no longer in any doubt that she had stumbled on something far larger than she had ever handled before: the fact that Lynskey had come—or been sent—all the way from Ireland meant it was big-time stuff. Treacy was the crux.

Back in the hospital corridor, Lynskey was again on to the chief superintendent in Dublin. "She's onto me. I don't know how—maybe she overheard something on the telephone when I was on to you a few minutes ago—but she's definitely onto me."

Chapter Twenty-one

The captain and crew of the *Agnes Monica* were weary. They had heard about the crash between the Hiace and the Starlet and, fearing increased police activity, were running for cover into a cave, the mouth of which was accessible to a vessel of the size of the *Agnes Monica* only at low tide.

They had lain low for twenty-four hours. A fishery patrol boat had passed twice, once in each direction and although they had not been detected, the captain was jumpy. Next time he got involved in something like this he would insist on better radio equipment: his stuff was not modern enough to intercept and decode signals from other vessels. But this was only a fishing patrol, for God's sake, not a nuclear submarine.

It was again low tide and the captain was preparing to come out into the open. Conditions had improved: after a dry spell in the early morning it was raining again, but the gale had lessened.

The crew had been primed to tell their colleagues back at Killybegs that they been forced to take shelter in an isolated bay along the exposed northwestern coast. They would even have a few white fish to show for their pains: they planned to trawl on the way home.

Before they ventured into the open, however, the captain sent out the dinghy to check that their way was clear. But the water level was rising fast and, with the considerable swell, the exit would soon be impassable. The men in the dinghy reported nothing untoward and the captain decided to risk it.

As he emerged into the open, the ship-to-shore link, silenced by the depth of the cave, crackled into life. The news was not good: Killybegs was crawling with cops. Some dunderhead had decided to destroy the evidence but, in blowing up the Hiace, had taken half the parking lot of the Gárda station and three Gárda cars. What was more worrying was that the Guards were saying they suspected a Loyalist attack in retaliation for one launched by the IRA on an RUC station in Strabane.

That meant they wanted to put the press off the scent. To the captain, who was a seasoned campaigner in many areas that had little to do with fishing, it also meant the authorities knew what they were looking for. Or thought they knew.

He was told to go back to base and face down the action there in case it was thought he was running. He knew better than to argue, especially on an open channel, even though he was using a well-tested code, but he did question the order, indicating the presence of the patrol vessel, before setting a southeasterly course. Half an hour after he left the cave, he saw a vessel of about their own size plowing through the brisk seas about a mile offshore. He recognized her as the *Slua Cailíní* from Burtonport and, to avoid attracting interest, slowed and ordered that his own nets be put out.

Unfortunately five minutes earlier the fishing patrol vessel, now more than twenty miles away, had pinpointed his location.

In northwest Montana, the sheriff of Mayville was also becoming impatient. He wanted his money and, with the trip to Ireland imminent, he wanted it now.

With expertise born of long practice, he opened a pistachio nut and scooped out the flesh. "Now, you listen," he said softly into the telephone receiver. "I've tried to scare the guy off the best way I know how. It's not my fault he's still snooping around. When am I going to get my fee, buddy?" He listened again, then, "Very well, but this is the last. I'll be in touch."

He broke the connection and considered, then punched out another number and stared into space for a couple of seconds. Then: "It's O'Connor. That errand you ran? We need more of the same. And it needs to be done now." He listened for a few seconds. "I don't care. The slate is clean when I say it is. And before you show me any more slices of your bleeding heart, that file is still in my drawer here. Right here," his eyes flicked downward, "locked, of course, but the key's on my ring. I could put my hand on that file right now. Cat got your tongue, O'Shaughnessy?" Then: "Good, here's the address . . ."

* * *

Nothing much happened in Choteau if you discounted its annual events: the Dinosaur Celebrations, its own Fourth of July rodeo, steak fry and parade, the 4-H Fair or Antique Steam Engine Threshing Bee. Apart from its pretty, wide open scenery, the nearby Egg Mountain—where a nest of fossilized dinosaur eggs was discovered virtually intact—was its main claim to fame. Yet Choteau's cottonwood-lined streets were wider than many a Paris boulevard and its well-kept green in front of the old quarrystone courthouse was so well trimmed it invited pause. Out-of-staters were seduced into stopping here sometimes, while motor-homing between the National Parks of Glacier and Yellowstone, to admire the dinosaur eggs and bone exhibits in the small privately owned museum. Some dawdled, spending a few days at the dude ranches which supplemented their owners' farming activities, but most visitors, if they stayed, overnighted in one of the four reasonably priced motels or two bed and breakfast houses.

Choteau folks minded their own business; but like all Montanans, who tended to be open-hearted and hospitable to a fault, they were not reticent about giving information. They would tell anyone who wanted to know that the beautifully presented ranch-style building a few miles outside town was one of those classy joints for rich nuts.

Now and then one or two in the town went further, muttered about the place being a waste-disposal unit for those elderly or awkward—but inconveniently strapping—relatives who stood in the way of some daughter's or son's rightful inheritance. And that its discreet but powerful security arrangements were not for the protection of the rich nuts' money but to keep them from escaping. Further, these cynics knew that many patients were checked in by their status-conscious families under assumed names.

The Teton sanatorium, as its medical personnel preferred to call it, housed no long-stay patients but was used purely for assessment purposes. With the exception of one or two miracle cases, or where the relatives had a change of heart, the inmates invariably moved on to permanent-stay asylums. While they were here, however, they were accommodated in suites, akin to those of a five-star hotel.

Luxury notwithstanding, Sunday was always a tedious day with a smaller than usual staff. Analytic and therapeutic activities were suspended, and the dull-eyed patients, never more than a dozen, lay around with little to do. For those *compos mentis* enough to realize where they were, the day must have been endless.

As it was to the staff—most of the nurses welcomed the dawn of Monday morning. The place hopped with cheerful queries about weekend activities as everyone buckled down to a fresh week.

"Good morning!" The smile on the face of the trainee died away as she came into the room and looked at the silent woman in the high, cot-sided bed. She came across and tweaked the already immaculate bedcovers. "Did you have a good weekend, Peggy?"

She was not expecting an answer, of course. At least, she thought, this one was not abandoned like many of the facility's inmates: in the short time Peggy McGovern had spent in the place, she had suffered a surfeit of visits. Her husband attended regularly at her bedside and had spent almost a fully day of the previous weekend with her, although she had been too sedated to know, and he had hired a companion for her, a gimlet-eyed young woman, who was staying in Choteau but who drove out to the complex every morning and stayed until nightfall. Peggy was bound ultimately for a facility in Oregon but while she was here, like all the other patients, she enjoyed—if that was the word—round-the-clock attention from the three nurses and the trainee dedicated to her care.

This trainee was as yet too green to have assumed the emotional armor of the fledged professional. Now, as she gave her charge a bed bath, she sang softly, hoping to penetrate the gray fog in which the woman seemed permanently wreathed. "Attagirl, Peggy," she cooed, when she was finished, "you take it easy," plumping up the pillows and then moistening a washcloth to clean a speck of food from a corner of the woman's mouth. "All nice and cozy? Would you like me to let your friend back in?"

She searched her patient's face for any sign of recognition or animation but saw nothing beyond the flickering eyelids which denoted disturbed or disturbing dreams. She knew she would have to toughen up: each case here was a hard case and she could not take them all to heart. She sighed and turned to leave. "See you later at lunch, Peggy, okay?"

But as she opened the door to admit the paid companion, who was seated on a chair reading a novel, the young nurse missed something. The eyes of the woman in the bed opened momentarily and swiveled after her but the tiny squeak of the door hinges masked her weak attempt to whisper something. Then it was too late. The girl was gone and in her place entered the silent companion.

The effort to speak had exhausted Mrs. McGovern and her eyes had again filmed over. But she was not sleeping. Her brain felt like mush. She could almost see it now: it looked like a mushy flying saucer balanced on the tufts of a soft, soggy cloud. Holding on to the image with difficulty, she imagined her brain bubbling, hillocks of air bursting sluggishly—*pop! pop!*—just under the inner surface of the bone. Then she became aware of a noise beside her bed. Making a huge effort she half opened her eyes.

That woman was there again: her face, a whitish blur, was wavering over an object. A book. The woman was reading.

Peggy allowed her eyes to close again and, for a second, her thoughts crystallized abruptly. She realized that she longed to die.

But, more than that, she desperately needed a drink.

Waves of half consciousness came and went and it was during one of the peaks that she became aware that the woman was no longer there. She forced her eyes open again. She was coming back in. She was leaning over the bed, saying something: Peggy tried to push back the fog in her brain and let the woman's words through. Something about her husband. He couldn't come today. What husband?

This was too difficult. Peggy's eyes closed of their own volition.

The paid companion sat back in her chair and reopened her book. She saw no point in repeating herself.

In the master bedroom of his pristine house, Daniel Treacy pulled aside the drapes, wincing at the brightness of the morning. Turning away from the glare, he stared at the phone beside the bed he had shared for so long with his wife, and wondered if she had understood the message.

The first call Sky made when she got back to the house was to her editor.

The time between her return to her mother's room from the parking lot and Johanna's being wheeled off for her operation had not been as difficult as she had foreseen. Saying

that he, too, could do with some fresh air and a change of
clothes, Lynskey had borrowed her car and gone back to the
hotel, returning only minutes before the transfer to the operating room. He offered to drive her home then and she could
see no way out of agreeing without making him suspicious.
She had her own plan as to how he should receive his come-
uppance and had no intention of tipping him off that he had
been rumbled. "Thanks, but do you mind if we don't talk?"
She pretended to be taking something out of her eye so she
would not have to look at him. "I'm exhausted and I'm worried about Mom."

"Of course." He had taken her arm as they walked down
the corridor and she had managed not to shy away. He was
now safely back at the War Bonnet and she did not plan to
see him again until after the operation. Now, as she waited
for Jimbo's wife to fetch him to the phone, she was congratulating herself on the way she had played it; smugly, she
felt that Lynskey could have no idea of her suspicions.

"Hello?" Jimbo sounded concerned. "How's your mom?"

"She's in the operating room. It'll be about three or four
hours before there's any news. I'll drop in the rodeo notes
before I go back to the hospital but I wanted to talk to you
about that Irish teacher. I think I know what you were going
to tell me about him."

"Go on." The editor's tone was cautious.

"He's not a teacher, is he? He's a reporter. Or a cop."

"The latter, I believe. How did you find out?"

"Who told you?" Sky found little satisfaction in being
proven right. She was having to fight waves of nausea.
To think she had considered this might be a long-term
relationship.

"Did Bill Collins get you?" Jimbo's multilayered mind led
him to answer questions with more questions.

"Well, yes and no . . ." Sky stared at the pad beside the
telephone. The funeral director's name had been written on it
several times. "Not in the sense you mean. I'm afraid I was
quite rude to him. He caught me at a bad time."

"Maybe you should talk to him as soon as your mom's
sorted out. Not that he has all that much information. But
someone tipped him off."

"Look, Jim," Sky's nausea and tiredness fell away, "I'm
mad at that guy, Lynskey. Let me at the story, will you? I
mean, don't give it to anyone else." Once before when a

mine disaster had threatened to overwhelm the meager resources of the newspaper, Jimbo had hired a young male freelancer. "I promise I won't let you down."

"You sure you can be objective? You even have a family connection . . ."

"Trust me, please?"

"The story's not going to go away." He remained circumspect. "Just concentrate on your mother for today, okay? One thing to our benefit, at least if he's a cop he's not going to blow whatever it is all over the *Washington Post*. He might even turn out to be useful."

Sky's febrile brain revolved at top speed while she was having her shower. She knew she was on the threshold of a bigger league than any in which she had played in her entire career: her day-to-day coverage of rodeos, community notes, obituaries, agriculture, zoning violations and local politics had not prepared her for this. Crime stories in Montana were largely to do with the relatively straight-forward reporting of court cases relating to drunk and disorderly charges and the occasional murder or rape.

She knew her skill was perceived as being vested in the writing rather than the ferreting out of stories; even in Chicago, she had never been marked to cover any felony bigger than a mugging or petty theft. "Get going and *do* it!" She turned off the water and addressed the chrome-plated shower head. "Just *do* it."

"Mr. Collins?" She was businesslike when she got through to the funeral home. "I'm very sorry we couldn't talk when you called yesterday."

In response to his inquiries, she brought the funeral director up to date on her mother's condition. She even managed a joke: "I'm afraid you'll have to wait a little longer, Mr. Collins, to look after my mother in a professional capacity." She waited while he chuckled at this and then asked him why he had wanted to talk to her.

"I have a little bit of news which might interest you, Miss MacPherson." Collins's voice sank to a murmur. "I've spoken to your editor."

"Indeed I know you have." Sky was too wound up for subterfuge. "You think Fergus Lynskey is a policeman. Why, may I ask?"

"I can't tell you that." He seemed miffed that Jimbo had stolen his thunder. "But I thought you ought to know he's not what he seems. You seemed pretty friendly together . . ." He paused, then, in a different tone, "You don't sound all that surprised, Miss MacPherson."

"I'd be interested to know why this man is here in Butte, pretending to be a schoolteacher." Sky hoped she sounded merely professional. "Is he on duty? Is something going on here that might interest him?" She held her breath.

"Let's just say that Mr. Lynskey *thinks* he knows something about something here in our city. But I would appreciate it, Miss MacPherson, if you would get it across to him that he is wasting his time. That everyone knows who he is and that there is nothing for him. That there never was. That he would be much better off enjoying his holiday or going back to Ireland. Much better off. I think too," his voice hardened, "that this man may have turned your head with some nonsense about Daniel Treacy and his deceased wife. It appears that you've been asking a lot of questions and it can only be as a result of what you've heard from him. But of course *I* know, and I've reassured others, that you are much too experienced to fall for libelous lies. I'm sure you know that Mr. Treacy has friends in high places, Miss MacPherson."

Sky half smiled at the ridiculous terminology. Friends in high places, indeed. But the threats, not only to Lynskey but to herself, were clear. It was one thing to be used by Fergus Lynskey, she thought indignantly—at least she had enjoyed herself with him while it had lasted—it was another to be told how to conduct her work. "Thanks for the tip, Mr. Collins." Her voice was now as hard as his. "I'll certainly watch my step. I have to run now—thanks again." She hung up before he could say anything more.

Then she called her grandmother and ascertained that the old lady would be arriving the following evening via Billings. After she hung up she checked her watch: she had plenty of time to pay another visit, a surprise one this time, to Daniel Treacy.

Chapter Twenty-two

The area between the ornamental iron gates and the façade of Government Buildings, "Versailles" to its Dublin critics because of its expensive restoration and fancy floodlighting, was as busy as a bus station on the night before a public holiday. Ministerial and Special Branch cars came and went and groups of lobbyists and public officials conferred. On the plinth in front of the entrance doors, an RTE television news crew was grouped around the Minister for Justice. Éamonn Vaughan, a reporter with large, sad eyes who was loved and hated in equal measure by the present government because of his professionalism, his approachability but his tenacious, in-your-face style, had just concluded an interview with the minister on a running story about Gárda recruitment, pay and overtime.

"That it, lads? I'm late—thanks . . ." But as the minister walked toward the front doors of the building, the reporter was still at his heels. "Minister, off the record." Vaughan's tone had sunk to a conspiratorial murmur. "Any further developments on the Killybegs bombing? Is it true there's a big operation going on?"

"No news yet, Éamonn." The minister waved to a party of schoolchildren being shepherded in crocodile formation past the ornamental fountain. "You'll be the first to know, of course."

"Minister—" The reporter tried again but the minister quickened his step and got into the building out of the man's reach.

The reporter had touched a nerve: the minister was on his way to a meeting to discuss the Killybegs episode prior to briefing the Taoiseach and the deputy prime minister, the Tánaiste, both of whose offices were in the building. He was being kept abreast of the developing situation in Donegal by the Gárdaí and, in deference to the involvement of the Navy, had invited the Minister of Defense to join with him in hearing what the Gárda Commissioner had to say.

The Defense Minister was in the room before him and so was the Commissioner. The latter had fresh news. "Nothing found on our trawler, Minister, but, then, that doesn't surprise us all that much. Our Mountie friends warned us that this would be slick and although we've been shadowing the stuff from the beginning, our manpower problem—"

"I hope the search hasn't alerted them?" The Minister for Justice interrupted rudely. He and the Commissioner had never hit it off.

The Commissioner's lips pursed. "As far as the crew were concerned we were looking for illegal nets—"

"You think they bought it?" The Minister again cut across, giving the Commissioner his most penetrating stare. "I have to tell you that that shyster Vaughan from RTE asked me out there about some big operation he'd heard about."

"He couldn't have missed it, Minister. As a cover we searched everything in the port. We gave it out that this was a new EC directive. The chief superintendent in charge of the operation traveled to Donegal but he stayed in the barracks. And the captain and crew of the boat were not brought in. We think we handled it."

"But you haven't found anything, have you?" The Minister for Justice had thundered from the podium, in a powerful, passionate speech at his party's last annual rally, the Ard Fheis, that, subject only to his prime consideration which, "first, last and always," was the protection of cherished family values, his ministry was laying heavy emphasis on ridding Ireland of the scourge of illegal drugs, "from crack to cocaine, from heroin to hash, until not a grain or a trace of it is left in Ireland. Until our cities can once again flourish and the streets and even the laneways are safe again for the little children." Indeed, *Safe for the Little Children* was the catch-phrase in the current poster and television campaign.

"We're really concerned about this, Commissioner." To compensate for her feeling of inadequacy, the Defense Minister spoke loudly. Both men ignored her. The Minister for Justice put his fingers to his temples, as though asking God to give him patience. "Do we have any idea where it is now, Commissioner?"

"I'm afraid we have temporarily lost sight of it, Minister."

The Commissioner, who had seen out at least five governments of all political hues and many more cabinet reshuffles, was not in the least rattled. "We followed the consignment from the time it was picked up and we know it was put aboard the *Agnes Monica* so, therefore, her captain either hid it somewhere along the coast during the twenty-four hours we lost her, or put it overboard to be retrieved later. Our lads will check every marker buoy and lobster pot along that coast. We've pinpointed to within a mile the place where she went out of contact. At the time, we thought she must have sophisticated jamming equipment but the search of her proved otherwise."

"So the solution is obvious, man." The minister's brows knotted incredulously at the obtuseness of all policemen. "She hid somewhere, in some small cove. Find that and you'll find what you're looking for."

"It's not quite that simple, Minister." The Commissioner stretched his legs comfortably under the desk. "Our American and Canadian colleagues tell us our fellas might have something new to this part of the Atlantic. At least, it's new to us. Apparently they can sink the goods in weighted waterproof containers with an electronic tag attached and recover it any time. All they have to do is activate this tag which releases the weights and the stuff comes back to the surface."

The Minister sighed heavily. "So lean on the crew."

"The recovery ship is rarely the one that dumps the stuff in the first place. It's almost certain this crew don't know who's involved at the top and possible they don't even know who would be involved in the recovery. We don't want to tip them off." The Commissioner cleared his throat ostentatiously as though he hated having to repeat himself. "As you know, the motivation of some of the creeps tied in with this is pretty mixed—and we'll be watching as many of the usual haunts as we can, not to speak of as many coves and inlets as we can manage in the circumstances." He let it hang.

"I have to tell you, Commissioner, that I'm very concerned and so are my colleagues in Cabinet." The Minister for Justice ignored the barbed reference to the recruitment and overtime dispute. "How do you think it appears internationally? After all, both the Mounties and the FBI were spot on. It is a little humiliating to admit, don't you think, that we lose it as soon as it goes on to a two-bit inshore coaster?"

"Yes," the Defense Minister chimed in. "My department's been cooperating fully, Commissioner, but this has been going on for sometime and our resources are scarce. We don't like them tied up like this at the height of the fishing season. It's time we saw some results."

"This is one of the biggest operations we've ever mounted. If more overtime for the Gárdaí could be authorized . . ." The Commissioner raised his eyebrows.

"You know damned well what your budgets are," the Justice Minister snapped.

"I'll have the costings of the overtime on your desk by close of business today." The Commissioner remained calm and stared into his minister's eyes. He not only knew damned well what his budgets were, he knew damned well that cracks were showing in the glue that held the coalition parties together and that drug-related crime was one of the issues exercising the minds of the electorate.

"Incidentally, while we're on the subject of budgets," the Justice Minister pushed his glasses up on his nose and stared back, "I'd like to know how much that one-man expeditionary force you sent to America has cost."

"I'll find out, Minister."

"Get a move on, Commissioner, and sort this whole thing out." The Justice Minister pulled toward him an unopened file as if he had better things to do. He glanced at his Defense colleague, then glared at the Commissioner. "Time is not on our side."

The Amnesty meeting was scheduled a few days' hence.

"Now," he said brusquely, "I have a constituency group in. And then I have to see the Taoiseach, brief him about this mess. He's taking a personal interest, as you know. I'm not looking forward to that meeting, Commissioner. I promised him we would have something positive at this stage. Something will have to be done if you and your men don't get a move on. Anything else on your mind?"

"Nothing else to report at present, and the Taoiseach can hardly blame the force for a car crash, which seems to have put a spanner temporarily in the works. But it has not affected our morale and you can assure him that we have things under control. I'll telephone you this evening, Minister."

As the Commissioner picked up his hat and gloves, he smiled and inclined his head toward the Defense Minister in a courteous bow. Poor woman: she had no idea what was going on. He knew that no one had briefed her about the possibility of a subversive strike from outside the state's borders. And as for the separate headache of a proposed royal visit, he doubted if she even knew there was an Amnesty conference in the offing, let alone who'd been invited.

The door closed behind him with a soft click as the Commissioner put on his hat. In the struggle between himself and his political masters over resources he held all the aces. A lot of unwelcome media attention had been paid lately to the fact that Ireland was being used as a clearinghouse for all sorts of criminal deals not only drugs. So with the bush telegraph positing an election sooner rather than later, this ailing coalition needed a big international press conference.

Sky telephoned Daniel Treacy's office to make sure he was in and was surprised to learn that he had not yet arrived. "I'll call him at home." She brushed off the secretary with a brusque guarantee that she was a personal friend. Then she grabbed her tape recorder, notebook and purse and ran to the Nissan.

She had no difficulty in finding the house; although no one she knew had seen inside, everyone in the city knew its location. What she was not prepared for was the view from the terrace at the end of the driveway. "Jeez," she gasped audibly as she let the Nissan coast to a halt before a spectacular Rocky Mountain panorama. The circular parking lot was large enough for at least eight cars, but only Treacy's Saab convertible was in evidence.

She heard the doorbell chime as she pressed the brass button, and then leaned toward the speaker grille set beside it. She waited at least ninety seconds, but when nothing sounded through the speaker, she reached for the bell again and was caught off balance as the door was opened. "Miss MacPherson—Sky—what a pleasant surprise!"

Without a jacket, the gray hospital-issue sling cutting into the flesh of his neck, Treacy looked thin and far older than she had seen him before. "Sorry to bother you at home so early." She stepped over the threshold in response to his silent invitation. "I did call your office. And I'm sorry about calling so late last night too. Did you get back to sleep?"

"Don't worry. I don't need much sleep these days." He sidestepped the question. "Have you had breakfast?" The

soul of courtesy, he closed the door behind her. The reporter
in Sky began to feel less intrepid than intrusive and shabby.

"As a matter of fact, I haven't." She remembered she had
not eaten for more than twenty-four hours. No wonder she
was suffering from mood swings: it was all that caffeine on
an empty stomach.

"This way." He stood back and indicated that she should
go through one of the doorways off the thickly carpeted
lobby. "Make yourself at home, and I'll get a fresh pot of
coffee." The telephone on a console table rang as he passed
it on his way to what Sky presumed was the kitchen. "I'll let
it be." He smiled at her over his shoulder. "A great invention, the answering machine . . ."

The electronically distorted voice of the secretary to
whom Sky had spoken earlier rang through the lobby as she
walked into the room to which he had pointed. Small and
elegantly appointed, it was decorated entirely in tones of
primrose and sparkling white, and contained the minimum of
furniture: a glass-topped marble table, on which breakfast
had been laid, and six graceful chairs, a matching sideboard,
over which hung an Impressionist watercolor of a spring
garden, and two upholstered rattan chairs in front of south-
facing full-length bay windows, which allowed in maximum
light from dawn to sunset.

The windows faced on to a sunlit Italianate terrace outside, and if the forest canopy beyond and below had been
blue instead of green, Sky thought she could have been
standing in a villa in Capri or the South of France. "My wife
and I did not entertain," the carpet was so thick that she had
not heard Treacy come back, "so we didn't need a big formal
dining room." He placed the coffee pot on a ceramic trivet in
the center of the table.

"It's beautiful." Sky meant it: the room exuded a sense of
peace and ease.

"Thank you." He waited politely, until she was seated
before he sat down. "I like it too. Rather fancifully, I suppose, we referred to it as the garden room." He waved his
uninjured arm toward the painting above the sideboard.

"We'll talk about my grandmother in a moment, Mr.
Treacy . . ." But then Sky hesitated: she was suddenly
unwilling to use her grandmother as a cover for her real purpose in being there. Treacy's courtesy made it difficult to
grill him about why he was attracting the attentions of an

undercover Irish policeman. Especially here in his own home. The blast of light from the windows revealed a network of fine lines all over his face, but it was the gray pallor of his skin and the tiredness in his eyes that were most striking. She bought time. "How's your shoulder, Mr. Treacy? Are you in pain?"

"Not really. Now, tell me about your mother. I hope you have not forgotten my offer of assistance—please help yourself to some croissants and fruit." He gestured toward the baskets on the table.

As she told him about Johanna, Sky thought that this was not the stiff tycoon she had met before. "I'm sorry I'm interrupting your own breakfast." She looked at the untouched roll on the plate in front of him.

"I'm afraid I'm not hungry." He pushed away the plate. "Please don't keep me in suspense any longer, Sky. What's the news?"

The effect of her telling him that her grandmother was arriving in Billings the following day was shocking. Treacy put his good hand over his face and she was afraid he might even cry. "Mr. Treacy . . ." she half rose.

"I'm all right. I'm sorry." He lowered his head and the words were muffled by his hand.

Sky was disconcerted: how on earth was she going to confront him?

As she wavered over what to say next, he coughed and lowered his hand. "Do you think she'll stay here?"

"One step at a time, Mr. Treacy." She was relieved that, although his eyes were brimming, he seemed to have regained his composure. Then, before she could stop herself, "You're very different here at home from what you are in public, do you know that?" Immediately furious with herself, she thought that if someone were to institute an academic course in how to control an unruly tongue she would have to be the first in line for registration.

"Am I?" The unshed tears still stood in his eyes but he smiled a little. "Who isn't different in his own home? " He seemed to come to a decision. "I'm going to tell you something I've never admitted to anyone before."

Suddenly, against all her training and reporter's instincts, Sky felt she did not want to hear. "Are you sure I'm the right person?"

"Yes. Midge hates—hated—this house. It was far too

open—I guess it made her feel exposed. It was one of the reasons she preferred the lodge, small windows, thick dark wooden walls. I chose this site, built this house, with your grandmother in mind. She always loved light and air. I knew she would probably never come here, but I lived in hope. Does that shock you?"

Sky was out of her depth, and she felt that to probe further would be voyeuristic. "Do you live alone?" She knew it was inadequate. "Does no one look after you?"

"You mean servants?" He seemed unruffled by the lack of a suitable response and smiled again. "My needs are few. A woman comes in to clean three times a week, and I send out my laundry. I don't like being fussed over. Any servants we had were in the lodge. Midge—" He stopped.

"What about Midge, Mr. Treacy?" Remembering why she was here and glad to be on safer ground, Sky kicked at her resolve.

"I beg your pardon?" He looked almost startled.

"Midge," she insisted. "You were going to say something about your wife."

"Yes." He paused a little and, again, the transformation was stunning: the softness and openness had vanished, replaced by wary reserve. "My wife was the one who had to have servants."

"I came here not solely because of my grandmother, Mr. Treacy. Or perhaps you might have guessed that."

"Oh?" He retreated further.

"Do you remember my Irish friend from yesterday's rodeo? The one who drove my car home?" His eyes did not blink or flicker but seemed to darken as, staring at her, he let the silence develop between them. For once, she chose her next words carefully. "I just found out he is not an Irish teacher at all, Mr. Treacy, but an Irish policeman. A policeman with a particular interest in you and in your wife's death." She looked at him as boldly as she dared. "Would you have any idea why?"

His reply was so unexpected it left her almost winded. "It is not news to me that he is a policeman. To answer your question, I have no idea what his agenda is. And I don't care, Miss MacPherson."

Something about his demeanour puzzled Sky. His words rang true and yet she knew he was lying. If, as he had said, he knew Lynskey's identity, he had to know why the

Irishman was going to so much trouble. What was it the funeral director had said? *"... He may have turned your head ... nonsense about Daniel Treacy. I've reassured others ... libelous lies ..."*

"The guy tricked me, Mr. Treacy." She decided she had nothing to lose by being honest. "I'm very angry. I wish you'd tell me what's going on."

She felt him weigh up the situation.

"You're the press, Miss MacPherson."

He was no longer as cold, however, so she pushed home her advantage. "I'm also Elizabeth Sullivan's granddaughter. Could you talk to me on that basis?"

He looked skeptical. "Come now! You're not expecting me to believe you wouldn't publish anything I might tell you?"

"Of course I can't guarantee that, but what I could do is make it so you'll suffer no damage." Sensing she was gaining ground, she pulled her chair closer to the table. "Somehow I cannot believe you're involved in anything illegal. You don't strike me as the type."

A ghost of a smile. "Is there a type?"

She cast around for something that would not pull down the shutters again. "Well," she grinned at him, "are you?"

Treacy had another shock in store. "I'm rather afraid I am."

As she goggled at him, he reached for the coffee pot and refilled his cup. "Mr. Lynskey has competition. If you look carefully and quickly when you drive out again through the front entrance you will probably see a diligent member of the FBI or it could be the CIA or even a private investigator—it's a matter of complete indifference to me—in a cream-colored Chevrolet making notes in a little notebook."

"You're being watched?" Then Sky remembered the two men in Stetsons who had almost knocked her down at the rodeo. "I saw them," she blurted out, "at the rodeo. I thought they might be your bodyguards."

"They're far from bodyguards. They're watching me round the clock." Treacy paused. "I can tell you it's rather an odd feeling. I would have thought it might be irritating but in a way it's a privilege. One feels a little like a celebrity."

"But what have you done, Mr. Treacy?" Sky forgot to behave like a reporter.

He let another silence descend, stroking the shiny fabric of the sling over his injured shoulder. "I'll tell you what," his accent sounded very Irish now, "I'll make a deal with you, Sky. I'll tell you what's going on—or as much as I know about what's going on—provided you agree to certain conditions."

"Depends on what they are." Sky tried to suppress her jubilation. She was there. She was sure of it.

"The first condition," he was weighing his words, "is that we work together, that I see what you're writing. If you agree, I think I do have a story for you, one that might make you famous, R. Sky MacPherson . . ." Again that trace of a smile.

Sky wondered how Jimbo would react to deal making. She had never before agreed to show copy in advance but, then, she had never dealt in this kind of stuff. "What's your second condition?" To help her think, she took a mouthful of coffee. Too much, too fast. She almost choked, just managing to swallow without spluttering it all over the immaculate glass tabletop. She was furious with herself for blowing the sophisticated, on-top-of-it-all Woodward-and-Bernstein image she knew she should be trying to convey.

He waited until she had recovered, then went on, "The second condition is that the name of one person involved in the story is for your ears only and is to be kept out of it. The name is integral, I'm afraid, but together we'll work out a way to do this.

"The third condition," he looked so intently at her that she knew this was going to be the most significant of the three, "is that is you must put a moratorium on publishing your story."

Sky considered. "Until when?"

"Until after my death."

She was about to protest when he held up his hand. "You won't have to hold the front page all that long. I have cancer."

Chapter Twenty-three

"So now maybe you can figure out why I'm so anxious to see your grandmother just one more time."

"How long?" Sky knew there was no point in being coy.

"I don't know. It may be weeks, a couple of months at the outside. It has spread to my liver. That will make it mercifully fast, apparently. Now," he became brisk, "perhaps since you know this, it makes it a little easier to hold off on publishing?"

Knowing full well that she should not take such decisions without consulting Jimbo, Sky agreed. She took out her tape recorder and switched it on. "No." Treacy had reverted to his businessman persona, "no tape."

She tried to get him to change his mind but he was adamant. "I think you'll have no difficulty in remembering what I'm going to tell you, R. Sky MacPherson." That offputting cold smile sent shivers of anticipation down her back; this man seemed able to switch at will between personalities. One second he was the perfect, considerate host, the next, a frosty, impermeable enigma. "Listen, Sky," he softened again, "when you hear what I have to tell you you'll see for yourself why I wouldn't want myself quoted verbatim. Even after my death."

She pressed the "off" button on the recorder.

As she listened to his low, intense speech for the next five minutes, she began to feel as though she was sitting in the back row of a movie theater. The scale of the revelations was so outlandish that Sky lost her sense of excitement about the scoop. She registered what he said but was unable to put it in context.

How could it be true, in pedestrian, nineteen nineties Montana, that Midge Treacy had not died—had not even been in that accident—but was in some upstate institution? That her husband had participated in the arrangements of her so-called death, had allowed the charade of her funeral to proceed—had even stood by a casket which did not contain her body. That he could stand there and accept the sympathy of Sky herself and every businessman in town. That some organization, for which the St. Patrick's Brigade was just a local front, had such power it could arrange this bizarre scheme, which obviously included police forces, medical examiners and even the judiciary.

"So there were three accidents." Sky tried to collect her scattered wits. "The one where your wife hit Sheriff O'Connor's Buick, the one where she hit the hobo—but didn't run away as you told me last time . . ." She allowed herself an accusing look to which he did not respond.

"Well, two really," she amended then, "and the third one was the staged one when your wife was already in Choteau . . ." It was so extraordinary that she could not sit still but stood to pace the room. "If it happened as you say, if the sheriff organized that her car went off the highway like that and caught fire, how did he square the hospital? Even with a phony accident someone must have called an ambulance. And with no body . . ."

"I left that to O'Connor. I wasn't there at the time." His tone had become conversational. They might have been talking about Ross Perot's chances in November. "Funny, when your life shrinks to a day-by-day affair, how little revelance that sort of thing seems to have. And my main concern was getting Midge settled. You haven't touched your coffee. Shall I fetch some more?"

"It's like something out of a thriller."

"It may well read like a thriller by the time you've finished with it." This time his smile was genuinely amused. "But I'm afraid it's all too true. What about the coffee?"

"I mustn't have anymore coffee or I'll go into orbit. Look, what was involved here?" Sky remembered her remark to Teddy Morzsansky about the oversized casket. "That casket was very big. Was it drugs?"

"I don't know. I didn't ask. I resented it, of course, and after Midge is finally secure I will go to the police—but, for reasons I've already explained, I did not—do not care what they did with the coffin. With Midge's condition and my own death imminent, I felt I had no option but to agree. And, of course, if I die before I go to the police, you will be free to tell whomever you choose. I'm being frank with you now so you will have the truth."

Sky's impression that she was caught somewhere in the middle of a thriller-writer's fantasy was reaching new heights. "How did they organize the funeral on the other side? I mean, I know it's not unusual for Irish Americans to want to be buried in Ireland but were there no formalities? What about your wife's family? Who was there to greet the casket? And if there was no one at the airport, would that not have looked a bit suspicious? And presumably you didn't go?"

"Hold on!" Treacy held up his hand. "You're going too quickly. To answer the last question first, I did not go to Ireland—for many reasons, not only the obvious one. You see, although the killing of your grandfather was an accident I had a manslaughter conviction against me and I should not have been admitted to the United States all those years ago. I got in only through the good offices of the friend of an uncle in New York. This man's name was Treacy. He had political and union connections. It was he who sponsored me and it was his name I took." He held up his hand again. "Don't ask how he swung it, I don't know. I've always understood it to be what we called in Ireland 'nod-and-wink' politics. He's long dead now and so is my uncle, so I'll never find out, and anyhow, it's irrelevant. But you understand now why I've never gone back—for fear I would be stopped coming back in again.

"I boarded the aircraft with the coffin and they put me off in Minneapolis. From there I went straight to Choteau to visit my wife. Before you ask," he had seen that she was preparing to launch another barrage, "I assume they have influence in airports too. As to what arrangements they made on the other side, I have no idea. And I don't *care*, Sky, I told you!" His voice rose momentarily. This was the first real evidence she had seen of the emotional stress he must be suffering, and she was tempted to back off.

Yet she had the nub of the story in her sights: having read and seen as much foreign current affairs coverage as anyone in her line of business, she was well aware of the allegations as to what some of the Irish-American organizations were up to. Gun-running, for instance, fund-raising for weapons for the IRA and INLA, for the Loyalist paramilitaries. "What about relatives in Ireland? You told me you'd put death notices in the Irish papers."

"And you believed me, Miss MacPherson." Again, he smiled, this time with something approaching affection. He might have been patronizing her, but she decided to give him the benefit of the doubt and smiled back. "I'm glad you're not cynical," he had meant no offense, "and I hope you stay that way, notwithstanding that what I am telling you might move you away from our own cozy little corner and out into the piranha pool of the national press."

"I doubt it, I'm afraid I'm a bit green at this, but—if I may ask you another question, Mr. Treacy, a crucial one." She took a deep breath. "Are you not concerned about what the contents of that coffin might have been? If it was drugs, for instance."

"I thought I'd already made my position clear to you, Sky." His eyes registered appeal. "Having heard what I've told you about my wife, do you think I was in any position to make conditions? You must understand, you *must*, that I could not allow Midge to stand trial, maybe go to prison. Can you not try to understand? This was my wife, Sky, someone I'd vowed to protect." He stared at her for a long time while, unusually, she schooled her tongue.

He seemed not to find comfort in her expression and looked away. "If it makes you feel any better, although I don't suppose it will, I was assured that any money raised as a result of my 'cooperation,' as they so kindly put it, would be going solely to fund legitimate businesses in the north of Ireland and for relief of hardship caused to prisoners' families." She had little choice but to accept his *bona fides* and, in any event, saw the moral dilemma in which he had been placed.

She went on to ask him for the names of the people involved in the deceit but he knew little. The only person who had spoken to him in any detail had been the sheriff, "And he gave me little information, said the less I knew the better. It was he who arranged Midge's admission to the sanatorium up by Choteau. And he is also arranging for her transfer to Oregon. I'll go with her, of course. So the only names I can give you are those of the Mayville sheriff and the funeral director, Bill Collins."

Sky remembered the call to Collins's mobile telephone the night she was killing time in the car park of the War Bonnet before going in to cover the Brigade's monthly meeting. "It was Bill Collins warned me about Fergus Lynskey. The man who's here from the Irish police. Collins tried to make me tell Lynskey to back off. What's more, it was he who called my editor to tell him too. In fact," she saw the irony, "I'd say he's the one who blew it because he actually tipped us all off, therefore *making* a story out of this whole thing."

"Bill Collins is a fool. He probably panicked. I may be wrong," Treacy spoke slowly as though working it out for himself, "but I think he's only small fry." He played with a piece of thread hanging from the sling. "I would say that the St. Patrick's Brigade are probably being used by a heavier crowd. The members of the Brigade believe they're helping what they like to call the Cause.

"You remember Jerry Flynn?" he asked slowly. "The Canadian in whose helicopter we traveled? You might check him out, although maybe I'm not being fair. I've never liked the guy—"

"If you don't like him," she interrupted, "why were you his guest at the rodeo that day?"

Treacy raised his eyebrows. "It's clear you don't know the way business works. Far more deals are made on golf courses and at lunch tables than in the boardroom."

"Sorry, stupid question. So what makes you think he's involved in something illegal?"

"Oh," Treacy looked off into the middle distance, "just some things he said, nothing I could put my finger on and it was more the way he said them than anything else. We were discussing something we had both seen on CBS the night before, a small news item about the Irish Prime Minister going to see the British Prime Minister and the two of them standing pleased as punch for a photo shoot. Flynn is third or fourth generation Irish and I can't even remember what it was he said. It was more a tone of voice, really, but I remember thinking at the time that there was a lot going on underneath."

The telephone rang in the hallway, again picked up by the machine. The door was open and Treacy cocked an ear: it was his secretary with changes to his appointments schedule.

While he listened, Sky checked the time. Although her brain felt sharp and she could think of nothing she wanted to do more than bite into this huge plum that had landed in her lap, she must not forget her mother. "I'm keeping you from work, Mr. Treacy," she drained her coffee when the bleep on the machine ended the message, "but you asked that a name be kept out of it. I assume you mean your wife's. I know I agreed in principle, Mr. Treacy, but I'm sure you can see it would be difficult to run this story without referring to her."

"I mean me, Sky. This is why I would not allow you to tape our conversation. By quoting me directly, there are those who might recognize figures of speech, vocabulary."

"But why? And how can I—"

"You have all the information," he interrupted. "It's up to you to find a way to write your article. You could find another—ah—source. Of course I'm central, I know that. All I'm asking is that I'm not quoted. No one must know that it was I who divulged all of this."

"But why?" she repeated. "What would it matter to you? You'll be—" She stopped.

"Yes, I will be." He interpreted correctly what she had been about to say. "But medical science is, as you pointed out earlier, making great strides. Too late for me, alas, but where my wife is concerned, although the alcohol had damaged her brain, she might recover some day. If she does, I won't be around to protect her from knowing what happened. But I can protect her from knowing that her husband was the prime source of her public humiliation."

Sky put her tape recorder back into her purse, preparatory to leaving. "One thing's puzzling me, Mr. Treacy. It's obvious, after what you've told me about your wife, why you didn't go to the police, but why, having covered up for so long, have you decided to tell me all this?"

"The truth is . . ." he shifted in his chair and she felt his discomfort in her own body. ". . . I don't take kindly to being blackmailed or treated like a simpleton, a blind, brainless pawn in someone else's game. Anything I can do to make life awkward for the good sheriff and his merry men I'll do. At the time I felt I had no choice but to go along with them because of Midge and I still feel that, because the arrangements concerning her are not yet complete. But that doesn't mean I'm going to lie down with my paws up in the air like some dumb lapdog. For a while I considered going to the police, despite the dangers, but I knew if I did that it would be likely that the charges against Midge would be reinstituted by O'Connor's successor. I've no idea how he managed to stop them in the first place. But he was right about the effect on her. I dread to think what she might have done. Even had you and I not spoken together because of your grandmother, I would have come to you, sometime before the end and when I was sure no one could touch Midge. I'm determined those crooks will not get away with it. I meant it when I said before that I admired your work, Sky. You're wasted in Butte."

"Thank you." Sky had received compliments before but knew that none had been so sincerely meant.

Treacy gazed away from her. The sun was still low enough in the sky to paint long shadows in the valleys between the mountain peaks to the west and under its fresh benediction, the green ocean that stretched to the foothills was full of light and shade. Yet despite all the architect's efforts to embrace the beauty outside, this ultrasilent, plush room remained isolated from it by suffering of its owner. For the first time Sky understood Daniel Treacy's loneliness. "It seems the authorities have now come to me," he said, almost to himself, "saving me the bother of making all these decisions. I don't underestimate those men outside. I wouldn't be surprised if they're also watching our sheriff and, with all my soul-searching, it may prove unnecessary in the end for me to give myself up and make my big confession." He smiled but his teeth seemed too big for his mouth. "You should ask your Irish policeman friend's opinion about how good he thinks they are." He winced then made an effort to turn his head back toward her. "Would you mind if I asked you to leave now? I find I'm already very tired and I still have a long day ahead of me."

"Of course." Sky reached for her purse.

"That's wonderful news about your grandmother." His eyes slid away from hers so he looked almost shy. "I'd appreciate it if you wouldn't tell her what I told you about the house."

"I won't." Sky knew there was little danger of that. It was such a private, intimate confession that she did not want to think about it.

"Did you extend my invitation to her?" He was still diffident. "Do you think she might agree to stay here?"

"Did you not ask her that yourself?" Sky paused in the act of closing the zipper on her purse.

Treacy swallowed. "I'm afraid I didn't have the courage to call her last night. It's been a very long time since we spoke. Look, Sky," he winced again and she felt sure this time it was not from physical pain, "I'm afraid I'll blow it."

"I'm sure she's looking forward to seeing you." Somewhere, during the course of this interview, Sky had changed sides.

"Do you really think so?" His face lit up from within and, his present appearance notwithstanding, she could see how handsome he must have been in his youth.

"I do." Instead of a professional journalist on the verge of her breakthrough story, she felt like a mother encouraging her son to ask his favorite girl to Homecoming. The hell with objectivity.

"There's just one more thing. I have no right to ask this, of course, but in return for what I have told you exclusively I wonder would you do me one more favor?"

"That depends."

"It would make me very happy if you did not allude to any of this in you grandmother's presence. If I get the chance, I'll tell her about Midge. And about myself. But I don't think she needs to know the ins and outs of what's been going on."

With the story on hold anyway, Sky felt there was little to be gained by making the poor guy's last few days more upsetting than they were already. She relaxed. "Done." She was shocked then to see his face contort.

"I'm sorry to be so rude," he gasped, struggling for control, "but you really will have to leave. I need to go upstairs—I'm afraid my medication is overdue."

The spasm passed and he made two more requests. He would be at the airport that evening in time for her grandmother's arrival but would hang back out of sight. Sky had gone so far down the road with him that she had no difficulty in agreeing to act as go-between and, if her grandmother was amenable, to take her to where he was.

She also agreed to keep the news of his cancer to herself. According to Treacy, the only people who knew were his doctor, his private secretary and his attorney. He had not yet told members of his various boards.

She took her time passing through the gate at the end of his driveway. The sedan he had talked about was there, parked on a strip of grass beside the highway. As Sky went by, the driver started up his engine and pretended to consult a map.

Chapter Twenty-four

Five thousand miles and eight time zones away, the *L.E. Aideen* was steaming slowly through moderate seas, captained by an ambitious young officer whose first command she was. He was proud of his ship, and her state-of-the-art communications and detection equipment, and was having no difficulty in tracking the *Agnes Monica*: his instructions were simply to continue to relay her exact whereabouts, heading and speed.

The fishing vessel was making headway; she had trawled for a while, then hauled in her nets and was now, the *Aideen*'s commander ascertained, traveling at full throttle.

He instructed his radio officer to report that the craft would be off Killybegs in approximately one hour and twenty minutes.

As she drove to the *Courier* offices from Treacy's mansion, Sky struggled to come to terms with her conflicting feelings. She knew her mother's condition should still be her prime concern but it was hard to contain her sense of exultation at the story she had been handed. "Get a grip," she said aloud to the dashboard of the Nissan, reminding herself she had gone to see Treacy not only in pursuit of the story but on a personal mission of revenge. To blow Lynskey's cover. Some hotshot she was. She had not yet decided how to handle the Irishman but on the journalistic side, she would let Jimbo dictate.

But, for once, he was not in his paper-dominated office. "Said he had a breakfast meeting but he's not back yet." The junior's languid hands were fluttering over an open filing cabinet in the main office. "Oh, and you had two calls. One was some man from the American Legion. I wrote down his name, Sky, it's on your desk. He wanted to know how you were going to handle the accident to Mr. Treacy."

Sky reached for the pad on her desk then changed her mind. "I've got to get to the hospital. Call him back for me, will you? Tell him to mind his own business."

"Really?" The junior's eyes widened.

"For goodness sake, no." Sky sighed. "Don't put it like that, use your judgment. Was the second call important?"

"He didn't say. I wrote down the number."

Unable to curb her curiosity about this one, Sky picked up the pad. The number meant nothing to her. And then she saw the name. After a second or two, she remembered: it was the driver of the logging truck who was alleged to have driven Midge Treacy off the road north of Mayville. "May I speak to Martin O'Shaughnessy, please?" As she waited for him to come on the line, she flipped through her notebook in an effort to find the entry she had made about the logger during the trip to Libby.

She had not yet found it when he spoke: "Yes?"

"Thank you for returning my call, Mr. O'Shaughnessy." She stopped realizing she should be cautious: the guy had to be involved in the fraud.

Something about his name, and not just that he was the logger she had been looking for, buzzed irritatingly inside her brain. What was it?

"The reason for my original call no longer applies," she hoped she sounded convincing, "because I was doing a story on road fatalities in the state and your name arose in connection with an accident near Mayville. But since you were on vacation I went ahead and wrote the piece without you. It's finished now and unless you have anything new to add, I don't think I need any longer to talk to you."

He did not immediately reply. Then: "I had no chance that night. You sure you have all the details right? When's your story appearing?"

His response confirmed that her instinct to be careful was correct. She told him she had no definite date for publication, that it was not a huge story—"just one of those perennials we do from time to time, you know?" She attempted to laugh.

"You sure I can't help you? Maybe if you could tell me what you're saying about that night?"

"I couldn't do that, Mr. O'Shaughnessy. I gather you weren't injured in any way?"

"I had a very lucky escape. She was driving like a crazy

woman." He hesitated just a fraction. "I had no chance to avoid her."

"So I've heard."

Sky waited but he said nothing more. "Thank you for calling," she said forcefully, "but I'm afraid I have to go to the hospital, my mother's quite ill."

The logger made ritual noises of concern and then: "That woman was a soak, Miss MacPherson. You'd be better off not bothering about her."

Echoes of Bill Collins's advice—or warning—to Lynskey.

"I appreciate the call." Sky wanted him off. "Now I have to go. Thank you." She hung up.

She discovered her hands were trembling. The logger was taking instructions from the sheriff of Mayville; yet Sky felt that he, like Collins, was just a minor player. What was it about that name? She said it aloud, "Martin O'Shaughnessy . . ."

"Yes? You want something, Sky?" The junior looked up, her bright vacant face enquiring.

"It's nothing." She proceeded to explain the cryptic notes she had made at the rodeo. "Just type them up first, that'll give you a sense of the story, but all you really need to get right is the spelling of everyone's name. Okay? Just do your best, it'll be fine. Tell Jimbo—Mr. Larsen—that I'll call him as soon as I can."

Johanna was still in theater when she got to the hospital and she installed herself in the empty room to wait.

She had been there only ten minutes when Fergus Lynskey put his head around the door. "Good morning, sleep well?" His expression was pleasant yet bland.

"Fine, thank you." Sky forced herself to reciprocate. "And you?" They might have been guests at a cocktail party.

"Is there any word?" He came into the room and sat down. Sky related what she knew about her mother's operation, which was precious little, and they lapsed into silence.

"I'm still half asleep." Lynsky yawned noisily. He stretched his legs, folded his hands across his stomach and let his eyes close.

Given his perfidy, Sky was outraged at his air of relaxation. Yet, as she glared at his prone body, she knew that, without Jimbo's input, she should not show her hand. "It may be hours yet, Fergus," she said, as sweetly as she could, "and you're so tired. Why don't you go back to bed and I'll contact you as soon as there's news?"

"Ah, no." He did not open his eyes. "I don't want to leave you on your own and I couldn't sleep anyway, during the day. I've hired a car, a Chrysler Topaz—if me ma could see me now! And it's the first time in my life I've ever had cruise control. Wonderful invention."

"I don't mind waiting by myself." Her exasperation was growing. If you're not tired, why don't you go somewhere? You said you'd like to see the Custer Battlefield, didn't you, that day we went to the rodeo?" It was a shock to Sky to realize that "that day" had been only yesterday. Lynskey's eyelids fluttered a little but he said nothing. "So why not?" she went on. "You're on vacation, after all. There's little you can do here and it's a pity to waste a pretty day like this stuck in a hospital room."

"Maybe." Still he did not open his eyes. "By the way how was Treacy this morning?"

Furious, she sprang to her feet. "Were you following me?"

At last he responded, shaking his head as though to clear it. He pulled himself into a more upright position and looked directly at her. "You're much too forthright for this game, MacPee. What's eating you?"

"I don't know what you mean—"

"Oh yes you do." His intelligent eyes were still. "One minute we're having the most fantastic time of our lives and the next it's igloo time. And you're too straight to carry it off. I wish you'd come clean."

"Why don't *you* come clean?"

"Ahh." His knowing tone inflamed her further.

She was trying to think of a retort when he got up and went to the window. "How did you find out?"

At least, she thought, looking at his back, he had the grace not to treat her like an idiot. Damned if she was going to let him run the show, she held out against him, letting the question hang. "Well?" He turned back from the window.

"Does it matter?"

"I don't suppose, it does, really." He walked back to his chair and turned it backward, straddling it. "So what are we going to do now? Are we going to help each other or what?"

Sky heard an echo of Jimbo's words . . . *he might even turn out to be useful* . . . "No, we are not."

* * *

Two simultaneous calls were taking place on different sides of the world. The logger, Martin O'Shaughnessy, was reporting into Sheriff O'Connor, while the captain of the *Agnes Monica* was standing in a drafty public phone box in Killybegs, talking urgently to someone in a Dublin hotel.

"It's done, but that's it now, no more, okay?" The logger sounded angry. "We're finished."

"Is that so?" Sheriff O'Connor's voice was silky, "I don't think so. We're finished when I say so." He smiled as the line went dead.

Anger had also fueled the trawlerman's rapid fire. "I don't give a shit who's listening. I'm fed up with this. You should see this place. Every shagging boat in the harbor turned upside down and the *Aideen* prowling up and down outside like a shagging sheepdog. EC directives, marya, I'm not going to be able to keep a lid on the crew much longer. This was supposed to be a simple. You promised it would lead to bigger things." The captain listened. "Me arse," he expostulated. *"Five percent?* You can stuff your extra five per cent. With the kind of hassle we're going through? I could lose my boat. *Stuff* your five percent."

Again he listened, then, "I couldn't give a shite who's on the line. I'm in it for the money, mate. And the fee's gone up by fifteen." He was so angry that it was only after he slammed down the receiver that he bothered to check again through the salt-roughened glass of the kiosk to see if anyone had been watching. The afternoon was bright and clear and, although the harbor area was busy with vehicles coming and going and activity on the quayside and in the boats, the cops seemed to have withdrawn to barracks.

Satisfied, he left the telephone box and walked away. He paid no attention to the yellow Electricity Supply Board carvan parked on the quayside near a public light standard.

The technician inside wound back the tape he had just recorded. Both he and the Detective Inspector sitting beside him knew it would not be very helpful as no names had been used. They knew that the telephone the captain had contacted was in the lobby of the Majestic Hotel but since it was in a public booth, that was of little assistance. The only thing of any promise was the captain's implied threat that his crew was becoming hard to control.

The inspector picked up his handset and dialed Dublin.

* * *

To Sky's relief, Hermana arrived shortly after Lynskey left her mother's room. She and the Irishman had not rowed overtly, but she had refused to thaw and, seeing that in her present mood he would get nowhere with her, he had yielded.

As strongly as she felt she had done the right thing, his departure had left her feeling raw and doubting whether she had behaved any better than he. After all, her conscience prompted, look at what she had done to poor Greg the minute another man had showed up.

Still anaesthetized, the patient was wheeled back into the room a few minutes later. Although Sky was shocked by the body cast, neck collar, and the scaffolding of tubes and drips with which her mother was festooned, she was assured by the nurse that everything had gone routinely.

For the next hour or so, Johanna drifted in and out of consciousness. From time to time she moaned softly but, according to the nurse, the pain was being kept to a minimum. "She'll be in and out of it all day," Hermana offered, "and tomorrow she won't even remember you were here. I'll be with her, in any case, so why don't you go home and get yourself some rest? After all, you have to be in form for your grandmother tonight.

Sky gazed at the motionless form in the bed. The word "sleep" conjured up a pleasurable feeling of longing and languor. And in anticipation that her grandmother would more likely choose to stay at the duplex than with Daniel Treacy, she knew she would have to prepare Johanna's room for her. "If you're sure," she smiled gratefully at the big woman, then, "See you later, Mom," gently kissing her mother's damp cheek. Devoid of any makeup, her hair flattened to her head, Johanna looked older than she was but as vulnerable as a baby.

Seeing her like this was difficult. Sky had believed that they had plenty of time to improve their relationship but now she saw with the evidence of Johanna's mortality all too evident, that she could postpone it no longer. *I'm sorry . . . I'll try harder, I promise. Things will be different, Mom . . .* Conscious of Hermana's bulk behind her, she blinked away tears, which stung at the back of her eyes. She must not get sappy, she had a great deal to do.

When she got home, the answering machine was flashing. The first message was from her uncle Francey who sounded concerned. He would wait in until he heard from her. Sky's grandmother was next: she was calling from Hubert H. Humphrey airport in Minneapolis: "I just got in from London, Sky. I suppose you're at the hospital." Her speech was hesitant, that of someone unused to speaking to machines. "I won't ring again now, but I'm looking forward to seeing you both." She paused and in the background Sky could hear the roar of the international terminal. "Goodbye now." A third message was from Jimbo Larsen's wife, asking after Johanna and repeating the invitation to come up "any time"; and a fourth was from Buffy, who said she had been delayed but would be at the hospital by lunchtime. Sky rewound the tape and reset the machine. Fatigue weighed her down to such a degree that she could not face seeing her grandmother's accommodation right away, nor even talk to Francey. He had the basic information, the money part could wait. The hospital was hardly going to throw out Johanna on her ear.

She fetched a camera and placed it on the telephone table near the front door so that she would not forget to take it with her to the airport. Then, although she was not hungry but knowing she had to eat something, she fixed herself a large bowl of Cheerios and milk laden with extra sugar. She took this into her bedroom, set her alarm for four hours hence, and, too tired even to undress, climbed into bed and forced herself to eat. She had not quite finished, however, when tiredness overcame her and she put aside the bowl.

When the alarm penetrated her consciousness, she struggled to rise through successive layers of fuzz until she recognized where she was and turned it off. She felt as though a steam-roller had flattened her body, reducing her dimensions from three to two.

Stumbling past the bedroom window toward the bathroom, she automatically looked out to see what kind of an afternoon it was. To her surprise, she noticed that the flag was raised on the mailbox at the end of the driveway. That was odd: with Johanna not here who could have put it up and why? It was not even windy . . . Unless some passerby had been lazy and had used their box instead of going to the trouble of walking to the public mailbox on the corner of the street.

She went into the bathroom where she had a shower. Afterward, feeling a little better, she belted on her robe and went outside to see what, if anything, the mailbox held. Perhaps it was a junk mail drop and the company wanted to attract her attention. If so, it was all to the good; her mother had always been tempted by free offers. The gift of a gold watch with the purchase of seven gallons of cleaning fluid or a set of nesting suitcases always sent her racing for her pen.

A minute later Sky was standing, horror-struck, with a brown padded envelope in one hand and a small cylindrical object in the other. In all the time she had dated Greg, she had never accompanied him on a hunting trip and it was the first time in her life she had touched a bullet. She held it for only a few seconds, then, as though it were some slithering creature covered in slime, threw it from her, recoiling at the "ping" it made as it landed on the blacktop of the driveway. From there it glinted malevolently up at her like the miniature rocket of death it was.

Chapter Twenty-five

As Sky stared at the hateful little piece of metal, the afternoon sounds—a dog barking, the thump of a basketball against a garage door—grew in volume until they seemed deafening. The sunshine which, only moments before, had seemed fresh and friendly, had become harsh and too bright. She ran back to the house and straight to the telephone, instinctively dialing 911.

But, even before her finger had left the buttons, she slammed down the receiver. Panicked through she was, she realized that, as a reporter, the police should not be the first in line.

Jimbo Larson remained composed. "Go back out there and pick it up—use your sleeve or the hem of your skirt to cover your fingers so you won't leave more prints on it—put it carefully back in the envelope and wait until I get there. Where's your Irish friend?"

"I don't know—when can you be here? I have to get back to the hospital, the airport."

"Calm down, Sky. Take a couple of breaths." His unruffled tone got through to her but, as she obeyed, the trembling of her knees became too much and she slid down the wall until she was sitting on the floor. "Are you there? Sky? Sky?" He at last betrayed concern.

"I'm fine," she whispered. "Come quickly."

By the time she heard him pull into the driveway she was dressed in jeans and the last clean white shirt in her closet. In deference to her grandmother's visit, she had tried to make herself look as attractive as she knew she could, piling up her hair and knotting the tails of the shirt at her waist. She added some of her mother's chunky gold jewelry, and hoped the overall effect was sort of Côte d'Azur, an early Bardot look the junior had recently copied from an old edition of *Vogue* for the *Courier*'s fashion page.

She opened the door, and when she saw his lugubrious but reassuring features emerge from underneath the roof of his car, she was tempted to throw herself into her arms. She held back, however, knowing that he would not welcome such a display.

"Where is it?" His expression was set and determined as he came up to her.

She handed him a bag, which he sealed into a *Courier* envelope he had brought with him. "What are you going to do with it?"

"Don't know yet." He put it in his jacket pocket.

"You look all right anyhow, nice outfit." He stood back briefly, eyeing her.

"Thanks." Coming from Jim Larsen, that had been a eulogy.

Knowing she could trust him with anything, as she made the coffee she gave him every detail. She even told him about Treacy's cancer because, in her book, the arrival of the bullet had called off all deals. He listened impassively but underneath she could feel the onset of journalistic excitement as febrile as her own.

She had finally remembered where she had seen an identical padded envelope to the one her bullet had arrived in.

The editor seemed unsurprised that Lynskey had received a similar warning. He agreed that for the present they would keep the police out of the story. A discreet friend of his at the University of Missoula could type the bullet for them. "What worries me most about it—thanks—" he took the coffee from her and sat at the kitchen table "—is not that it was sent and what it represents, although, of course, that's bad enough, but that they see a need to warn you off. They whoever 'they' are, know we're on to something. I wish I knew what, though. But who's watching and where? I'm sorry, now, that I got you mixed you in this."

"You couldn't have known." Despite his words, Sky felt he was not all that sorry. "I still can't believe it's the shamrock lot." She sat opposite him and bit into a rye bread and banana sandwich. "I mean, look at them, Jim, average age sixty-something, those stuffy meetings, those formula notes?"

"I think they're mostly just a bunch of sad middle-aged people whose knowledge of Ireland and patriotism is hopelessly out of date." He stirred his coffee morosely. "But I always suspected one or two of them would go further than that. I didn't think until yesterday that Collins was among them."

"Well he must be. He made the call about Fergus Lynskey, didn't he? But Treacy reckons Collins is small potatoes, that all those shamrock lot are—"

"My guess is he's right. And we're not talking about any of the registered organizations we all know and love. This is something bigger and I'm even wondering if it has much to do with Irish republicanism. But that being said, Sky, I insist you take a break. You need a few days off—you've had enough excitement in the last week to last the lifetime of the average hack."

When she objected he looked seriously at her. "It's not only that, Sky. It's that much as I'd love to be able to run with this as quickly and as comprehensively as possible, I'm wondering if the *Courier* is up to this kind of story. I have a hunch that it's going to need a lot more resources than we have. I'll have a chat with our intellectual friend," he used the disparaging epithet by which they referred to the paper's proprietor, "but I'm not sure he'll authorize the kind of money I think we're going to need. How would you feel about sharing the legwork with a bigger newspaper, in Minneapolis, say, or Detroit? I have contacts—"

"Jim, that's not fair." Every competitive instinct in Sky's body reared up against the notion. "It's our story."

"Yes, but when we started we had no idea how long its legs are. It seems they travel oceans and international borders. And not only that. Close to home it's inconceivable that this story doesn't cross state lines. To my certain knowledge no organization in Montana is big enough to pull this off. Those watchers on Treacy? He's right, they have to be FBI. And there's the safety consideration. That bullet should have given you some idea of what we're up against, Sky."

"I still think you should give us a chance. We can work together on it, maybe hire in a researcher."

"Perhaps now's not the time to talk about this. We can discuss it again." He finished his coffee in a long gulp. "One thing I can do is try to locate the guy who gave us the original tip-off on those coffee coupons. Maybe I'll be able to shake a bit of information out of that airhead back at the office as to what he looked like. She's still typing up those notes you gave her, by the way." He smiled and Sky saw that he thought he had gone too far. "To be fair," he admitted, "I suppose she is making some sort of fist out of that fashion page. Now," he patted himself down to find his car keys, "as for you, young lady, I insist that you take time off."

When she objected again, he stood up. "Look, the story's not going to go away. And Treacy's not going to die tonight, is he?"

"I'll take a day or two but I'll call you." She recognized temporary defeat, and remembered simultaneously that her grandmother was probably even now boarding her commuter aircraft for the short flight from Billings to Butte.

"What about Lynskey?" Jimbo hesitated.

"What about him?" Sky frowned.

"Well, as far as I can see he knows as much as we do—probably more. I know you have your personal agenda with him, Sky, but I'd like to meet him."

"Provided I'm there." She had no intention of letting the story move on without her.

Sky had been expecting Elizabeth Sullivan to look well for her age but was unprepared for the tall, erect figure carrying a tote bag, who came through to the small airport concourse.

Sky's grandmother was dressed in a pencil-slim skirt and toning knee-length coat in shades of avocado. Her cream-colored blouse draped softly from a cowl neck to a neat waist, her gray hair was sleeked like a ballet dancer's into a heavy bun at the nape of her neck and her pale shoes, far from being "sensible," had court heels.

Sky was taken aback. She now realized that, photographic evidence to the contrary, she had spent a lifetime visualizing her "Irish granny" as a cross between Maureen O'Hara in *The Quiet Man* and the mother from *The Waltons*, to whom this smart sophisticate bore no relation.

"Grandmother?" she stepped forward.

"Sky!" Her grandmother's fine-boned face, set off by a pair of heavy gold earrings in the shape of Roman coins, lit up. "At last! I've so wanted to meet you again. It's not the same in letters or on telephones, is it? Anyway, as you've probably noticed by now," her smile broadened, "I'm not the greatest writer in the world."

"I've no excuse—I'm supposed to be the professional here." They hugged, but to Sky's confusion she felt oddly shy. She put it down to fatigue.

"Let me look at you." Her grandmother, who was

suffering no such qualms, stood back. "You've grown up to be beautiful, Sky, everything I imagined and more. You were a lovely little girl but now . . ." Her accent, although soft and distinctly Irish, was nowhere near as thick or rapid as Fergus Lynskey's. As they smiled at one another, to add to her sense of unreality, Sky felt she was seeing into her own future. Those photographs again: she had never noticed before how much she and her grandmother resembled one another. They were even around the same height, with perhaps an inch or two favoring Elizabeth Sullivan. Given Sky's espadrilles, however, this could be put down to the older woman's high heels. Recollecting that she was supposed to be looking after her grandmother Sky said, "You must be exhausted." Then she took the tote bag and the older woman's arm, and led her to where the bags were already arriving.

"I am a bit," her grandmother admitted. "A person really has to work very hard to get from Cork to Butte, Montana. Or from anywhere, I suspect."

Echoes of what Daniel Treacy had said when he had offered the use of a private plane, Sky thought.

"Thank you, Sky, yes, that one there." She pointed to a neat tartan case, and her expression became serious. "Now, tell me about poor Johanna. I tried to ring you but I got that awful machine."

"I got the message." Sky picked up the bag and, as they walked toward the exit, told her about her mother's operation. Then, as they arrived at the door: "There's something I have to prepare you for."

"You haven't told me the truth about Johanna." Her grandmother's face creased with alarm.

"No, nothing like that." Sky pulled her aside a little so as not to block the entrance. "It's Daniel Treacy, I mean McCarthy—" Her grandmother stiffened. "He's waiting out in the lot."

She had passed Treacy's parked Saab on her way into the airport lot, but, as she was running late, had not stopped to talk to him. "He's hoping you will see him, Grandma. He's repeated his invitation to you to stay with him." Somehow she avoided blurting out the news of Treacy's illness.

"I see." From her grandmother's mask-like expression, Sky could not make out whether she was pleased or not at the news of Treacy's presence. "I can go out ahead of you, if you like, and tell him you're too tired tonight," she offered.

"After all, you've every reason. You've been flying for the best part of sixteen hours."

The older woman's face cleared. "To tell you the truth I'm dying of curiosity." Her smile took thirty years off her.

As she accompanied her grandmother out into the warm evening air, Sky knew she would remember everything about this moment: the laughter and the serial explosions of car doors slamming throughout the small airport parking lot, the mackerel sky streaked with pale pink and primrose, the smell of warm tar and automobile metal overlaid with the sweetish odor of burnt aviation fuel.

Treacy was standing beside the Saab and straightened as he saw them. He touched the breast pocket of his dark jacket then checked the knot on his tie. His clothes stood out in exotic contrast with most of the other people in the lot, who were clad in cutoffs or denims.

The two of them came to within feet of one another and then stopped. They did not embrace or even shake hands but stared at one another. At least, Treacy was staring: Sky, who was behind her grandmother, could not see her expression. "I'll wait in the car, Grandma." She touched her elbow. "Let me know what you decide."

Her grandmother turned her head slowly and looked at her as though not seeing. "Grandma?" Again Sky touched her arm. "Are you okay?" The older woman's eyes swiveled back toward Treacy. "After all these years. I wasn't prepared for how you look, Daniel."

Sky thought it tactful to retreat immediately. "I'll take your bags, Grandma."

She threw them in the backseat, then got in behind the wheel and wound down the window to watch them. Still they were not touching. All that restraint, she thought, even after all this time . . .

But although neither had moved, he was bent slightly forward at the waist and was making urgent gestures. He appeared to be pleading and Sky, trying to put herself in their shoes, wondered how she, or even her mother, would behave in such a situation. Johanna, no doubt, would handle it with circumspection: so her lover of five decades ago had resurfaced, that was lovely, and, of course, it had been preordained. Sky, on the other hand, would no doubt be melting like an emotional greasespot all over the parking lot. Or would she? Sky faced her sense of anticlimax on seeing her grandmother. Something was missing from this historic meeting: should she not be crying with joy—or, at least, with something? Was she just a cold fish? But Sky realized that her dominant feeling was of shock, as though she had stepped on what happened to be rock only to discover it was cardboard.

Over the past few days, even when reading between the lines of Daniel Treacy's staggering revelations about the Elizabeth Sullivan he had known and continued to love, she had held on to her own storybook vision of her grandmother. Its dissolution was traumatic. This slender, elegant person, who would not have looked out of place in the more fashionable eateries of Manhattan, could never have been a real grandma, apple-cheeked dispenser of domestic ease and presider over sink, stove and knitting basket: a person who, even if physically absent, was always there in the background and could have provided alternative mothering. True mothering. As in *Little Women* and TV sitcoms. Sky had placed Elizabeth Sullivan at the opposite pole to that of her mother's fascinating yet self-absorbed free spirit. Now no one would ever scold her for putting a dirty hand in the cookie jar.

For Christ's sake, she thought, recognizing the ignoble stab of self-pity, she was hardly a kid anymore. And how could she be so disloyal to her mother? What sort of daughter—or granddaughter, if it came to that—was she? What kind of adult? Abruptly, for no apparent reason, Sky longed to see her father.

Moments later, she saw her grandmother touch Daniel Treacy's lapel, whereupon he seized her hand and raised it to his lips. Great, she thought, lighting on the distraction from her own maudlin thoughts, progress at last. But she was mistaken. Her grandmother extricated her hand, then they turned toward her and came across the lot. The old lady was walking briskly, a little ahead of Treacy. Sky could have wagered that his case had been unsuccessful.

She was right. "She won't come home with me, Sky, in spite of all my blandishments." Treacy attempted to smile as they came up to the car, and Sky felt so sorry for him that she was tempted to weigh in with her own advocacy. His dark eyes burned in their sockets and, notwithstanding the elegant clothes, or perhaps because of them, she believed that even since this morning she saw a deterioration in his condition: a yellowish tinge to his skin, the shrinking of his neck size so that his shirt collar looked too big. Then she chided herself for being dramatic: she saw this now, she thought, because she was aware of the true state of his health. She got out and went round to the other side of the car to open the passenger door for her grandmother, "She's very tired," offering this to him in an effort to make his rejection seem less severe.

"Sure won't we see each other tomorrow, Daniel?" Sky's grandmother hesitated before following her round the hood, then: "You won't mind driving me over, Sky?"

"I'll pick you up," Treacy interposed and, before Sky's grandmother could react, made a time.

Except for expressing a desire to go to the hospital immediately after depositing her bags and freshening up, the old lady was silent during the short trip to the duplex and Sky let her be. But as they pulled up in front of the door, she turned to her granddaughter. "It's been fifty years, Sky. Can you understand?"

"Yes, of course, Grandma," Sky said, although she knew she could not.

It was not that she could not understand how a youthful romance had died a natural death in her grandmother's heart over the course of such a long time. It was that she could not conceive of the intensity of the passion Daniel Treacy had sustained over that time.

Chapter Twenty-six

"It's a place called Killybegs." The Helena lieutenant had more bad news for his boss in Vancouver and, for a woman who made a virtue out of staying calm in all circumstances, the degree of irritation she showed was remarkable.

In response to her anger, the lieutenant had to agree that perhaps the money so far committed to the test operation might prove to have been misplaced. In support of his own judgment, however, he explained that with Ireland being a new territory, he had had to rely on local sources to identify people who could help.

"I tried to call you," the woman spoke even more softly than usual, "but you were not available. This is bad."

"There was a fault on my telephone. It's fixed now."

The woman took a quick, deep breath to calm herself. "Please continue."

Irritation, however, was not what she felt about what she heard next. She was horrified that, on being instructed to deal with the setbacks in Montana, some subordinate, a sheriff, had threatened two people by sending bullets to them. That was crude—and stupid. One of the recipients had been a reporter for the meddling newspaper: no matter how insignificant this one was, all newspapers were bad karma.

Provided that meticulous precautions were taken against discovery of her own involvement, the woman had no objection to quick, clean violence. Indeed, this very lieutenant had been responsible for the disappearance of one or two people whom the police had never been able to trace. If people stepped out of line, violence, she felt, was justified. She treated people fairly; she expected fairness in return. But sending bullets to policemen and newspaper people would draw the authorities. "Pay off that person. And if you think it necessary, please deal with those two people who are being inquisitive. Only, however, if you think it necessary. I'll let you know if we decide to go ahead. *If* we decide to go ahead. So far Ireland has not been what I hoped. And don't do anything else until you hear from me. I'll call you."

The detective who had been monitoring the woman's calls since the raid in Ottawa conveyed the information to his superiors, who in turn passed it down the line to Lynskey.

As she helped her grandmother out of the car and pulled out the bags, Sky's eye was caught by a movement at the end of the driveway. She glanced over her shoulder to see Fergus Lynskey loping toward them.

Her grandmother followed her gaze. "Someone you know, Sky?"

But, before she could explain, Lynskey was on top of them. "Hello there." His cheeriness did not seem in the least forced. "I thought I'd drop in to see how things were going down at the hospital. This must be your grandmother, Sky." He stuck out a hand and beamed. "How do you do? I'm Fergus Lynskey. As a matter of fact, we're neighbors, I know your part of the country well. I'm from Kerry myself, just across the border. But, of course, you live in the big smoke now, don't you?"

"How do you do? I do. Live in Cork, I mean."

"You must be exhausted," he said, reaching for the suitcase. "In fact you must both be wrecked, here, let me," and she knew it would seem churlish not to relinquish possession. He led the way toward the front door, as though he owned the place, and stood on the stoop, waiting for her to produce the key. As she opened the door, Sky thought she could murder him without a second thought.

When they got inside, he offered to make coffee, a proposition accepted with such alacrity by her grandmother it made Sky fume. Where women were concerned, did Fergus Lynskey's charms recognize no age boundaries? "This way, Grandma." She shot him a disdainful glance that he appeared not to see, and showed the older woman into Johanna's room. She left her to unpack, then telephoned the hospital. There was little change in her mother's condition: she was "comfortable."

Reluctant to go into the kitchen to face Lynskey alone, Sky went into the living room—little used by herself and her mother. Here, the landlord's taste in wallpaper, which was bad enough in the bedrooms, ran to oak leaves and unrelated berries in shades of tan and ocher, the furniture was early fifties leatherette and the room's single window faced north. Both Sky and her mother hated this room and rarely used it except at Christmas, when they made an effort to act like something resembling a normal family. The room had a real fireplace, however, and more to kill time than because it needed attention, Sky used a hearth brush to groom the wooden surround.

How was she going to get out of this situation? She could hardly be overtly rude to Lynskey in front of her grandmother, who was buying his act as readily as had the Bliss Sisters and every other woman within a million-mile radius. He was a regular Don Juan, she thought, her sense of betrayal building toward white heat as she scrubbed at nonexistent ash.

"I think your grandmother's gorgeous, a real lady."

Hearing the stage whisper behind her, she straightened and spun round, but Lynskey put a finger to his lips. "Ssh, we don't want her to know we're talking about her."

"We're not talking about her." Sky lowered her own voice. "I'm not talking to you about anything. Please go away."

"Come on, MacPee, where's the harm in talking?" His expression belied his jocular tone and he came toward her. "There's something I have to tell you and its going to be a bit of a shock. Don't say anything, please, until you hear me out. You have to get out of here temporarily."

"What? You must be joking."

"I mean it. You're in danger."

"Even if I am I wouldn't take the word of anyone so— so—" To her annoyance, she couldn't find a word to describe the depth of his duplicity.

"Tricky?" He was not being facetious. "Yeah—fair point. But *think,* Sky." He tried to take her wrist but she resisted violently and he let it drop. "Put yourself in my shoes. At the beginning, all I was doing was figuring out my own line of inquiry. I had no idea I would . . ." He trailed off. "This is a complicated situation," he amended. "You yourself told me so. Endlessly."

"Sorry if I bored you," but Sky hated petulance, even her own.

"Just as a matter of interest, purely academic, how did you find out?"

"I had a call from Bill Collins." She watched him, then said, her voice laden with irony, "I assume there's no need to explain who he is."

"Ah . . ." Lynskey nodded as though he had guessed as much.

"Stop saying that!" Sky wanted to slap his face.

In lieu of reply, he stepped closer toward her and, although he did not touch her, when he looked down into her eyes, she felt his presence surround her like a cloak. "I'm sorry." He did touch her then, brushing one finger across her lips. "But I'm deadly serious about this. You have to get away to somewhere you'll be safe. I can't tell you why just now. But I will. I promise."

"Go away." She batted off his touch. "Can't you understand English? My grandmother's just arrived, my mother's in the hospital. I can't go anywhere. Please leave, Fergus, I don't want you in our house." But she was uncertain now and she knew that he knew it.

"You understand why I couldn't tell you?" It was as though she had not spoken. "I didn't know what I was going to be dealing with at first but then, when I met you—"

"I suppose that so-called novel in your briefcase is a heap of surveillance equipment and a transmitter?" Sky, unwilling to acknowledge the subtext of what he was saying, was stalling.

Lynskey did not flinch. "Not quite, I'm not the KGB. But something like that. I'll show you, if you like."

"I don't want to see it, Lynskey. I don't want to see *you* again. I don't think you know just how upset I am."

"I can imagine. Normally I would say something stupid like all's fair in love and war. But, I wasn't expecting— well—" Before she had anticipated it, he had lowered his head and kissed her on the lips. For an instant her body responded but then her mind kicked in, and she broke away in fury.

"I can't believe you did that." She took a step backward away from temptation. "Is this how you do all your police work? Make love to people to get information."

"Never before, I promise." He followed her.

"Go away, Fergus." She stepped round him and made a run for the kitchen. He followed her again. Then, as she reached the kitchen and turned to face him, the picture of the bullet popped into her head. And, of course, her big mouth framed it and let it out.

His reaction was to throw his arms up in the air. "Jesus! Why the hell didn't you tell me straight away? Now will you believe that you have to leave here for a while." The more heated he became, the more clipped his speech became.

"I wasn't speaking to you, if you remember," she stared him down, "but while we're talking about warnings in brown padded envelopes, I know you got one too. Don't bother to deny it. And *you* didn't deem it necessary to tell *me*."

His expression was so serious now that she began to run out of steam. She reminded herself then that she had done nothing of which she should be ashamed. "And I might jog your memory about the small fact that you're standing in *my* house, and not at my invitation so please don't treat me like I'm a—a—a *suspect*." She sat down. Suddenly she felt woozy—too little food and sleep, too much caffeine and drama.

"You must see how important this is." He pulled up a chair and sat beside her. "Bullets are not playthings, Sky." His speech became even more deliberate. "Where is it now?" He frowned when she told him. "Look, I'll deal with it. Are you sure you didn't see anyone hanging around, get any odd phone calls? No one hung up when you answered?" It was only then she remembered the call from the logger. With all that had happened, it had slipped her mind.

"That's it, Sky." When she had finished telling him as much as she remembered about it, he folded his arms. "I'm instructing you not to follow this story any further. I'll tell your editor too."

"You're *instructing* me?" She was too astonished to take offense this time.

"I mean it," she could see only too well that he did, "and I'll have you stopped if necessary. You're out of your depth."

"How dare you? How dare you dictate—"

"I dare because this is my line of work." He cut her off. "I know what I'm talking about. Think, Sky. *Think*. Do you want the next bullet turning up from the barrel of a gun? Can you shoot? Have you got a gun? Do you know who your enemy *is*?"

"My editor will assign me to stories, not you," she hissed.

Lynskey unexpectedly took both her hands in his. "Your

editor will be told to take you off this one. Please, Sky, listen to me."

"Don't touch me! Take your hands *off* me!"

She attempted to pull them away but he persisted. "Listen, listen ... shhh, Sky, *listen* ..." They struggled but as she had already found out, he was strong and within a minute or so, her forearms ached with strain.

She tried to intimidate him with her eyes while maintaining the haul. "I won't be treated like a child, Fergus."

"Are you listening?" He waited until she was still then, softly, "If you won't listen to reason, listen to unreason. I love you. I don't know how it happened, I certainly didn't plan it and it's damned inconvenient, but I do. I don't want you putting yourself in danger."

It seemed to Sky that a nuclear explosion had detonated somewhere near her solar plexus.

"Did you hear me? I love you." He was as composed as if these were ordinary words.

"I heard you." She heard someone else speak in her voice. Quite calmly too.

Then she heard a sound behind her. It could have been a sigh, or a gentle cough, and she looked round to see her grandmother framed in the doorway. "Excuse me ..." Lynskey let go of her hands.

"Sorry, Grandma." Sky stood up and went to the stove to fetch the coffee pot. She averted her face, which she knew must be as white as milk.

Behind her, she heard the chair scrape as Lynskey stood up. "Come on in, ma'am."

The sheriff of Mayville did not take kindly to criticism. "Screw you," he said softly into the receiver as his caller hung up.

As far as he was concerned, his end of the drug deal had gone admirably, smooth as cream. Treacy had not kicked up and was unlikely to, seeing that he would be dead when that wife of his was out of harm's way. Because Brian O'Connor had no intention of drawing any attention to himself by leaving a single loose end. There remained a slight possibility that Midge Treacy, who was at present nothing but a vegetable, might resurface; and since he had more at stake than being middleman for some private profiteer he had identified someone at the Oregon facility to which she was to be moved who would ensure that she did not.

But now these suits were disposing of him. Who did they think they were? The sheriff had been absentmindedly shelling a pistachio nut and crushed it in anger. It was hardly his fault if some loolas in Ireland messed up. And as for the bullets: he had been instructed to scare off the meddlers in Butte. It had been his experience ever since he had begun to walk on the shady side that one ballistic reminder was enough to scare off amateurs. Even professional amateurs like that Irish cop.

And now the Helena guy was losing his cool. Well, the telephone warnings from good old potato head Collins hadn't worked, had they? If these people wanted velvet gloves they should have said so.

He stood up and tossed the spoiled nut into the trash can. That done, he shook himself like a dog. He was going to be paid the full amount of what he had been promised and was not going to take shit from some jumped-up jerk in Helena.

"Well?" the chief superintendent snapped.

"Things are heating up here," Lynskey's voice was quiet on the phone. "There's been a development in Vancouver."

His superior hesitated, then spoke again less belligerently. "Is that all? I know that. Our friends there tell us the principles might pull out altogether. The natives here are more restless than they're used to coping with. I think our lady head honcho might be beginning to think she's bitten off more than she can chew in Ireland."

"I think we should move in on them right now. We have enough on tape with all those monitored telephone calls, surely."

"Not yet. She might go ahead—and why catch the sprat when you can have the mackerel? Everything's set, though."

"Look, are we still keeping a tight grip on this other thing—Omega?" The word seemed to stick on Lynskey's tongue. "And are we any way closer to finding out who's the villain on our side?"

"Only myself, yourself, the Commissioner and the two Ministers, Justice and Foreign Affairs know about the first item so far, unless you've shot your big mouth off, to your—how did you put it?—your friend the reporter, for instance?"

Lynskey let that pass and his superior resumed: "No, I

haven't figured out who our canary is yet. I'm getting jittery, Fergus, time's moving on."

Down the hall from the chief superintendent's office, Rupert de Burgh worked busily at his desk, studying his notes. He had taken to wearing headphones connected to his Sony Walkman: he had told the others in the clattering room that to listen to music helped him concentrate while he was reading or writing reports.

Sky had no chance to react to Lynskey's declarations, either of love or danger, until much later that evening.

First came the trip to the hospital, during which he stuck to her like a parasite. She insisted on leaving him outside the room, however, and went in ahead of her grandmother in case the shock of seeing her mother after all these years might prove too severe for Johanna.

She was asleep, although her body was still punctured with the drips and drains. Standing beside the bed, Sky floundered. The last of the evening sun floated through the west-facing window, highlighting the woven texture of the body cast and neck collar so that her mother looked like a sickly caterpillar, an impression reinforced by the pallor of her skin. "Mom?" She touched the back of the hand which, curled like a child's, lay on the sheet.

Her mother's eyes opened. "It's you, Sky!" Her voice was scarcely audible and, accustomed as Sky was to the lilts and musical swoops, it was terrible to hear. As though she were sweet-talking a baby, she squatted at the side of the bed to bring her head level with the pillow. "Guess who's here, Mom?"

Making a great effort, Johanna focused glazed eyes.

"It's Grandma," Sky swallowed hard. "Grandma's here."

Johanna's eyes moved slowly toward the doorway. Then her whispery voice cracked even more, "Mammy?"

Sky's grandmother came forward slowly, her erect carriage faltering only as she reached the bedside. "Hello, Johanna." She clasped her hands in front of her as though touching might not be allowed—or in case touching her daughter might bring down some delicate edifice between them. "I'm sorry—here's a thing—I never thought—"

"I'm sorry too, Mammy—I thought I'd never see you again—"

Johanna's hoarse croak and the emotional rigidity of both

women finally pierced Sky's armor. She knew it was only a matter of seconds before all three would break down and, unable to bear the prospect, she fled.

Lynskey was coming back from the telephone booth and saw her agonized face. "What's wrong?"

"Nothing." Sky, reluctant to give into her weakness, scrubbed at her eyes. "She's fine, everything's fine, it's just that—" Only her pride saved her from caving in completely and weeping like a mermaid against his chest. "I'll be all right in a minute." She groped in her purse for a tissue and blew her nose. "It's just that they haven't seen each other for such a long time."

"Of course." Lynskey had the wit not to embrace her and looked away to give her time. "I feel like a cuppa, how about you? It must be at least ten minutes since you had your last caffeine fix." She nodded gratefully and he loped off to the machine. She blew her nose again and gave herself a mental scolding for being such a weakling.

She had just managed to compose herself when one of the nurses sat beside her and engaged her in chat. This was followed shortly afterward by the emergence from the room of her grandmother. "She can't stay awake." Her eyes were red-rimmed but the whites were shining. "I told her I'd be back first thing in the morning—that will be all right, will it, nurse?"

"Of course." The nurse stood up. "Please don't worry, either of you. It'll take a few days but she's going to be fine. Here comes your coffee," she smiled at Lynskey who was just arriving, "hello again."

Another conquest, Sky thought, seeing the way the nurse twinkled up at the Irishman, and her good humor reasserted itself. What was it about this man? This man who had told her he loved her.

All the way to the hospital that four letter word had reverberated. While he, behaving as though he had lived here all his life, had cheerily drawn her grandmother's attention to the Butte landmarks, the statue, the High School, the Civic Center, the Court House, Sky let the words *I love you* roll around the perimeter of her consciousness, bouncing them away every time they came too close to her heart. Love with this man was not on her agenda.

Love with no man. No agenda.

Relationships, perhaps, that overused word, but not love.

Greg had insisted he loved her, but, in Sky's opinion, he was far too macho to know what he meant when he said it.

Love with Lynskey? She had the feeling she was fencing with something very dangerous indeed. Sky had once fallen in love, with her feckless husband. That had been enough.

And yet the barrage of feelings Lynskey had released by the mere utterance of the word had shaken, no, had excited her in a way she found difficult to define.

For the second time in two hours, having thought little about him for months, maybe years, Sky longed for her father.

Chapter Twenty-seven

Sky had to face the love conundrum head on when they got back to the duplex. Lynskey asked her for a quiet word outside as her grandmother went in and she could think of no excuse to refuse. As she walked beside him and searched for something to say, the short driveway seemed to stretch into infinity.

It was a beautiful evening, with air as soft and warm as velvet: that time, just before dark, when every sound seems to spurt a little before muting for the night. Canned laughter rippled from the open window of the neighbor's house across the fence, to be subsumed by noise from the outside traffic—once by the cacophony from the faulty tailpipe on a pickup, once by the exuberant whoops of a crowd of boys on the prowl in a powerful convertible. And as they reached the sidewalk, sparrow wars exploded like firecrackers from a nearby tree.

She pretended to be fascinated by the overhead brawling and made as though to walk over to the tree, but Lynskey was having none of it. "So what do you think?" He spun her round and took her hands in his, pulling her toward him.

"So what do I think about what?" She studied the gutter between the wheels of the Topaz and the curb and remembered the bag of marbles, perfect glass eyes with rainbow irises, sent to her from Ireland when she was a child. They were still pristine in her bureau because when they arrived she had found no one except Johanna who knew what to do with them. "Look at me, Sky," he tugged insistently at her hands, "you know perfectly well. About where we were before we were interrupted in the kitchen." He searched her face then said, gently: "What is it? What are you afraid of?"

With these words, he had hit on the truth. "I don't know."

"It wasn't a declaration of hostilities, you know, or a

request that you hang up your freedom shoes. It was, and is, quite simple. I love you. Simple."

"It's not simple." She felt her palms begin to tingle with perspiration and hoped he could not feel it. "I mean it's not *that* simple—"

"It's very simple indeed. I love you. End of story, no demands, no nothing."

"But I don't want you to love me, I didn't ask you to love me." In spite of her best efforts her voice rose until it was almost a wail.

He regarded her for the longest five seconds of her life and for once his eyes were grave. "Nobody but a fool asks for love." He released her hands and kissed her softly on the forehead. "Nobody deserves it or earns it or is owed it. At your age you should know that."

"But we just met . . ." Sky, so self-contained, so sophisticated felt lost.

As she vacillated, his mood changed and hardened. "That's something for another day, perhaps, but don't worry, I won't mention it again for the foreseeable future. We have to talk now about your safety. If you won't cooperate, Sky, I'll have to take other measures, for your own good."

The transformation was so sudden that she was taken by surprise. So much so that she could not resist when he informed her he was going to stay the night in the duplex. "On the couch, so don't worry." He got into his rental car and wound down the window. "I have to go to the hotel and pick up a few things. Don't answer the door, don't answer the telephone. I won't be long."

She watched his retreating taillights until he rounded a corner and all that was left of him was an echo of the engine. As she turned to go back into the house she tried to make sense of what she felt. Or even to put a word on it. She almost settled on *maelstrom* but then discarded it as being too melodramatic. Yet *maelstrom* was the one word which exactly fitted.

As he drove away, Fergus Lynskey was attempting to sew up the wound in his heart. She was not interested. He had been a fool.

Superconscious of Lynskey's presence in the living room, Sky slept badly, her dreams punctured with monstrous caterpillars, chases and falls, and vague, slithering fears. Several times, just as she felt she was about to be consumed, she awoke with a jump.

Heart hammering, she switched on the bedside radio and tuned to an all-news station, turning the volume low, reasoning that the murmur of human voices in the background might soothe her back to sleep.

It was not to be, however, and while it was still early she was delighted to hear her grandmother moving around. She was relieved to get up.

She tiptoed toward the living room and, opening the door as quietly as she could, peeped round it. Lynskey's bag was in the middle of the room but the comforter she had given him was neatly folded and draped across the arm of the couch. Pinned to it was a note:

Sky: I'll be back in less than an hour. Please don't forget, don't answer the door, don't answer the telephone. I'll buzz the doorbell five times so you'll know it's me. F.

His handwriting was as neat and precise as the folds in the comforter.

After a quick shower, Sky dressed and went into the sunlit kitchen: the day promised renewed heat, and the brightness and kitsch normality of her surroundings seemed bizarre in the context of what was happening all around her. As she brewed her first pot of coffee, her grandmother appeared clad in one of Johanna's kaftans. When her mother wore these relics of her hippie youth they inspired only ridicule, but somehow, Sky thought, the bright patterns and flowing lines gave her grandmother a regal air. "Are you hungry, Grandma?" She opened a cupboard to see what—other than birdseed—she could muster. To her relief, she saw a carton of pancake mix, one of her own defiant purchases.

"I could eat something," the old lady admitted. "Airline food isn't wonderful, is it?"

"About ten minutes?"

The pancakes were ready when her grandmother reappeared. She had changed and looked cool and fresh in a dark blue linen dress with a white collar. Sky glanced disparagingly at her own outfit, the gray silk suit she had worn to dinner with Daniel Treacy in the Copper King Mansion.

Although she had hung it up, it could have done with the touch of an iron.

"Thank you, dear. And if I may return the compliment, gray suits you—it does wonders for your hair. It's a color I used to wear myself." They smiled almost shyly at one another.

"Oh, Grandma, it's great to have you here." Sky reached out and hugged her, then realized this was the first spontaneous gesture of affection she had been able to make.

Her grandmother hugged her back and then stood away a little. "We've got a lot to catch up on, you and I. I'm ashamed of myself I didn't come before now."

"The onus wasn't on you," Sky protested. "Every college student I know has been to Europe at least once. But you do understand that I had had quite enough of going about when I was younger, don't you? It seemed like heaven just to stay in one place."

"Of course." Her grandmother laughed. "But let's stop all this. At least we managed to connect again before I went down to start pushing up the daisies."

"Grandma!"

"Oh, for goodness' sake, Sky, I'm seventy-whatever-age-I-am and I've had a full life," the old lady's expression became wry, "some of which has apparently come back to haunt me. What time are we going to meet my fate?"

"I'll call him after breakfast."

They had been eating for less than five minutes when Lynskey's five-buzz signal sounded in the hallway. "It's very early for callers, isn't it?" Her grandmother looked startled.

"It's Fergus. I'll explain later." Sky went to open the door. With the old lady around, she knew she could not talk seriously to the Irishman but, without rancor, she made it clear to him as she let him in that she was going to go about her business as though he was not there.

"No problem." He was freshly showered and shaved—he must have been back to the War Bonnet—and dressed in yet another faded T-shirt, this one advertising the rock group U2.

He chatted to her grandmother in the kitchen while she, reckoning seven thirty was not too early, telephoned Daniel Treacy's house to find that he, too, was up and about and anxious to see her grandmother. "And Sky. . . ?" He seemed about to broach something else but changed his mind. "No, forget it." She was too intent on ticking projects off her mental list to pursue it.

She reached Francey, who offered money, access to medical expertise in Harley Street, anything that might help Johanna. When she told him about the pile of useless checks, he laughed so hard she had no choice but to join in. "That's our Johanna, all right," he spluttered. "Hasn't changed a bit, has she?" Sobering, he outlined plans for himself and Sky's aunt Hazel to fly to the States within the next few days, but Sky, who felt she had enough to do with commuting in the hospital and looking after the guest already installed in the duplex, persuaded him to wait until her mother was stronger.

Lastly, she called Jimbo and found to her annoyance, that Fergus had already spoken to him and their meeting was set for nine o'clock. "You have to come along too, Sky." Jimbo's normal abruptness on the telephone had given way to gravity.

Half an hour later, Sky and her grandmother were in the Nissan: the nearer they got to Daniel Treacy's house, the greater the tension Sky sensed from the passenger seat where the old lady sat, erect as a queen. She chatted about her job, about the beauty of Montana, about anything that might put her companion at ease—and keep Sky herself from glancing in the rear view mirror, which showed the ever-present hood of a Chrysler Topaz. At least Lynskey had the tact to pull onto the shoulder and did not follow her up the driveway to Daniel Treacy's house.

Her grandmother's response to her first sight of the view from Treacy's car park was similar to Sky's own. "My God," she breathed, her eyes widening, "I thought the Béara Peninsula was lovely." Then, virtually to herself, "Hasn't he done well for himself?"

This morning, Daniel Treacy's panorama would have done justice to the ritziest Montana tourist brochure. Although the sky was limpid, the sky had not yet burned off the mist. Insubstantial as angel hair or a quilt crocheted from cobwebs, it drifted just yards above the deep green of the forest canopy and piled like sheared wool against the flanks of the Rockies so that the peaks appeared to float free. "If you think this is good, wait till I take you up to Going-To-The-Sun-Road in Glacier." Sky, enjoying her grandmother's reaction, gave her a few moments to take it in, then, "Shall we go in?"

"You don't have to come with me, you go off to your office."

Recognizing that she wanted to be left alone, Sky did not insist. "All right, see you later." She could not resist delaying her departure, however, driving slowly enough away from the house to see, via the rearview mirror, Treacy open the door within seconds of her grandmother's arrival on the stoop.

As she turned out of the gateway into the road, she looked for the plain sedan but although she continued to drive slowly, searching on both sides of the road and using all her mirrors, she saw nothing—except a blue Chrysler Topaz. She must not let him get to her. She gritted her teeth. She must not let him get to her.

The first thing Elizabeth Sullivan noticed when she stepped across Daniel Treacy's threshold that morning was the mass of flowers. All white. Banks of white roses—dozens, maybe hundreds—drifted out of vases and urns in every corner and on every surface of the lobby. There were more in the drawing room, augmented here by Casablanca lilies and baby's breath, still more in the garden room where she and Treacy settled to talk.

"All these flowers—they must have cost a fortune, Daniel." She looked around.

He dismissed them with a wave of his hand. "Are you sure it isn't too cold for you in here?" The windows along the terrace were all open so nothing stood between where they sat and the forest beyond the lawns. Butterflies skidded about on the warm drafts of air and the loudest sound was from a passing bee.

"It's beautiful." Throughout the extensive tour of the house she had been sincere in her admiration. "I feel like a princess in a fairy tale."

"I hope so. Do you really like the house?"

"You know I do—what is it?" The fervor of the expression in his eyes alarmed her a little.

"I know nothing can ever happen between us again, Elizabeth, but having you here is a dream come true. I wanted to see you one more time. And I wanted to see you here in this house."

"Why? Do you have a dungeon you can lock me up in, Daniel?" Afraid of his intensity, she endeavored to make light of it.

"No," he said softly, "no dungeon. No tower either. This is your house, Elizabeth. I built it for you."

It took a while for that to sink in. "My house? What do you mean?"

"Every piece of wood and glass and every tile, every blade of grass outside was chosen with you in mind."

She was so nonplussed that she sat further back in the cushions as though afraid he might physically try to bend her to his will.

He recognized the truth instantly, and sorrow enlarged his dark eyes. "It doesn't matter now, Elizabeth, it's too late anyway. But having you here like this ... Just once is enough."

"What do you mean?"

He told her then about his illness, and while she struggled to take it in he came across and squatted in front of her, taking her hands. "I said it doesn't matter now, Elizabeth, and I meant it. Now I've had everything I ever wanted, you here in your house with the flowers all around. I don't mind dying now. What I dreaded was that I would go to my grave thinking you hated me. I can see now that you don't—you wouldn't have agreed to come here otherwise." The sadness in his eyes was replaced with tenderness. "Please don't think I expect anything more. That you don't hate me is all I need to know." Painfully, using the armrests of the chair for leverage, he stood up. "There's just one thing I want you to do for me ..."

He went out, leaving her stunned. Another woman would probably have cried. In her late years, however, Elizabeth's emotions, so unruly when she had been younger, had acquired a patina of rest, although not without a great deal of effort. Somehow, during those last years, she had achieved peace both inside and out.

"I want you to have this." He was back, carrying a square jewelry case. "I've kept it for you for many years."

"I couldn't." Her hard-won calm was threatened.

"Open it and look at it at least," he insisted softly. "If you don't like it, that's one thing, but I think you will. I was going to leave you this house I built for you, because even as they were putting the furniture in I knew that if Midge

survived me she would sell it straight away. But then I
thought such a bequest might be a terrible imposition, not to
speak of an impertinence. This is an alternative."

She stared helplessly at the case as though it were a lethal
weapon and saw that he was holding it so tightly his hands
shook a little. It was made from sumptuous black leather,
tooled with gold, and she knew that whatever was inside
must be valuable.

"Will you not just open it?" The shake became more pronounced. "If you don't like it, you don't have to take it. But
it would make me happy to see it on you, just once. And if it
makes you feel any better, it's not the Koh-i-Noor diamond
or anything like it." A trace of a smile passed across his
white face. "It's not the value of it that's relevant, it's what it
represents."

Slowly she took the case and opened it, conscious of his
scrutiny. "I had it made for you, Elizabeth. I've never forgotten that blue dress you wore the night we danced. Do you
remember?"

The Oriental woman had made up her mind. It was raining in
Vancouver—probably an omen.

She had thought a great deal since talking to her lieutenant
in Helena the previous evening and had reviewed her assets.
Even with absorbing the loss on her investment in the trial
run, she would have enough to be comfortable for the rest of
her life. For two lifetimes in fact. The extra, which would
have come had she continued the operation in and through
Ireland, would have been the cream, but no point in tempting
fate, she had decided. She had had a smooth, uneventful
career over the past ten years and so much had gone wrong
recently that it would be wise to interpret the signals.

Perhaps she was losing her touch. Searching for new ways
in which to run drugs into Europe, it was she who hit on the
casket idea. And she had chosen Montana from which to
originate the operation as it was hardly seen as the drugs
capital of the world, or even of the U.S. In retrospect, neither
the casket nor Ireland had been good ideas. Perhaps it was
the combination of the two that had proved so disastrous. It
was time to cut her losses and end it. She made the call to her
man in Helena.

He was surprised, but accepted his orders to stand down
the entire operation, even the test. The woman made her

financial arrangements with him and, although she had no intention of talking to him again, told him she would be in touch the following day about something new, that she was running a little late now as she had an early appointment downtown.

She was careful to the last on the telephone: somehow the line was almost too clear. During her time in Ottawa, she had learned enough from certain former lovers to know that someone who has something to hide should be wary of a connection that never crackled. Even when it was made through supposedly secure cellphones. "Have you dealt with those other matters? I don't like leaving loose ends."

"They're in hand."

"Thank you. Your consideration may be collected in the usual manner."

After she rang off, the woman, who was dressed in a silk *cheong sam* and matching turban, as though she was going to see someone important looked around her apartment for the last time. She would leave without regret. It had never become home. Vancouver, with its long winters, its damp and grayness, had never been anything but a staging post: she hated cold and rain and her eyes had always been firmly fixed on the blue and white world of the tropics.

She put on a voluminous cotton raincoat and placed her airline tickets, passports and the most personal of her financial documents into a largish leather purse, switched on her answering machine and, having made sure the gas stove was off and the windows to her terrace secured, left the apartment, every inch the business woman on a mission.

"Have a pleasant day—thank you, ma'am," the doorman responded as she handed him a tip while he held open the cab door.

"Thank you, Mel. You have a pleasant day too." She smiled at him. "See you later."

As her cab moved into the rush hour traffic, downtown, the detective was reporting to his superior on the call he had just monitored. The two men had a relatively brief discussion. The superior decided that, since the big deal they had been waiting for had now been aborted, they should pull her in. "Where did she say she going?" He walked ahead of the detective toward his own office.

"She didn't say, it could be anywhere. She has no regular haunts, as you know."

"Put out an APB with her description," the senior ordered. "It shouldn't take too long. And put people on her apartment. If we miss her, we'll get her when she comes home."

What the detective's superior did not know, of course, was that the woman's meticulous planning was paying off. She had given the doorman the name of a downtown restaurant to pass to the cab driver but, once inside the vehicle, seemed to change her mind and asked him to drive her instead to a shopping mall, which was just opening. She paid him off and walked purposefully inside, then seemed arrested by a window display of shoes. She used the glass as a mirror. No one seemed to paying her any attention.

Moving away from the shoe store, she strolled along until as if on impulse on passing the washroom, went through the door marked *Women*. Once inside, she locked herself into a cubicle.

Underneath the coat she had concealed a lightweight nylon knapsack, the type children take to school. Unzipping it, she removed from it a boy-sized jacket and trousers in dark polyester, socks, soft boy's shoes and a wig.

When she emerged less than ninety seconds later, she was a small Oriental man with cropped gray hair.

The *cheong sam*, turban and clutch purse had been jammed into the sanitary can, the raincoat, with empty pockets and from which all labels had been removed, remained hanging on the purse hook behind the cubicle door.

The only point of danger was in leaving the washroom, but her luck held. No one was near the door from which she emerged except a bored cleaner pushing a wide floormop. And he had his back to her.

Chapter Twenty-eight

It was when she—and the trailing Lynskey—were almost at the office that Sky remembered what it was about Martin O'Shaughnessy's name that had been bothering her. It was simply that it was Irish. Treacy, or McCarthy, Collins, O'Connor, O'Shaughnessy, Flynn. All Irish. And an Irish cop over here snooping around. It did not take a genius to work out the connections. No wonder the FBI was involved.

Jimbo and Lynskey greeted one another like cousins and settled in to talk. Since much of what was being discussed between them was familiar to her, Sky watched the Irishman. He was outwardly relaxed, although it was obvious he had decided that the editor of the *Butte Courier* was a man to be reckoned with. So far he had not mentioned his outlandish suggestion that she had to be taken off the story.

The editor was ultra serious too, to a degree she had rarely seen. He kept darting glances at her, which was odd. "Let's see where we are with this," he said. He pushed his computer terminal to one side and reviewed the single sheet of paper in front of him. "It's a pity you can't be more specific about certain aspects."

Sky went over to the cooler to get a drink of water but then discovered it had run out of dixie cups. Even though she had not been listening closely, she had heard enough to know that Lynskey had not advanced the story one iota. All he had done was to acknowledge the accuracy of some of what Daniel Treacy had told her and what she and the editor had deduced between them. "Could I say something?" Instead of resuming her seat, she leaned against the wall beside the cooler.

"Sure." They turned to her expectantly.

She stared at the Irishman. "Everyone we know so far to be involved is of Irish descent. I think we're talking about terrorists, isn't that right, Fergus?" To give Lynskey his due, he did not even blink.

"Why do you think that, Sky?" This was Jimbo.

Lynskey had still not reacted, but as she was watching him so closely she saw that his expression had become, if anything, even more bland. "Why don't you ask Fergus, Jim?" She came back to the desk and sat down. "I think he might know the answer. I'm only putting two and two together—and ask him, while you're at it, if this is the reason he wants me to hide."

The editor looked from one to the other. He had not responded in a way she thought her statement warranted. "Did you hear what I said, Jim?"

Lynskey splayed his hands on his knees. "I'm sure you understand why I can't be specific—in fact, I shouldn't be talking to you at all, but believe me," he looked across at Sky, "I'm not exaggerating or being dramatic. On the assumption that everything said here is confidential and will remain unattributable—"

"Of course." Jimbo put one foot up on his desk.

"I will tell you that what you have discovered is only the tip of the iceberg. There are, we believe, two operations in tandem here. Whether they are deliberately linked or the linkage is just fortuitous, I don't know yet. My guess is the latter."

It was beginning to dawn on Sky that somehow Jimbo already knew about Lynskey's proposal that she should make herself scarce. Disbelieving, she tuned in again to what the Irishman was saying. ". . . and I'd say motivations are mixed. I would not be surprised if, to take Sky's point, a certain—ah—national fellow-feeling binds the Sheriff of Mayville, for instance, to his Irish colleagues. I don't see him taking these huge risks just for his own benefit. A nasty piece of goods, sure, into anything he can get for himself, yes, but up to now he was just a slimeball. What is going on now," he was picking his words again, "in my opinion is beyond ordinary villainy."

"Excuse me?" Sky again, still leaning against the wall and so incensed she wanted to give both men enough rope to hang themselves—and to see how far they would go without including her. "If the FBI knows all this, as you've admitted they do," she asked conversationally, "why don't they just pull in a few people?"

Lynskey hesitated, then: "The FBI and ourselves are in consultation. We want to wait a big longer to see what exactly is happening but we can move at any time. I can't go into any more detail, I'm afraid."

So much for confidentiality. Sky saw then why the watching sedan was missing from Treacy's house this morning: "I suppose it was you who pulled the watchers off Daniel Treacy after I told you the story?"

"You did clear up a lot of things for us, thanks."

For nothing, Sky thought. For being the patsy as usual. Aloud, she asked who now had the privilege of being watched.

"Yes, who? Bigger fish, perhaps?" This was Jimbo.

Lynskey clammed up further. "You know I can't say."

"Well, where, then?" Jimbo again. "In Montana? I've made a few inquiries of my own and the Montana state police don't seem to be involved in any of this."

"Perhaps," Lynskey studied him, "the state police are aware of the Bureau's presence but are not playing any active role. Not yet, at any rate. This, as you've already guessed and as is self-evident from the involvement of both myself and the FBI, is an international operation."

"All this—you here, the FBI, police and the Navy all chasing their tails in Ireland—for one casket load?" The editor placed his pen at right angles to the margin of the paper, lining it up precisely with the point touching his pants leg. "Hardly likely, is it?"

Lynskey did not move. "No comment."

"I see." Jimbo picked up the pen again and began doodling an interlocking series of figure eights. "It was definitely drugs in that casket, was it?" He drew flower petals around his figures.

"No comment again." Lynskey remained still. "But if I could get to why I believe Sky here needs to make herself scarce for a little while?"

At last. Sky was so angry now she felt calm. "I am *not* making myself scarce—"

"Let him talk, Sky." Jimbo raised his eyebrows at her.

"All right, I'll let him talk, it's a free country, but I'm not going anywhere, not with my mother in hospital and my grandmother—"

"If I said that I'd take you with me to Ireland?" Lynskey glanced at the editor and then back to her.

Sky stared at them both.

"Don't fly off the handle, Sky." Jimbo's expression was disingenuous. "It was me who proposed it. This is a huge story. I've been on to our intellectual friend and, miracle of miracles, I've convinced him to authorize the expenditure."

Sky sat down. The arrogance of these two men having discussions behind her back on how she should or should not conduct her life and career was breathtaking. "Good for you, Jim," she said coldly. "But you can unauthorize the money now. I'm not going anywhere."

There was more to come as she discovered when, jointly, they set to work on her. Apparently not only was she being sent to Ireland, she was to be out of Butte "for her own good" until her plane left. As soon as possible. Like tonight. They had chosen a venue for her vacation: she was to visit her father for the night. They had even made travel arrangements. Apparently Daniel Treacy had been telephoned by Lnyskey during his brief absence from the duplex earlier that morning and had agreed to lend one of the small company planes to fly Sky to Yaak, thus saving driving time. One of the summer airfields the company used was on a valley floor in the Purcell Range and was only ten miles from the town.

"Purely academically, of course," Sky was having to work hard now to suppress excitement that at last she was getting the big break she had so long wanted, but she did not want them to have everything their own way right off, "would I not be in as much so-called danger in Ireland as I would in Butte?"

"Definitely not." Lynskey's statement was flat and brooked no rebuttal. "I'll be able to look out for you better over there. It's my territory and I have a better chance of recognizing any strange villains. I'll have my colleagues to help too."

"You really think my life is in danger?" Despite everything that had been said and the bullet in her mailbox, she found that difficult to credit. When he did not reply, she looked from him to her boss. "Come on," she appealed, "you don't believe that, do you, Jim?"

"I'm not the expert here. He is. And I'm worried." Jimbo looked it. She tried one last angle although her excitement was now growing apace. "How are you going to get next week's edition of this rag out if I take off?"

"The same way we always do. I'll write most of it, we'll

expand the advertorial, the kid can have the time of her life with a fashion spread and we'll lift stuff from the nationals. Piece of cake."

Eventually she agreed, on condition that she could make adequate domestic arrangements.

Shortly afterward, Lynskey departed. "I've to see a few people, make a few calls. I'll see you later, Sky. Stay here until I come back for you and then I'll take you to lunch."

But she never got to eat lunch that day.

The moment the door closed behind their visitor, Jimbo shot to his feet. "It's drugs all right. Ireland's currently fashionable in that line of trade." He came out from behind the desk and began pacing the small acreage of floor space not taken up with piles of paper; she had not seen him so animated since she had joined the *Courier* eight years before. "That would explain his agitation about your safety." He cracked his knee against a corner of the desk and massaged it. "But there's definitely more. He wouldn't be here if it was just one casket load of drugs—or even guns." He resumed pacing. "There are easier ways to get guns into Ireland. Remember he talked about two intertwined operations? He's here because of the second part. Look," he turned to her and she saw the lines of his face had lifted until he looked almost happy, "I know you hate people making arrangements on your behalf, but think of the story, Sky. We could even *make* money with this story, syndicate it. For sure nobody else is on to it. Lynskey'd help us—you like him, don't you?" He was nearly shouting with joy. "You get on with him okay?"

He was so excited he did not wait for her response which was just as well because she had been about to laugh. "Aren't you getting a little ahead of yourself, Jim?" she asked, when he had calmed down a little. "And I know I've provisionally agreed to this madness but a drugs story? Not to speak of the other unknown you both keep talking about. I wouldn't know how to start. I don't even have a passport. I've never done work like this, you know it—"

"He'll help you. I'll help you." He went behind the desk, opened a drawer and rummaged through the hundreds of business cards jumbled up inside. "Remember that Salt Lake City seminar I went to on business investment in Ireland, the one that was addressed by their Taoiseach—I have the name of someone here from the Irish television station . . . Where is it? Never mind, I'll find it—and leave the passport situation to me. He said you weren't to be left on your own, although personally I think you're all right in daylight—"

"Well, that's nice—"

"So I'll come downtown with you. You'll need to get photographs taken before you head up to the northwest and I'll have a passport for you by tomorrow morning. And while you're gone I'll be making a few inquiries so that I'll have more for you for when you fly out. You won't be on your own. Look, Sky," he parked himself on the front of the desk, "we all know there're huge drug deals going on all over the world, and if it was *only* that I wouldn't think twice about it. Okay," he shrugged, "if Montana's become a center for it that's news, but only within the state. No, I'd bet my bottom dollar it's something much bigger than routine passage of drugs. We have most of the bits, I know we do. We just need to find a few more and then tie them up. You have to go to Ireland."

Sky forbore to remind him that only a matter of hours ago he had been insisting she take time off. "You forget that I've no training as an investigative reporter," she reiterated, thinking that he should be given the chance to pull her off in case she screwed up.

This energized Jimbo looked at her, impatiently, and said, "For goodness' sake, just go and get the story."

For a while, he tried to teach her how to act on a foreign assignment. Then, just as she thought her head would burst with contact names and dates and historical data, he gazed out at her from his tottering paper grotto. "Now forget everything I said, okay? Use the contact numbers I gave you, get as much help as you can but, above all—I can't say this often enough—above *all*, keep your eyes and ears open. Trust yourself, Sky, I trust you. And if you can't think where to start, start with that casket. Find out who met it, where did it go. Your friend Teddy at the funeral parlor will probably be able to help you there—there must be *some* legitimate documentation stored over in Collins's. It's like nuclear fission, Sky. One item of information will lead to the next and there's no stopping it once it gets started. But *trust* yourself. Oh, and enjoy yourself too—I wish it was me."

Reeling with plans, she went with him to get the photographs taken and then they drove to collect her grandmother from Treacy's house.

The old lady herself came to the door in response to the

bell. "I'm not ready to go, Sky," she said simply. "I can get a taxi or Daniel can drive me."

"How are you getting on?" Standing there on the stoop and conscious of Jimbo waiting for her in the Nissan, Sky, feeling absurdly like an interfering mom, longed for details: what she really wanted to know was whether or not the two old people were renewing their love affair.

But her grandmother gave her no clue. "We're getting on grand." She was pale but composed: whatever was happening in there was restrained.

"That's good." Sky hesitated and then, seeing she was not going to be invited in, cast around for a graceful way of making an exit. Her grandmother saved her. "I've got to go in now, darling. Tell Johanna I'll be up to see her sometime this morning. See you later."

As Sky and Jim Larsen descended again into the city, she was struck by how odd it was that after all these years just as her grandmother arrived in the States, she was going to Ireland. Maybe they were fated not to get to know one another.

And she found that Lynskey, with all his conspiracy theories and dire warnings, had gotten to her. For the first time she felt uneasy. With the sun shining gaily, the Rockies like sentinels on the horizon, the notion that someone was out there planning to kill her was preposterous . . . or was it? It felt bizarre to have her editor babysitting her. "Do you *really* believe that I'm in danger?" she asked him.

"He convinced me." Jimbo's tone was sombre. Sky checked her rearview mirror again. Nothing to be seen except the glittering, empty highway

The controller of the Irish side of the drug-running operation now bitterly regretted ever having heard of this deal. He had been approached originally through an intermediary in the Department of Agriculture in Dublin who, over the years, had been dealt a proportion of the profits from the controller's agrarian activities: as a rule he dealt in pig-smuggling across the border, angel dust, fertilizer for the lads in the IRA. Nice, safe, traditional criminality. Although he had recognized the extent of the leap he was being asked to make, he had found the big money impossible to resist.

But now, having lost control of his troops, he was boarding the ferry at Dun Laoghaire to make a run for it to England.

* * *

The *Agnes Monica*, shadowed at a distance by the *L.E. Aideen*, was steaming slowly with nets out toward the cave and the heroin. The captain knew that he had attracted the attention of the patrol vessel but she was at least a mile and a half away and his plan was simple: the crew would take the *Agnes Monica* as close as they dared to the cave's mouth—the water was deep so they could get within twenty yards. He and another man would be in the dinghy, tied close to starboard and invisible from the ocean sea and to their stalker. At the last minute he would cut loose and dash into the cave. The *Agnes Monica* would continue on her way without pause, pulling the unsuspecting *Aideen* with her.

By the time the *Aideen* or anyone else suspected anything, the stash would be buried and the skipper and his mate a couple of miles farther east toward Killybegs, calmly checking lobster pots.

And so it happened.

In Dublin, hours later, the chief superintendent looked slowly around his assembled troops over whom silence hung like a mushroom cloud.

"After X number of conferences," he began, "Y amount of resources, Z hours of missed sleep, we have no drugs, no big deal in the offing, no arrests. Just Gárdaí running in circles all over the effin' country, four corpses and a few innocent fishermen. And the humiliation of having to ask the Brits to watch out for our man on the ferry." He glowered, leaving no one in any doubt that this last was the worst of the lot. "Let's hope we get to him first. Oh, and I nearly forgot," Daly spoke slowly, "we have an apoplectic Commissioner, not to speak of what's going on in the Department of Justice and beyond." He paused then: "Would any of you geniuses have any ideas as to what we should do next?"

The telephone on his desk rang and he snatched up the receiver. "What is it? I said no calls."

Then: "Wonderful. We might as well hear his great thoughts on the matter. Put him on conference." He waited a few seconds. No one in the room dared move. Then, when Fergus Lynskey's amplified and distorted voice dropped like lead into the room, "Hello, hello?" Daly inclined his head toward the small black box set in the center of the table.

"How about you, Lynskey? You've heard what's been going on over here? Any brilliant ideas?"

"I heard, and I'm afraid I'm fresh out." Lynskey sounded as brisk as always. "But I want to talk to you privately after this conference."

"Well, since this so-called conference has progressed precisely nowhere, I propose to dismiss it so you can talk now." The chief studied his fingernails.

The others shuffled their notes together and as they filed out of the room, to the ominous crackle of static, the chief superintendent pulled so hard at his ear lobe that anyone watching might have worried he would do it a permanent injury. "This'd better be good," he exploded, as the door closed behind the last of them. "I greatly appreciate you returning all my calls—where the hell have you been? Apart from the circus here there's been another development in Vancouver." He berated Lynskey for a full minute.

In his bedroom at the War Bonnet, Lynskey waited imperturbably for him to run out of steam and fiddled with the clutch of telephone messages from a "Mr. Harvey" in Dublin—Bill Day's sense of humor was as transparent as Elwood P. Dowd's imaginary rabbit. But as the chief's funnybone was not much in evidence now he decided to keep quiet about his proposal to bring R. Sky MacPherson to Ireland with him.

"So, for Chrissakes, get a move on your end." He gathered that the wigging was coming to an end. "The Commissioner is getting antsy about all of this. And guess whose turn is it to get it in the neck?"

Lynskey remained calm. "What new development in Vancouver?" He listened as the chief filled him in, and then told him about his meeting with the editor of the *Courier*.

"Jesus, Mary and Joseph," Daly roared. "I don't bleddy believe it! Why don't you just put up a notice about our activities on the Great Wall of China? Then everyone'd know."

"Keep your hair on. I had my reasons and it's to do with why you sent me over here in the first place. Now I'm ready to come home. I've been checking around with the men who listened in to all the telephone calls and I'm as good as convinced now that these stupid buggers over here have no knowledge at all of what you persist in calling Operation Omega. You're probably in the clear to give the go-ahead for the visit. By the way, those bullets. The hotel porter who took delivery of mine remembers a man in the tractor of an articulated truck. If it's who I think it is there's no point in going after him. He's small fry. Anything from Ballistics yet on the one I gave the feds?"

"No," the chief snapped. "Get back to this newspaper guy."

"Yeah, well, he's to be trusted."

"I feckin' hope so, given people are about to be pulled in both here and over there. In Vancouver they're waiting for that woman to show up at her apartment any minute now and if the media gets hold of it—"

"The media won't. So it's all right if I come home tomorrow?"

"I'm sorry now we sent you over there in the first place." The chief superintendent slammed down his receiver and Lynskey was left with an earful of static.

The Varig flight carrying the Oriental woman from Los Angeles to Rio De Janeiro was climbing out over the ocean. Naturally she was traveling economy as befitted a dowdy peasant Filipino going for the first time to visit her servant daughter who worked for a rich family in Rio. Humbly, she accepted the tomato juice and peanuts offered by the stewardess, then glanced apologetically at her seat companions as she tore the top off the packet. It seemed she was worried about upsetting them with the noise. They were going to South America on the trip for which they had saved for decades. They felt sorry for the poor little woman. She seemed so frail and timid. "You got family in Rio?" the man asked.

The Oriental woman looked terrified.

"Not to worry, ma'am," the man smiled kindly at her, "we won't bother you none. But if you need help with customs or immigration or anything, you just holler, okay?"

The Oriental woman's face broke into a shy smile of gratitude and the man exchanged compassionate glances with his wife.

Chapter Twenty-nine

Breaking the news to Johanna about the possibility of Sky's trip to Ireland was not difficult. She was still drowsy from pain medication and accepted the notion with equanimity. "Be sure to go and see everyone, tell everyone I said hello."

Buffy did not balk when Sky asked if she and Hermana would step into the breach her departure would occasion, "if I go at all." There was still her grandmother to consider, but when the old lady arrived at the hospital, she would stand no argument. "I live alone at home. For goodness' sake, don't you think I can look after myself?"

Sky's secret thrill that she was off on the story of a lifetime was tempered only then by the thought that if she was in danger in her own home so was her grandmother. She did not want to alarm either her or Buffy, however: she would discuss it later with Lynskey.

When Lynskey arrived to escort her on the short trip back to the duplex, she drew him aside and hissed, out of the hearing of the others, "This has gone beyond a joke. It's broad daylight, the middle of the day. This is Butte, Montana, in 1992, not Chicago during Prohibition."

"I'm driving behind you and there's an end to it." She had no option but to agree.

When they got home, the digital display on the answering machine showed two messages. The first was for Lynskey, asking him to telephone "the usual number" in Washington, D. C. Sky was outraged. "You're giving out my home number?" She was so incensed that she let the second message proceed without listening to it. "Well, that's the limit, Lynskey, it really is—"

"Ssh," he put his finger to his lips, "let's hear what this one is. Roll back the tape." Furiously, she did so.

The second message deflated her. It was from a man who gave his name only as Matt. He asked Sky to meet him at

nine o'clock that evening in a coffee shop on Highway 15,
just beyond the outskirts of Butte. He had crucial information for her on a story. "You're not going, I'll go," Lynskey
insisted. Which set her off again. They had another argument—*sotto voce,* because she did not want to upset her
grandmother.

Yet Lynskey held all the cards, would do as he saw fit,
because the visit to her father had now become a reality. Sky
was looking forward to it, not only for itself, but as a respite
from the drama around her. The Treacy Resources plane
would be ready for her in just over two hours' time.

"This suits us fine, Sky." Lynskey loomed over her like a
whispering angel—or devil, she could not decide which. "If
this guy's talking to me he can't be stalking you. Although I
looked at all the angles and couldn't see how he could have
found out where you'd be, I was worried about you going up
to the backwoods. If they think you're here, you'll be fine."

The implicit threat seemed outlandish in the context of her
own home. Sky felt at a loss. She went into her room and
took down a small bag and a suitcase: she might as well start
getting ready for Ireland too.

"Can I use your telephone? I'll pay for the calls." Lynskey
was still standing in the hallway.

"Go ahead." Stalking past him, Sky lugged her suitcase
and the ironing basket into the kitchen and started the irritating business of packing. She closed the kitchen door
ostentatiously, in case he thought she might be listening in.

The Prince of Wales's trip to Ireland was in danger of being
aborted, partly from security considerations but also because
the FBI, which was monitoring the calls and activities of the
Sheriff of Mayville, had discovered that O'Connor had suddenly decided to take the vacation he was owed. The Bureau
passed this nugget of information to Lynskey when he called
the number in Washington from Sky's duplex.

He immediately telephoned Dublin. "I thought we'd heard
the last of you. Aren't you on the way home?" The chief
superintendent sounded unusually weary. "The stuff just
came in on those bullets, the one from that university with
the name like cooking oil—"

"Missoula."

"Whatever. And the one you gave the FBI. They match.

Nothing remarkable about them. No prints, they hadn't been fired, could have been bought in any gunshop."

"Surprise, surprise! I'm coming home tomorrow." Lynskey was speaking as low as he could while remaining audible. "I can't stay long because I'm on a private telephone, but our friend in Mayville is on the move. The day after tomorrow. I think we're on course. And although this is a problem," he hesitated a little, "that Butte newspaper I told you about is sending a reporter over to Ireland. A Miss R. Sky MacPherson if you remember."

"What the—"

"Don't worry. They have no idea what they're looking for." He lowered his voice still further. "All they know is that it involves something big and probably subversive."

"They could really make a mess—"

"Look, I told you, they don't know what they're looking for. And the newspaper's main contact in Ireland is Éamonn Vaughan. He's too busy chasing day-to-day stuff for RTE's television bulletins to have any idea either. I think it's time we told the Brits about this group."

"Would they tell us?"

Silence hung between them and Lynskey let it hang. Although, for public consumption, cooperation between the Special Branch of the Irish police force and Scotland Yard was superb and ongoing, in fact it was riddled with rivalries, xenophobia and post-colonial resentments on both sides.

"They're already laughing at the circus we're running here at the moment over that drug bust," the chief super's voice was tight, "and for once I don't blame them. Leave it with me. On your side, I've already discussed it with the feds and they're ready to do a round up over there. They're waiting until they're sure they have all the names and then they'll move on everyone simultaneously. After that, we'll make the decision about Operation Omega. If this group is out of action it'll be okay."

"You're the boss." Lynskey winced at the loud crack when the chief superintendent put down the phone.

Jim Larsen had decided to begin at the beginning, to look for whoever had started the ball rolling. It was clear that the black tramp, the guy who'd delivered the misspelled note, had known about Midge Treacy's hitting the hobo that night and might be able to put the Sheriff of Mayville on the spot.

Firstly, however, in the vague hope that Mrs. Treacy might be *compos mentis* enough to help, he tried the clinic in Choteau, where he ran into a blank wall of officialdom. "No one of that name here, sir, who wants to know?" If he had had time to go up there he was sure he could have swung something, but time was in short supply.

"All right." He called the kid into his office and spread out the coffee coupons on the desk in front of her. "Now think hard, Lindy. You told us before all you knew about the guy's height and weight and so on, but we need more. You said the guy was black?"

"Yeah—well, I think he was black."

"Coal black? Brown black or chocolate black or mahogany black?"

"Sort of brown black, I think. I'm sorry, Mr. Larsen." The junior picked nervously at the cuticle of her left thumbnail.

Jimbo gave her what he hoped was an encouraging smile. "Now, could he have been Native American, do you think? What was he wearing?"

"Sort of a jogging suit, I think, no . . . yes . . . And he wasn't Native American. I'm absolutely sure of that. His cheekbones weren't anyway."

"Do you remember the color? Of the jogging suit?"

The junior's face cleared instantly: this was her territory. "It was indigo—you know, that sort of very dark blue, not quite midnight blue but that's nearly black? It was quite new. And it had a very unusual boat neckline. To tell you the truth, Mr. Larsen, it looked like quite an expensive garment for someone like him."

"You mean, for a tramp?"

"Well, he wasn't a tramp, exactly. I mean, he didn't smell or anything like that. Well actually . . ." She reconsidered.

"Go on."

"He didn't smell *bad* although I did think I caught a whiff of alcohol off his breath but there was another smell from him too. Kinda like burning? As if he'd been in a fire?"

It was not much to go on but it was something. "Thanks, Lindy, that'll do for the moment, but if you think of anything else, anything at all . . ." He dismissed her and sat for a moment sunk in thought. Then he called the police station. His buddy there was out but before Larsen could leave a message he found himself switched to the desk sergeant. As time was so short, he decided to take a risk. "Jim Larsen, of the *Courier*."

"How can I help you?" Although respectful, relations between the newspaper and the police had never been ultra cordial. Larsen knew he was regarded as being far too independent. "I'm trying to locate a black tramp, someone who might pick up a bit of work here and there, maybe at an incinerator, maybe a dump. Or someone who likes to hang around fires, even in summer. Anyone you know fit that description?"

"He done something?"

"Not that I'm aware of, but he gave us some information and I would like to trace him again."

"Information concerning what, exactly, Jim?"

"Oh, just a story we're working on."

"I see. Well, no one comes to mind right away. But if you come across a bit more information about the guy or what you're looking for, maybe we could help you out."

The editor thought quickly. He didn't want to reveal too much but the death of Old Leon was in the public domain anyway. "The guy left a note in at the front office here. Apparently some friend of his called Leon died by the side of the road upstate and he wants us to commemorate him, write an obituary, that sort of thing. We'd like to facilitate him— it'll make good human interest copy—but we can find out very little about his friend. We need to talk to the black guy again to get a bit of material."

"I'll ask around," the sergeant was noncommittal, "but I'm not all that hopeful. Haven't never seen a black hobo in Butte."

With time ticking away toward her departure for Yaak and her suitcase for Ireland less than a quarter filled, Sky was becoming panicky. Her grandmother reappeared in the kitchen. "Sit down, Grandma." Sky cleared a space on the table. "Have you eaten?" At least her self-appointed bodyguard had had the decency not to come into the kitchen. After his telephone call, she had heard him go toward the living room.

"I have." Her grandmother sat in the chair indicated.

"I'm sorry, you don't mind if I continue with this?" Sky indicated her ironing. "I don't have much time," and when her grandmother shook her head, "So come on, Grandma, tell me. I couldn't ask you at the hospital in front of the others but I'm dying to know what happened between you and Daniel."

In response, Sky's grandmother drew a jewelry case out of her purse and placed it on the table. "Have a look. It nearly finished me altogether."

Sky placed the iron on its heel and opened the case. Spread out on the black velvet was a necklace of emerald-cut gems of pale blue set in a flexible band of white gold. It was modern yet timeless, the most beautiful object she had ever seen. She picked it up and draped it across the back of her hand from which, catching the light, it poured like tassels chiseled from the blue-white core of an iceberg. "It's very heavy." She could think of nothing which would adequately describe such beauty.

"The stones are so pale I thought at first they were aquamarines," her grandmother touched the necklace, "but they're cornflower sapphires, apparently. He searched until he got the color exactly right. They're yours, Sky. I can't wear them."

"Why ever not?"

"Because of what he said but not what he meant. What that necklace represents. To him it's a talisman of something long gone. For me it's a reminder of too much pain, his— then and now—mine, everyone's, even his poor wife's. I certainly remember that night and that blue dress." Talking to herself now, she picked the necklace off Sky's hand and let it cascade through her fingers. "It's uncanny how he matched the color." She looked back at her granddaughter. "That dress was the one I was wearing at the dance the night he shot your grandfather. Daniel and I had danced together for the first time."

"But that shooting was an accident, he told me—Mom told me—"

"Yes. But it's a chapter in a closed book. Take it, Sky." Decisively, her grandmother put the necklace back in its case, snapped the box shut and pushed it across the table. "I'll be leaving it to you in my will anyway. Just don't tell Daniel I've anticipated a little, will you? Anyway," she brightened up a little, "white gold looks awful on old skin."

Sky cradled the case in her hands. She would decide what to do with the jewels later. "Tell me, Grandma, from the very beginning. I saw him answering the door when I was driving off . . ."

The story came out slowly and, while relating it, Sky's grandmother stared at the formica top on the kitchen table. She looked up now. "He had just given me the necklace when you came to the door to collect me. What was I going to say? Such dreams, such love. I felt unworthy but at the same time I didn't want all this, I'd put it behind me years and years ago."

"Don't you think it's wonderful, though, Grandma, all this time he's kept this torch alive?"

"It's a responsibility I cannot accept. I feel awful about putting that so bluntly, but what can I do? The poor man is dying, I know that, and I'll do what I can for him but at my age, Sky, death is . . ." she searched for an analogy, "not a friend exactly, more like a neighbor, liable to drop in at any stage of the day or night to borrow your remaining time. Although you don't think about it all the time, it's always there, living right next door, in the next room. It's impossible to avoid because it's already called on other neighbors, good friends from school . . ." She trailed away.

"So if you couldn't tell him how you felt about this business with the house, are you able to tell me?"

"How did you think I felt? Moved and shocked and sad and yet flattered. All at the same time. I did love him, Sky, I was a foolish and headstrong young woman. He was gorgeous then—you should have seen him."

Her grandmother smiled in a way that showed Sky how she had been as a young girl. She could see the two of them, in one another's arms. "And now?" she breathed. "Now that you've spent a morning with him?"

The smile died away. "How could I not love Daniel McCarthy? But not the way he loves me. He saw it straight away. It was very sad. I could have pretended. After all," she avoided Sky's gaze, "what had I to lose? I could so easily have pretended for the few weeks he has left. But then I thought that would not be worthy of either of us. Or of his poor wife up there, wherever she is."

Sky opened the jewelry case again, and examined the sapphires. "When are you seeing him again?"

"Later today. He's taking me out to dinner. And tomorrow too, Sky. I'll see him as much as he likes until—" She stopped then went on, briskly, "This is why, although I'll miss you, there's no problem at all with your going on your trip. It's funny, isn't it, that we'll have sort of swapped places again? Seems like we're forever destined to miss each other. Anyway, Johanna's going to be in hospital for a long time yet so apart from visiting her, I'll be available for Daniel. In fact, as it looks like your mother's lovely friends feel they have to baby me to extinction, it'll be nice to have a project of my own. He's going to take sometime off. Apparently when he received the prognosis, he set up his work so it practically runs itself. He's going to bring me up to visit his wife."

"I see." Sky, who had not spent much time considering elderly people's motivations or their behavior among themselves, wondered which of them had come up with such a bizarre idea but thought it better not to ask. Maybe when you got to be over seventy neither ordinary niceties nor taboos applied. "So what happened after you took the necklace from him?"

"Nothing, we just talked. He offered me tea—can you imagine? After all these years, Daniel McCarthy offering me tea just like we gave our visitors in the old days. It's all coffee and cocktails now, of course. Twining's." She smiled affectionately. "Apparently that's the nearest thing to real Irish-style tea you can get over here. I was touched."

In the absence of a mirror in the kitchen, Sky held the sapphires against her forearm to see how they would look against her skin. "They're beautiful on you, darling," her grandmother said softly. "Wear them, and remember I wasn't always so old."

Chapter Thirty

After making his call to the reporter's home, the Helena lieutenant had set off quietly for Butte. He always worked alone. He had not yet decided what to do with this reporter woman: like his employer, he believed in violence only when it was necessary.

This appointment to meet her was really a reconnaissance mission. Or, at least, it would start out that way. If he managed to scare her into submission, well, everything was probably going to turn out all right.

He would know within minutes if she was prone to heroics. Most reporters had egos as big as redwood trees and were used to having things all their own way, imagined they were invincible: that their ability to place things in the public domain gave them power.

The Helena lieutenant knew all about power. Middle-aged, he had retired early from his post as an assistant district attorney at the DA's office. Ostensibly, his retirement had been because of an ailing heart, but in reality his work for the woman in Vancouver had started to make too many demands on his time. He still saw his former colleagues, however. It was how he continued to keep up with everything that moved in the state of Montana. How he knew where most of the bodies were buried.

He planned to confront this R. Sky MacPherson, not at the coffee shop, but on the pretext that it was too crowded—it always was—to take her somewhere a little more private.

He did not doubt that she would turn up. No reporter could resist the carrot of an anonymous tip-off.

Across the border in Canada, the elderly Jerry Flynn—the first of the plotters' group to start making the move to Ireland and the richest by millions—was walking to his limousine to be driven to the airport.

Unlike the rest of his coconspirators, he was motivated less by the more recent events in Irish history than by vivid memories of stories told him by his Irish great-grandmother who, as a girl, had survived her trip to the Americas in one of the aptly named coffin ships that brought the starving and destitute across the Atlantic during the potato famine of 1847. Eight members of her family had started out from County Galway, but she was the only one who had arrived. To the end of her days at the age of ninety-four, through her late marriage to an Irish-American cop, through the move to Canada and the upbringing of her single son, the arrival of grandchildren and then great-grandchildren, she implanted in the minds of all around her tales of the heartless brutality of the English masters and the suffering of the Irish.

Jerry Flynn had polished those stories until they shone in his memory like jewels. He felt the hunger pangs of his great-grandmother and her neighbors, vomited with them the green slime of grass torn from the roadsides and stuffed into their mouths, watched sullenly as the carts laden with yellow grain harvests rumbled away from their homestead toward the ports and the tables of England and India in payment of English taxes. For many of Flynn's coconspirators, the crucible of the present impasse in Irish affairs was planted in the failure of the 1916 revolution and executions of Pearse and the other patriots. Their motives had been simple too: to get England out and let Ireland run her own affairs.

For Flynn, everything that had happened in Ireland had flown directly from the injustice of the famine. Now he was embarked on vengeance. For his great-grandmother, for all his ancestors. Those who now ran the Irish parliament, and bent the knee to loyalists and unionists, must be humiliated. Flynn's heart beat fast under his snappy business suit as he emphasized to his chauffeur that he would be in New York for about a week.

Three hours later, he took a cab into New York City and had his hair cut short. "And while you're at it, buddy," he told the young barber, "take off this mustache. I feel like giving myself a new image for the ladies." The boy, hiding a snicker, shaved him so tightly his skin squeaked. Then Flynn went to a prearranged rendezvous on 42nd Street half a block from Times Square and had his photograph taken. He went for a short walk, enjoying his anonymity among the rubber-neckers, skateboarders and seedy lowlifes with whom the area was infested. Then he went back to the office where he had posed for the camera, and was handed his new passport.

When he got back out to Kennedy and presented his passport and ticket at the Aer Lingus Premier Class desk, he was John Mulqueen, American senior citizen. But he felt twenty years younger already.

"I'm glad you're taking this seriously at last, Sky." Lynskey was driving her to the airport. "I know you think I'm a nuisance but if you won't think about your own safety, someone has to. We have word back on those bullets but they were clean of clues as to who was behind the sending of them."

"It's the sheriff, you know it is."

"You're probably right but we've no proof. But whoever it was won't be shy. They mean business, Sky."

"Talk to my editor about it." She summoned as much hauteur as she could.

"You can bet I will," Lynskey promised as he turned into the parking lot and stopped. He turned off the engine and shook his head. "What am I going to do with you at all? You're a big eejit, do you know that, MacPee? Ah well," changing tone and mood a full 180 degrees, he bent to kiss her cheek, "go off and see your da and have a great time. I'll take care of things down here."

She had stared at him. This man was a stranger of less than a week's acquaintance: what had happened that he was now "taking care of things here"? He noted her expression, guessed the reason behind it. "Sorry, I'm being a bossyboots again, right? Can't help it. I love you."

Once again, she felt that flutter of terror. She fiddled with the shoulder strap of her overnight bag, pretending to check that the buckle was secure. "One thing I'm worried about. Will you make sure my grandmother's all right in the house? If I'm supposed to be in so much danger . . ."

"She'll be well protected. Have a good flight now."

She raised her mouth for a kiss but he sideskipped and planted a second one on her cheek. "See you soon, MacPee."

"I'll see you when I get back." Unreasonably, she felt a little piqued as she got into the sunshine.

The single-engined Treacy Resources plane was already on the runway and the young pilot, whom she reckoned to be at least ten years younger than herself, took her on board.

As they banked after take off, Sky tried to relax, yet she

could not avoid facing the sludge of corrosive emotions which had been stirred up in the past week. She felt as raw as a scraped carrot: at heart, for the moment at least, she was a little girl who wanted her daddy.

The butterfies began to stir in her stomach as they crossed the wide flow of the Kootenia river, northwest of Libby, and then flew along the smaller and more tranquil Yaak. Northwest Montana unrolled beneath the wing like one of those bright relief maps she used to make from *papier mâché* for geography class in grade school: rivers glinting like threads of gold and copper between lush, steep banks of deciduous and coniferous trees; occasional, widely spaced glimpses of a cabin built from logs or a long, low, ranch-style house; a spooked horse galloping, tail up, across a bright green pasture, a brown clearing alive with loggers and their yellow, dinosaur-like machinery.

Parallel with and above the plane's wing, in a long lazy line, the frosted, dreaming heights of the Rockies.

They were making their final approach to the field. Now that she thought about it, Sky could not understand why she was taking this trip. Eight years was a long time, and now that she was faced with it, what was she going to say to her father? She could hardly throw herself into his arms—as she had earlier felt she would like to do—and ask him to fix everything: all her anxieties—about the trip, about Lynskey, about her mother. Larry MacPherson had never lived for a single day under the same roof as she and Johanna, much less had he had anything to do with their emotional well-being.

For the first time it occurred to Sky that not once had it crossed anyone's mind to let Larry know about her mother's accident. Least of all had she herself thought to tell him, although it was she who had spoken with him. She felt guilty about that: she had been bubbling over with the prospect of seeing him, of going to Ireland, and had forgotten.

Or could she have deliberately withheld the information for reasons she did not now care to analyze? As the aircraft flashed along the crushed-cinder runway past the Nissen hut that served as waiting room and service center, she caught a glimpse of her father lounging in the doorway. The butterflies went crazy, although at least a few were dancing for joy. She would tell him now, first thing.

To banish the sensations in her stomach she bent double,

leaning hard on her solar plexus and making heavy weather of retrieving her shoulder bag from where she had stowed it between her feet. She regained control of herself as the aircraft swung around and began its short taxi run toward the hut. She reminded the pilot that he should pick her up again early the next morning, jumped out and ran across the gate toward her father. "Dad! Thanks for coming to meet me," as she buried her face in the hug. The smell of him—tobacco, old leather, an overriding scent of the woodsy outdoors—soothed doubts about the reasons for this trip.

"Stand back there and let me see you." He held her by the shoulders and looked her up and down.

"Will I pass?" She had to raise her voice to be heard over the pilot's take-off run behind them.

"Rainbow Sky MacPherson," his voice was like pouring chocolate, "you're a sight for my eyes."

"You too, Dad. Let's see you, now." He was dressed as she had always remembered him: checkered shirt, jeans faded to a whitish gray, boots of hide so scuffed it looked like ancient suede. "You've cut your hair! Last time I was here you looked like Davy Crockett!"

"And didn't you just let me know it." He grinned. The white tanmark around the sides and back of his neck under his baseball cap showed that the barbering was recent: she was touched he had had it cut just for her. "Well, let it grow again, Dad. I take it all back, I preferred it long."

"There's no pleasing women." He threw his eyes to heaven in mock exasperation. "Here, give me that, truck's just here." He took the bag and threw it into the rear of a newish Daihatsu 4-track, which, with all four doors open, stood beside the hut.

"This new?" The last time she had been up he had been driving a pickup, held together by its own rust.

"Yep, business was good, last coupla years. How's your mom?" He closed the two rear doors of the jeep and folded himself, lithe as a big cat, into the driver's seat.

Sky climbed in beside him: "Mom's in the hospital. I should have told you, I know."

"She all right?" Larry turned the key in the ignition.

"Well . . ." Sky was a little put out that he did not seem all that concerned.

"You would have told me if it were anything serious,

yeah?" He engaged the gears and reversed away from the hut.

"It's serious enough, Dad. She's broken her back."

Her father whistled, a long note, like a harmonica player's. "She's going to be okay, though, ain't she?"

"What would you say if I were to tell you she won't?" It was out before she could contain it.

"Come on, hon, I know you'da told me." Her father spun the steering wheel and took the jeep out on to a wide track that seemed to lead directly into a forest. He glanced across at her. "Hang on to your hat, it'll be a bit bumpy for a spell."

Sky was silent. Wanting him to ask about her mother's operation. Wanting him to be frantic. Instead, he seemed content to concentrate on his driving as the jeep, engine roaring, jolted and juddered across the deep ruts in the track.

They came out on to the highway after about two miles which, to Sky, seemed more like forty. It was not the physical discomfort: rather, she felt almost in shock. She tried to put this in perspective as the jeep picked up speed: her father and mother had never married—had never even lived together. Why shouldn't he take this news casually? What was Johanna to him now?

"You're very quiet, Dad." She could not keep the provocation out of her voice.

"Up here you get used to silence and your own company," he responded equably, "you should know that, darlin'. It's you folks in the big cities make more noise than a posse of foxes." She knew his penchant for silence: he was the type of man who would retreat to his own dreams at his own time.

They came to an intersection and turned left into Yaak proper, which comprised a store, two telephone booths and the Dirty Shame saloon. "She'll be in for quite a while," she said quietly. "Mom," she added as he looked across at her, incomprehension written all over his craggy, handsome face.

"Oh, yeah . . . She needs anything while you're gone on your trip, you just tell her to let me know, okay, hon? With one hand, Sky's father extracted a spindly roll-up from a tin on the dashboard and put it in his mouth. "Hey, there's a thing. My little girl's going to be a foreign correspondent— how 'bout that!" He grinned across at her while patting himself down in a search for matches. "Hang on." He came up empty, braked hard, then reversed to the front of the general store. "I have to go in here for a second. My little girl a big newspaper star." He chuckled, shaking his head. "Who'da thought? Want a soda or something? They got ice."

Sky did not trust herself to speak. After he had gone into the store, she got out of the jeep to sit on the wooden glider set on the verandah under the eaves. It was the Yaak evening rush hour: a pickup stopped in the middle of the street, its engine left running as the man in the passenger seat went in for supplies; on the far side, with a hiss of air brakes, a huge articulated rig overshot the Dirty Shame and stopped opposite where she sat. The driver hopped down from the cab and stretched. "Howdy," he called across to Sky, "how's your day goin' so far?"

"Fine," she called back, and did her best to smile.

"You bet." The driver shook himself like a bear coming out of a river and walked briskly toward the saloon.

"Here you go." Her father was back with two Cokes and two dixie cups. "Want to sit awhile?" Taking her silence for assent, he went to fetch a bag of ice, pulling it open with his teeth as he came back. He filled first her cup from the contents, then his own, before cracking the top off both Coke bottles against the rim of the glider. "Nice here," he sat beside her, "nice and cool."

It was the last evening and the trees at the edge of the forest at the other side of the highway exhaled a quiet, green breath. It had been dry up here for weeks: the breeze stirred little eddies of dust around their feet and the two water-feeders slung from the rafter beside them were in constant use by hummingbirds, their wings blurring as they sipped from the tiny pipes. "I prefer it in winter," her father's slow voice was reminiscent, "never a breath of wind, two feet of powder. A blue and white world, so clear.

"Lovely little things, aren't they? Bet you don't see many in the city." Hunched over, elbows on knees, the better to watch the activities of the hummingbirds, he gazed at them with such tender pleasure she could not square it with his seeming callousness toward her mother's plight.

"It was because of a hummingbird that Mom's in the hospital."

"Oh?" As she explained what had happened, Sky was trying to decide from his expression whether he was more interested in the fate of the bird caught in Moondancer's mouth than her mother's accident. She finished the story and pretended to bury herself in the Coke.

What had happened in eight years? She had been twenty-six when last she saw this man. An adult. Old enough, experienced enough, to see and hear the truth. Had he always had this *laissez-faire* attitude toward the mother of his child—or was she just now seeing it because of her own reaction to Johanna's brush with death?

Even as they entered her head, Sky heard the pompousness of her thoughts and would have dismissed them if she had not been so taken aback. Because it was only then she realized she had been hoping that, somehow, Johanna's accident would have brought Larry MacPherson rushing to the hospital.

Happy ever after.

It was also why she had not told him on the telephone: she had needed to confront him about it. All these years she had held him in a web of dreams: her lovely, absent father, so beautiful, a Peter Pan in a fairy castle. Even at *her* age.

And now, dimly, she saw that the whole caboodle was tied in someways with goddamned Fergus Lynskey. "I've met a man, Dad."

"Oh?" At least that had got his attention. "A better deal than that Randy, I hope?"

"Not much," she admitted. "Well, he's amazing, but he's a—a *trial* as well. I'm not sure I trust him, Dad—in fact, I know I don't. But he loves me," she rose from the glider and wandered over to the water feeder, which was temporarily unattended. "At least, he says he does, and I'm really worried about that." She twanged at the pipe. "I mean, what kind of a man says he loves a woman after only a few days? And just because he sleeps with her just *once* . . ."

"I see." Her father's tone was wry. "Sounds like an all together guy!"

"Oh, Dad, what'll I do?" She turned round to face him.

He was watching her, his eyes soft. "You'll make the right decision, Rainbow Sky, you always do."

"My life's a mess."

"Of course it's not a mess. You're a big success, aren't you? And you left that Randy."

"That's another thing. You didn't even come to the wedding."

"Wise decision, as it turned out."

"And you hate Mom."

"But I don't hate your mother . . ." She could see he was genuinely mystified and something in her, perhaps her childhood, broke.

Chapter Thirty-one

Sheriff O'Connor, who was divorced and therefore free of busybodies who might question his comings and goings, told no one why he had decided to take off. Neither his deputy nor anyone else connected with his office even asked. On the contrary, they danced metaphorical jigs of delight. Brian O'Connor was not popular in Mayville. Anyone who talked about the snap vacation assumed that since his ex had moved to Florida some years ago, he was probably going down there to see his kids. Apart from himself and British Airways, the only people who knew he had bought a return ticket to London were federal agents. He planned to buy the Dublin ticket at Heathrow.

If his staff were delighted at his projected absence, the sheriff's own heart had expanded with fierce exultation. They were on the move at last. No more telephone calls, just action.

Now, on his final afternoon before the adventure began, he sat on the back porch of his clapboard house. The yard was dusty and overgrown; he had no interest in gardening or in tending to the shrubs and flowering trees planted so optimistically by his wife when they first moved here more than twenty years ago. He was brooding as he stared through the screen door but he neither saw nor thought about the tall weeds and rampant ivy. His excitement had been short-lived: payment for the part he had played in the casket deal had come through that morning, but when he had opened it he saw he had received only a token amount, less than a third of what had been originally agreed. It was enough to fund his trip and his part of the ancillary expenses, but barely so.

The sheriff was sore: he had made plans for the rest of that money. He had been screwed around, something to which he had never taken kindly.

What was more, it appeared that the newspaper had

ignored his warning to butt out: within the past hour he had gotten reports from people who owed him favors in both Helena and Butte that the *Courier* was still snooping around. He had to watch his back: the Lord only knew what damage they could do to him if they tried. Or got lucky.

He wished like hell he could think of some way to get back at the guy in Helena who had gotten him into this mess with the drugs. Not only at him but at the *Butte Courier*. Not only at them but at the whole world. The more the sheriff thought about the fix he had been put in, the madder he got.

He heard the metallic drone of a small airplane over head, a little to the west. He looked up: the plane, in the red Treacy Resources' livery, was traveling south. It was not all that odd to see the company's aircraft in these skies but, as far as he knew, Treacy's logging and mining activities in the northwest were dormant. The company operated a "rolling" vacation system for its staff whereby the workers went away at the same time and the entire sites were closed down.

Could Treacy himself have gone back up to his lodge? The sheriff hatched an idea. He would have plenty of time to go up there and get back—it was only a matter of fifty or sixty miles.

He put in a call to the company's headquarters in Butte and asked for Daniel Treacy. He was told that Mr. Treacy was taking a little time off, but if it was urgent messages could be gotten through. Declining to leave his name, the sheriff hung up and grabbed his hat and gun. He hurried around the police car and got into the little Hyundai loaner he still had from Deke and Skippy, whom he had caught fiddling mileage clocks on some of their used stock and who were therefore most amenable to giving him anything he wanted for free.

Maybe something could be salvaged from the wreckage. Geese could sometimes be induced to lay more than one golden egg.

The journey from Yaak to her father's cabin, about six miles to the west, passed silently for which Sky was grateful. Larry, humming quietly to himself as he drove, had no idea what had happened between them back there on the verandah of the store.

"Here we go." He pulled the jeep off the road through a rough, ranch-style entrance arch made from three lodge pole trunks lashed together. An ancient mongrel hound lolloped forward to sniff at Sky's hand as she got out.

"You have a new porch." She was pleased to have some material for ordinary conversation, although the porch in question was a shiny aluminum excrescence on the lovely wood from which the house had been constructed.

"Yes." Her father swung out of the driver's seat. "Me and the old dawg here decided we were fed up with the wind whistlin' through the cracks in our front door, weren't we, dawg?" He fondled the hounds' ears and then took Sky's bag from the back seat of the jeep. "Would you like a beer?"

The interior of the cabin was exactly as she remembered it. It was warm, although not too much so, from the big wood stove kept burning winter and summer, and the living room bristled with hunting trophies and artifacts. The huge stuffed grizzly, more than eight feet tall, continued to snarl from one corner. Fixed to the log walls, heads of other animals, moose, deer, raccoon, otter, beaver, even an ancient buffalo, still stared down. Up here, there was no point in being a bleeding heart on behalf of all the creatures who had donated them—her father would have looked at her with incomprehension. The display of Native American wall hangings, everyday and peace pipes, bear claw and shell necklaces, even a tomahawk, would have done justice to a small museum.

She kicked off her sneakers and luxuriated in the feel of the soft fur rugs on her bare feet. "Is that new?" She pointed at a beautiful rawhide shield, hung with eagle feathers and decorated with what looked like a brightly colored pyramid.

"It was a big honor," her father said, almost shyly. "I was presented with it at a Crow gathering last year."

"This new too?" Dwarfing the serving bowls and jugs on the table by the cabin's window was an enormous CB radio.

"Must keep up with the times." He smiled his long, slow smile and headed toward the kitchen.

"Business must be really good—it must have cost you . . ." She followed him as he opened the refrigerator and removed two cans.

"Yep. All those city businessmen going native for two days once every three or four years. Some of 'em wait ten years for a license for one moose, you know." He shrugged. "Can't see it myself. And then when they get one, all they want's the antlers to bring back with 'em to put on the roofs of their four-wheel drives. Me and my neighbors up here don't mind, though. We sure do love passing that meat counter in the store!" He opened the lid of a big chest freezer beside the fridge. "Look here." The cabinet was packed to the brim. "All wild."

They took the beers outside and sat at a picnic table set up in a little clearing he had cut into the dense forest. Out here among the trees the coolness had a sharp green edge to it and the quiet was unlike that in the national forest around Butte. There it crackled and hopped busily; here where the trees were virgin, the silence was stealthier by far, as though the creatures all around knew that they must be extra quiet or get killed.

Although their meets had been so rare, Sky had never before felt like a stranger with her father. Some of the scales through which she had viewed him all her life had peeled off her eyes at the Yaak general store, and the rest had fallen away in the past five minutes. In noticing the big CB radio it had hit her for the first time that he had never even telephoned her. It was a phenomenon she had somehow overlooked. Sure, he had paid what he could toward her maintenance and had remembered birthdays and Christmases now and then, even her high school graduation. Sure, he said he loved her, said it in the same affectionate tone he used when talking to his coon dog. Sky wished she had not come. It would have been so much nicer to have kept him intact in the fairy castle of her memories. With her newly awakened sensibilities she saw that Larry MacPherson's self-sufficiency was so all-encompassing it excluded her. Not only her, but all human beings. He did not need anyone.

"I've been interviewing Daniel Treacy." She was unable to let the silence go on. "He says his lodge is near here."

"Not far—want another one?" He held up his empty can.

"No thanks." She had barely touched her own. "How far is it?"

"Oh, 'bout ten, eleven miles, right on the Idaho border."

"It's closed up now, yeah?"

"So folks say. Guess I'll have another myself." He stood up. "Are you not curious about *anything*, Dad?"

A small frown creased his otherwise unwrinkled forehead as he looked down at her. "Not especially—maybe things like how fast the snow plow'll get here after the first fall, that sort of thing."

"How about people? Aren't you interested in people at all, Dad?"

"Sure I am. But people always mess up, don't they?" He looked at the beer can in his hand—enlarged and cracked from manual work—and then went inside to get the next.

Because she could not bear to fret alongside him, locked into inactivity while he remained oblivious to her feelings, she asked him to take her to see Daniel Treacy's hunting lodge when he had finished his second beer. To justify it, she bent her mind to the expedition in a journalistic way rather than with any personal interest—although now, with her grandmother in the picture, she had every reason for the latter.

The trip to Treacy's lodge took less than a quarter of an hour. They came to a big wooden billboard welcoming them to Idaho. Her father veered off the highway and drove slowly toward what seemed to be a large, spreading bush. "Want to go right in?"

"Sure." She was surprised he had to ask but still could not see any road. "Driveways 'bout a mile." At the last minute, the foliage gave way and she could see the dirt track winding uphill away into the distance. The camouflage was masterful: the track was hidden to any but the most knowledgeable. Expertly, her father drove through the leaves so that not one touched either side of the vehicle.

In the *Courier* office, the junior's brain was whistling at her: it had not worked so hard in years. Her job was to call every public building in Butte—schools, churches, utility offices, banks, office buildings and apartment blocks—every single place that might have given a job to a black guy, even for a few days, to tend their incinerators.

The editor was out walking the streets and back alleys. And although in the course of an hour and a half he did not find the man for whom he was looking, he did find something.

He was walking down Dublin Gulch when, passing the liquor store, he saw Sky's boyfriend, Greg Landos. On impulse, remembering the junior's mention of drink on the messenger's breath, he went inside.

"Hi, Jim, what can I get you?" He was surprised at the guardedness of Greg's welcome but did not give the younger man's coolness more than a passing thought. "I'm wondering if you can help me?" Briefly, he described the quarry.

To his delight, Greg did remember something. "Black, you say?"

"I guess so."

The tramp had been in only once but during the few minutes he had spent in the store, he had picked a verbal fight with another man, an elderly janitor, who was one of Greg's more frequent customers. "I threw them both out," it was in Greg's nature to be helpful, "but about an hour afterward, I saw them both, the best of buddies. They were sitting on a bench together over by the civic center. The old guy works there."

The janitor was not at work that day but finding him was easy. Armed with his address, the editor drove off to Walkerville in the city's suburb. The house was a tiny ramshackle two-up two-down in the shadow of one of the defunct pithead cranes. Only the outline of a door bell remained and flakes of rotting paint and wood showered him when he knocked on the door.

It was opened by an elderly man, no bigger than a schoolboy and wearing oil-stained overalls. His breath reeked when he spoke. "Not buying nothing today." He went to close the door but Larsen put a hand on it, introduced himself and explained why he had come. "I ain't seen that guy but the once." The janitor tried to close the door again but Larsen persisted.

"I have to find him, Mr. Schindler, it's very important. Have you any idea at all where he was headed?"

"He said something about Anaconda."

After about half a mile, the dirt track into Treacy's lodge ended in a little "S"-shaped bridge, which spanned two tumbling loops of a deep, brown stream. As the jeep negotiated the second of the bends, the forest suddenly opened out in front of them and Sky saw the house.

In the sumptuousness of its design and the external appointments, Daniel Treacy's so-called "lodge" rivaled his elevated mansion outside Butte. It was dominated by the rounded spine of the mountains, which, like a cyclorama, defined it and gave it majesty. Her father engaged a lower gear as they began climbing an arrow-straight road between a pair of lawns. At the crest of this hill, the house was set into a semicircle of ornamental trees. Long, low, and roughly crescent-shaped, it was constructed of the same wood as her father's house but Sky had lived long enough in Montana to know that the difference between the two log cabins was about a million dollars.

The windows were shuttered and blind, however, and the entire place had already taken on the forlorn look of a house abandoned. Not completely foresaken, however, as a little Hyundai was parked off to the side. "I guess he's still having it maintained." Larry let the jeep coast to a halt. He got out and stretched. "Want to see around the back?

"No." Sky wanted, more than anything now, to be alone. "I think I'll go for a little walk in the woods, Dad."

Her father leaned into the jeep and unsnapped a lock box under the back seat. "Take this." Pulling out a rifle, he checked the breech. "You know how to use it?"

"I couldn't possibly—" Sky recoiled.

"Then I'm comin' with ya." He shouldered the gun. "Bear," he explained, as though to a two-year-old. Sky laughed, inappropriately as always.

Around the back, the sheriff was in a quandary.

He had arrived at the house only minutes before and had gone straight to the rear, but with no automobiles out front or in the garages the place was obviously unoccupied. Then he had heard the engine of the approaching jeep and reckoned he had not come up here on a wild goose chase, after all.

He had debated whether to reveal his presence right away—his auto out front was a giveaway that someone was here—but, on instinct, he hung back. Better to wait until Treacy was in the house. Slowly, he made his way to a corner of the house and listened for his quarry to go inside.

Instead, as the sound of the engine died away, he heard two voices. To his horror, one of them was that reporter from the *Butte Courier*. He recognized it instantly: outside of public service TV, how many women talked in that fruity, lah-di-dah way?

He heard the unmistakable sound of a gun being breeched, the voices again and then her laugh. The unmistakable laugh of a bitch.

It was that laugh . . . The sheriff had to hold on to the side of the lodge to keep himself from running after them.

His rage had been bottled up for many, many years. After a few hothead explosions when he was young, he had recognized that rage made a person lose control and control was what success was all about.

Internally, though, the rage fermented. Rage against the crooks and conmen who got away, sometimes literally, with murder because of smartass lawyers. Rage against his dumbass parents, who had beat him senseless, against his ex-wife who had turned his kids against him. Rage against the federal government, which was restricting the rights of American citizens in favor of foreigners, spongers and left-wing agitators. Rage against the rich, against men better looking than he. And against the bitches who laughed at his attempts to seduce them so that he was reduced to sleeping with whores.

He had been able to channel some of his rage against the Brits who would not get out of Ireland. But now, for the first time in decades, on hearing that laugh the rage boiled over.

The sheriff shook as he held on to a down pipe at the corner of the house; he shook so hard that he was afraid the gutters might come down around him but he knew if he loosened his grip he would do something stupid. He struggled to control himself. After a minute or two, he loosened his hold. The pressure of the down pipe had rubbed his hands raw and they started to throb. Walking stiffly, the sheriff came around the side of the house.

The jeep was carelessly parked behind the Hyundai, three of its four doors open. Unconcerned that he might be seen, the sheriff walked over to it and raised the hood. He identified the wires and cables and then, as though he had all the time in the world, joggled and pulled at the front brake cables. His hands and forearms were strong and it was only a matter of seconds before they snapped loose. The Daihatsu had a dual line system so he had to perform the same operation with the second set of cables that ran to the rear wheels.

He closed the hood and checked to make sure that fluid had not leaked out conspicuously from under the jeep, but if it had, the raked gravel had absorbed it.

The sheriff got into his rental car and drove away.

By the time he had crossed the little bridge half a mile from the house and the forest had closed round him, the rage had ebbed away. He felt empty. And puzzled. Why had he done that? They had obviously seen the Hyundai; it would not be difficult to trace him.

He did not know why he had done it. But, somehow, it had been cathartic.

When he reached the end of the dirt track and was turning on to the highway, he was calm. Even regretful. Now he would have to race back to Mayville to return the rental and to lean some more on Skippy and Deke. The sheriff sighed. There was no accounting for human behavior.

Chapter Thirty-two

"It's getting dangerous." It was almost midnight and Rupert de Burgh was speaking from a telephone box at the corner of his suburban road. "From the way they're talking I think they know someone's leaking. I may have to take the—ad— you know, out." Although he always called his brother from different telephone booths and not at his London flat, he was never less than circumspect. "But don't worry," he rushed to reassure him, "they haven't a clue who it is. Our little device has served its purpose and we're still on course. Anything your end?"

"I've been thinking about this."

De Burgh, who knew his brother like he knew himself, heard the unease in Toby's voice. "It's too late to back down now." He concentrated on projecting energy and authority. "We're dealing in cyphers here, not humans, remember? That man is honorary colonel of the Paras, Toby. Remember what the Paras did that day in Derry?"

"I remember." His brother's tone had dulled again.

"Talk to you soon. At the club, lunchtime tomorrow. Not long now. Try to get me some more information your end, like times, routes. You're clear about what you've to do the moment he takes off?"

"Yes."

"Three different telephone booths, the same code word. You have the numbers I gave you? You remember what the code is?"

"I'm not a child."

De Burgh sighed. He was glad it was coming to a head. "Think of history, Toby." He tried to sound bright. "Our place in history."

When Sky's father braked about fifty yards before reaching the little corkscrew bridge at the bottom of the hill that led away from Treacy's lodge, nothing happened. The jeep was not in top gear but was gathering speed. He swore, jabbing at the useless pedal, then crashed into a lower gear and pulled at the parking brake.

The engine screamed but the gradient was too steep for the emergency brake. They had one second before they entered the bridge, wide enough for only one vehicle.

"Hang on," he yelled letting go of the brake and directing all his concentration into steering.

As Sky, petrified, gripped the sides of her seat, her father accelerated—and they successfully negotiated the first bend on the bridge. He accelerated harder, sending the tachometer way into the red, but on the second bend, the rear fender struck the wooden guardrail, splintering it. The smell of burning oil filled the cab as, ignoring the impact, Sky's father pushed the jeep to its limit and soared off the bridge with the needle of the tachometer stuck at the top of the danger zone.

Once through, he took his foot off the accelerator and let the vehicle coast to a shuddering halt about a hundred yards or so into the bumpy dirt track where the engine cut out amid clouds of swirling brown dust. He looked across at his daughter. "You OK, darlin?"

"Yes." She could only whisper it. After the screaming and the terror, the rustling trees and little breeze were as loud in her ears as a pounding ocean.

"I just don't understand it." Larry, who seemed relatively unshaken, jumped out. "This baby was serviced only two weeks ago. She's never given me trouble, not since I bought her. I hope I ain't burned her out." He raised the hood and looked inside.

Sky, whose legs felt like rubber, fell out of the Daihatsu. The full horror of what might have happened dawned on her now and she felt sick. She went to the side of the rack and sat on a soft carpet of moss and pine needles, bending her head to her knees.

"Would you like a drink, honey?" Her father was standing over her, "I got a little flask of bourbon. Always carry it." He fetched it and sat beside her. "Who do you know drives a Hyundai?"

As she looked at him with incomprehension, he expanded. "Whoever drove it disabled my brakes. Cables are disconnected, front and back, all the fluid's gone."

"Can it be fixed?" Sky took a mouthful of the whiskey; it burned her gullet but the effect on her stomach was miraculous, almost instant. It was hard to believe that someone had deliberately caused the crash.

"I carry most stuff," her father did not even sound angry, "but not enough brake fluid to be safe. And the cables are damaged. We'll finish our drink and I'll call someone. Guy that sold me that jeep told me for sure that telephone'd come in handy someday."

Sky's fright yielded to anger. Who would dare to do that to her—to them?

The same person who had dared to have a bullet delivered to her mailbox, of course.

By Montana standards this place was not far from Mayville and it should not be difficult to prove who was driving a Hyundai right now. She was so damned furious she could not even remember her fear. "Dad, when you make your telephone call, tell whoever's going to fix the brakes to bring pliers, rubber gloves and *new* cables."

"What?"

"Fingerprints. It's a long shot, I know, but maybe not so long. And may I use your telephone before you call anyone?"

When she reached the *Courier* offices, the breathless junior told her that the editor was out looking for the man who had delivered the Folger's coupons. "I'm assisting, Sky, but I can't stop to chat. I'm only halfway through my list of calls."

"Thanks, Lindy. Get him to call me at this number *immediately* you hear from him." Next she tried the War Bonnet for Lynskey, but he, too, was out. She left the number there too, and tried to impress on the receptionist how urgent it was that he call her.

The approach to Anaconda is dominated by the huge smelter stack that towers over the town. Not only that but, on arriving from Butte, the visitor sees first not the wonderfully wide parkways, and houses neat as buttons, but an enormous slag heap, almost big enough to be called a mountain. The city, proud of its illustrious mining past, had turned it into a tourist attraction, selling "bags o' slag" in its visitors center.

Jim Larsen had passed the slag twice, first on driving into the city, then on foot as she searched for anyone who had seen or heard of a black hobo wearing an indigo jogging suit.

He was on the point of giving up when he decided to try the shops and coffee bars one last time.

He got lucky. An old lady, walker by her side, was sipping iced tea at a table in Donovan's restaurant, a long, narrow room dominated by the buzz and ring of pinball machines near the bar. "Excuse me, ma'am." He waited while the woman lowered her newspaper, which featured a large photograph of Princess Di on the front page.

"Yes?" Her voice was slow and quavery, as though she had had a mild stroke, but behind the glasses, her eyes were sharp.

Larsen launched into his routine of questions but this time, instead of the blank stare he had received so far, the woman pursed her lips. "Yeah, I know the guy. He ain't here, though—he's working at a little bar up by Georgetown." Larsen could hardly believe what he was hearing. "He was there yesterday. My son took me up to the lake for my birthday and I saw a guy like that take out the trash. I remember because you don't often—"

"I know, I know." He just wanted to get going. "You don't see that many black men in Montana. Thanks for your help, ma'am."

He ran back to his automobile, passing a telephone booth on the way and wondering briefly if he should call in to the office to see how the young dipstick had got on. Maybe this black man was not the right one.

He decided not to call until he had checked it out.

By the time Larry MacPherson and his daughter were arriving back at the cabin in the repaired Diahatsu it was almost nine o'clock. Sky had supervised the removal of the damaged cables. Then she had used the pliers to place them on the backseat of the jeep and planned to put them in a freezer bag as soon as they got into the cabin.

Since leaving her messages, she had tried both the War Bonnet and Jim Larsen's home several times and was agitated at the lack of response. She considered calling a cop acquaintance of hers at the station in Butte, then reluctant to let go of the story without consulting Jimbo, she decided to hold off.

She was also aware that she could not expect Lynskey to call, at least for a little while: he was due to keep the appointment with the man called Matt.

Lynskey had been in the parking lot of the coffee shop for half an hour. But this time he was not working alone. With the seriousness of what was at stake, and with no jurisdiction here, he had informed his FBI contacts of whom he was planning to meet and why. Four agents, two to a car, had turned up but they were so conspicuous, in their clean-cut suits and conservative haircuts, that Lynskey despaired. If "Matt" recognized what was afoot he'd take off straight away. And Lynskey had no doubt that this man was for real. His federal contacts confirmed that no calls had been made to or from the Helena man since early that afternoon.

The agents wanted Lynskey to let them take it from here but he convinced them that he would learn more than they would and they agreed to hold off until he gave them the signal. Now they were seated inside and Lynskey hoped that in the homogeneous bustle, they might somehow blend in: it seemed to be a popular venue, not only for local teenagers but for adults as well. Tourists, bikers, and RVs were attracted to its vast parking lot and the free showers offered along with the steak dinners.

Before taking up his position he had studied the restaurant both inside and out, the bathrooms, all entrances and exits, and as much as he could see of the kitchen from the dining area.

Now, as he lurked outside the shadow of a giant Winnebago, he saw it was five past nine and although three lone men had arrived in the past twenty minutes or so not one had aroused his suspicion. One arrived in a pickup so battered that Lynskey doubted it could have made it even from Helena, and one, in a brand new Porsche, he dismissed as being too attention-grabbing. The third drove a huge twelve-wheeler loaded with candy bars. The graphic picture on its side of two children tucking into chocolate, made Lynskey's mouth water; he had not eaten since lunchtime. But then another vehicle arrived and his antennae twitched.

The car did a slow three-sided tour of the lot. When it was temporarily out of sight, Lynskey flitted over to the candy carrier and—the driver had left it unlocked—hopped into the cab. It was dusk and from up here he could see the faint sweep of the newcomer's lights along the perimeter of the lot until, at the far side, they went out. He shrank down in the seat but resurfaced to get a glimpse of the automobile driver just as he pushed open the door to the coffee shop: medium

height, probably middle aged, dressed in the Montana uniform of jeans, check shirt and boots. Then the restaurant
swallowed him up.

Lynskey counted slowly to ten and followed. He spotted
"Matt" immediately he got to the glass door. He was parking
himself on a stool at the counter and, with the plastic-coated
menu in his hand, was perusing the crowd. Out of the corner
of his eye, Lynskey saw one of the agents sit up a little
straighter as he came in and paused, looking around expectantly as if searching for his date. The man at the counter
registered his entrance and passed over him without interest.

All the stools but one along the counter were taken. The
man in the check shirt had sat between two pairs of teenaged
girls.

Lynskey strolled over. "Excuse me—Matt, isn't it?"

"No," the man replied shortly. "You got the wrong guy.
My name's Pete."

"Is it now?" Although every instinct was telling him he
had guessed correctly, the man's demeanor was perfect. "I
could have sworn your name was Matt," he continued pleas-
antly. "The voice is right anyhow. Although you never can
tell, I suppose, with those answering machines."

The man slid off his stool. "I said you got the wrong guy,
and I don't want to talk with you, now or in the future." He
turned on his heel but Lynskey was too quick for him,
catching his arm and squeezing hard. "Sit down there now,
like a good man, I want to talk to you. You don't want a
scene here, do you? Bring the police maybe in on top of us?"
He was much bigger and stronger, and the man yielded.
"That's better." Lynskey sat in beside him. "Would you like
coffee or what?"

"Forget it." The man was watching him closely.

"Very well, I'll have a cup of tea myself a bit later on.
Now, Matt, or Pete, or whatever your name is—"

The man jumped and ran toward the door but, as he did so,
all four federal agents leaped up to intercept him. Heavily
outnumbered, the man did an about turn and ran back toward
the kitchen. Finding Lynskey again blocking his way, he
brought up a knee, jamming it hard into the Irishman's groin.

Gasping with pain, Lynskey doubled over, knocking a
stool and its occupant to the ground. The man veered past,
pulling a small handgun from an inside pocket as he ran.

The four girls at the counter began to scream, as the four

FBI agents upset everything in their path in their rush to the kitchen.

Brandishing his gun, the man was still ahead of his pursuers. As he raced through the metal swing door an elderly porter, lugging a tray loaded with dishes toward the sink, skipped aside but the overladen tray crashed to the tiled floor. The gunman lost a precious second as, skidding on shards of broken dishes, he struggled to keep his balance.

Now the agents were through, their own guns out. The fugitive grabbed a young busboy and put the handgun to the boy's head. "Stay back," he shouted at the agents.

Everything stopped. The three chefs stood transfixed. A waitress who had been putting mash onto plates let the scoop fall.

The terrified busboy, who was only about fifteen, was too shocked to cry out as, breathing hard, his captor backed slowly toward the doorway away from the agents.

One of them, however, inched forward. Putting away his gun, he smiled. "We can work this out. Let the boy go."

"Stay away." The man pressed the gun barrel tighter to the boy's temple and continued backing toward the doors.

In the restaurant, Lynskey, although winded, nauseous and still racked with pain, half ran, half limped toward the entrance grabbing a handful of cutlery as he went.

Outside, he inhaled a lungful of fresh air, which, if anything, seemed to make the pain worse, but helped his nausea a little. He limped around the side of the restaurant toward the kitchen exit, praying he was not too late.

An overloaded cart stood a few feet to the left of the kitchen door and Lynskey stepped behind it. Almost immediately the door was pulled open and the gunman, with the busboy held across him like a shield, backed through. He was followed by one of the agents who had both hands in the air to show he was not armed. "Come on," he was saying softly, "we can talk about this. Let the boy go—"

"Back off, back *off*." "The gunman was in control but more jittery than Lynskey would have liked for the boy's safety. He tensed, ignoring the pain which still radiated from his groin.

As the agent stepped free of the door and continued to hold the gunman's attention, Lynskey came out from the shadows and moved swiftly up behind him, jamming the heel of a spoon into the man's neck as though it was a gun.

"Drop it!" Simultaneously, he grabbed the gunman's wrist, twisted it, and the weapon fell harmlessly to the ground. With a sob, the busboy broke free and ran screaming around the side of the building.

Two seconds later "Matt" was on the ground beneath Lynskey and the agent, just as the other three FBI men came rushing round from the front.

Chapter Thirty-three

At last! Sky, who had telephoned the War Bonnet so often she knew she was wearing out her welcome at the front desk, rushed to grab the telephone beside her father's CB radio. It was not Lynskey, however, but Jim Larsen. He had located the originator of their anonymous message and, while the man's grasp of detail was hazy, he was willing to swear that Midge Treacy's Volvo had hit his friend that night.

He and his friend had both been drinking earlier in the afternoon but no way, the man insisted, had either of them been drunk. They had been heading up the highway toward a barn Leon knew where they would spend the night. After the accident, the black man had made himself scarce—the law always made him nervous. But when he had heard on the grapevine that the woman who had hit him was not going to be charged and that his friend was supposed to have died, drunk on the side of the road, it had been too much for him. In Butte for a spell, he'd decided to do something about it.

"I have news for you too . . ." She told him about the brake cables and the Hyundai.

"That's going to be real easy to check." Jimbo was elated. "We have him, Sky. Well done."

"Shouldn't we tell the police?"

"I already have."

"Well, I suppose that means I don't have to go to Ireland." Sky could not decide whether she was glad or sorry. She had begun to get used to the idea and the trip, with Lynskey along, meant she could postpone any definitive thinking about him. It would be a different matter if he were to vanish across the Atlantic alone.

It's not over yet, Sky—I'd bet you a million dollars. I've been talking to Lynskey . . ." He hesitated.

"The rat. Why didn't he call me? I've left two thousand messages for him at his hotel."

"He's not at the hotel. He's actually gone up to Helena with a few of the FBI men. Turns out his warnings to you were well founded. I think I should let him tell you, though."

"Tell me, Jim."

She listened, dumbstruck, to how Lynskey had probably saved her life.

Sky was unable to sleep during the night of distressing self-discovery she spent under Larry MacPherson's roof. It was bad enough to have found her relationship with her father so wanting, but to compound her confusion Lynskey's long face and merry eyes were floating above her every time she woke. The guy was a twenty-four carat here.

But still he did not call . . .

As she tossed around under the tumbled bedclothes, she tried to find a way to categorize what was going on between them. The sex had been terrific, there was no doubt about that—her body burned with the memory of it. Good sex, however, was a long way from love; with her ex-husband it had been wild—and look where that had gotten her—and with Greg it had been good too, almost up to the end.

In the depths of that night, Sky's lifetime of sexual encounters paraded before her one by one, and pretty pathetic they had been, starting with the fumbles in the backs of T-Birds and beat-up Chevys during high school and college. The more sophisticated couplings during the early years of her career had been even emptier.

The greater proportion of those encounters had led to what she had thought then was falling in love. But her heart had been too quick and needy and the boys and young men to whom she exposed it had always been scared off. Until Randy came along. After him, she had bricked up her heart.

She had gotten by perfectly well without love for most of her adult life and she had a lot for which to be grateful. She had her career, which although it had its downsides, sure beat working in an office in Detroit or Chicago or, perhaps, as one of the army of women realtors who showed condos and split-level houses to couples who could not afford them; she lived in one of the most beautiful parts of planet Earth, with some of the best winter skiing on her doorstep, no pollution and a relaxed lifestyle. She did not need to be in love.

Fergus Lynskey, however, had made a mess of her carefully constructed defenses. Extraordinarily she had not recognized this at the time: the progress of the realization had been like a slow burn, smoldering on even through her anger at his deception—not to speak of his bossiness. She ground her teeth with frustration: she was not mad at Lynskey anymore but being in love with him was out of the question.

And yet, at three o'clock, four o'clock, five o'clock in the morning she did want to be in love with Lynskey. By six, though, when the alarm shrilled on the nightstand, she was afraid again. She looked at the gray-faced, tousle-haired wreck in her father's bathroom mirror and wanted to hide. From everything and everyone, from this editor who expected too much, from this father who expected nothing. Did she really want to run from Lynskey as well?

Suppose she did not run, her uncooperative reflection suggested. Suppose she trusted him and let him in? But suppose it did not work and he abandoned her? Anyhow he lived in Dublin, Ireland, she lived in Butte, Montana. "You're a goddamned mess, R. Sky MacPherson," she harangued the mirror, "do you know that?"

The sheriff of Mayville was shaving. Although his shuttle flight to Denver, via Billing was not due for take-off until early afternoon, he had always been an early riser because he slept badly.

As he regarded himself in the speckled mirror of his run-down bathroom, he was trying to retrieve the feelings of well-being he had enjoyed just twenty-four hours earlier. But that had been before his underpayment had arrived, before he had fixed the brakes of that jeep. Idly, he wondered what had happened after he left. Had the vehicle gone into that little river? He must make inquiries. Then, he remembered that he would not have time for that today, and cheered up: only a few more hours and he would be off on the adventure of a lifetime.

The bell rang and he peered out through the bathroom doorway. Outlined against the glassed upper half of his front door, he recognized his colleague. What could he want at this hour of the morning? "Just a minute, Ed," he called.

Hastily wiping foam off his face with an old towel, the sheriff stepped into his pants, which were draped over the side of the tub and, still in his T-shirt, suspenders around his hips, went to answer the door. "This is a fine time—" he

began, before he was hustled out onto the porch by FBI
agents, who read him his rights and handcuffed him. The
sheriff knew enough not to bluster or to deny. Instead, he
asked if he could be allowed to put on a sweater.

Minutes later, in the car, he offered to cut a deal.

Two hours after the sheriff had been driven away, in Helena
another man, seatbelt on, blinker flashing—everything
legal—was pulling out from the curb in front of the splendid
public library, into the flow of the morning traffic when two
cop cars screeched up beside him. In Chicago, a third was
apprehended as he walked toward his automobile in the
driveway of his house in the suburb of Park Ridge; a fourth,
waiting for his prescription dramamine, was taken out of the
line in front of the pharmacist's high counter in a drug store
in New York; a fifth was lifted as he answered the door of
his house in Nashville, Tennessee; a sixth as he was dropping off his grandson at the local high school on his way to
Dallas airport.

Three more members of the group named by the sheriff of
Mayville were temporarily missing, although American
agents called at both the homes and places of work of two:
one, who was a cop in the LAPD, would be easy to trace, but
in Santa Barbara, the plumber Joe Mason was not at home.
Single with no dependents, no one kept tabs on him except
for his answering service, which had recorded no callouts for
him that day.

At Jerry Flynn's huge spread north of Calgary, Alberta,
the Mounties came up empty too. Because, in the small
Immigration area at Dublin airport, the Canadian was
standing in the long line for people holding passports issued
outside the European Community. Of course, he was no
longer Jerry Flynn but John Mulqueen.

He had arrived in Dublin four hours late. After check-in at
New York the airline announced that the flight had been
delayed due to technical problems and, although the lounge
was comfortable and he had even dozed a little, he was tired.
He had not been informed that there would be an hour's wait
at Shannon before the twenty-minute flight to Dublin.

Momentarily forgetting that he should be blending into the
background, Flynn reverted to type and became irked at the
delays, and at having to stand in line for so long. And he was
also irritated that there was no special treatment for first-

class passengers in this dumb holding pen. He was fed up with having to listen to gabby Americans jingling coins continually in the pockets of their polyester pants and complaining about the way they did things in Europe.

Most of all, he was annoyed that his money and status seemed to count for nothing in the land of his ancestors.

He realized he was second next and snapped to. The American at the desk in front of him was still in full flow: "Why don't you get more people on these desks? Only two of you for two full 747s, for God's sake." The official was patient. "It's beyond out control, sir. One of the flights was late."

"Yeah, but Jiminy Christmas, look at this ..." The American waved at the line snaking behind him.

"I apologize for the delay," the immigration officer was unruffled, "but I'm afraid we're short-staffed these days. Enjoy your stay in Ireland."

Flynn's mouth dried as his own turn came at last. He touched his breast as though to reassure himself that the proclamation he would read for the world was still intact in his inside pocket then dropped his hand quickly in case anyone should notice. No one did, apparently. "Good morning, sir," the official opened the passport, "and what is the purpose of your visit?"

"Just a va-vacation." Flynn smothered his nervousness with a cough.

"Nice time of year for it. The weather's not too bad at the moment." The official turned a page in his Suspect Index Book and ran an eye through it. Flynn's heart started to thump.

"How long are you planning to stay?"

"About three weeks, I reckon." At least that had come out good and strong.

"That's grand." The official closed both the book and the passport and handed back the latter. "Have a pleasant holiday."

He was in.

He took the public bus into the city center and booked into a small hotel by the bus station in a rundown part of the city center.

Half an hour later, which was much later than it should have been, because holiday time was aggravating the chronic staff shortage in the public service, several new names and passport numbers were inputted into the Suspected Index Book, which was frequently updated by the Department of Justice. Flynn's name was on the list, along with that of a policeman and a plumber, both from California.

By that time, "John Mulqueen," wearing beige polyester pants and a new windbreaker in serviceable navy, middle-range Pentax hanging around his neck, had merged with the throngs in the streets of the capital and was strolling along Talbot Street toward O'Connell Street and the personal mecca he had heard and read about all his life, the GPO in Dublin, scene of the Easter Rising.

The only name not confirmed to the FBI by the sheriff of Mayville in his bid to save his own skin was that of Rupert de Burgh. The sheriff still nurtured hopes that as the Irishman was on the spot, if he could evade detection the plan could somehow go ahead. And like the rest of his group, the sheriff refused point-bank to divulge any detail of the plan or the motivation behind it.

Because she was so tired and stressed, the parting of Sky and her father that morning was quick and without the resonance she might have expected after the trauma of her disillusionment. As her father drove her back to the airstrip, he seemed again to have little need to talk or to have the smallest inkling of what had passed forever out of his relationship with his daughter.

Sky could not imagine now why she had wanted to talk to him about anything to do with her life. After she had blurted out that she had "met a man," he had not brought it up again and neither had she. "I'm sorry about your brakes," she said tentatively, when they were only a mile or so from the airstrip. "That was because of me."

"Forget it." He smiled his easy smile. "But it looks like reportin' is a much more dangerous game than I thought. Be careful in Ireland, won't ya?" She could see, though, that his mind was already miles away in his beloved wilderness.

The aircraft was on the runway when they pulled in beside the Nissen hut. Larry put her bag in her hand and hugged her. "By now, sweetpea, have a great trip. Love ya!"

"I love you too, Dad," she replied automatically as she hugged him back, then broke away to race to the waiting plane. Looking through her porthole window as the little craft took off, she saw that the jeep had left.

She had no time to brood as the trip was short and, from the moment she landed, the rest of the day took on a kaleidoscopic quality.

She half-expected Lynskey to be at the airport to meet her and felt vaguely disappointed when he was not. The hell with him, she thought, and yet, perversely, she longed to talk to him. Nevertheless, she put off calling and took a cab home.

To her surprise, the duplex was empty although it was not yet eight o'clock in the morning. She checked her mother's room and the bathroom: both, although neatened, showed evidence of having been used overnight. Sky decided she could trust her grandmother's assurances that she could look after herself. She was probably at the hospital.

In fact Elizabeth Sullivan and Daniel Treacy were in Choteau.

To Daniel's surprise, she had agreed with alacrity—"Everyone should try everything at least once"—to his proposal that they should take a helicopter to save time.

"Maybe this was a mistake." He watched her carefully as they walked from the lawn at the far edge of the grounds where the chopper had put down to the sanitarium building. The staff were expecting his visit so there had been no problem with the security, which was usually tight.

"Of course it's not a mistake. Daniel, only young people make mistakes. People like us just live what's left of our lives."

"Afterward, if you like, we can go down into Choteau itself. It's very pretty."

"That'd be nice but this is pretty enough." She looked around appreciatively and, seeing it through her eyes, he had to admit that the architects of the Teton Sanitarium had chosen their site well: the single-story complex was shingled with weathered cedar and blended seamlessly into the greens and golds of the prairie. This countryside was not spectacular like Yellowstone or Glacier: rather it was airy, rolling in wide swathes to the western foothills. It was the type of landscape that had lent Montana its affectionate nickname of Big Sky.

Daniel was nervous about seeing his wife. When he had

tried to work out why he was bringing Elizabeth up here, he could come up with only a visual image: that with death imminent, it was necessary to bring ends together, or to close off a circle.

Although he was endeavoring to keep it from her, he was not feeling well this morning and, as they walked slowly toward the facility, was having to struggle to breathe normally: perhaps the end was even closer than he had thought. "Are you all right?" She stopped. "Are you in pain? I can hear you wheezing."

"I'm fine, never better." He attempted to smile but the pain did threaten now: it rumbled like a gathering storm, and he could see he did not fool her.

"Let's sit for a moment." She looked around for somewhere suitable. "Over here." She took his arm and led him toward a raised flowerbed, the front of which was grassed. "Sit down, Daniel, we've all the time in the world."

As he lowered himself gratefully on to the coarse, spongy material which passed for grass in this part of America, memories of the soft, velvety grasses of his childhood in Ireland swarmed unbearably into his mind. "I know I promised I wouldn't be maudlin, but since you came here, Elizabeth, I can't stop thinking of all those years ago on Béara." Even as he said it he regretted it.

But she came to sit beside him and folded her hands in her lap. He had remembered her as restless and always moving, but in the years since he had seen her she had learned the art of stillness. "We can talk all you like, Daniel, and about anything you like. So long as you know that what was between us is long over. It's not gone, it's just locked away in time. Like those lovely sapphires you gave me: what was alive in them, what made them beautiful millions of years ago is now sealed in there and cannot change or grow anymore. Do you understand? I hope I'm not hurting you."

"You're not hurting me, Elizabeth." He looked at her lovely, tranquil face and wanted to cry: "You can't imagine how happy I am right now."

The the gods caught him in hubris and the pain struck like thunder. Although he strove hard not to grimace, she saw it. "Have you your painkillers with you?"

"I'm afraid I've taken as many as I'm allowed," he gasped. "I probably need an injection—" He doubled over as the spasm ripped through again, so powerful and all-encompassing he could not have located its site.

Alarmed, she half rose. "Daniel—"

"Hold on, it'll be over in a minute."

A third one. But then the pain rampaged away, leaving him weak and bled of energy. "I'll be fine now, honestly," he panted as soon as he could find his voice. "This is the way it is these days."

"You should be in hospital, Daniel."

"No."

She saw there was no point in arguing and did not pursue it.

They were about two hundred yards from the parking lot beside the first building of the complex and, although they could see leisurely activity as people came and went, they could hear nothing except the swift hallabaloo of a bee, gone as quickly as it came, and the faraway, oddly muted twitterings of birds that served only to emphasize the delicate susurration peculiar to wide, quiet spaces.

Although he was week after the onslaught of pain, he found courage. "Look, I've never apologized for your husband, Elizabeth."

She would have none of it. "It was all a long time ago. Please, Daniel, don't rake it up. We were all young and silly—at least, you and I were."

"I have something for you."

That upset her even more. "You've given me enough. And I want nothing at all."

"It's just something I'm giving back, really. It never belonged to me in the first place." From the inside pocket of his jacket he extricated the silver case containing her family photograph. "I've carried it with me everywhere but now I've no need to anymore."

"Where did you get this?" She had opened the case and was staring at the picture.

"I spent a fortune tracking down negatives through contacts in Ireland, but in the end, I did what I should have done right from the outset. I asked your daughter."

"Johanna gave you this?"

"Don't be annoyed with her, Elizabeth. I'm afraid I put a lot of pressure on her, and she's a lovely, soft-hearted woman."

When she asked, then, why he was giving it back now, he told her that it should be obvious. "I can't take it with me to the grave, can I? And, anyway the real you is now stamped forever in my heart—don't stop me talking like this, please." He had seen she was about to try. He gazed at the coarse grass now, matted from too much care and feeding. He was not afraid to die, but the prospect of leaving her behind, now that he had found her, flooded him with almost unbearable sadness. "Don't stop me saying what I feel, they're only words, Elizabeth. I don't have time now for anything but the truth." He thought he might have gone a step too far and risked a glance at her, but she was staring away, toward the shimmering sea of automobile roofs in the parking lot. There was something else he had to say and now was as good a time as any. "Did you mean it when you said we could talk about anything?"

"Yes." It was as though she knew what was coming.

He gazed at her profile, acutely conscious of the overpowering, musky scent from the carpet of wallflowers in the bed behind them. If she gave the slightest sign of abhorrence or upset, he was ready to stop. "I've a stock of certain drugs in my house." As far as he could see, she betrayed no adverse reaction. "When the time comes, will you be with me?"

"You're not asking me to . . ." Still she watched the cars.

"No. I just want you to be with me."

She dropped her eyes to her hands, still folded calmly in her lap. "What about the legalities?"

He had been expecting that. "I'll make absolutely sure you're not implicated."

"Can you?" She looked at him then, almost surprised. "Is that within your power?"

"I've thought it out, and I've talked to an attorney who knows about these things. You won't be anywhere near when I actually take—"

"Please don't say anymore." She blinked hard. "I'll do that for you, Daniel."

"I think it will be soon." When he felt strong enough, she helped him up and they continued toward the sanitarium.

Chapter Thirty-four

Once unleashed, the full might of U.S. authority swept not only through the sheriff's *ad hoc* group of conspirators but also the more formally organized and more mercenary band who worked for the Oriental woman, formerly of Vancouver.

Once he had been overpowered at the coffee shop, the woman's Montana lieutenant was driven from there to the FBI office in Helena. There, on being told his boss had taken flight, he had seen no reason any longer to be either secretive or chivalrous and gave enough information to engender predawn swoops on previously unknown houses in Anchorage, Los Angeles and Orlando. The FBI's sister force in Mexico had organized a similar raid in Mexico City.

In Ireland, to the chief superintendent's relief, the cattle smuggler had been intercepted on the ferry by one of their own men before disembarkation onto British soil—avoiding the humiliation of having the Brits do it and having to go through the rigmarole of extradition.

After that small triumph, however, they were no nearer to finding the drugs. The controller steadfastly refused to reveal where they were hidden. He would neither confirm nor deny any of the names put to him. The skipper of the *Agnes Monica* and the funeral home owner who had claimed the coffin had also been arrested but were playing similarly dumb.

As the demoralized Irish police demanded greater resources to handle their growing problems, a hydroplane touched down on the shallow, cobalt-shaded sea which surrounded Santa Tomas, so named by its new owner.

Between the Dos Abrolhos archipelago and the Brazilian mainland, from which it was less than ten minutes' flying time, the island, which appeared on no international maps, comprised only three hectares of trees and scrub. The small beach, however, which was shaped exactly like a cockleshell, boasted sand of the consistency and color of talcum powder, while the artesian well, which the Oriental woman had had bored, offered reliable fresh water. Regular as a metronome, rain fell every afternoon in February, enough to ensure a year-round supply. Except for that one month, the island's climate offered nothing but sunshine, sunshine and sunshine.

As the hydroplane coasted to a halt, a powerboat set off from the shore and the pilot threw open the door to the warm, slightly sweet sea breeze.

As she waited for the launch to arrive, the woman could see her house. Of modest size, but constructed from the most durable and expensive materials available in Brasilia and Rio de Janeiro, it was set back a little from the edge of the beach and surrounded by shade palms. To the right and left of it were similar buildings. The first was the servants' quarters, the second the storehouse, which also housed the generator; the third and largest served as hangar and boathouse.

For the first time in her life, the woman felt she had a real home, somewhere she could spend the rest of her days in comfort and solitude, unharried. Especially by such bothersome documents as extradition warrants.

The visit by Daniel Treacy and Elizabeth Sullivan to the former's wife was depressing. They found Midge alone in her room, and when Treacy made angry inquiries, he was told the paid companion had quit. At least, it was assumed she had quit: when she had not turned up for work and the manager of the facility had telephoned the motel in Choteau where she had been staying, he had been told she had left in a hurry and with no explanation.

Midge, who was still under heavy sedation, could not have cared less who was with her. Only semiconscious, she showed no interest in either her husband or the woman he had brought along. Instead, she moaned incessantly while mouthing a litany of words which meant nothing: *egg salad, trees in the middle, total wipe-out, black without walls* . . .

"I'm sorry," Treacy whispered. "I'm truly sorry. I don't know, now, why I brought you here."

"You brought me because you brought me." Elizabeth took his arm. "She must have been a beauty in her day."

Daniel looked down at this raddle-faced woman with thinning hair and cracks at the side of her mouth. "She was."

The woman in the bed sighed noisily and rolled her head from side to side: *shame and the old stuff, millions, trillions, twenty-five and little bread and butter* E

"Don't upset yourself, Daniel." She touched his arm.

"People liked her, you know." The face he turned toward her, already ravaged from his illness, was tragic. "She was gentle and kind underneath it all. Poor Midge."

They walked back to the front door in silence but as they emerged once more into the sunshine, they saw a police car. A young officer, pink with embarrassment, got out. "Mr. Treacy?"

"Yes."

"I'm afraid I have to ask you to come with us, sir. There are a few questions."

"Am I being arrested?" Treacy looked from the youngster to Elizabeth and back again.

"No, sir, it's just a few questions."

The businessman slumped visibly, then, recovering somewhat, "If I give you my word that I will report to the Butte police station within one hour, may I take my friend back to the city? She's a visitor and—forgive me, Elizabeth—" he smiled briefly at her "—quite elderly. I have a helicopter."

"I don't know, sir." The young policeman glanced nervously toward his colleague who was standing by the automobile.

"Call in," Daniel suggested. "Ask your superior officer. I'll tell you what—here's my wallet as security." He took it from his inside pocket. "It contains not only cash but all my credit cards." He smiled a little. "I won't get far without them."

Both policemen visibly shrank from the proffered wallet. "Do what he says," the older one ordered. "Call in."

Treacy's word was accepted, without the security of his wallet, and he and Elizabeth walked slowly back to the helicopter.

Sky was trying to persuade Teddy Morzansky to search the files—behind his employer's back—without telling him why. "Trust me, Teddy. Remember we pledged each other, senior year?"

"That's below the belt, Sky."

"Yeah. Come on, Teddy, just this once."

He did what she asked, most unhappily, but when he called her he was reeling. Nothing remained of Midge Treacy's records in the files of Collins Brothers' Funeral Home. "I can't understand it. Nothing like this has ever happened before and Melinda keeps *meticulous* files. I can't even find a copy of the invoice for the casket. This is extraordinary, Sky. What's going on?"

"Tell you later, Teddy." Sky was not surprised he had come up blank.

This had made him more curious still and she had had to improvise. "I thought, since I'm going to Ireland, I might do some research on a book I'm thinking of writing. You know, the Irish in Butte, that sort of thing? I have to dash, Teddy. Just remember not to tell Bill Collins I asked you to do this, okay? Or even Melinda. It doesn't seem proper, somehow, Mrs. Treacy being so recently dead and all . . . But if you do come up with something, if you remember anything you might have seen or overlooked, will you let me know? Jimbo Larson will have the number of the place I'll be staying at in Dublin."

"You owe me a big one for this, Sky MacPherson. Have a good trip."

Her grandmother arrived back at the duplex just as she hung up. Sky was struck by how subdued she seemed. "You've been at the hospital, Grandma?"

"Not yet, dear. I was hoping you'd drive me."

Sky changed her mind: She was more than subdued, she was sad. "Sure I'll drive you, but are you okay? Where have you been?"

Sky listened as her grandmother told her what she was sure were "edited highlights" of her visit to the Choteau sanitorium, and was simultaneously getting on with her ironing, putting the folded clothes directly into the suitcase at her feet. Then something Elizabeth said clicked into sharp focus. "What was that, Grandma? Mom gave him a photograph?"

"This one." From her purse, her grandmother pulled out a flat silver box, like an old-fashioned cigarette case, opened and passed it across the table.

Sky knew the photograph, but it was not that which made her purse her lips. She remembered Johanna's sudden flight to see Freda Little Calf when the subject of Daniel Treacy had first been mentioned. Her confusion when she returned. Now it was all clear as day.

When she and her grandmother got to the hospital later in the morning, however, she had not the heart to tax Johanna with it. Her mother, although still immobilized, proved fully alert and more cheerful than Sky could have thought possible.

Overnight, her room had been turned into what could only be described as a shrine: candles, their flames dim because it was full daylight outside, had sprouted like stalagmites from the windowsill and the bedside locker; favorite snapshots were grouped on top of the TV where she could see them easily, a huge pot of amaryllis scented the stuffy air, and over the bed, instead of the hospital-issue spread, was draped Hermana's fringed Indian shawl, which glowed with the colors of a peacock's tail. "Isn't it wonderful, Sky? I'm so privileged." In the middle of it all, Johanna, who could not turn her head, beamed like a lighthouse. "No pain. Not a twinge." Swiveling her eyes, she aimed a brilliant smile toward Buffy who was sitting beside the bed. "My lovely friend here went all the way to the reservation to fetch a herbal infusion from Freda Little Calf and it has worked wonders. You're amazing, Buffy. Do you know how much I value you?"

"Oh, hush." Buffy's pleasure showed through her embarrassment. "You'd do the same for me."

"Did you check with the doctor before you took it, Mom?" Sky had long suspected that Freda Little Calf's concoctions had less to do with medicine than with hallucinogens, an impression borne out now by the glitter in her mother's eyes.

"Oh, pooh! Of course we did, didn't we, Buffy?"

"They're quite understanding here," the other woman reassured Sky. "Your mom's specialist works up at the reservation hospital. He knows what's in most things and he says that as long as we tell the nurses so the conventional drugs can be adjusted, there's no problem."

Sky let it be: Johanna was lucid and happy, so who was complaining? If Freda Little Calf's potion could make her smile like that while it took away the physical discomfort, why not let her have it? "I don't want to change the subject, Mom, but Grandma has just gotten back a certain photograph . . ."

"What photograph?" Johanna looked genuinely puzzled and Sky suddenly had no desire to continue. Maybe she had grown up some in the last few days, but the emotional tension between her and her mother seemed to have evaporated. And she had a hunch it was not simply their separation since Johanna had been in hospital. She had no time to analyze it now though. "It doesn't matter. Grandma'll tell you. I'm sorry I can't stay long." She placed a bunch of yellow roses on the bedspread; in the face of the Bliss Sisters' loving and opulent care, her contribution seemed inadequate. "I'll put these in water before I go, but is there anything else you need?"

"Not a thing, dear. This accident has been such a blessing. I know now how loved I am. Just imagine, Buffy," again she turned radiant eyes on her friend, "my mother coming all the way over here. And we were just saying before you came in, darling, that I couldn't have a nicer daughter, isn't that true, Buffy?" Back to Sky: "And guess what, Sky. Francey called the hospital. He's told them to send all the bills to him. And Buffy and Hermana say I should let him pay because he can afford it, so I'm going to. Can you believe it? Everything's perfect, I'm so happy."

"Oh, Mom." Sky could have wept with guilt, "it shouldn't have taken an accident to make you feel loved."

But of course it had. And that was what had changed between them.

Hermana came in then to relieve Buffy, and a little later, Sky kissed her mother and left the hospital with the *bon voyage* blessings of all three Bliss Sisters ringing in her ears. "I'll see you later, Grandma—will you take a cab?"

"I will, yes." There it was again, that note of ineffable sadness.

It was as she was getting into the Nissan that Sky realized she had not mentioned her visit to her father and not one of the women had asked.

On the way back to the duplex, she zipped into the office of the *Courier* to pick up the passport and new charge card Jimbo had had delivered. "Oh, Sky," the junior breathed, eyes like saucers, "you're lucky you missed it here yesterday. It was incredible. You wouldn't believe the number of telephone calls I had to make—and isn't it wild about Daniel Treacy?"

"What about Mr. Treacy?" Sky, who had been practically running down the room toward the editor's office, came to a swift halt.

"Didn't you know? He's been arrested. Oh, and there's a message for you from Mr. Lynskey. I wrote down the number, he's in Helena."

Arrested? Before she could consider this, Sky punched out Lynskey's number.

All he wanted, however, was to make sure they were on the same flight out of Minneapolis that evening. Hearing his voice, and with so much having happened since she last spoke to him face to face, Sky felt oddly shy. "You heard about Treacy, I expect?" deliberately brisk.

"It's just a formality." Lynskey was cheerful as always. "The guy's not going to be charged with anything—everyone knows his days are numbered. Anyway, he's a victim rather than a perpetrator. Take it from me, he's more than likely on his way ome now."

"That's good. Hey, Lynskey, I hear you're auditioning for Superman."

"Perfect. You, of course, can be my Lois."

"Seriously, congratulations. You were right and I was wrong about last night. I'm sorry."

After a pause he was back. "Come on, MacPee. Don't spoil it. I can't stand good losers."

Behind the jocularity she could hear uncertainty. "What's the matter?" Glancing at the junior, she lowered her voice. "You can give it but you can't take it? I mean it. I'm sorry."

"Apology accepted." Again, that uncertain pause. "I'll talk to you on the plane."

"See you, then!" Smiling, she hung up and then collected the stuff from Jimbo. Then she was on her way.

Daniel Treacy went straight home from the police station. He was feeling vile: his medication was overdue. It had been humiliating to be confronted like that in front of Elizabeth—and it had brought back fears and memories he had thought long since banished. At least she had promised to come to the house for dinner. He felt so tired and low that he planned to take a long nap between now and the time he would have to shower. He would order in—he knew she would not mind. And food for him was academic now anyhow; the medication was so strong he found it difficult to differentiate between tastes, even the spiciest of foods. Everything tasted of metal.

He let himself into his chilly, beautiful house and climbed

the stairs, each step of which felt like a mountain. At least he would be dead before he was reduced to the indignity of installing a stair elevator to reach his bedroom.

He sat on the side of his icy white bed, breathing heavily, feeling every insidious little cancer cell traveling and multiplying and eating into every part of him. He could visualize them chomping and masticating and spewing out bits of him and deciding which organ they would feast on next. Death would come as redemption. He had not been lying when he said he did not fear it.

He had been lying about something else, however, during that blessed time when Elizabeth sat in his garden room surrounded by flowers. He had told her that now he had found her again he was happy to die. It has been the cliché of the century, prepared for the eventuality that she would not feel the same about him as he felt about her.

And so it had proved. But he could not be "civilized" or "mature" or "adult" about this. The knowledge that she did not return his love caused him such keen agony it rivaled the pain of the cancer. He was not happy to die, to leave her. Now that he had found her again, he wanted to cleave to her, for her to cleave to him. At rock bottom he did not care whether she wanted him or not. Given time, he could probably have led her into seeing she did love him, after all.

But, of course, time was the one luxury he did not have.

His stomach contorted with such acute pain that he cried aloud. He had been taught to take fast, shallow breaths during these spasms, rather as a woman is taught to do in labor. He curled up on the bed and started to count the breaths—one—two—three—four—five—six—seven—eight—from experience he knew that by seventeen the spasm usually waned—fifteen—sixteen—seventeen—

He waited but, instead of abating, the pain intensified. He grabbed his bottle of pills from the nightstand and shook two into his mouth, swallowing them with a mouthful of saliva. The pain became worse. He forced himself to start panting again, to start over, almost hallucinating now: one—two—three—four—five—six—seven—eight—nine—ten—eleven—By twelve the agony was banding his chest with white-hot steel and sent a rippling sheet of it through his upper arms and into his neck . . . his jaw . . . his head. Thirteen—

It was happening now. Please, not yet . . . It was happening too soon, too soon ... She was coming to dinner. One—two—three—four—

He grabbed again for the pills but could not reach them.

In stretching, his entire body seemed to rip open. He curled up as tight as he could, trying to contain the pain but it was too late. The pain had won. One—two, one—two ... He screamed aloud. One—two—

Then something, fireworks maybe, detonated all around his face and exploded through the back of his head.

Daniel Treacy died at one fifteen in the afternoon. His body, coiled in the fetal position on his blood-soaked bed, was found just after eight o'clock. His eyes were wild and staring; his mouth was wide open and contorted; both his fists were clenched. In each hand, like a fat white rose stained with red, bloomed a handful of the silk spread that covered his bed.

That night the paramedics, who lifted him off his bed and cut away the silk, opined to their wives that he must have had a most terrible death.

It was certainly the loneliest.

Sky's grandmother came home from the hospital to say goodbye and, at the last minute, on impulse and much to the old lady's delight, Sky clasped on the sapphire necklace, not caring if it looked incongruous worn with a white silk shirt and Levi's. "I'll keep it on all the time I'm in Ireland. It'll be my good-luck charm."

"Don't let Daniel see it," her grandmother warned. "I wouldn't like him to be hurt."

Outside, Sky heard the honking of the cab horn and threw her arms around her grandmother's neck. "Goodbye, Grandma, wish me luck."

"You know I do." Her grandmother hugged her tightly. "You're a lovely girl and I'm very proud of you."

"Are you sure you'll be okay here without me?" Sky stood back. "Your mother's friends will probably not let me alone for a second." Her grandmother smiled. "And I told you I'll be spending a lot of time with Daniel. I'm going up there for dinner tonight. To tell you a little secret, Sky, I might even stay over. Just one night. What harm can it do? I know I said I wouldn't but it would make him so happy. Don't tell your mother, though, will you? She mightn't approve."

"Mom? Not approve?" Outside, the cab horn sounded

again. "I have to run. Enjoy the dinner—don't do anything you wouldn't want the baby Jesus to see!"

Her grandmother laughed. "Get away out of that—you'll be late for your plane."

Chapter Thirty-five

Sky was half an hour out of Minneapolis that afternoon when she finally allowed herself to believe she was on her way to Ireland. She checked her watch: five o'clock.

Jimbo had been true to his word, utilizing his contacts to the fullest so that not only did she have a brand new passport and charge card, she had been upgraded from economy to business class. Now, as she sipped her drink in her wide, plush seat in the upper deck of the 747, she felt chagrin, guilt and satisfaction knowing that, somewhere down the back, Fergus Lynskey was having to jam his knees under his chin.

She had no seat companion, which was just as well because it was a long flight and she could not have beared to have to talk to some stranger. She had forgotten to bring a book and, although she had been offered newspapers and magazines, had decided that for once she would relax and do nothing. She stared through the window, identifying shapes—castles, a whale, a roller coaster, a crouching rabbit—in the dense clouds below.

Thirty-six thousand feet above the ground, she was even more nervous than she had been when trying to assimilate all the information Jimbo had thrown at her. At long last she was getting the chance she had dreamed about, but now that she was staring down at it, it was terrifying. There was no going back—not after all the moaning about how frustrated she had been for the past eight years. She prayed that she wouldn't make a mess of the story—and waste all the *Courier*'s money into the bargain.

To reassure herself, she placed her drink in the little indentation on her seat tray and reopened the wallet containing all the contact numbers Jimbo had given her with a summary of what she was supposed to remember.

She still did not know, however, what she was to look for when she landed in Ireland. On the telephone, this Éamonn

Vaughan character had been pleasant and sympathetic but
more than a little baffled; although he knew about the drugs
connection—he was working on it right at the minute—he
seemed unaware of any other big story brewing in Ireland
that might also involve players from Montana. It was clear
that he was not aware of the FBI's second wave of arrests
and she did not tell him.

Yet Jimbo, who had clearly been taken by the guy, had
advised her to confide fully in him. "You'll find you can
trade with him what you know for his contacts. He'll have
the best in the business and I'd be willing to bet he'll share
with you. You'll be no threat, being foreign."

Vaughan had been intrigued and had agreed to meet her.
That was a start.

Lynskey held the key to the story, both she and Jimbo
knew that. She was to stick to him like a leech. "Use your
feminine wiles." He had been quite serious. "After all, he
used you." Jimbo, great newspaperman and all round good
egg, had never been insightful when it came to affairs of the
human heart.

"You never told me how you got on with your father."
Sky, drowsy with the airline's alcohol, opened her eyes to
find the Irish policeman plumping comfortably into the seat
beside her. "How did you get up here?" She did not know
whether she was pleased or sorry to see him.

"The lovely Sherrilyn down the back in steerage said I
could come up to visit you." He was again the cocky, flip-
pant character she remembered. "I told her you were my
fiancée—"

"*What?*"

"But that I was just a struggling musician and your lousy
company wouldn't pay for me to go with you on your business trip. I told her we had only recently become engaged
and that I couldn't bear to let you out of my sight even for a
few hours." He grinned. "Want to join the mile-high club?"

"*Lynskey!*" Sky looked around involuntarily in case he
had been overheard, but all the other passengers were either
wired into their headsets or dozing. "You'd no right," she
expostulated.

"I know. Ain't I the limit? That's lovely on you." He
became serious and touched her necklace. "It goes really
well with your eyes."

"Thanks." Sky stroked the sapphires: they felt as smooth as butter.

Lynskey activated the footrest on the seat and stretched his long legs with a contented sigh. "This is sure the way to go."

"You'll have to go back to your own seat now, sir. We're about to serve dinner." The steward, who clearly didn't approve of social climbers, was standing in the aisle.

"In a minute." Lynskey brushed him off.

"Now, sir," the steward insisted.

"Listen, pal," the Irishman's voice was low and intense, "I shall go back to my seat in a minute."

Something in his eye quelled the other man who, nevertheless, leaned across him, "Excuse me, ma'am," and flourished a linen cloth over Sky's dinner tray. "We're serving *right now,* sir."

"I'll be back," Lynskey whispered, "or maybe you could slum it with me for a while?" Before he could say anymore, the steward arrived with the hors d'oeuvres, serving fork and spoon raised above his tray. Lynskey stood up. "I'll see you later."

As Sky watched him lope toward the staircase that led to the lower deck, Jimbo's instructions returned to haunt her: "Use your feminine wiles . . ." She knew it would be impossible.

The seventh coconspirator in the Bodenstown plot, the man from the Los Angeles Police Department, was being hauled down to the station in LA just as the eighth, Joe Mason, was pulling himself together for disembarkation at Amsterdam. Like the ninth, Jerry Flynn, Mason was traveling under an assumed name and with a well-forged passport. Although his sight was perfect, the photograph showed him wearing glasses.

Now, as the captain of the KLM jet applied his brakes after landing, Mason scoured his eyes as though he was rubbing sleep from them and put on the glasses. The frames were of nondescript dark plastic and the lenses were a little scratched, as though well worn.

Of the ten originally involved in the plot, only three now remained operational: Mason, Flynn, who was safely ensconced in his seedy hotel, and Rupert de Burgh. And of these three, only the latter knew what the prize really was.

* * *

The Taoiseach of Ireland, thinner than his love of good food
and fine wine warranted, took a tissue and rubbed at a dried
water drop that had marred the gleaming surface of his desk.
A man of fastidious personal habits, he worked until no trace
of the stain remained and then, task completed, he folded
the tissue in half before depositing it in the wastebasket
beside him.

The others in the room, two civil servants and two
advisers, a secretary and the Minister for Justice, waited for
him to speak. He had less than two hours to decide whether
or not to give the go-ahead for the republic's visit from the
heir to the British throne. Last night the visit had almost
been declined on advice from the department of Justice but
then, at the Taoiseach's personal request, a stay had been put
on the veto until lunchtime today.

It had been in Brussels, during an EC dinner, that the Irish
Minister for Foreign Affairs had been sounded out infor-
mally by his British counterpart about the Prince of Wales's
desire to pay a visit to Dublin for the Amnesty conference.
The issue was so sensitive that the Irish minister, not telling
even his most trusted advisers, had come straight to the
Taoiseach's office on his return. Only a few were aware of
it—the two politicians present, the Gárda Commissioner and
one or two others. Up to an hour ago even the civil servants
in this room had not known. Now, with only twenty-four
hours to go, the decision had to be made.

No member of the British Royal Family had made a
formal visit to Ireland since independence in 1922, although
some had slipped privately in and out of the republic, to
attend horse shows or to visit distant relatives. An appearance by the heir to the throne, however, was a different
matter. Although technically it would be a private visit, the
conference was high profile, especially with Naboom Kebele
coming, and there would be no question of the Prince's presence being unobtrusive.

The stakes were high: despite the IRA and Loyalist cam-
paigns which continued to roil on in the north, behind the
scenes relations between the British and Irish governments
had improved steadily during the Thatcher years, which
looked set to continue under John Major. This was a sensitive time: it was beginning to dawn on some leaders of the
nationalist community in Northern Ireland that perhaps the

way toward what they wanted lay not in violence, which, over nearly a quarter of a century, had produced nothing but more violence, but in democratic means. The Taoiseach had to weigh up whether the Prince's visit, even in a private capacity, would enrage Northern nationalists to the extent that this small opening in the blank wall of despair known for so long as "the Troubles" could be closed over again.

Like most politicians, who would happily claim public credit for a week of sunny days, he was inclined to look favorably on the idea. Opinion poll after opinion poll had reaffirmed that the British Royal Family continued to be a source of fascination to many in the republic and there was no doubt that this visit would spawn acres of newsprint. Yet, the consequences of anything untoward happening to the Prince while he was in Ireland were unimaginable: the Taoiseach's party could probably wave goodbye to domestic power for a very long time, not to speak of the loss of international prestige.

He cleared his throat and looked round the room. He was kept informed about the progress of the investigation into the conspirators discovered in the United States. So far, those captured had not revealed anything much but, like his advisers, the Taoiseach tended to agree that whatever the plotters were about could have had nothing to do with the Prince.

In fact, the whole thing was a mystery: it seemed to make little sense for people with ultranationalistic leanings to want to harm the nationalist seat of power. Yet, in the Taoiseach's experience, no one ever went broke underestimating the cockeyed fervor among certain far-out fringes of Irish America. "What do you think?" His eyes caught those of his Minister for Justice. "I'd let it go ahead but I'll be guided by you. You say most of these so-called plotters have been rounded up?"

"Seven at last count." The Minister for Justice lowered his voice as though they were being overheard. "Two more probables have temporarily gone missing. Five so far, would you believe, are cops or ex-cops."

"Doesn't surprise me." The Taoiseach flicked at a speck on his Boss suit. "With seven out of it I'd say they've collapsed. What's your best guess, Minister? Is it safe or is it not?"

"Well." The minister hesitated and then cheered up. "He's

only going to be here for a couple of hours. We can fly him in and out of Baldonnel," naming the military aerodrome twenty miles from Dublin, "and sure didn't even His Holiness manage to get in and out of here without a problem, and millions around him all the time?" The Pope's visit to Ireland in 1979 had been the highlight of the Minister's life. "I mean, what can happen in a couple of hours?"

"Fantastic—*fan-fuckin'-tastic.*" Jill Tuffy, the organizer of the Amnesty seminar at which Naboom Kebele was to be the star speaker threw the telephone receiver back on its cradle. She was so excited that she got up and jigged around the floor.

Amnesty was in serious fund-raising mode. Her invitation to the Prince had been one of those four-in-the-morning inspirations which, in the cold light of day, had seemed so unlikely to bear fruit that she had not nurtured even the slightest hope of his acceptance. But as days and then weeks went by without rejection, she had let herself dare hope the tiniest bit. And then the barrel had started to roll.

She sat at her desk, making herself calm down. The instructions were specific. Only four named people were to know that the Prince was coming. If a single advance word appeared in the newspapers about it, the whole thing was off.

How to get around that one was the problem . . .

There had been considerable local interest in the conference from predictable sources: all the worthy Irish newspapers were sending representatives. But Ms. Tuffy had a wider constituency in mind: she wanted a conference sexy enough to attract the world's media. She had been jubilant when Kebele had accepted, but then appalled that the international take up of press invitations was almost nil. Only *The Economist* was sending. Global media was looking to Eastern Europe and the election run-up in America. Africa, poor old starving, dying, waring Africa, was now old hat.

She thought hard. The only way to get them here without jeopardizing the Prince's appearance was to do a selective leak about a surprise guest. And if one bit, they would all bite—afraid to be scooped. She lifted the telephone. "Hello, RTE? Newsroom please—Éamonn Vaughan . . . Thanks— I'll hold . . ."

* * *

At the Natural History Museum of Ireland, half a mile away, the reaction to the Taoiseach's call was more muted.

The awed man who took the call from Ireland's Prime Minister gathered his thoughts sufficiently to say that the museum's director was in Iceland, "But I think I know where he's staying and I'll try to get him back."

When he hung up, he stared at the old-fashioned black telephone on his desk as though it had rabies. Then he went to the door of his office and looked down at his two-hundred-old domain, which slumbered quietly in a cramped narrow building between the Dail and Government Buildings. Generations of schoolchildren and their parents had thundered and tramped along these tiled floors and wooden staircases, marveling at the giant deer and the whale skeleton, suspended from the roof, horrified by the bullet hole in the skull of the polar bear, thumping the elephant and stroking the giraffe, or recoiling in disgust at the insect pinned to paper or the tentacles of the octopuses in glass jars. So old-fashioned and untouched was it that it was now world-famous as the best nineteenth-century cabinet museum extant: a large proportion of the collection, which had grown to encompass over four million specimens, had been donated in 1857 by Livingstone himself and was preserved intact. Naturalists and zoology students loved the place and, in teeth of modern museum display science, begged that it be kept exactly as it was. Apart from a major clear up and a yellow paint job on the walls a couple of years ago, they had been granted their wish.

In this man's lifetime the museum had never had a state visit from any important dignitary—none that made him or herself known, anyway. The problem with this one was that it was happening tomorrow and that the newspapers had been more than a little premature in touting the Eskimo curlew exhibit. With the cutbacks in public service biting hard, the staff, reduced now to four—which meant that the ratio of people to specimens was one to a million—were behind with everything: the top gallery, which housed the invertebrates and the priceless Blaschka Collection—handmade glass reproductions of marine specimens—had had to be closed off to the public for lack of personnel.

Perhaps they might be able to rustle up a modest exhibit, he thought gloomily—*very* modest exhibit: although the museum had the two birds, the documentation and habitat

material was far from ready. All stops would have to be
pulled out.

The man went back to his desk and reached for the telephone to begin the process of locating his director. He
brightened a little: after years of neglect—it was all archae-
ology these days—it was nice that someone was taking
notice of the lovely old place.

Jill Tuffy was on her second call, to a reporter in the BBC
television newsroom who had only recently moved there
from RTE. "No, I can't tell you, I really can't. The papers
aren't to hear a word of this, do you understand? But, believe
me, if you're not here you'll miss out on one of the stories of
the century." She listened, then, "Have I ever given you a
bum steer before?"

She sat back, satisfied. Whatever about Éamonn Vaughan,
she knew the BBC reporter, who lived with a *Guardian*
subeditor, could not keep a secret to save her life. They'd all
be here tomorrow evening.

Chapter Thirty-six

Sky's mental image of Ireland, fed by the Irish Tourist Board and her mother's sepia-toned memories, had not prepared her for Dublin's modern, swarming airport. The culture shock was intensified as she and Lynskey made their way into the city by cab. This was not the city of posters, where tourists clopped through misty, elegant squares in horse-drawn carriages or strolled hand in hand across a graceful, lacy bridge. Instead, this was a city where gridlock threatened, which seethed with crowds, preponderantly young, and where people took unleashed dogs with them into the center: the cab narrowly missed killing at least two which, kamikaze-like, darted across the street through the traffic.

Having come prepared with sweaters and raincoats, the bright sunshine, as hot as it was in Butte, was another revelation. Lynskey agreed the weather was uncharacteristic, which was confirmed by the number of sunburned shins and shoulders she saw under shorts and sleeveless dresses.

She sweltered in the back of the little Volkswagen cab, and debated crossly whether she would be better off with the window open or shut since each offered roughly equal horror. The outside air was choked with diesel fumes and the hot, acrid smell of melting tar, not to speak of dust from a plethora of roadworks and building sites. To add to the ambience, Gardiner Street, which seemed to be the main artery into the center from the airport, was either in the process of being demolished or rebuilt along its entire length: the thunder of pneumatic drills competed on equal par with roaring bus engines. When she closed the window, however, the heat became intense and she almost choked on the smoke from the front of the cab as the driver, despite a prominent notice on his dashboard thanking her for not smoking, puffed away like a crematorium chimney.

Sky knew she was tired—and irritable because of it—and

decided to suspend judgment on Dublin until she was in a
better mood. As they inched forward through a monumental
traffic jam at a complex series of junctions and bus stops
near the bottom of the street, she glanced across at Lynskey,
who, head lolling, was dozing. Why should he sleep while
she suffered? "I could do with a shower. How about you?"
She dug him in the ribs.

"Are we home?" He started awake and looked around, his
eyes clouded with sleep, then: "Ohh," he jerked a finger over
his shoulder, "that *is* where I live. I've an apartment on the
top floor."

Sky looked across him at the five-story brick block, neat
as a set of egg cartons, on the other side of the street. "Nice."

"No need to be sarcastic." He smiled and closed his eyes
again. The plan was that he would drop her at her hotel and
go on immediately to a briefing—or a debriefing—session at
his office.

It was coming up to lunchtime and the newsroom at RTE
was hopping. "Hold on, I'll transfer you to his extension."
For the umpteenth time that morning, the secretary pressed
four buttons and hung up.

"Yes?" Two desks away, Éamonn Vaughan, who had been
battering his keyboard as though his life were at stake,
snatched up the receiver as it rang. "What?" He put his left
hand over his ear, then, to the people nearest him, "Would
you keep it *down* there, please!" and into the mouthpiece,
"Sorry about that. What was that you said?" He listened,
then, "I see." Thoughtfully, he replaced the receiver. It was
the second so-called tip-off in as many minutes. And the
subject matter of both could not have been more uncon-
nected. He gave credence to anything that came from Jill
Tuffy but the second caller had been anonymous.

On the previous night's *Nine o'Clock News*, Vaughan had
broken the story about the botched drugs operation and
chaotic follow-up investigation. The morning papers had
seized on it with glee as the Guards continued to chase their
tails up and down the country. The anonymous informant
had told him that the drugs could be found buried in the
grounds of Glengarriff hotel. Glengarriff was in the extreme
southwest of the country: almost the full length of the
country lay between it and Killybegs.

After a few seconds, Vaughan got up and trotted off down

the length of the newsroom—he never walked anywhere—
toward the security correspondent. "Bella, who's the best
person to talk to about a tip-off in this drugs affair?"

"Me." She looked up, frowning.

"Yeah, you." Vaughan did not smile. "I know that but give
me a name, not the Minister, not the Commissioner, certainly
not the chief super in charge of the investigation. Someone
who'll cooperate with us in return for information."

"What information? You're encroaching on my territory,
Eamonn." He had gazumped her with the drugs story on last
night's bulletin, and she glared at him. "At the very least we
should be sharing the information. At the last chapel
meeting—"

"Sorry I asked." Vaughan turned and hurried back to his
desk. He thought again then, reluctantly, put a call through
to RTE's Cork office. He was as ambitious as anyone but the
story always came first. If the tip-off was accurate and the
police already on the way, he could not possibly get to Glengarriff in time to film. Better that a camera be there than not,
even if he was not behind it. "Be sure and call me back, even
if there's no activity." He said goodbye to the reporter in
Cork and checked his watch. Now he regretted having to
meet that woman from Montana. He had far too much to do.

Turning his thoughts back to Jill Tuffy, he pulled a piece
of paper toward him and quickly, stream of consciousness,
scribbled names of famous figures and world leaders who
might pose a security headache. The more outlandish and the
more unlikely to attend an Amnesty International conference
in a little country like Ireland the better: Yasser Arafat, John
Major, Mother Teresa, Saddam Hussein, Robert Mugabe,
Nelson Mandela, the queen of England, President Bush . . .

Vaughan was still adding and subtracting names as he and
his crew traveled to the city center hotel for a news conference. By the time he arrived, he had it down to three, John
Major, Yasser Arafat, Moshe Dayan.

As he was walking into the Shelbourne, he reconsidered:
John Major had been in Dublin for a European summit the
year before so his presence here was no big deal. But this
depended on what he was going to say—and a British leader
on Irish soil was always a prime target for subversives. He
put a question mark beside the Prime Minister's name and
decided to begin his quest with the British embassy, if for no
other reason than to eliminate him.

The conference was late starting and, taking advantage of the delay, he went to a quiet place in a corner of the foyer to begin making his calls.

The Prince of Wales was walking around a car components factory, being shown a machine which was pressing little disks out of a river of gray metal. He uttered appropriate words of fascination and was shepherded to the next stage of the process where the little disks were falling off a sort of waterfall and being lined up so that holes could be punched through them.

As the entourage moved along the production line, a palace functionary moved forward and murmured something in his ear. The Prince's expression did not change but at the end of the line, the managing director of the plant was told that, unfortunately, the Prince would not be able to stay for lunch. Within minutes, the directors and staff found themselves saying goodbye to their visitor on the helipad at the side of the plant.

The Prince's diary for tomorrow was blank. Officially he had a day off. In reality, it had been left clear for the possible trip to Ireland. Now that this was a going concern, the palace and Foreign Office officials were anxious to get working. Each syllable of each word—indeed, each emphasis on each syllable—uttered by His Royal Highness during the few hours he would spend in Ireland must be pulled apart and scrutinized by all sides. Although he would be speaking to the Amnesty constituency, the historical significance of his visit could not be ignored. It was still to be decided if he would say anything public during his courtesy visit to the Irish Dáil. And if so, what.

The officials, both in Britain and Ireland, did know that they had to build a visit to the Natural History Museum into the schedule. In the Prince's book, the attraction of seeing an Eskimo curlew was irresistible. Fortuitously, the museum was right beside Irish Government Buildings.

Rupert de Burgh knew that the story would break sooner or later about the Prince's visit but it suited him for the moment to keep it from his coconspirators. Given their depleted numbers, the scale of what they were unwittingly planning might intimidate them. He wanted everything so far advanced that it would be impossible to pull out. His Semtex devices were ready and he knew where he was going to deploy them. The locations would be made secure in advance, like all areas the Prince was to pass through, but this was where he himself would come in. The operation hinged on whether he could get himself assigned to that security detail and, so far, he saw no reason why he should not be able to swing it.

Laying his hands on the explosive had been simple. Under the guise of police research he had sourced it through an ODC—Ordinary Decent Criminal—in one of the Dublin gangs which had contacts with the IRA and who, he knew of old, would keep his lip buttoned. Anyway, de Burgh knew the chances of himself surviving unscathed were not high. At the very least, he was sure of jail so whether the ODC kept quiet about it or not, *after* the event, was irrelevant.

Never a great sleeper, the previous few nights had been so disturbed that he was having to resort to drinking copious quantities of coffee and eating lots of sugar to keep himself going. Yet this had its drawbacks since he could not appear jumpy or nervous with his colleagues. The effort to behave normally was a strain, and even his wife, who rarely noticed much and to whom he knew he was a puzzle, had asked him that morning if anything was wrong.

He had avoided projecting what it would be like to go to jail, to leave his family. Whenever the prospect entered his head, as it had a moment ago, he forced it away. He did not want to weaken. The Cause that had obsessed him for so long was omnipresent, like his own shadow; it had taken over the places in his heart that he knew other men reserved for their wives and children. De Burgh's motivation was higher and finer than mere personal gratification. To him, the Damascus conversion he had undergone, when he went to Trinity and learned the truth about Irish history, was as profound as a vocation for the priesthood.

Although he was fond of his children, and the youngest boy in particular, he had long ago ceased to love his wife—if he had ever loved her in the first place. She was quiet, with a calm disposition which he felt had a great deal to do with lack of imagination. She had been a clerical assistant in a government department when he had met her at a Gárde Club dance when almost everyone in his immediate circle was getting engaged. Hating her job, she, too, was surrounded by friends showing off diamond solitaires and clusters on their ring fingers, was eager to marry—and happy to

find someone interested in her. After marriage she settled
to bring up their three children efficiently and without
complaint.

Wearing his Walkman, de Burgh wrote busily, stopping
occasionally to chew the end of his pen, or to consider. What
the others in the noisy room did not know, of course, was
that his personal stereo was tuned to the tiny transmitter still
stuck to the underside of the chief superintendent's desk. Bill
Daly was in session with the Gárda Commissioner. He had
asked Lynskey to be present.

Through his earpiece de Burgh heard the tinny ringing of
Daly's telephone, and the chief answering. Then "thanks for
the call. No, no comment at present," the chief's voice was a
little indistinct as he sat across the desk from the bug, "but
we'll certainly follow it up."

"That was RTE." The chief spoke again. "A reporter in
Cork asking us about an anonymous tip-off Éamonn
Vaughan got in Dublin. Same tip-off about the drugs being
buried in Glengarriff, which was telephoned anonymously to
de Burgh—he's one of my men here."

Down the hall, de Burgh bent his head as though he could
not read what he had just written on his pad.

"Are you taking it seriously?" This was the Commissioner, who was positioned right over the device and whose
voice boomed as if through the cello stops on an organ.

"Are you joking?" Lynskey, viola, quite clear too. "The
same anonymous tip-offs, one to us, one to the media? Glengarriff's the last place I'd be looking for those drugs. I'd be
much more interested to know who's making those calls and
why he wants us to go down there."

De Burgh's knuckles whitened around his pen. It had been
a misjudgment to ring Vaughan: the only mistake he'd made
so far. But it was not insuperable. So they wouldn't go to
Glengarriff. Although he did not have much time left, he
would find another way to keep them thin on the ground in
Dublin. The Gárda overtime ban still threatened and
although it was not seriously affecting anything yet, with the
swelling crowds in Dublin city, would be bound to within
the next twenty-four hours.

"De Burgh, wake up!" To his intense irritation, de Burgh
saw rather than heard the other man standing in front of his
desk. Pointing at the headphones, the detective mouthed,
"Take those things off," as though facilitating a lip-reader.

"What is it? I'm busy." He lifted off one of the earphones while trying to follow the conversation in the chief's office through the other.

"You're wanted on the downstairs public phone." He was already walking away. "The fella said it's important—he sounds American. And he's on a public phone himself so he can't hold on all that long."

De Burgh had no choice but to go. He took off the headphones and slipped them around his neck as he left his desk. It would be too much to walk through a nest of detectives and not expect them to wonder at why he needed to listen to music while walking down a corridor and into the front hall to take a telephone call. It had to be Flynn: few people in Ireland could tell the difference between American and Canadian accents.

And it had to be an emergency. All of them had that number only for emergencies.

While he was on his call, the atmosphere in the chief superintendent's office had become leaden. "You know as well as I do," the Commissioner had put on his grave public voice, "that we have to keep up the pressure." All three men indeed knew it, and so did everyone in the country, because of the Justice Minister's personal crusade against drugs. "With the amount of bad publicity we've had in the past few days," he added, "we've got to at least be *seen* to be doing something."

"It is my considered opinion," Lynskey butted in again, "in fact I feel very strongly, that we should not take this tip seriously about a hotel in Glengarriff. Let RTE go off. If they find heroin buried under some fuschia bush there, well, they'll have their scoop and it'll be a bonus for us. These tip-offs are either hoaxes or an orchestrated attempt to get resources as far away as possible from Dublin. I don't think it's a coincidence that someone is trying to move us just at this particular time."

"For once I agree with this man here, but it's up to you, Commissioner." Bill Daly folded his hands and waited.

The Commissioner thought for a minute or two, then picked up his gloves. "On your head be it. If RTE finds the stuff we'll be made to look fools. About that other thing, at least make sure you've crossed every 'T.' I know what they've rounded up in America and although my inclination is that they couldn't possibly know about yer man coming over here, I'm still uneasy." He looked at a spot on the wall over his subordinates' heads. "I'm long in the tooth and I know when something feels wrong. Apparently this plumber fella has done this before—vanished, I mean. But the other one who's gone missing, Flynn, he has so far been a model Canadian citizen. I hate model citizens, you know. They're always the ones to watch."

"Going through the passport records for every departure from the United States to Europe—assuming he didn't necessarily fly directly in here—is taking a great deal of time," he said.

The Commissioner ceased his examination of the spot on the ceiling. "If it was up to me this visit would *not* be going ahead and I've strongly advised against it. In the name of God," he shook his head, "how can we manage it all? Kebele, the Prince of Wales—and the town hopping with rogues, pickpockets, all these conventions and dancers and tourists? And Bodenstown in the morning as well. But, then again, I'm only a humble policeman."

"Could we circulate a photograph of him, sir? Flynn, the one we know?" This was Lynskey. "I took one of him."

The Commissioner looked from one to the other. "Do that, I suppose—not that it'll do much good. He's rich, apparently. He's probably had a face-lift." He stood up, as did the others, then slapped the desk with his gloves. "Between ourselves, gentlemen, your man's visit here is going to be a political three-ring circus. They want to parade him like a prize bull. Which I suppose he is." He smiled for the first time since he had entered the office. "Geddit? John—Charlie—Bull?

"Very droll, Commissioner." Lynskey did not dare look at Daly. "Just one more thing, sir. What about our canary?" He stifled a yawn. "With those two still not accounted for, and since all the raids took place at exactly the same time, is it possible they were warned? The only reason I bring it up is I'm wondering if the telephones here are bugged."

"They could be." The chief superintendent involuntarily reached for the instrument on his desk and then withdrew his hand. "Certainly impossible in here, no one has access to this office. I lock it every time I leave it."

"Not even cleaners? The oldest gag in the book." Lynskey raised a cynical eyebrow.

"Have the whole place checked," the Commissioner interjected. "Phones, computer terminals, everything, even the light bulbs. And question all the cleaners, particularly part-timers. It's unlikely but taking the worst case scenario, if you *are* being listened to, have you said anything in here about . . ." He hesitated, then, "Operation Omega . . . I damned well hate that. Sounds like a bad film."

"The only time the name was ever used in here, Commissioner, was when you yourself used it not five minutes ago."

The Commissioner stared at the chief superintendent as though trying to ascertain whether or not he was being subjected to insubordination. Then he drew on his gloves. "Sweep the place and put off telling people for as long as possible. Just make your plans and put everyone on standby. No names until tomorrow morning. Until then they can be told it's John Major or someone—use your own judgment. What time is the strategy meeting?"

"Eight tonight."

"I'll be there. Let's hope the press don't hear about it before tomorrow."

Downstairs, it had turned out that Jerry Flynn wanted to tell Rupert de Burgh nothing he did not know already and the detective could have strangled him. This was what came of getting involved with geriatric idealists who had never before put a foot in the country. Constrained as he was by his surroundings, however, he had to watch not only his tone but his body language.

Jerry Flynn, or John Mulqueen, was calling from the bus station. He was expecting Joe Mason, due in on a flight from Amsterdam, to arrive into the hotel any moment. "Unless he's been arrested too. We can't do our work with only the two of us, Mr. de Burgh."

"We won't have to. I haven't heard that there has been any problem with that, but thanks for the call, Mr. Mulqueen." For the benefit of passersby, he tried to sound cheerfully normal. "Leave it with me."

Flynn got the message. "The reason I'm calling is to tell you that the flight was on schedule. And to check that the meeting is still as we arranged. Three o'clock?"

"As is. Don't worry. Thanks for letting me know, Mr. Mulqueen, I'll be in touch as you say. Bye now."

Before the Canadian could say anything more, de Burgh

cut him off and raced back up the stairs. As he passed the
chief superintendent's door, he nearly collided with the
Commissioner who was just coming out of the office. "More
haste less speed, detective." The Commissioner was not
amused.

Chapter Thirty-seven

Sky's initial impressions of Dublin city had changed already. Her hotel turned out to be a small private establishment located between two Georgian squares on the south side of the city where the traffic, although still heavy, was at least not intimidatingly so. Here, too, though, the pneumatic drills were hard at it: it seemed nowhere in the city was safe from them.

The receptionist in the little foyer was apologetic about the noise. "It happens every summer."

What was more upsetting was the reason for the drilling: apparently the water mains were being repaired and the hotel's supply was temporarily cut off. "It couldn't be happening at a worse time for us." The receptionist redoubled his apologies. "All our rooms are full—the city is crammed to bursting point with visitors this weekend. But they promise we'll have normal service by six o'clock. In the meantime we've put a jug of water and a basin on your dressing table, madam, so you can at least have a wash after your long journey. And please take this with our compliments." With her key he gave Sky a little card on which was written the name of a hairdresser's, just round the corner. "They'll send the bill to us."

The room was comfortable, if a little too lacy and flowery for Sky's taste, and it had a direct dial telephone and TV. She unpacked quickly and, as much as the limited water resources allowed, brushed her teeth and washed. Her appointment with Éamonn Vaughan was not for another two and a half hours and, too wound up for a nap, she decided to avail herself of the hotel's offer: with the long series of flights and the heat, her hair felt unpleasantly oily.

The hairdresser's, on the second floor of one of the tall

Georgian houses, was small and busy, but they could take her if she was willing to wait for a few minutes. While she sat in the tiny, overheated reception area, Sky selected the only Irish magazine she could find from the selection of publications on offer, although it was almost six months out of date. And she almost missed the fact that it was Irish because, oddly, the cover picture was a paste-up of Princess Diana and her husband who, superimposed on one another, were staring glumly in opposite directions. She was curious to see them used as a lead here: it had not occurred to her that, given the history of the two countries, the Irish would be interested. She opened the magazine but the article was standard stuff about marital difficulties, mostly speculation, and, to her experienced eye, compiled from features already published elsewhere: paragraphs about Diana's bulimia and lightweight tastes in music contrasted with Charles's more solitary pursuits of ornithology, an interest in nature and painting watercolors. Sky was turning to her horoscope to see if what it forecast six months ago might have been accurate when she was called to the washbasin.

She felt much better when she emerged again into the sunshine and, with ninety minutes still to go until her appointment with Éamonn Vaughan, she decided to take a walk.

She got no farther than a lovely little park, where among the flower beds, office workers on their lunchbreak lounged around on emerald-colored grass to listen to a poetry reading. The atmosphere could not have been more different from that of the city center during the cab ride in from the airport. Although the top storys of the terraced houses in the square were visible on all four sides outside the railings, and if she listened hard she could hear the muted sound of engines, among the trees and greenery, the poet, who was standing on a grassy hillock which provided him with a natural platform, needed no amplification and had to compete only with birdsong.

A bearded man in his thirties, with large, hypnotic eyes, he read love poems that spoke of secrets and dark longings, which did not seem incongruous beside the brilliance of the sunshine and the holiday poses of his listeners. Gritty-eyed, disorientated from fatigue and jetlag as she was, Sky was enchanted and almost forgot her one thirty appointment with Vaughan. Along the way she stopped in a bank to change her dollars into Irish currency. The girl behind the counter was helpful and, in response to questions about the public telephone system, offered to give her a bag of the coins she would need but recommended that she purchase telephone cards, which were now in wide use.

When she got to the Conrad Hotel, situated across the road from a large concert hall advertising an Amnesty International rally for the following evening, she saw that it rivaled any such establishment she had encountered during her days in Chicago. Resplendent with modern plush, polish and glitter, it was far beyond anything she had expected in Dublin.

She was early so she went to the foyer shop and bought a fifty-unit telephone card, then sat in a squashy couch behind an enormous flower arrangement and began to search the face of every man who entered for a resemblance to the description Vaughan had given her over the telephone. She need not have worried. She would have known he was a reporter by the anxious way he came into the lobby, eyes searching before the door swung closed behind him. "Mr. Vaughan?" She stood up and was rewarded by a clearing in the thicket of lines along his forehead.

"You must be Miss MacPherson."

"Sky, please."

"Éamonn." He headed up the stairs toward a mezzanine area, leaving her no choice but to follow. "Sorry I'm late and I'm afraid I don't have much time. I was covering a new conference at the Shelbourne down the road. We should have met there, only I didn't know where to find you—Coca-Cola, please," this to the girl behind the small bar at one end of the mezzanine, "how about you, Sky?" He was dressed in a snappy suit and his shoes were polished; TV reporters here obviously dressed as formally as at home. And she was glad she had shed her jeans in favor of a wrinkle proof summer dress.

"The same." She nodded at the girl.

"How can I help you?" He obviously believed in wasting not a second. "Are we on or off the record?"

"Whichever you want." Vaughan shrugged.

"Off." Sky took a deep breath. "What I'm proposing to you is that we work together. I have some leads into two stories that connect Montana and Ireland."

"We already know about the drugs connection."

"Do you know about the second one?" Their Coca-Cola arrived and she insisted on paying.

"Try me." He grimaced and took a slug from his glass. "What is it about Montana, all of a sudden?"

"The deal is," Sky did not want to let him think too much, "I give you my leads in return for your help with local contacts. We progress the stories together and, if it works for us, we break them together, me in the States, you here."

"That's the kind of offer I've never had before. I must admit it's original."

"Well, have we a deal?"

"Is this something I couldn't find out by myself?"

"I don't know. But before I go any further, I need you to agree—even if you're not interested—to keep this between us. That you will not run with it by yourself. If you pass on what I'm going to tell you, I'll have to start over with another reporter." She dredged up what she hoped was a charming smile.

She had succeeded in making him curious. "Give me a hint anyway." He swizzled the ice around his glass with the tip of his finger. "I give you my word that if I'm not interested I won't queer your pitch. But I must warn you that as I'm an employee I can't go haring off on my own."

Sky decided she had no option but to trust him. As quickly as she could, she told him everything she knew about the conspirators.

"Any more?" He looked at his watch as though to remind her that his meter was running.

"We know that the police here are on to something," she refused to rush, "enough to send one of their detectives to Montana to snoop around. That's how I got involved. Something I'd written caught his eye."

"Who'd they send?" He was definitely interested now.

"A man called Fergus Lynskey. You know him?"

"Not socially. I know of him—the names of all those Branch men pop up in court reports."

"I mentioned terrorists to him and he didn't jump out the window denying it. All the people they've rounded up have Irish names, seven at last count from various states. But here's the interesting thing, Éamonn. Even *before* these guys get arrested, Lynskey suddenly decides to come back. He was on the same flight as me and he didn't even go home to change his clothes. He went straight into his office."

"How well do you know him?"

"Fairly well." Sky managed to keep a straight face. "I'm meeting him again quite soon—apparently his office is near this hotel and he said if I waited for him here after our appointment, he'd come to collect me."

"Don't tell him you're talking to me, all right? Not yet." Vaughan pulled out a notebook. "Have you got the names of these people who were picked up in the States?"

"Only one so far but my editor will have the others when I next call him." Vaughan noted the sheriff's name and the states and cities where the other six were brought in.

"We have a starting point, I suppose." He looked dubiously at the scribble in his notebook. "Any idea if anyone's involved in this country?"

"Not yet but it would stand to reason, wouldn't it? Anyway, it's your turn now. Will you point me toward some people who might know something about the kind of area we might be talking about?"

"I will, but funny enough, you're timing could be brilliant. I've just heard something else which might turn out to be interesting but it's my turn to insist that you keep something under your hat—not for long. If my hunch is correct it'll be all over the shop soon. I don't think it's connected with either of your stories. There's someone very big and hush-hush coming here for that Amnesty rally in the hall across the road. I've been ringing the embassies—the British embassy was so coy I'm beginning to believe I'm on the right track."

"Who do you think it might be?" Sky stifled a sigh. If it turned out to be a story, she could cover it but the thought of all the work ahead was already overwhelming. He told his ideas and then the names of his contacts. "I'll leave it to you to be discreet. You don't want to alert them by asking too many questions. If you get anything you'll ring me immediately? Here's my mobile number . . ."

He watched her write this, then cocked his head to one side. "Maybe you could help me with your friend, Lynskey, on the identity of Mr. Big at the Amnesty conference. Where can I find you later?"

She told him where she was staying.

They arranged that she should come out to RTE at
around seven that evening for them to compare notes and
he hurried off.

Sky decided to call Jim Larsen collect while she waited
for Lynskey to pick her up. It was just after six a.m. in
Montana and she knew that he was an early riser. The hotel
operator came back to her, however. "It's an answering
machine, madam, no one there to accept the charges."

She should have remembered: both Jimbo and his wife
always began their day with a run. "Thank you. I'll call
again later."

She toyed with the idea of calling home but decided
against it. It was far too early, and her grandmother, *if* she
was there, might think she was checking up on her. Although
Sky did not see herself as romantic or sentimental, she had to
admit that the notion of two old people getting together
again after all these years was a blast. The only sad part
was that, with Daniel Treacy's illness, they would not have
much time.

She was about to return to the couch where she had waited
for Éamonn Vaughan when she decided she might as well
use the time until Lynskey came. It took her a while to
master the intricacies of the Irish telephone directory—and
then she ran up against the Irish lunch hour. It was now just
after two but incredibly, after five calls, she had still not
found anyone at a desk. The sixth switchboard operator who
was a friendly soul, confided that with the sun splitting the
stones, as it were, people were finding it hard to work. "But
he's not due back until two fifteen at the earliest anyway,
love."

"How long do people normally take for lunch?" Sky was
bewildered.

"Well, *technically* we're all supposed to take an hour and
a half, but no one really minds a few extra minutes, especially on a day like this. Will I give him a message for you?"

"No thank you. I'll call back later." An hour and a half for
lunch, never mind longer, was such a bizarre idea. She had
never been very interested in food and would not have
known what to do with all that time.

Still no sign of Lynskey. She looked up the Amnesty
number in the directory and, ignoring the man in line behind
her, who sighed ostentatiously, punched it out. Then she

changed her mind, "It's all yours, sir, sorry I've been so long," and retrieved her card.

She would go across the street to the concert hall. If the rally was tomorrow evening, there would surely be someone around making last minute arrangements.

Chapter Thirty-eight

The foyer of the National Concert Hall was airy, lofty and virtually deserted, although a few people dawdled at tables in the coffee shop. The girl at the box office pulled her longing gaze away from the sunshine outside when Sky approached.

As far as she knew, she said, none of the Amnesty organizers were around—"No, wait, I tell a lie, there she is," pointing across the foyer at a woman just leaving the coffee shop.

"Excuse me." Sky ran over to intercept her.

"Yes?" The woman, petite and curly-haired with merry black eyes, stopped on the steps in front of the doors.

Sky established she had the right person and introduced herself. She came straight to the point. "I hear you're having some VIPs here tomorrow evening?"

"What paper did you say you represented?" The woman fiddled with one of her glass earrings.

"The *Butte Courier*—you won't have heard of it, Miss Tuffy, it's in Montana, U.S.A."

"I can hardly believe it. That didn't take long." The woman laughed. "Well, you're right there—er ..." she glanced down at Sky's card ... "Miss MacPherson. We do have an exciting evening ahead of us. Would you like some of our literature?"

"Could I ask you who is coming?" Sky took out her notebook.

"Naboom Kebele—" The woman stopped, looked sidelong at Sky.

Pen poised, Sky looked politely interested. "Yes, I saw his name on your poster—and anyone else?"

"You didn't come here especially for this, did you?" The woman's expression was skeptical.

"No, I'm afraid not."

"Do you know any of our local hacks? Éamonn Vaughan, for instance? Or anyone at the BBC in London?"

"No. I was passing and saw your notice."

"So where did you hear we had someone big coming? Apart from Naboom Kebele, I mean."

"Oh, word travels," Sky improvised. "Let's just say that although you've never heard of my newspaper, many people have." Inside her shoes, her toes squinched with embarrassment: she could not believe she was behaving like this.

"Let's put it this way, Miss MacPherson," Jill Tuffy said slowly, "if you're here tomorrow evening about fifteen minutes before our meeting begins, I'll personally give you a briefing. I'm *dying* to give you a briefing." She dropped the façade of detachment. "You won't be disappointed, honestly. He's really going to be big news—" She stopped, realizing she had just confirmed that it wasn't a woman.

Sky pretended she had not noticed. "Montana is eight hours behind, and if this person is really as newsworthy as you say, we'll be scooped by the East Coast papers. You couldn't give me just the tiniest hint?"

"All I can say," the Amnesty woman hesitated again, "is that this person has never been here before. And no one, in the republic of Ireland especially, ever thought they'd see the day when h—this person'd set foot here. I can't say anymore—I've said too much already."

Sky agreed to meet her before the conference, although she doubted that she would be there, depending on whether she found bigger fish in the meantime. As she stood on the curb waiting for a gap in the traffic to cross back to the Conrad, she saw Lynskey. Her heart leapt and she quelled it instantly.

He spotted her and waved but as he got closer she saw that instead of the cocksure man-about-town image he normally projected, he looked harassed. "Have you had your lunch?" He kissed her cheek.

"The whole of Ireland is having lunch as far as I can see."

He did not respond but took her arm and propelled her, none too gently, along the street. "We'll go to O'Dwyers, they'll do us a decent sandwich."

"Whoa." She pulled her arm away. "What's the rush? Maybe I don't want to go to O'Dwyer's. I've work to do."

"Oh, yeah, sorry. Look, will you not come for just ten

minutes, Sky? I could do with a bit of decent company." He looked so dejected she capitulated.

The pub, which was done—or redone—in lots of shiny brown wood, was less than half full. Lynskey remembered to consult her before ordering and, on his advice, she decided to try a glass of Guinness. When it came, however, she found its unusual nutty taste and thick texture quite unnerving. "Is this very strong?"

"One glass won't do you any harm." He took a deep swig from his own pint glass. "It's great for the old nerves. How did you get on with Vaughan?"

She told him, selectively, but realized he was not listening when he reached out and touched the sapphires. "They really are beautiful."

Her body, reacting to his touch, told her what was happening between them as he stroked not the sapphires but the skin underneath. Sky had noticed before that air travel always heightened her sexual desire and perhaps it was this, rather than his fingers, which sent all the old signals. Whatever the source, she wanted him badly right now. "Stop it, please."

"Stop what?" He ignored the plea and, leaning forward, kissed her.

"This isn't fair." She glanced around but no one in the bar was paying them any attention. She looked him directly in the eye. "You know we can't—we're both too busy."

"Your hotel is only ten minutes away."

"I have to *work*, Lynskey."

"Do you think I don't?"

She could almost see the sparks in the air, could certainly feel them.

They sat facing one another. The barman came over, heel tips pounding on the wooden floor. "Two ham and cheese?" He put the sandwiches on the counter.

"Thanks." Lynskey did not remove his gaze from Sky. "Just leave them there, we'll be back for them later."

He put a handful of money on the counter and they slid off their stools in balletic unison. They did not speak again until they were in bed.

The young widow of the van driver killed in the crash in Killybegs was frantically weeding a flower bed in her front garden. She could not stand to stay in the house, was finding it increasingly difficult to deal with the well-meaning but upsetting and never-ending expressions of concern from everyone around her. She had no privacy: every member of her large extended family was inside, drinking tea and discussing her future. Tears—of grief and of anger against the world, her husband and God—dripped down her nose as she wrestled with a stubborn dandelion root, bigger than a carrot. It broke in two as she pulled and she cried aloud with frustration.

She straightened up to push the hair out of her eyes and saw, coming along the road toward her, the skipper of the *Agnes Monica*, who had just been released from the Gárda station for lack of hard evidence against him. Judging by his expression, he seemed to be coming to offer sympathy.

The heart of the driver's wife exploded with hatred and jealousy that he was alive and free and her darling husband was dead, imprisoned for ever in a wooden box.

She ran inside.

The hotel bar where Rupert de Burgh met his American and Canadian coconspirators had been renovated recently and was too open for comfort: the hotel, booked by the Canadian, was also too close to Store Street Gárda station. It was one detail de Bugh had overlooked. He took the two men across the street into Connolly railway station. Here, the crowded platform café smelled like a cattery.

He ordered three coffees and brought them over to the table he had managed to secure. Flynn was carrying a brand new Adidas sports bag, which he clutched to him as though it contained pearls without price. Never having met the Canadian before but knowing him to be wealthy, de Burgh had been taken aback at the man's chicken neck, skinhead haircut and cheap clothes. His eyes were sharp and clear, however, and de Burgh knew that, appearances notwithstanding, this man had to be more formidable than he appeared and that it would be a mistake to underestimate him.

Joe Mason was almost exactly as he remembered, burly and pot-bellied, with a long, Connemara man's face, the genes of which always seem to survive from generation to generation. De Burgh's assessment of him, formed during that long night of talk in California, was that he was intelligent but pigheaded, always a dangerous combination.

"What's in the bag?" he asked Flynn.

"My wallet and stuff. I just thought it would look touristy."

"It does that. We mustn't stay too long." He passed out the coffee. "I have the parcels for you." He had brought with him a suitcase in which he had packed two pistols and two semiautomatic machine guns, together with ammunition. "Both of you know how to use the hardware?"

"I got tutoring," Flynn announced.

"I know them, no need to ask how." Mason grimaced on tasting the coffee, gray and weak as dishwater.

"You're aware that these are backups." De Burgh sized up a couple of new arrivals, who took the table next to them, then lowered his voice. "They will be loaded, of course, but I hope you won't have to fire them."

Of course you won't, he thought, lifting his coffee cup to his lips. *You won't know what you're going to do until I tell you tomorrow morning . . .*

He spoke then over the rim of the cup without moving his lips. "The details of the Bodenstown timetable, who's going to be there, all the rest of it, are in the bag too. You've seen the place already?" He turned to Flynn.

"I was out there this morning and Mr. Mason and I are going again later this evening. A lovely spot, I must say, with the hills in the background, although," he frowned, "my cab driver had difficulty finding it. Imagine! One of our national shrines and he'd never been there."

He paused, then went on: "Something is bothering me, Mr. De Burgh. I'll be blunt. Bodenstown cemetery is quite an open venue, far more open than I had imagined. Are we engaged on a fool's errand? Can the three of us do what was planned for ten?"

De Burgh studied both men. Both pairs of eyes facing him had one thing in common: the subdued glitter of fanaticism. "Let me be equally blunt." He pushed away his cup. "It's not going to be easy and the situation has drastically changed but if our plan is to make a point, a *strong* point, which will have serious impact, then yes, we can still do it. Although the police presence will be substantial, because of the presence of known subversives in the march, no one expects trouble at Bodenstown these days. We will be armed and we will have the element of surprise on our side." He paused to let that sink in and, to his satisfaction, saw them exchange glances. "But it's up to you," he went on. "You will be the ones in the front line. Please don't feel we have to continue. There'll be another day."

They looked at one another. "I believe someone has to do something. We have stood by long enough." This was Flynn, his conviction absolute.

Mason was more circumspect. "I suppose I've nothing to lose," he muttered finally, "and I agree that someone has to stand up and be counted. But I'm not so sure now that we'll succeed . . . With only three of us . . ."

De Burgh was alarmed. He needed both of them as diversion if his own scheme were to have any chance of success. "Let's not make any decisions until I have the final list of who's going to be there." He hoped he sounded soothing. "And we needn't make our minds up tonight. Nothing is so far advanced that we can't pull back if you're too nervous to go ahead. I'll be in touch after a meeting I have to go to tonight at eight o'clock. And I'll come to see you tomorrow, early as we arranged. You found the pub all right?" Their last meeting was to be in an early house quite near their hotel which, given that it would be a Friday morning, was guaranteed to be swarming with customers.

"Okay by me." Flynn spoke again, but Rupert noticed that Mason said nothing. "Right." He stood up. "We'll talk later." He glanced at the tables around to check that no one was listening. He raised his voice. "Have a safe journey now . . ." Leaving the suitcase at Flynn's feet, he walked out of the café and down the steps into the echoing station.

He had waited too long to let the Prince slip through his fingers now, and it was far too late to recruit more help. He *had* to keep these two on his side—without them he had little chance of success. From the outset he had never considered letting them go through with the original plan. They might have captured the Taoiseach for a few minutes, even have read their proclamation. But even if all ten were to have launched the Bodenstown operation de Burgh knew far better than his transatlantic partners how their actions and declarations would be received by the rest of the world. Their notions of Ireland had been preserved in amber for generations whereas what he had planned with the Prince was in the realms of *realpolitik*.

He would reveal the role they were to play only at their final planning meeting tomorrow morning and was confident he could persuade them to stay with him. But before he did

he needed to know exactly when the Prince would be visiting
the National History Museum. It was there that he planned to
make his final move.

Perhaps part of what made their lovemaking so special was
that it always took place in inappropriate circumstances. Sky
rolled over and pushed her hair, damp and sticky again, out
of her eyes. As she lifted her elbows, she loved the way the
skin all along her flanks tightened, the way every inch of it
felt as pliable as silk. Luxuriating in the sensation, she
stretched up one arm until it was at right angles to the
shoulder, then the other. Her thoughts drifted like straw on a
quiet lake.

She should be getting dressed: she was due to meet
Vaughan in less than an hour. Her clothes, Lynskey's too,
lay scattered to the four corners of the room, which was
dappled with lace-diffused light from the room's two sashed
windows. She had packed only two summer dresses and
hoped idly that the one lying crumpled on the floor was still
wearable. Now, however, she did not care, wanting to float
on and on like this into gentle, lengthy sleep.

Lynskey, lying on his back beside her with legs spread,
was only now recovering his breath. "Jesus, Mary and
Joseph," he breathed, "I thought that would never stop, I
thought I was dying . . . That was the best." He levered himself up on one elbow and kissed her shoulder. "You're
amazing. *We're* amazing."

"Mm." She nuzzled his damp collarbone. "By the way
who's the mystery VIP coming to the Amnesty meeting?"

He looked at her in dawning horror and then recoiled as
though he had been shot. "This is not clever, Sky."

She had not meant to say it, but now that she had let it out
there was no going back. "Just tell me, please, Fergus." She
attempted to stroke his back. "Had it anything to do with
why you were sent to the States?" She, too, got up on one
elbow and cuddled in to him.

"This is not fair," he cried passionately, shaking her off
and sitting up. "You know I can't tell you." He reached for
his shirt and started to put it on.

"Come on, Lynskey." Her sense of languor was fast evap-
orating and she was becoming annoyed. "It's no big deal.
You know you did the exact same thing to me in Butte. You
milked me about Daniel Treacy."

"Are you saying the only reason we did what we did just now is because you wanted to get information out of me?" He faced her, incredulity lengthening his already long face.

"Aha!" She sat up too. "So now we're getting to the truth! Are you saying the same about what we did in my bed in Butte?" They glared at one another, recent intimacy banished—or too painfully bared, Sky could not tell the difference.

Lynskey looked away from her toward the window and sounded almost lonely. "You've got it the wrong way round, Sky. The French have a saying about this kind of thing. Something about the woman should ask for what she wants before, the man after . . ."

While he was going along the corridor to his desk at Gárda headquarters, Rupert de Burgh was appalled to see a man he recognized from outside his work environment. Just vanishing into the chief superintendent's office was a professional security expert whom he had seen at computer and electronics exhibitions. Rupert, in whose imagination that lethal piece of gum under the chief's desk now grew as big as a rhubarb crown, could think of only one explanation for his presence.

But having caught only a glimpse, he did not know if the expert had been carrying his equipment. Before he had thought out what he was going to say, he found himself knocking at the chief superintendent's door.

"Just a minute," the chief called from inside. After a pause, the door opened. "Oh, it's you, de Burgh," he seemed hassled, "what do you want?" De Burgh took a lightning glance over the chief's shoulder, but could see no equipment. "Sorry, sir," he mumbled. "I see you're busy, I'll come back." He backed away and then half ran toward the office he shared with the others.

"Oh, hold on, he's just come in." One of the others transferred the call.

"Who is it?" Ruppert picked up the receiver and held it to his chest: he did not feel like dealing with anything other than his immediate problem.

"Someone in Killybegs, she says it's urgent."

"Hello?" With a sinking feeling in his stomach, de Burgh listened as his informant told him where the missing drugs could be found in the cave. This was the last thing he needed today. He looked around but three of the other four men in the room were on calls and the fourth was writing. "Thanks," he said quietly. "It's hectic here today but we'll get on to it straight away. Could I have your name—where I can get you later?" He was left holding the buzzing telephone.

He toyed with the idea of ignoring the call but the informant had asked for him by name. If she saw no police activity within the next couple of hours she might call again and go higher next time.

Then he saw how he could turn it to his advantage.

Galvanized, he raced out of the room and back down the corridor. This time, when he knocked, it was with much more confidence. "What is it?" The chief superintendant's roar could have been heard in the street.

De Burgh opened the door and put his head round it. "I know I said I'd wait, chief, but I'm afraid this is very urgent." Then, to the electronics man, giving no indication he recognized him, "I'm sorry to interrupt, sir, but it really is important." He prayed that the chief would ask the intruder to leave rather than come to the door or out into the corridor. His prayers were answered.

"No problem." The security man got to his feet. "I'll go for a cup of coffee—I know where the canteen is."

De Burgh smiled apologetically as the man passed him in the doorway, then went in and sat in front of the desk. He retrieved the gum within three seconds. What he had not bargained for was that he was now ordered to Killybegs.

"May I ask you a favor, sir?" His brain raced.

"What now? Just go, de Burgh, do it. This is not a good time."

"May I speak in confidence?" He stared across the desk, willing his superior to listen.

The chief superintendent sighed. "I'm very busy, de Burgh."

"I appreciate that, sir, but I wonder if someone else could deal with Killybegs, at least until I get something personal sorted out."

"This'd better be good."

"My wife discovered this morning she was pregnant."

The Chief regarded him in silence, eyes narrowed. "So?" he said at last. "And anyway, I thought it was your wife's sister who was pregnant."

"She is, sir, she's about to pop any day now, but the news this morning has upset my wife very much. *Very* much."

Two minutes later, reprieved and almost giddy with relief, he was back in the corridor.

Chapter Thirty-nine

The crowds in the RTE canteen, a single story, open-plan building with floor-to-ceiling windows on three sides, clattered and chattered like a cageful of cockatoos as Éamonn Vaughan, with Sky in tow, searched for a free table. "Over here." He found one near a window. Sky, whose legs ached with fatigue, watched, bemused, as he shook little white showers all over his fried eggs and french fries. Shades of Lynskey: salt seemed to be an Irish obsession.

She and Lynskey had parted, if not as enemies, certainly not as lovers. He had continued to be upset at what he saw as her exploitation of him and the more she tried to point out that this was rich coming from him, the more he clammed up. She could barely believe they had known one another for such a short time: although the words "days" and "weeks" had ceased to mean much to her, she reckoned it must be only a week, maybe ten days. They fought not tentatively as new lovers do but as though they had known one another for years. She tried to shake him out of her mind and took a mouthful of her lasagne.

She and the Irish reporter had progressed their story not at all. Vaughan had been too busy all afternoon with routine work for his television bulletins; for her part she had shaded the truth a little to him, confessing that she had been so tired after the journey that she had gone to bed for a couple of hours.

"Never mind." Vaughan larruped into his meal. "I'll have a bit of time now. You can come back up to the newsroom with me and we'll hit the telephones." He seemed to be one of the stars of the station, and popular with it. Throughout the meal they were interrupted by a stream of people coming across to their table with tidbits of gossip. "Everyone's very nice here," she said, when they were alone for a few moments. "Must be a lovely place to work."

"You're a stranger here, all right. Give yourself time." Vaughan finished his tea. "Shall we go?"

Before they could get up they were interrupted again by a man who could have been the model for the ubiquitous smiley face that had swept the world. Sky did not catch his name, but he was a children's TV presenter and wildlife artist. "Butte, Montana?" he repeated. "It's one of the places I've wanted to go all my life." He went on to discuss a project in which he had been trying to interest the newsroom for a long time, a wildlife slot to be included once a week as a tailpiece—"no pun intended, Sky"—to the bulletins.

"Or even once a month, people would be interested, Éamonn, I promise you. Even urban people. Magpies, foxes, mice, you should see my mailbag."

"You're preaching to the converted here. I told you, I put it up and no one was interested, Vaughan said ruefully.

"Try again, please?"

"All right." He rose and Sky followed suit.

The three walked together out of the canteen and across toward a colonnaded building where the newsroom and television studios were apparently housed. "Saw an extraordinary thing today," a wildlife man said as they approached the carousel doors. "I had a group of kids in the Natural History Museum and for the first time in all the years I've been going there I saw what can only be described, in museum terms, mind you, as a frenzy of activity." He laughed. "That means, of course that there were at least three people running around. That's the entire staff—the director's away. Could I interest you in doing a story there, Éamonn? They're shamefully neglected, you know."

"What was going on?" Vaughan was waving at another colleague across the lawn.

"You may well ask. They wouldn't tell me, although they'd taken one of my little favorites out of his glass case— maybe it's something to do with the exhibit they've promised us. I don't suppose you saw anything about another little Eskimo curlew they found recently?"

"No." Sky could see Vaughan was not in the least interested and was just being polite. By now they were at the doors and, as the wildlife man was not going inside, they stopped. "It's a little bird which was thought to be extinct— oh, never mind." He finally yielded to the fact that his enthusiasm was not being shared. "It's of interest only to ornithologists."

"Maybe I'll get along, bring my kids—see you around, kiddo . . ." Vaughan pushed the doors and then stood back to let Sky go first.

All the way up to the handsome, cantilevered staircase, which led from the lobby to the second floor of the television building, Sky was being bothered by the word "ornithologist." It has some resonance she could not grasp, but she had a feeling she had come across it somewhere recently and that it might be important.

The newsroom was busy but hushed, the clicking of keyboards the predominant sound. Vaughan installed her in a small side office. "Carry on here—no one will bother you. Dial nine for an outside line."

When she reached him Jimbo had little to offer besides the names of those arrested, but as she wrote them to his dictation, Sky thought she detected an unusual undercurrent in his voice. When he had finished, she asked him if anything was wrong.

"Have you called home, Sky?"

"No." It was as though something cold slithered down the back of her neck. "Not yet. I was going to call after I spoke to you—why?"

He hesitated, then: "I'm sorry to have to be the one to give you bad news, but Daniel Treacy died yesterday afternoon."

"Oh, no." Even as she reacted, Sky was relieved that it was not someone close to her. She had been afraid the news might have been about Johanna. Then she immediately thought of her grandmother. "I've got to call home, Jim. My grandmother—"

"You won't find her there right now. It was she who found Treacy last night. She's taking it remarkably well. One of your mother's friends—I can't remember her name now."

"Hermana? Buffy?"

"That's the one—your grandmother's at her home."

Then, quickly as she could, Sky gave him details—pitifully few—about progress in Dublin. "But although I can't say too much about it right now, there's a possibility—we—" she glanced out at Éamonn Vaughan, who was whispering into his own telephone and paying no attention to her, "we may be about to discover why Lynskey was sent to the States."

"More than to do with why these guys have been arrested over here?"

"Maybe." She lowered her voice. "I'll know for sure tomorrow."

She took the liberty of calling Buffy's number, at which there was no reply, but just as she replaced the receiver, a wisp of memory floated to the surface, so weak and intangible that she almost let it go. Somehow she knew it was vitally important that she catch it and place it in focus.

Not caring who saw her or what they thought, Sky put her forehead against the cool wood of the desk and shut her eyes, squeezing tightly to force the memory higher into her consciousness. Something really significant . . . Something to do with that word "ornithologist" . . . She pressed harder so the bones of her forehead hurt . . .

Then it burst through. Like tumblers in a combination lock, everything clicked into place: the out-of-date magazine article, the Amnesty woman's little hint about their VIP never having been here before and never expected to be here, Vaughan's comment about the coyness of the British embassy, the running around at the Natural History Museum mentioned by the wildlife man who had linked it with birds, Eskimo birds.

"It's him!" she cried, so loudly that Vaughan stopped his whispering and looked across at her. "I have it, Éamonn! I know who it is."

"May I remind you there's an overtime ban due to start tomorrow, sir?" Unusually, the speaker was Rupert de Burgh, an officer not known for public contribution at meetings.

It was not going well for the planners. All Gàrda leave had been canceled for the weekend yet with the city stuffed to bursting point and the security risk at the Amnesty conference increased tenfold, the Commissioner still doubted that they had adequate cover and quailed at the thought.

"Can we not know who it is we're supposed to be protecting, sir?" This from a detective inspector well down the table.

"No!" The Commissioner's response had been more violent than he intended. "Not yet," he said more quietly. "We'll be letting you know, still on a confidential basis, of course, early tomorrow afternoon. In the meantime, just take my word for it, gentlemen—and ladies," he nodded in the direction of the women in the room, "this will be an unusual situation but one I'm sure we'll all rise to as we always do." As he looked at lines of serious faces, he was not half as confident as he appeared. He passed the chair to the chief superintendent.

After he had allocated the security personnel, and spelled out the plans for advance screening of the places through which their mystery guest was going to pass, the chief seemed to remember something. "De Burgh," he barked, "keep in touch with Killybegs, keep it spinning. At least we'll have something good to report to the press for a change."

"My fella's in at a meeting." Éamonn Vaughan threw down the telephone. "Why don't you try your friend?"

"Sure." Sky steeled herself. Although she and Lynskey had parted with plans to meet the following day, it would not be easy to open the subject that had caused such dissension.

She was secretly relieved to discover that, like Vaughan's contact, Lynskey, too, was in a meeting.

"Must be the same one they're all at." Vaughan drummed his fingers on the desk. "The only thing to do is to ring the Ambassador directly."

The British ambassador to Ireland was at a function that night and was therefore unavailable to take Éamonn Vaughan's call. Lynskey had gone to ground and had not returned Sky's, and neither had Vaughan's friend in the Branch returned his.

Two hours had passed, they—or, rather, Vaughan—had called everyone in his book and still they were no nearer confirmation. Buffy was not answering her telephone in Butte and Sky was reluctant to call the hospital in case is disturbed her mother.

"We've got to pin it down, we've just go to." Vaughan was pacing the small cubicle to which they had repaired after the return of the inhabitants of the office they had first occupied. Sky, sick with fatigue now, was concerned that they were attracting too much attention. She saw how her scoop would grow wings and escape beyond capture, should any other reporter tumble to what she and Vaughan had been chasing: RTE ran radio bulletins through the night.

On the instant it rang, Vaughan snatched up the telephone

in the little cubicle. "Yes? All right, put her through. Oh, hello!" His voice dropped, sweetened. "Talk about a blast from the past. What can I do for you?" Then: "Funny enough, I heard the same thing. I wonder if we have the same source? No . . . you go first . . ." He pulled a face in Sky's direction. "I see. Well, I was thinking along the same lines and I think you're right . . . Come on . . . You don't seriously expect me to tell you, now, do you?" He listened, then, "Sure I'll see you when you come over then, all right? Come into the newsroom. Maybe we'll both have a bit more news to tell each other."

He threw down the receiver. "That was a BBC reporter, a girl who went over there from this place. She got the same tip-off I did but she has no clue. All she's found out so far is who it's definitely not. And it's definitely not John Major. But she did say something interesting. The British Foreign Office went ballistic when she rang them. Sky, I'm beginning to believe that you're a little genius."

Sky summoned a smile. She certainly did not feel like a genius: she felt like a rabbit brought down with an elephant gun.

He saw it. "You're dropping on your feet. Why don't you go and get a good night's sleep? I'll order a taxi. I promise I'll ring you straight away if I hear anything. Anyway, there's nothing we can do in the middle of the night—the Ambassador certainly won't thank us for ringing him up at this hour. I'm going to call it a day, start again in the morning. But I think now you've got it right."

"Spare me the details, Toby. Just ring as soon as you have anything concrete. So long as you know that, here, I won't be free to talk." De Burgh was on his bedroom extension. His brother's Foreign Office friend was coming to his flat for a late supper after helping the Prince with his speech.

De Burgh put his head in his hands. Now that it was so close he had to keep his nerve even as all those around him—Toby, the plumber—were threatening to lose theirs. Even Jerry Flynn had been showing signs of softening when he had telephoned earlier.

At least he was on the security detail assigned to guard the mystery guest. Unfortunately, so was Fergus Lynskey. If de Burgh could choose any of his fellow officers to leave off that detail, it would have been Lynskey.

Copy to follow????
Copy to follow????
Copy to follow????
Copy to follow????

But he was realist enough to know that not everything would go his way and, when the crunch came, it would be just himself and the Prince anyway.

De Burgh opened his wallet and reread the letter he had written earlier that day to his family.

His wife was at the movies with a friend, and his three children, who were all on holiday from school, were taking full advantage of her absence. Downstairs, the television blasted out some sitcom and, in the bedroom next door, the stereo was booming away: his elder son, a taciturn enigma to his father, playing nothing but Metallica.

"Turn that down." De Burgh banged his fist on the communicating wall. Nothing happened. In normal circumstances he would have stormed into his sons' room but tonight, most probably the last night he would spend here, he decided to leave it be. For a few seconds, he stroked the letter gently with one finger, then put it back in his wallet and went downstairs.

He walked through the kitchen and out into the back garden, down the path to his shed, always kept locked and to which he had the only key. His family knew that when he was in here, rebuilding hi-fi speakers from salvage stock, tinkering around with the model planes, boats and other electronic gizmos which were his only hobby, they were to leave him alone.

He let himself in, locked the door and took a long, deep breath. He always felt calm in here, almost happy, although happiness was not something he could easily identify. The last time he could say he had been happy was in those heady, high days of his short Trinity career. He liked the smell in here, though—a combination of sweet, decaying wood, Airfix glue, and a sharp, musty scent he associated with opening the packaging around new electronic components.

From a high shelf, he took down the Semtex devices, packed neatly in butter foil and, to all intents and purposes, if anyone saw inside his briefcase between now and when it was planted, just innocent packets of butter. He was hedging his bets here: a quarter of the amount of explosive he had used would have been enough, but he had to cause maximum panic and superficial damage although without injury or death. If anyone asked, his wife had asked him to pick up the butter—she needed extra to seal her containers of home-made pâte.

He also took down two other, more unusual and far smaller contrivances, packed into flat, teardrop shapes, each no longer than three inches and designed to self-combust at a pre-set time.

The detonator on the main bomb was activated by TV remote control. At first he had toyed with a car alarm remote, which he could have kept on his key ring without arousing suspicion, but was unable to find components small and powerful enough to fit into the housing. He would carry the TV remote in his pocket and, if it came to light, act surprised—one of his children must have put it there during a game.

Someone knocked on the shed door. "Dad?"

"What?" De Burgh paused in the act of putting the devices into his briefcase.

"I just want to say goodnight, Dad, I'm going to bed." It was his younger son, thirteen years old and the only one of his three children who seemed now to have any time for him.

"I can't open the door," he called gruffly. "I'm in the middle of something—goodnight."

"Night, Daddy."

De Burgh listened at the door as the sound of his son's running footsteps faded on the concrete path.

No matter what disaster now befell him or his plan, he was determined to go through with it—alone if need be. If he had been asked to describe what it was that was pushing him, he would not have been able to put words on it. All he knew was that his concentration had been refined to focus only on that single point tomorrow when he would confront the Prince of Wales. It was as though his being had become as thin and elegant as a laser beam, which cut through his family and all personal considerations. Everything in its path was insubstantial.

Sky got back to the hotel ten minutes after leaving RTE and was paying off the cab when a figure emerged from an auto-mobile a little way along toward the park. Lynskey.

"I'm sorry," he said simply. "Will you forgive me?"

"I shouldn't have said it. It was crass, you were right. But you should know by now that my tongue runs away with my brain."

"You'd every right to say what you did, I was as bad as you. You were dead right, Sky."

"No, I was the one—" Sky stopped. "What does it matter? You're here now," she said softly. "Kiss me."

He did, and for the first time it was as though they were kissing not as sexual partners or people mutually and overwhelmingly attracted but as a couple of human beings who needed one another. "Maybe we shouldn't meet again until all this is over?"

Then he catapulted her right back into the problem between them. Holding her a little away, he looked down at her. "It won't be long now, I promise. By this time tomorrow night we can be together without any hidden agendas or conflicts of interest."

Final confirmation.

Chapter Forty

Sky looked at her watch: although it was still only five thirty in the morning, the room was already suffused with quiet, milky light; she had not drawn the swagged curtains, preferring the more open look of the lace underneath.

She lay for a few moments in the deep comfort of the bed then, for the sixth time since coming to Ireland, reached for the telephone and called Buffy's number. This time it was answered.

"Oh, Sky." The older woman was guarded. "We're all fine. How are you, dear? How's Ireland?"

"Buffy, I know about Daniel Treacy. How's Grandma taking it?"

"She's here beside me." Buffy's relief was unmistakable. "I'll put her on to you."

Sky's grandmother was calm and controlled. "You're not to be worrying about me. Buffy here couldn't be nicer, neither could Hermana. The two of them are looking after me as though I was royalty." Treacy's wake was to be held the following evening and she was not looking forward to it. "I'm sad, of course, and a little guilty."

"Guilty? What have you got to be guilty about, Grandma?"

The old lady's tone brooked no follow-on. "What are you doing up so early? How are you getting on? Do you like Dublin?"

"Dublin's fine, I think, as much as I've seen of it." Sky did not feel like going into everything that had happened—or had not happened—since her arrival. "And as for being awake, I can't sleep any longer. The change in time I suppose. I'm going to call the hospital next. How's Mom?" Johanna was well enough, her grandmother said, then, "I'll let you go, dear, this telephone call must be costing you a fortune."

"Not at all," Sky protested. What was it about the Irish and telephone calls? "The *Butte Courier* is paying."

"Don't forget to ring your aunt Maggie in Lahersheen, will you?"

"I'll do better than that. I intend to go down there when I've filed my story. Ancestral pile and all that."

After she hung up, Sky lay, staring at the snowflake patterns on the lace at the nearest window. Easy to reel off a few confident words about filing stories. Different when it came to the actuality.

Mentally, she listed what she knew: the drug story, which was common knowledge and of little interest in Montana, except for a couple of paragraphs under a sub-heading: "Helena and Mayville Men Implicated"; some plot involving terrorism and an Irish-American group in the States in which "Mayville Man Implicated" also figured; the Prince of Wales arriving in Dublin today for an Amnesty conference and probably going to visit a bird show in a museum. The more she thought it out, the more she saw the connection between the Prince and the putative terrorism: this was undoubtedly what had sent Lynskey to America.

She sat up, sleep forgotten. It had to be the story. Charles was the planned target.

And since the Amnesty conference was going to be so heavily guarded, that couldn't be the venue. She had to get the whole of the Prince's itinerary. She was reaching out to call Éamonn Vaughan's number when she remembered it was still not six o'clock.

Rupert de Burgh was also awake, going over and over in his mind what could and could not happen in the course of the day, and what would have happened to him by its end. He had covered every eventuality: his will was updated and his letter to his wife and family safely locked in his shed. It would be the first place his colleagues would pull apart for clues as to why he had acted as he did.

At six thirty, he stole out of bed and, taking his clothes with him, tiptoed toward the bedroom door. Behind him, his wife stirred and sighed. He froze: she was accustomed to his coming and going at odd hours but he did not want to answer any questions this morning.

It was nearly time to meet Flynn and Mason in the early houses. It would be a short encounter because he had to be home in time to drop his younger son to summer camp on his way in to work.

Bambi was a Rottweiler whose handler, or so his colleagues always said, had a sick sense of humor.

Not so, the handler would retort: Bambi, although vast and with a mouth like a bear trap, was as gentle as his namesake and lived indoors with the family, frequently sleeping on the children's beds. Now, as the man stumbled into the kitchen, he wagged his stumpy tail and ran to the back door to be let out.

"Good morning, fella." The handler plugged in the kettle, then padded across and patted the dog's velvety head. "Big day today." Where explosives were concerned, Bambi's nose was infallible.

"I wonder how he'll react to all the bones. Anyway, there'll be no problem, I'm sure—I hear they're very well trained." The director of the Natural History Museum, who had cut short his visit to Iceland, and one of his subordinates had had no sleep: it had taken all night to mount the Eskimo curlew exhibit. Now, as morning light flooded through the glass ceiling of the three-tiered exhibition space above the ground floor, the two stood back to admire their work.

"Have we ever had a dog in here before?" The director rubbed his tired eyes.

"Not that I can remember." The other man yawned. "Well, I'm going home for a bit of kip. We've done all we can do, I think. How long'll yer man be looking at it, anyway? About a minute and a half?"

"I hope he'll spend longer than that." The director frowned. He looked around his domain, the walls of which sprouted so many heads, horns and antlers that they might have been in the presence of a Rajah's trophy collection. "The cleaners are due for a last go around."

"Not to speak of the Branch and their bloody dog. I'll see you in a couple of hours."

Jerry Flynn had slept well and felt buoyant, if a little tense. This was quite an adventure: he had stayed in five-star hotels and resorts all over the world but he was experiencing more true happiness in this little hotel in a run-down part of Dublin than ever he had in Toronto, New York or even Las

Vegas. The shower might be a trickle, the noise from the
bar downstairs might be disturbing but, by and large, he
felt good.

Dublin itself had been somewhat of a disappointment to
him, though: it was littered and the air was smoggy. To be
fair he knew that the city was not Ireland and he also knew
that this part of Dublin, rancid with trains and traffic and
roadworks, was not the real city either. What was more dis-
appointing was the flavor of the place: he had always felt
you could taste a town by walking around its streets and
watching its TV. These streets were not relaxed and friendly
as he had hoped. And as for the Irish, they showed a lot of
British and American imports. Even their local news seemed
to bend over backward to be "fair" to the Unionists and Loyalists and the British, while giving a disproportionate amount
of air time to people who were condemning nationalist
action. In fact nowhere—except on amateur posters affixed
to lamp posts and among the young people selling the
nationalist newspaper *An Phoblacht* outside the General Post
Office—could he find sentiments sympathetic to his own
views. The Irish seemed to have obliterated the sins of the
past from their collective memory. Nowhere, except among
those young idealists, had he found an echo of his own
burning sense of injustice. As far as Flynn was concerned,
this collective amnesia and indifference were symptomatic
of why he had had to come here. They were certainly justifi-
cation for it.

Deeply religious, he had been disappointed to learn that no
Masses were celebrated early in Dublin—or early enough
that he would be finished and out in time to meet with Joe
Mason and Rupert de Burgh. He had grown up with the
image of the 1916 leaders attending the Sacraments on the
eve of their own sacrifice and thought that hearing Mass this
morning would have been a nice touch. Although he did not,
deep down, think he was going to die, he felt that he had
little left to detain him on this earth: he was a widower, he
had lived a long, useful life, his children were grown and set
up in their own lives. He was ready.

As he shaved, he admitted to himself that he was a little
worried about the commitment of his colleague from Santa
Barbara. Several times on the previous day the plumber had
expressed reservations about the likelihood of their success.

Rupert de Burgh would sort it out. The Irish policeman

seemed to share his own passionate conviction that they were doing the right thing.

When the twin-belled alarm clock jangled beside his ear, Fergus Lynskey did not so much as flutter an eyelid. He continued to breathe deeply and evenly and, after a minute or so of vigorous effort, the bells ran down. As it was on the top floor, the one-bedroom apartment was hushed; the bedroom window was open, but the early-morning traffic on Gardiner Street was light and the road crews were not due to start work for another hour or so. The alarm, however, had goaded Lynskey into semiconsciousness and he felt as though he was caught weightlessly in a hammock slung between dreams and reality.

After a bit, the second clock started its intermittent, five-second on-off bleeping, which he knew would persist. He held out for a short while but the sound became so annoying that he had to get out of the bed to turn it off.

He hung over the dressing table, both palms flat on its surface while toying with the notion of resetting it for fifteen minutes hence. Then the realization of what day it was roared in like a tornado and he stumbled into the shower.

His private secretary brought the Prince of Wales a copy of his speech for the Amnesty seminar and left it with him so he could go over it. Of necessity it was short: as heir to the British throne, he would not refer openly to anything political. And as for the subject of the meeting, "Political Repression, The New Global Holocaust," a future leader of the Commonwealth could reveal little of his true thoughts and feelings on that.

The Prince was being flown directly in an RAF plane to an Irish military aerodrome and then helicoptered to the President's residence, which was apparently in the middle of a big park. Given the short time scale, it appeared, unfortunately, he would not be able to see much. Everywhere else he was to be taken—the Government Buildings, the Natural History Museum, the Amnesty meeting, the Department of Foreign Affairs—were all in the center of the city and within half a mile of each other.

"Excuse me, sir," it was the secretary again, "Mr. de Burgh is on the telephone. Shall I have him put through?"

The Prince took the call.

All Toby wanted was to wish him well for the trip.

Toby knew Dublin, and they chatted for a couple of minutes about public buildings in Dublin for which the Prince should keep an eye open if he had a chance. Then the heir to the throne said goodbye and turned his attention to his speech.

It was just after half past seven but the air in the early public house was already so blue, both metaphorically and literally, from cigarettes, that de Burgh, who detested smoking, felt it could have been cut with a machete. To the night workers this was tea time and relaxation, to the revellers not yet gone home, it was just a continuation of the party. But at least the din was such that no one could follow anyone else's conversation.

He edged himself on to a bar stool between a bright-eyed Jerry Flynn and the Californian. Although a couple of other tourists were there, Dutch or German to de Burgh's experienced eye, these two could not have been mistaken for anything else—at least, Flynn, who still clutched the Adidas sports bag, could not. Once he had established the normality of his presence and ordered a glass of Guinness, de Burgh dropped his voice a little. "We need to talk."

"Oh? Something wrong?" Joe Mason immediately picked it up.

De Burgh adopted his most persuasive tone—the one he used to keep Toby in line. "Nothing wrong. As a matter of fact it's precisely the opposite. I've just learned that we've been presented with an opportunity beyond our wildest dreams." Mason, he saw, was suspicious and Flynn simply startled.

"What is it, Mr. de Burgh?" the Canadian asked.

"We won't need to go to Bodenstown. The Prince of Wales is making a surprise visit and I've amended our plans."

"But I thought—"

Mason's lips were tight but de Burgh immediately cut off any protest. "Imagine the impact around the world if, instead of taking the Taoiseach hostage, we were to take the heir to the British throne. I've been working it out. It's eminently possible." He held his breath.

"I'm not agreeing to anything until I hear what you have in mind."

"Just let me tell you what I've planned. At least listen." He looked down from one to the other, slowing his voice, hypnotizing them. "I guarantee that if we do what I say, we will hit TV screens all around the world tonight, front pages tomorrow. No one will be able to ignore what we ask. Sometimes the most complex tasks can be solved with the simplest of plans."

To her frustration, Sky found that the National History Museum, which was just a short walk from her hotel, did not open until ten o'clock. It was just before nine now and she was wound tighter than a new watch.

She had tried twice to contact Vaughan but his home number rang unanswered and both his office and his mobile numbers had taken messages. With nothing much to do until the museum opened, she wandered into the park where the poet had been reading the previous day. On this overcast morning, the atmosphere was different: the immaculate lawns were deserted except for people with briefcases hurrying through. When she emerged at the other side of the park, a double-decker bus was just pulling up at a nearby bus stop. Still with an hour to kill, she decided to hop on.

Ten minutes later she was standing by the brown river Liffey.

She walked up toward what appeared to be the main bridge over the river. But when she got to it she saw that, across its six lanes, the Friday morning rush hour was in full, roaring disarray. To cross seemed like too severe a test of speed and nerve and she decided to turn left in the direction which should bring her back to the hotel and the museum.

As she walked by a long stone wall topped by railings, she was looking ahead toward a curved, stately building—and bumped straight into an elderly man standing stock-still in the middle of the pavement. "I'm very sorry." Flustered, she disentangled herself.

Another tourist, she thought, noticing the Pentax round his neck. He seemed about to smile but turned away. His bullet head was covered in white stubble and he was thin but, although his appearance was not unremarkable, something about his near smile—perhaps it was the quick flash of gold teeth—got to her. "Are you sure you're okay?" She touched his arm to detain him while trying to work out the connection.

He inclined his head to indicate he was fine then turned on

his heel and walked away in the direction from which she had come. Still puzzling, she looked after him.

Flynn's heart was thumping as he hurried along by the wall, which he knew ran around the perimeter of the Trinity College campus. What was that girl doing here? Of all people to bump into in a city of a million people! Had she recognized him?

He was distressed at his own reaction: if he got this nervous after such a simple accident, from which no harm could come, how was he going to deal with the big stuff later on today? He consoled himself with the thought that this evening he would be following instructions. The unexpectedness of the encounter had shaken him.

He looked around: in his panic he had walked blindly and, although he was not exactly lost—when he looked back he could see the first stones of Trinity's wall—he had to get his bearing. He was opposite a public house on a corner of a side street, which petered out to nothing: that had to be the river. From there, he knew how to get back to his hotel, which was on its north side.

Feeling a little better, he crossed and set off toward the water.

The traffic-clogged street was narrow, with tall apartment blocks on one side, a derelict garage and lock-ups scattered along it. He was standing at traffic lights at a cross street when he felt a sharp pain between his shoulder blades. Simultaneously, the shoulder strap of the Adidas bag was jerked, hard.

He tightened his grip and whirled around. It was two kids of ten or eleven. He kicked out, hard, and connected with the shins of one, but the boy came back, swinging a large stone in a length of nylon stocking. Flynn ducked and the other boy, chucked hard at the strap, pulling him off balance. As he fell, a motorist and a cab driver, both halted at the traffic lights, jumped out of their vehicles and ran toward the fracas.

The boy with the stone swung it so it cracked across the back of Flynn's hand. He roared with pain and dropped the bag, whereupon the child snatched it and ran.

As the motorist reached him, Flynn looked to see that the cab driver had taken off after the two boys. As all three vanished into a nearby entryway, the motorist helped him up off the ground. "Little gurriers! Are you all right?"

"My bag—my bag—" Holding his injured hand with the other, Flynn started to follow the boys and their pursuer, only to see the taxi driver emerging, shaking his head, from the entryway.

"Is your hand okay? I've the car here—would you like me to take you to a hospital Casualty?" The panting cab driver reached them.

"No, no, it's all right, really." Flynn was frantic, not only at the loss of the bag and what it contained but at the attention the incident had drawn.

The lights had turned and the air was full of the cacophony of horns from those stalled behind the two driverless vehicles.

"Did you have your money in the bag, Dad?" the cab driver persisted.

"Yes, but it's all right, really, it's all right." Flynn tried to back away only to be stopped by the cab driver.

"Wait a minute."

"I'd better move my car." The first man glanced behind him at his fellow travelers.

"Yeah, you go on." The cab driver dismissed him, then turned back to his captive. "You should have that hand seen to."

"I will." Flynn, drawing on every ounce of the authority gained over years in management of a large staff, calmed himself. "I'm really fine. I will go see a doctor."

"And the Guards. They're only around the corner here in Pearse Street. You should ring the American embassy too— they're in Ballsbridge. Look, Dad . . ." As the Canadian moved off, the cab driver followed him. "You've had a terrible shock. Why don't you just get in the car and I'll take you to—" he broke off. "Oh, great! Thank God. Here's what we need." Under Flynn's horrified gaze, he hailed a uniformed bank guard who was just turning into the street.

Chapter Forty-one

As Rupert met up with the dog handler and his charge, Bambi sniffed his hand but backed off, sneezing violently.

After packing the Semtex in the briefcase the previous night, he had washed carefully in the juice of a dozen lemons. He repeated the exercise this morning before his wife got up and this time added a dollop of pepper dust. "What's on your hands?" the handler asked curiously.

Rupert explained that he had been working with creosote on his garden fence the previous evening and that some had got under his nails. The lemon juice had been his wife's suggestion. He looked at his hands. "Nearly as good as Fairy Liquid."

Before going to the museum, Sky called Lynskey at work from a telephone booth. He was guarded: "I can't talk now."

Indeed, Sky could hear the hubbub in the background. "Could we meet for lunch?"

"I'll try, a quick one. Where can I contact you?"

"I'll be at the hotel at twelve thirty."

He rang off without saying goodbye.

The sun came out as she walked to the museum, an oddly blinded building because of three unfilled niches and two blank window spaces above and on either side of the stone doorway.

Her initial impression of the place was its singular lack of color, or rather a play of darkness on light: dark wooden cabinets, dark bones, the fat dark body of a stuffed basking shark suspended from the ceiling. As she moved around, however, that somewhat doom-laden impression of suspended decay was dispelled by the iridiscent feathering of a kingfisher, and the soft mottled honey of an exhibit of fox cubs in their den.

Upstairs was a series of the most extraordinary rooms she

had ever seen. The creaking wooden staircase came out on a large gallery with two further, minstrel's galleries overhead, dominated by the skeleton of a whale. The place was filled with bears, lions, a giraffe, a pygmy hippopotamus, monkeys, elephants, fish, birds. Then there were the invertebrates and octopuses, butterflies, beetles, spiders and flies, whitening in phials and jars or spreadeagled over black velvet display cases, while fixed to every vertical surface not made of glass were heads with or without horns or antlers.

"Excuse me." She walked up to a man in his shirtsleeves.

"Yes." The man looked flustered.

Sky produced her most charming smile. "I'm an American visitor. Could you direct me to whoever's in charge?"

"I'm afraid the director is not here at present." The man adopted a hunted look. "What can I help you with? You've come at a bad time."

"I know I have." Sky continued to smile. "Perhaps if I told you why I'm here. I know you're receiving a very important visitor today."

The man's eyes widened in horror. "No one's supposed to know. We were told not even to tell our wives."

"I know from my relatives in England." She tried to adopt a simultaneously knowing and aristocratic expression. "But don't worry, I just want to see the little Eskimo exhibit for myself." She could not remember the precise name of the bird used by the wildlife man she had met in RTE, but hoped that by tossing it off quickly it might sound like insider jargon.

The man looked hard at her, then, "I suppose that's all right. First, though," he recollected his security duties, "could I see some form of identification, please?"

"Sure." Sky rooted around in her purse. She was thinking fast. To know she was a reporter would send this functionary running for cover. "Will these do?" She pulled out her brand-new charge card and her membership card for the camera circle, the latter of which showed her photograph.

He examined both cards closely then said, "Follow me." He led her downstairs and to the back of the exhibition space on the first floor, where he showed her a largish glass case in which were two medium-sized birds. One appeared to be nesting in what looked like lichen or moss, the other was perched on a stone. As far as Sky could see they were unremarkable creatures, brownish beige with spindly blue-gray legs and beaks like miniature scythes. Certainly not worth creating a fuss about.

"What do you think?" They were joined by another, much younger man.

The first man's face cleared with relief. "She said she knew who was coming." He turned to Sky, "This is our director." Then, again to his boss: "She's an American student, I checked."

"Don't worry about it." The younger man smiled. "Not much anyone can do about it now, the word is probably out—this town is a village. You haven't been here long, obviously. After a few days you'll find yourself meeting the same people everywhere." He held out his hand. "I'm Declan Corkery, the director."

"Sky MacPherson." They shook hands.

He turned to his handiwork. "Do you approve of our efforts? The case had to be specially made and we had the devil of a time getting the habitat material."

"Very nice, er—Declan." She hesitated. "Could we talk?"

"Sure, I've a few minutes, come on into my office."

"I'll come straight to the point." Sky took a deep breath after he closed the door behind them. "I think you're wrong when you say that probably everyone knows about who's coming here today. The only people who know are the police and the authorities, yourselves, the Amnesty International people and me."

The director was shrewd: "So what are you asking me to do?"

Here it came. "I'm not a student. I'm a reporter. I represent a small and impoverished newspaper in Butte, Montana. I would be no threat to any of your local reporters here, but it would be a lucrative coup for us if I had an exclusive—any exclusive—concerning the Prince of Wales." On tenterhooks, she stopped. He had not reacted to the name. Further confirmation.

"Go on."

"Could you arrange for me to be here when he comes? I will not approach him or speak to him unless he speaks to me and, even if he does, I'll not reveal I'm a reporter. I'll just write a color piece about him being here, how he reacted to your Eskimo birds."

"Eskimo curlews. If you're pretending to be a wildlife researcher, at least get your names right."

"Please, Mr. Corkery, please." She leaned forward, engaged him with Johanna's cornflower eyes. "The rest of the press pack will have other opportunities—at the Amnesty conference, for instance. I'd be only one of many there. You've no idea how important this would be. It's a matter of life and death to our newspaper because we'll be able to syndicate it. I'll be out of a job if we don't get some money soon. But it's not my job, Mr. Corkery, it's that our newspaper *needs* to be saved. We're one of the last independent voices in Montana, in the whole United States, maybe. We represent small local and environmental interests against the big boys—" Thinking she might be gilding the lily she stopped.

Watching from under her lashes to see if he'd bought it, she was delighted to see him smile. "I've got to admit it's a pretty impressive pitch. What would you say if I told you my wife's a reporter and I wouldn't let *her* in?"

Sky was crestfallen.

"I'm joking, Miss MacPherson, I'm not married." But when she sat up eagerly he held up a restraining hand. "I'm afraid it's out of the question. I'm a civil servant, I'm not my own boss."

"Isn't there anything I could do around the museum? As a researcher? Even a typist? If there's any inquiry afterward, I'll take full responsibility. You can say I deceived you and I'll back you up."

"You clearly have no idea how the Irish civil service works." He smiled wryly. "To get in here—anywhere, really—requires the equivalent of an Act of the Oireachtas—in triplicate. I would like to help but I'm afraid I can't. Our orders are clear, I'm afraid, and the police are due here any minute to clear the place."

Behind her, Sky heard a soft knock and then the door opening. The older man she had met previously came halfway into the room. "They're here with the dog, Declan."

"Speak of the devil. Show them in." He stood up.

Sky stood up also as two men, accompanied by a large dog, came in. The dog, panting a little, immediately lay down quietly beside its master's feet. And uncomfortably close to Sky's. The other man looked suspiciously at her: "We've no woman on our list." She hated the way his light-colored eyes seemed to drill straight through her.

"This is Sky MacPherson, from America." The director

glanced at her and then back at the policeman. "She's here purely by chance, I assure you." Sky flashed him a grateful smile, but his expression was bland.

"I'm afraid I'll have to ask you to leave, miss," the policeman with the light eyes said crisply. "May I see some identification?"

She fished out the same two cards she had shown the attendant. Although both had photographs, neither showed her address. "I'm on holiday. I was taking a walk in the park and just wandered in here. May I complete my conversation with the director?"

The cop handed back the cards, "You can remain until we get as far as here. We'll be starting upstairs on the top floor and working downward."

The policeman seemed to lose interest in her, and asked the director if all the side offices and storerooms were open. When the latter replied that they were, he said; "They must be locked immediately they've been cleared. Will you come with us with the keys, please?"

The dog stood up as soon as the handler twitched the leash. "Please stay here, Miss MacPherson. I'll be back as soon as I can." The director took up the keys from the desk and all three men, with their four-legged companion, left the office.

Instantly, Sky picked up the telephone on the director's desk. "Éamonn," she whispered urgently when he answered his mobile, "can you meet me? As soon as possible?"

"Jesus, Mary and Joseph! Oh shit, oh *shit* . . . I don't fuckin' *believe* it." The two boys were safely tucked into a small rubbish-strewn space beside an electricity transformer and were rifling through the Adidas bag.

It was more than they had bargained for. Not only had they bagged a wad of cash, but something else, too. Reverently, the bigger of the two pulled out a pistol, which was impressive enough, but the second item was really the business. Although he had never handled one before, the boy recognized a submachine gun when he saw it. "Are they real?" The smaller one's eyes were as round as plates.

"Of course they're real, dickhead." The older boy put both weapons back in the bag and sat with his back snugly against the transformer to think.

* * *

"Would you like another cup of tea, sir?" In Pearse Street Gárda station, Jerry Flynn was being killed with kindness. At least the interfering cab driver had finally been inveigled into leaving but the policewoman who had walked him in here was still hovering solicitiously. She was buxom, with a fresh, country face and, in other circumstances, Flynn would have liked her.

He ached with anxiety to escape but as he was supposed to be an elderly tourist with time to spare, he had to play dumb. At least he had had the presence of mind to give no name and he had said he was staying at the hotel where he had had a cup of coffee the previous day which was in a much more salubrious area than his. "I really must be getting along," he stood up, "and thank you kindly for all you've done. I truly appreciate it."

"You're sure now you don't want me to ring Victim Support for you? They're very good. Would you like someone to drive you back to your hotel?"

"I'll walk. Truly."

As he left the police station he got an even worse shock than had been doled out by the two little thieves. Laid carelessly on top of a pile of ledgers was a glossy eight-by-ten photograph of himself in rodeo gear.

He was shaking when he got outside, so much so that he began to feel woozy. By a supreme civil act of will, he got himself across the road and to a little plaza in front of a cinema. He sat down on a parapet surrounding a flower bed but rather than lower his head, which was what his instinct told him to do, he pretended to be enjoying the sunshine. The last thing he needed was another bout of do-gooding from someone concerned that he might be ill.

Bit by bit, he began to feel more normal. He flexed his hand: it was sore and already swollen, but he was pretty sure nothing was broken.

His heart was, however. He had waited so long for this opportunity but there was no avoiding the bitter fact that his dreams were in shreds around his feet. Jerry Flynn was an idealist and a patriot but not a fool: he knew his role in the mission was over.

At least he still had his plane ticket and false passport back at the hotel.

He had to get out of Dublin.

* * *

Fergus Lynskey met the chief superintendent in the gents' lavatory at Headquarters. "How're we going to handle the press? As soon as they know who's here it'll be open season. I'm not worried about the print media—it'll be too late for them—but you can be sure it'll break on radio and that'll draw crowds."

"I'm scheduling an impromptu press conference downstairs about the drugs find in Killybegs at the same time as the Amnesty conference. That'll divert some of them, but not for long, I suspect."

"Why here?" Lynskey, who was combing his thatch, looked disparagingly at his reflection in the mirror. "We've no facilities—why not in town?"

"Because Harcourt Square is too close to the concert hall, dummy!" The chief ran water into the basin and soaped his hands. "Where's de Burgh? He's the liaison man with Killybegs, he'll have to be there."

"He's out with the dogs. He shouldn't be too long but I'm not his keeper."

"You're not anyone's keeper. How's the little American?"

"No comment," but Lynskey caught himself grinning into the mirror.

"Yeah, yeah, who do you think you're fooling, Fergus?" The chief dried his hands and came across to punch his friend affectionately in the ribs. "If you see de Burgh before I do, tell him to come in to see me, time's getting on."

Rupert de Burgh, Bambi and Bambi's master had finished their sweep of the museum, and had joined up with another dog unit to check out the Dáil.

They had put it about that the reason for the security activity was that Naboom Kebele was making a brief visit but the rumor wheel had already started to turn. During ten minutes in the kitchens, they had been asked several times who was really coming. Although a porter had the correct name and one of the commis chefs said he had heard it was the Duke of Edinburgh, most of the hot money seemed to be on the Duke of York. Having spent more than half his life here, Rupert de Burgh still marveled at the way information spread in Ireland. It gave a new twist to what folklorists liked to call the Oral Tradition.

Chapter Forty-two

When they had finished in the Dáil, Rupert walked with his colleague back toward their cars. He had taken his own under the pretext of having to register a letter for his wife at the GPO, and not having wanted to drag along his colleague and the dog. "Damn," he felt around in his pockets now, "I can't find my car keys. There's a hole in my trousers' pocket—they must have fallen through. You go on, tell them I'll be along as quick as I can."

"Sure," his colleague patted Bambi, "see you back at the salt mines."

De Burgh searched the ground for his keys until the handler's vehicle had gone and then walked quickly to his own, which he had parked far enough away so as not to attract the dog. From the trunk, he removed the briefcase containing the Semtex and handcuffed it to his wrist.

"I thought we'd got rid of you." The museum's door attendant was cheerful.

"Just one last check." Now out of earshot of his colleagues, De Burgh's tone was equally lighthearted. "Can't be too careful. You might have put a bomb in the elephant's trunk since we were here!"

He walked upstairs and tramped purposefully all around the upper galleries, looking up at the ceiling, gazing at light fittings. When he came to the director's office, he knocked once then opened the door. "All seems in order."

Declan Corkery looked up from a booklet he was showing the woman reporter. "I'm afraid I need to use your lavatory," De Burgh said apologetically, "sorry, I know it's locked, but it's a bit urgent. Bit inconvenient too," he added, "with this attached to me," indicating the briefcase.

The men's washroom was on the first floor, to the left of the staircase. The director unlocked it, handed the key to the door attendant, and went back toward his office.

Once inside it took only a minute for de Burgh to place his butter packs, strung together by the detonator wire, in one of the two stalls. He locked the door from the inside, stood on the toilet seat and climbed out over the partition into the neighboring cubicle.

He washed his hands then, employing generous streams of Jif lemon juice, as a precaution against running into Bambi or one of his mates.

The attendant was waiting when he came out. "That's better." He assumed a jocose smile. "It's just as well I came back, we forgot these." He locked the door, returned the key to the attendant and, out of the briefcase, took two pieces of yellow police ribbon, the type used to seal off crime scenes. He fixed lengths across the door frames of both the gents' and ladies' washrooms. "Now don't forget not to let anyone, even the Pope, in there until after the famous visit."

"The staff toilet is sealed off too—what happens if we want to go?" the attendant objected.

"There are plenty of hotels and restaurants around," de Burgh offered. "Can I rely on you to tell your boss? I've somewhere else to go and I'm running late." He had to assume that staff, even directors, of a place like this were unused to security alerts.

He was not wrong: "Don't worry," the attendant waved an airy hand, "you can count on me."

De Burgh went downstairs and as he left, again checked quickly behind both the inner and outer entrance doors. He had previously noted that while the inner door closed with a Yale lock, suitable to his purpose, the outer was secured with both bolt and turnkey. As before, there was no sign of the key. "Pretty impressive." He saluted the attendant and left.

As he got into his car he realized his palms were sweating and took a moment to compose himself.

He drove into town and down Abbey Street, turning right into Liffey Street and parked outside the back entrance of Arnott's department store. He switched on his revolving light as though answering an alarm call, locked up and walked quickly through the Friday shoppers into the store.

The menswear department of Arnott's had managed to retain the old-fashioned atmosphere of a country draper's and the staff, although attentive, were not pushy, allowing customers to browse unmolested. De Burgh walked along the rails, pulling out here a suit, there a sports jacket, as he made his way toward the expensive raincoats. He chose one at the end of the rail, size 54. He slipped it off the hanger, which was made from molded plastic, each end spread like a pad to fill out the garment's shoulders.

He tried on the raincoat and moved to a mirror, carrying the hanger. This morning, the department was busy but not crowded, with older men predominating, and no one paid him any attention as he twisted and turned as though assessing the fit of the coat. As he did so he pressed one of the teardrop-shaped packages into the hollow under one of the hanger's shoulders.

He checked the coat again from a different angle, then, "No, I don't think so."

"Excuse me, sir." A salesman came toward him, "that one's too big. Let me get you one in your size."

De Burgh had been prepared for this. "It's for my father. Arnott's is one of the few places he can get decent coats in this size. But I'm not sure about this color. I'll have to bring him in, I'm afraid."

"Do that." The salesman lost interest and looked away for the next prospect.

He took off the coat, replaced it on its hanger and put it back exactly where he had got it. In that size it was unlikely to be tried on again before the incendiary went off in just over four hours' time, unless he was very very unlucky. He repeated the exercise two hundred yards away, in Clery's of O'Connell Street.

As he drove back to Headquarters he felt relieved, almost jolly, now that the gears of the operation had engaged. Stuck in traffic in College Green, he called into the office and was told that the chief supereintendent wanted to see him urgently. "On my way," he said, "had a bit of trouble with the car. Be there in about ten minutes."

Sky was talking to Éamonn Vaughan in the latter's automobile, coincidentally a Nissan but far bigger than her own. "So you think there's no point?" She was downcast. "None of your contacts could help? He's a nice man, I think he'd let me stay if he got permission."

He shook his head slowly. "No one I know'd help me out for something like this. If they let just one journalist in they'd be in trouble with the rest."

"How about a pool arrangement? I'd share my stuff with everyone."

"That happened when Reagan was here but we all had to have security clearance in advance, stand behind ropes, all that sort of thing." He twisted his lips in bitter recollection. "We've got to think of some other way. He's definitely going there before the Amnesty meeting?"

"Definitely." Sky had been able to garner that much from the director. "But please, Éamonn," she sat up abruptly, "I'm trusting you not to show up with all the TV paraphernalia. Whatever chance we have, we'll have none if you do that. If you help me get in, I promise I'll rush straight up to the meeting and I'll give you every single tittle-tattle, every wag of his head or his little finger."

She was glad she had not told him her suspicion that there might be some incident involving the so-called plotters and the Prince.

"I could always send down another crew—I gave you this story in the first place—" he began.

"But I was the one who discovered the Prince's identity—and it's something I would have found out from my contact, Fergus Lynskey anyway."

Seeing she was getting upset, he relented. "You'll share everything with me? All Lynskey's information?"

"Everything I can legitimately find out." She nodded.

"Give me a moment." He stared through the baking wind-shield of the car and she could almost hear the clicking of his mind.

Then she had a brainstorm. "What's the name of that wildlife TV presenter you introduced me to last night? I never caught it."

"Rory Traynor. Ye-yes," he looked at her with admiration, "I see what you're at. And, by the way, it's not only the museum. Rory's very well got with the Taoiseach, who's given to making statements about our priceless natural environment."

"Where can I find him? Can I use your telephone?"

He switched on the mobile and handed it to her. "Here's the number."

To her great joy, Traynor himself answered and remembered immediately who she was. "Look, Rory," she said quickly, "you may or may not be able to help. But you did say Montana was one of the places you always wanted to visit and if you can help me with what I ask, when I get back home I will do my utmost to get the Montana Parks and Wildlife Service to sponsor you out to Yellowstone or Glacier National Park." She was skating on thin ice, but all too aware of the smirk on Vaughan's face, she intended to honor the pledge.

Rory Traynor chuckled and said he wished he could be bribed every day.

Encouraged, she explained what she was asking him to do. "I hear you keep exalted company sometimes. Could you ask the Taoiseach first? I'm sure he'd say yes to *you*, Rory!"

"Don't I bring you to nice places?" Lynskey grinned. He and Sky were eating up in Abrakebabra, a fast-food restaurant that specialized in kebabs. "What's the matter? You're not with me."

"Sorry, I was just thinking." Sky, who had told Rory Traynor she would call back in an hour, was peppering for the hour to be up but there was still fifteen minutes to go. She attempted to concentrate on her food. "Well, at least they give you lots of meat—ughhh." Some of the kebab sauce oozed out of its wrapping and down the front of her dress. "I'll have to go back to the hotel and change."

"Want me to come with you?"

"I thought you were busy—hey! I've just remembered!" Sky put down the kebab.

"You've just remembered what?" Lynskey stopped mid-chew.

"The rodeo, you were eating fast food at the rodeo."

"Yes?" He looked mystified.

"That's where I saw him."

"Who, for God's sake?"

She glared at him. "Forget it. If you can't be civil—"

"All right, I'm really sorry, but I'm under desperate pressure and you're behaving like a lunatic. Who did you see at the rodeo that I remind you of?"

"It's that Canadian, Jerry Flynn. I saw him today. He doesn't look at all like himself, Fergus, he's cut his hair and he's shaved off his mustache but it was definitely him. I *knew* I knew him from somewhere. It was the gold teeth that did it. Lynskey, he's in Dublin."

Immediately he forgot the rest of his meal.

* * *

Gárda Headquarters gave every appearance of being close to organizational meltdown: police vehicles shot off with tires squealing and people ran, rather than walked, through the offices.

In the chief superintendent's office, the atmosphere was no better: Rupert de Burgh was being bawled out. Despite his quiet and steadfast insistence that he could not be blamed for a puncture, or that the tightness of the wheel nuts had defied all efforts to remove the wheel, the chief was not having any. "You could have called in, you pillock. Today of all days! Four people already have not showed up for work—"

"It's the overtime ban, sir."

"I know it's the bloody overtime ban." The chief's tone contrasted with his subordinate's in much the same way as those of an elephant and a cat. "Don't tell me what I know!"

"I'm sorry, sir, but I was so intent on changing the tire."

"Look," the chief waved impatiently, "forget it. What's happening with the drugs recovery in Killybegs? I want a detailed report on my desk in fifteen minutes. And I will also want to know what *exactly* we will be saying at that press conference in four hours' time." The telephone on his desk buzzed and he picked it up. "What is it now?"

As he listened, all the bombast left him. "I don't bloody believe it." He collapsed against the back of his chair, "When? How long ago?"

De Burgh started to back out of the office but his superior stopped him with a glance. "Ring me back as soon as you have any more details," he said quietly into the telephone. He hung up, looked up at the other men. "That was the detective unit in Mountjoy. There's been a bungled supermarket robbery in Finglas. A Securicor van. The driver's injured and so is one of the villains. We know them, a father and nephew. But as if that wasn't enough, turns out this villain's gun is an AK-47. And get this, the other one's got away on a mountain bike—a *mountain bike*! There go more of my resources . . . Apparently half of the northside squad cars are at present careering around Finglas."

It was clearly the last straw and de Burgh almost felt sorry for him but this couldn't have come at a better time.

At first, he did not make the connection. When he did his heart jolted.

It settled down again. Although one of the weapons he had given the plumber and Jerry Flynn had been a Kalashnikov AK-47 automatic rifle, "borrowed" from the Gárda stores of gear confiscated from IRA weapons dumps, it could not possibly have been used to rob a supermarket in Finglas. AK-47s were not thick on the ground but they could be found without too much difficulty.

"Go and do that report," the chief superintendent said quietly. "And then you and Lynskey go out to Baldonnel. You can peel off for the press conference after I find a replacement for you. But stay in touch!"

"Yes, sir." As he left the office, de Burgh was fingering the comforting outline of the TV remote control in his jacket pocket. As soon as he got to his desk, he called the hotel. Neither Mr. Mulqueen nor his friend were in. "No message." He hung up.

"It's like World War Three." A woman pushing a supermarket trolley had stopped on the path at a safe distance from the action.

"It's a disgrace, with kids around and all," her friend agreed. The two settled down to watch as, across the wide green in front of them, a mare galloped, closely followed by her terrified foal. They were bolting ahead of a desperate young man on a mountain bike. In pursuit and closing fast were three squad cars, sirens blaring, rooflights blinking in the bright sunlight.

Suddenly the youth bucked the bike and doubled back toward the main road. The pursuing squad cars skidded on the soft grass and the cyclist gained precious seconds. Still paced by the frantic horses, he was now traveling so fast his feet were just a blur on the pedals. The traffic along the main road was brisk enough, with cars traveling in both directions on or just above the speed limit. The youth hesitated just long enough to judge an infinitesimal gap between a car and a truck traveling in opposite directions, and shot across between them, reaching the other side of the road before either had a chance to brake.

The police drivers, seeing their quarry speeding downhill across a stretch of reclaimed land which led steeply to the Tolka river and Dublin industrial estate on the opposite bank, screamed to the roadway, which curved toward a bridge half a mile away. A Gárda motorcyclist, lights and siren blasting, now joined the chase.

Sky could not believe her luck.

When she got back to Traynor, five minutes before her hour was up, he had good news. "I was honest. I told the Taoiseach I wanted to be there too, and about your promise to get me to Montana. He knows how much I've wanted to go there all these years. I've to keep an eye on you. But the deal is you're not to tell a single other reporter, all right?"

She felt like dancing. "Oh, Mr. Traynor, I could kiss you."

He chuckled again. "Is that another promise? Just get me to Glacier. That'll be plenty."

As soon as she hung up she called Jimbo but his response deflated her. "All right, it's a scoop of sorts, I suppose," he acknowledged grudgingly, "but come on, Sky, the British Royal Family? Who cares?"

"This will be a *world exclusive*, Jim. You'll find our readers care. You'll be able to syndicate it."

"I suppose so." He was still reluctant. "Now what about the real story? Are you any closer?"

"Oh, sorry, I've run out of money, I'll call you back." Sky was so angry she cut him off even though the visual display still showed twenty-three units left on her card.

The windy acreage of Baldonnel aerodrome was not Fergus Lynskey's favorite location. He was uneasy that Jerry Flynn was in town and wished he was nearer the city—in Government Buildings or Áras an Uachtaráin, the Irish President's residence in the Phoenix Park.

The airfield bristled with security. All roads leading to it were closed off and the fields around were being patrolled by the Ranger unit of the Irish army—a highly trained response unit; a convoy of army helicopters was lined up on the tarmac, ready for the transfer to the park. That was another thing: Lynskey hated traveling in helicopters, hated their weightless, stomach-dropping maneuverability. Some private, low-key visitation this was. Again he scanned the crowded apron: although there was no honor guard or color party, there had to be nearly fifty people there, from the British ambassador to the Ministers for Justice and Defense, civil servants, a few supposed close associates of the Prince and a contingent of army and police brass with more stars and stripes on their uniforms than the American flag.

"Excuse me a minute," he said, to no one in particular, and moved away a little to a spot where he would have space to call into Headquarters.

To say that the chief superintendent was hassled was the understatement of the millennium. Every short-staffed police station in the city was filled to the gills with rogues and thieves. One lot, the chief said, had even employed a Kalashnikov in an attempted supermarket robbery. "That's all we need, the IRA."

"Did you say attempted?" Lynskey covered his free ear with his hand as a burst of raucous laughter erupted near him. "Did you recover the gun?"

"Yeah. It's with Technical now but won't do anything with it until next week."

"Here we go, gentlemen." The Gárda Commissioner and a chief superintendent from a division other than Lynskey's were standing nearby. Lynskey looked to the eastern sky: he could see the landing lights of the RAF plane. "I've got to go. I'll call in again when I get to the park."

"Let's try one more time. Where'd you get the gun?" The detective sergeant tried to intimidate his captive with sheer bulk. The youth, who looked as though he could do with a decent meal, stared up at a spot at the wall behind the detective's head. After the chase he had been found hiding in a car parked in one of the factory lots on the industrial estate. "You uncle's in bad shape, son." The other policeman tried a more confidential approach. "It's all over. Why don't you tell us? You never know, if you do, it might even go a bit easier on you in court. 'He gave us full cooperation, Judge,' you know how it goes."

The youth interrupted his contemplation of the wall and darted a look at his interrogators. "Look, can I have a cigarette?"

"Here you are." The sergeant shook one out of a packet of Benson and Hedges and passed it over. The youth took a deep drag and exhaled, filling the small interview room with fumes. Neither detective blinked.

He told them then where he and his uncle had hired the guns.

At about that time, a Gárda officer from the severely under-resourced Technical Branch had just labeled the AK-47, wrapped it in a plastic bag, and was putting it away in the strongroom at the Gárda depot in the Phoenix Park. "That's funny." He looked at the metal shelving, then back at the package in his hand.

He went to check records.

Chapter Forty-three

The tension in the museum had quickened. The unfortunate door attendant had so far had to deal with two disappointed parties of schoolchildren—and their teachers—who had booked a tour, as well as several academics and irate tourists who, brandishing information leaflets and printed guides showing the opening times, had demanded to go in.

Sitting with Rory Traynor and the director in the latter's office, Sky mentally reviewed her options. She was going to get something interesting, even if it had to be a bottom-line, first person, "How I Talked My Way Into Seeing The Prince" piece, which was not the *Courier's* style. Better that than nothing—she was already winning.

She quailed, however, at the task of pulling everything together for her mainpiece: leaving the Prince aside, an article spanning drugs and guns and conspiracies linking Montana and Ireland was not going to be easy to encapsulate. She would probably need a *New Yorker* word count.

At least it was happening quite fast, so she would not be costing the *Courier's* skinflint proprietor too much of a bundle. "Not long now, eh?" The director had gone home at lunchtime to change and had returned dressed up like a haberdasher's window. They had been told to expect the Prince at three o'clock.

"Alone and palely loitering . . ."

"What?" Rupert de Burgh spun as though on ice skates.

"Relax, de Burgh." Lynskey looked at the Englishman with surprise. "I was being ironic." He surveyed the ranks of Gárda and army outriders lined up outside the President's residence. "I think this is a hoot, to tell you the truth. Here we are with a so-called anonymous visitor, who's supposed to remain that way, about to scream through the city with all the traffic lights turned off, the whole shootin' gallery. Sure half the press corps'll be after us before we hit Parkgate Street."

To save himself the necessity of replying, de Burgh walked over to the car he and Lynskey were to share in the motorcade. He was aware that he was betraying how tightly strung were his nerves. As he reached for the radio handset, he forced himself to breathe deeply. Only another quarter of an hour or so . . .

Behind him he heard a shuffling on the gravel as approximately six dozen booted feet got ready to mount their bikes. He replaced the handset without using it and straightened up to look toward the door where the Irish President was coming out alongside her guest. Instead, he encountered the puzzled eyes of Fergus Lynskey.

The organizers of the Amnesty conference, due to start at five o'clock to facilitate the nine fifteen start of the *The Late Late Show*, whose only guest would be Kebele, were in a tizzy. Their chickens had come home to roost with a vengeance, not least because it was now widely known that a mystery guest had been flown into Baldonnel in the presence of the British Ambassador and had been helicoptered to Éras an Uachtaráin in the Phoenix Park. It was also known that half the motorcycle policemen in the city had been diverted to traffic duty. It did not take much of a leap of imagination to know who was in town.

And it was not only the newshounds who knew: the efficient, village-style grapevine in Dublin had ensured that a respectably-sized crowd was already present outside the concert hall. "I hope they're not going to blame me for this." Jill Tuffy looked with satisfaction at the film crews scrabbling for ladders and stools and tripping each other with lead wires and cables. "I told no one."

"It doesn't matter now how it got out." Her colleague glanced sidelong at her. "I only hope our other guests aren't going to feel left out."

"Nonsense." The woman checked a list on her clipboard. "This conference is going to be the lead this evening on every bulletin in Europe. The world, in fact. What time is it now? I want to listen to the three o'clock headlines."

Toby de Burgh was sweating. The three telephone booths from which he was making his calls were in close proximity to one another near Leicester Square but he had to walk fast if he was to complete his task in the six minutes his brother had allowed.

Two down.

He had called the Dublin radio stations, using the recognized code word given to him by his brother. To the first, he had called in a bomb warning in McDonald's O'Connell Street, to the second, McDonald's of Grafton Street.

Now, he moved as fast as he dared without breaking into a run, glancing fearfully over his shoulder as though people could read his mind. The sweat was stinging his eyes and, under his loose-fitting silk shirt, he could feel uncomfortably cold streamlets running from his armpits to his waist. It was one of those intensely hot London days when the air seemed thick as lint, when taxi drivers, resigned to the stifling traffic jams, hold conversations with one another through their open windows. "Christ, Rupe," he mouthed as he side-stepped around one of these conversations, "why did I agree to this . . ." Then he looked over his shoulder again, afraid someone might have heard him.

He reached the third booth, one of a row of four at the top of an alleyway.

Inserted two pounds coins. They dropped.

The third radio station on his list, RTE, did not answer until the fourteenth ring and his heart felt as though it was exploding by the time he gave his message. This one located the bomb at Bewley's of George Street.

All three restaurants were located in busy areas. All three were crammed to the doors and evacuation would be difficult.

Task completed, the adrenaline drained away like a falling tide and Toby felt so weak he thought he might faint. He looked at his watch. Right on the button. Ten minutes to three.

At ten minutes to three, a hunched old man wearing a woollen cap, gloves, and a scarf wound so tightly around his neck that it covered part of his chin, in spite of the glorious sunshine, got into a taxi beside the central bus station. He carried no luggage, yet he asked the driver to take him to the airport. "Do you take credit cards?" When told this was out of the question, he reached into his pocket and took out a fifty-dollar bill. "I always keep this for emergencies."

"I can't change it. I'm not a foreign exchange bureau."
The driver looked at him through his rearview mirror.

"It doesn't matter." The old man hunched deeper into his
scarf. "Would fifty dollars cover the fare to the airport?"

"I suppose so." The driver shrugged and drove off.

Flynn relaxed a little. He would have moved earlier but,
fearful of discovery, had spent more than an hour sitting in
his room trying to second-guess his decision to abandon the
operation. But the more time ticked by, the more he saw that
he was trapped. Each minute increased the chances of his
being found. It was not only the unfortunate incident with
the guns, he was sure that that reporter girl from the rodeo
had recognized him.

If only he could have reached de Burgh: he had telephoned
twice, but each time his office had said he was out. By the
third call, Flynn had left a message: John Mulqueen and his
friend had been urgently called away and would be in touch.
It was the best he could manage under the circumstances.

The cab driver cursed the traffic in which he was stalled at
the junction of Gardiner Street and the North Circular Road
but Flynn cheered up somewhat: just because *this* adventure
had not worked out did not mean there would not be another
day. The Cause was still there, still waiting for someone to
espouse it. He heard police sirens in the distance and tensed
but they were receding. Only another hour or so and he
should be in the clear.

Joe Mason, wearing his scratched glasses, was already at the
airport, boarding a flight for Amsterdam. He had wasted no
time in introspection but had left the hotel as soon as he had
heard from Flynn what had happened to him.

Rupert de Burgh was now on his own.

In checking the records, the policeman who was logging in
the AK-47, confiscated after the supermarket robbery, had
discovered that it had been logged in before—less than a
month ago. He found no record of it having been removed.

And as he went on, he found something else peculiar:
three other guns were unaccounted for too, two pistols and a
second assault rifle.

The Gárdia had been recently successful in locating and
raiding IRA arms and ammunitions dumps in the republic,
and there were so many weapons in storage that it was not

surprising that the absence of just four had been overlooked. Especially with the resources situation as it was.

He reported the discrepancy to his superior, who immediately passed it up the line.

The Prince's entourage was coming down the North Circular Road and crossing the big junction at Dorset Street, to the complete apathy of most of the pedestrians who were used to having their thoroughfare turned into a scene from *Starsky and Hutch*. Motorists stuck in the already heavy Friday afternoon traffic, who found themselves being waved peremptorily to the side by the advance riders, were not so sanguine.

De Burgh, with Lynskey beside him, was driving one of the lead cars. Such was the racket from the outriders behind them that the latter felt, rather than heard, his mobile ring against his thigh. He drew it out of his pocket and yanked up the tiny rubber aerial. "Yes?"

All he got was static and interference. "I can't hear you, whoever you are," he yelled. "Call back in a couple of minutes. We're just coming into Mountjoy Square."

He switched the telephone to standby, looked across at de Burgh and shrugged.

Outside the concert hall, Éamonn Vaughan and the BBC reporter who had been the lucky recipient of Jill Tuffy's second telephone call the previous afternoon, were closeted in Vaughan's car. Their crews were part of the mêlée inside.

As they compared notes, a squad car, which had been passing at a sedate pace, suddenly spurted, tires spinning. Then, lights flashing and siren blaring, it squealed around the corner out of view.

"What was that?" Vaughan jumped out of the car and listened. He heard another siren join the first. "It's nearly three o'clock. Quick! Turn on the car radio!" He whipped out his personal stereo and put on his headphones.

"Oh my God!" The woman browsing through the men's raincoats in Arnott's Department store jumped back and snatched her baby from his buggy as a tongue of flame shot through a coat at the end of the rail. She screamed as she pulled the buggy after her, cannoning into a display of Viyella shirts, which collapsed as staff and customers started to run. A quick-witted trainee manager grabbed an extinguisher and

put out the small fire, but it was too late to avert chaos. The woman continued to scream, her baby, too, and a stampede began for the doors.

In Clery's, less than a quarter of a mile away, a middle-aged Texan tourist was not so lucky. Tall—he had been a basketball player in his youth—and broad now that had turned to fat, he was just reaching for a coat when the incendiary went up, catching the side of his face and setting fire to his abundant snowy hair.

It happened so fast that his wife, browsing thirty feet away, did not know anything had happened until she heard a girl scream. She turned round just in time to see someone throw a heavy wool shawl over her husband's head. One side of his face looked like a piece of grilled steak.

The information was coming in too fast: the chief superintendent put his head in his hands. The bomb scares had distracted him from a picture he saw hovering vaguely just outside his ken. He pulled a pad in front of him:

—AK-47 turns up at the supermarket robbery
—so does handgun
—handgun hired from kids who got it in mugging
—chances are AK-47 part of same mugging
—Jerry Flynn recognized by Lynskey's girlfriend. Fits
   description of mugged tourist.

He picked up his telephone: "Find out who signed in to that storeroom at the depot in the last week. I want an answer NOW." He flung the receiver back in its cradle where upon the telephone rang again.

In the museum, Sky felt absurdly like a teenager. She had tried to persuade herself she was feeling this way because she was about to get a world exclusive—but if she was honest she had to admit the excitement was prompted by the prospect of meeting a real live prince.

"What is it about royalty?"

The director reacted as though she had struck one of his own specimen pins in to him. "What do you mean?"

"Oh, it doesn't matter. Are you sure you don't want us to be in the background?" She looked at Rory Traynor who seemed as calm as though he did this kind of thing every day.

"You're fine where you are." The director glanced at his watch. "Any minute now."

As if on cue, Sky heard the bagpipe wailing of sirens.

"Jesus, he's here!" The director half ran toward the door and then back to the place he had allocated himself.

"Relax, Declan." Oddly his agitation calmed Sky. "It'll all be over in three or four minutes."

"He'd better stay longer than that. After all we've been through . . ."

"Who?" The chief superintendent rose in his seat. "Quickly! Are you sure he was the only one not actually working there?"

Whatever the person at the other end said caused him to drop the telephone and race out of the room. He was punching at his mobile as he ran toward the general office. "Lynskey," he hissed urgently into the mouthpiece, "are you alone?"

"No, chief," Lynskey pulled a face, "as you can hear we're surrounded by the third army. We're just pulling up now outside the museum." The outriders came alongside and the rest of what the chief had to say was drowned in the thunder of motorcycle engines. "What, chief?" Lynskey got out of the car as, behind him, the Prince and his entourage, to the heart-stopping amazement of the rapidly growing crowd, got out of theirs. All he could hear now was static. The chief was no longer on the line.

Rupert de Burgh looked toward where Jerry Flynn should have been. He was to have hijacked a bus and its passengers from outside Trinity College and have it at the intersection of Merrion Street and Merrion Square just before the Prince's party arrived and then driven it straight toward Government Buildings to distract the police from what he was about to do. But as he followed Lynskey toward the Prince's party, his heart pounded. There was no sign of any bus.

He saw that the Prince, instead of walking straight through the iron gate that led into the museum, had stopped just outside to shake hands and chat with Dublin citizens and thrilled tourists who were being corralled by a phalanx of policemen.

"He's got a gun." Improvising wildly de Burgh ran after Lynskey and caught him by the sleeve.

"Who's got a gun?" Lynskey wheeled.

"That man over there!" He pointed up the street toward where an unkempt youth, curious about the commotion, was running toward them.

The mobile telephone in Lynskey's hand shrilled again. "What?" he yelled into it, while keeping an eye on the fast approaching boy. He could see no gun.

More crackle, then, distinctly: "Don't let de Burgh near the Prince." The voice in his ear was low and commanding. "He's our canary."

The Prince and his bodyguards were now through the gate and walking up the path. Lynskey saw that de Burgh was now right behind them and closing fast. The youth indicated by de Burgh, he knew now, was harmless. He started to run through the crowd.

He got to de Burgh just as the policeman reached the Prince and his group. They were only feet from the door now and the welcoming party which included—to Lynskey's horror—Sky MacPherson. Then he saw de Burgh's hand snake into his pocket.

Lynskey launched a flying tackle through the bodyguards, connecting with his colleague's back and knocking him off balance just as the Semtex erupted through the building. The bodyguards wrestled the Prince aside to safety but the momentum of Lynskey's tackle carried him and de Burgh through the doorway into the dust and debris flying through the gallery. Lynskey caught a brief glimpse of Sky's startled face before he and his colleague fell to the tiled floor.

De Burgh's plan had been to shove the Prince into the museum ahead of him as the bomb exploded and to slam and lock both the heavy outer door and the inner. He would have about five minutes in which to force the Prince to sign a statement apologizing for British atrocities before he shot him. Just as his paratroopers had gunned down thirteen innocent civilians in Derry.

Instead, he found himself fighting for his own life.

Twenty years of planning and patient waiting all gone for nothing.

But twenty years of suppressed fury lent de Burgh a sudden spurt of strength and determination. He gouged at

Lynskey's eyes and as his colleague instinctively arched his back, threw him off.

Lynskey spun through the inner doorway, giving de Burgh time to spring to his feet and bolt the outer door. In the split second before Lynskey came at him, he raised his gun.

Slowly, Lynskey lowered his gun and backed inside.

With a flick of his shoulder De Burgh closed the inner door.

Chapter Forty-four

Everything had happened so fast that Sky did not even have a chance to scream. One moment she had been standing on tiptoe to see over the museum director's shoulder as the Prince approached, the next there had been a huge explosion, which had blown Lynskey and another man into the museum. The neon lights overhead had gone out and half of the ceiling had crashed down along with waterfalls of glass, while something huge and dark descended to fill her peripheral vision. Transfixed by the two men fighting on the floor, she was afraid to try to see what it was.

The contest had lasted only seconds and then Lynskey's assailant had leaped to the door.

She could hardly breathe: the air was choked with fur, feathers, and ancient dust. She covered her mouth and nose with one hand and dared to look over it. Through the waning hailstorm of fragments she saw the second man standing against the closed door pointing a gun at them. The huge dark object was the skeleton of the whale from the gallery overhead. Most of it dangled by the tail bones through the destroyed ceiling.

Beside her, she could hear someone moaning. The director was on his knees, blood streaming from a gash at the temple, just under his hairline. Without thinking, she moved to help him, but the gunman roared at her: "Stay where you are!"

"Let her be, de Burgh." Shoes scrunching on shards of glass, Lynskey pulled himself upright and came over to her. He, too, had a gun but it was held loosely by his side. Paradoxically, because his voice was so calm and matter-of-fact, Sky's heart lurched with fear. "She's a civilian," Lynskey said quietly, "they're all civilians here except you and me. Let them out."

"Stay where you are. *All of you, I'm warning you* . . ." The man called de Burgh bent his knees a little and pressed the small of his back harder against the door. He raised the gun, which he now held in both hands.

"How many rounds do you have, de Burgh? There're seven of us in here." Lynskey stepped in front of Sky.

"Get back behind her *and drop your gun*." His face contorted.

Lynskey extended his arm to its fullest extent and let the gun fall, theatrically, from between finger and thumb.

It occurred to Sky then that less than a minute could have passed since the door was shut. Dimly, she discerned that the attendant, the assistant director, Traynor and the other two men on the staff, were huddled together behind herself and Lynskey. Absurdly, the police ribbon taped across the door of the ladies' washroom was still intact, like a gay yellow flag. She remembered where she had seen this man before. He was the policeman who had questioned her about her ID.

Now only the director's harsh, half-sobbing breath could be heard. She did not dare look at him again. "So now what, de Burgh?" Lynskey's voice was low, almost hypnotic. "You can't kill us all, you know that. Why not just let them go? I'll stay in here with you. Just let them go. I've no gun now, even. There's no way out for you, you know that, so why not let them go?" He took a step forward.

"Stay *back*! De Burgh lifted the gun higher, aiming at Lynskey's face. "Back beside her."

"Come on." Lynskey took another step.

De Burgh lowered the gun and discharged it. Sky leaped at the intolerable level of sound in the enclosed space and at the detonation of glass just in front of Lynskey's feet. This time she screamed and so did one of the men behind her.

"Okay, okay." Lynskey raised his hands and stepped back beside her.

The director collapsed into the glass under him.

"He's hurt, he needs help."

Sky's yell unnerved the gunman: "Shut up, shut up, *shut up*!" He fired again, toward the ceiling this time, and hit the suspended whale skeleton. At such close quarters, the force of the bullet dislodged the remains and the giant cradle of bones cascaded to the floor, destroying what remained of the glass cases below it with earsplitting impact.

Sky closed her eyes and reached into her reserves of courage while the reverberations of the shot and the bursting glass continued. Beside her, the director whimpered softly.

"How many left now, de Burgh?" This was Lynskey, as the air gradually stilled.

His quiet tone seemed to calm the gunman. "All right, you three," his voice was decisive as he waved the gun at the staff members cowering behind their boss, "pick up the injured man and take him outside. You, Lynskey, step over to the wall while they're doing it." He hesitated, then: "You can go with them," pointing to Rory Traynor.

Then he motioned to Sky. "You stay here, but first pick up that gun and hand it to me."

From outside, Sky heard an amplified voice but it was too muffled for her to distinguish what it was saying. At least someone was thinking about their plight. The gun felt like ice as she picked it up and, holding it in front of her like a votive offering, she walked across the strewn no-man's-land to give it to the gunman.

He took it almost casually and placed it in his belt under his open jacket; he seemed to be regaining confidence with every second. "Now," he said to her, "you stay here beside me. You three, pick up that injured man now and take him out. If there's any funny stuff while the door's open, I'm going to shoot this girl. And please don't think I'm not serious. I've nothing to lose."

"Let her go too, de Burgh." It was Lynskey again, from his position by the wall. "Why are you involving her?"

"For the last time, Lynskey, will you shut up? I've been listening to your blather now for more years than I care to remember."

The three frightened men shuffled over to their director and picked him up, two at his shoulders, one at his feet. Blood had soaked into both sides of his shirt collar before spreading to the rest of his clothes and Sky had to avert her eyes: in the dim light, his mouth open and head dangling as though half-severed, he looked as though his throat had been cut.

"Now, here's what you're going to do." The gunman's voice was right beside her ear. "I'm going to open the door a little and you're going to appear in it. Not one step outside, understand? You're going to tell whoever's out there that an injured man is coming out. That's all. Then you're to step back inside. I'm going to be three inches behind you with a gun pointed at your head. Is that clear?"

"Yes." From some reservoir she had not known she possessed, Sky found the courage to speak.

The gunman stepped sideways so he could cover not only her, but Lynskey at the far wall. He opened the inner door slowly and she felt his hand at her back, pushing her forward.

Slowly, with his back to the outer door, he reached up and pulled back the bolt. A crack of daylight appeared.

Then she could see, only feet away but to both sides of the door, several policemen all with guns drawn. About fifty feet away was a statue on a large stone plinth. Behind it were more policemen, and outside the railings she could see about twenty police cars. The man with the megaphone was in plain clothes, standing by the gate.

As the door opened wider, a number of policemen dropped to their knees and took aim. Birds sang in the branches of nearby trees as if nothing had happened, but everyone outside was as frozen as the bronze statue on the plinth.

She felt the pressure of the gunman's hand on her back. "Excuse me," she said, "there's an injured man coming out." The hand in her back pressed harder and, although for one blazing moment she considered making a dash for it, she backed through the opening. Just before the outside world vanished from her view she saw Éamonn Vaughan arrive at the railings.

In the museum again, she was ordered to stand beside Lynskey while the three men, followed by Rory Traynor, left with their burden. Then de Burgh closed the door and she was with him and Lynskey. She pressed close against Lynskey for reassurance and was conscious of something, a piece of paper, being crushed into her hand. "Stand away from each other." De Burgh waved the gun to emphasize his point.

"Now what?" As he stepped away from her, Lynskey was again speaking in that calm, mesmeric way. "There's no way out."

"Oh, yes, there is." De Burgh smiled, "I'm not stupid enough to think that it'll all work out happily ever after but at least I'm going to make my point."

"What is your point?" Searching her palm with her curled fingers, she was now sure that Lynskey had passed a note.

"You're not going to catch me as easily as that—" de Burgh began, when Lynskey's telephone rang.

De Burgh reacted to the shrilling as though shot by his own gun. "Turn that thing *off*!"

"You're very jumpy." Lynskey disabled the telephone and then, still holding it, leaned against the wall, crossing one foot over the other. "Look, de Burgh, all your friends are rounded up, every last blessed one of them. There is nothing you can do by yourself. You know it, I know it, so why are we all wasting our time?"

Outside, the muffled instructions, or whatever they were, continued unabated.

While keeping her eyes fixed on the gunman, Sky was surreptitiously unravelling the balled note with her bent thumb and little finger. She was sure it contained instructions and, when the opportunity arose, she wanted to be able to read it at a glance. Her concentration on such a small, but vital task, as well as Lynskey's close, warm proximity and calm demeanor, gave her some small assurance.

The world had shrunk to the dimensions of this murky room; and somehow it felt appropriate that the setting for such a bizarre act was in itself so fantastic: the gigantic whale pancaked like collapsed scaffolding on the floor, half of an antler at the gunman's foot, and beside her own, the small glass eye which stared at her from a nest of dust.

"All right." De Burgh had recovered his composure. "She's staying in here with me. Lynskey, you go outside and tell them that I want to see the Commissioner. In here. Unarmed and alone."

"You're the boss." Lynskey started to move forward.

"Slowly, hands above your head where I can see them." De Burgh raised his gun, covering every inch of the other policeman's movement.

Slowly, step by step, hands above his head—Sky noticed he still held the telephone—Lynskey advanced toward the door.

De Burgh never took his eyes off him. As Lynskey got closer, he circled away, always keeping a distance of about six feet between them. Lynskey was almost at the door now, was reaching out to open it—

Sky screamed at the top of her lungs. De Burgh glanced toward her. Lynskey hurled the telephone into his adversary's face while unleashing a flying, two-footed tackle at the gun, which dropped to the floor and discharged, the bullet passing harmlessly through the frame of the men's washroom. Then he leapt on De Burgh in an assault so quick and professional that the gunman did not have a chance. He was brought down and flipped on to his stomach. Lynskey twisted his colleague's gun arm up behind his back while retrieving his own weapon from the waistband underneath.

The door crashed open from outside and dozens of armed men poured through it.

It was dark but not quite night and, for several seconds, Sky had no idea where she was. Then she heard Lynskey's deep, even breathing beside her in the narrow bed. To judge by the quality of the light, they must have slept for hours.

She lay quietly, listening to the sounds of the city below. The events of the afternoon seemed like a dream. After the rescue, she had refused to go to the hospital, or even to see a doctor, although she was familiar enough with psychobabble to expect some sort of physical or mental reaction to what had happened. At present, however, she felt nothing but a numbed peace.

In the immediate aftermath of the event she had insisted on filing verbatim copy immediately from the nearest telephone, which proved to be in the museum director's office. It was odd to do so in the presence of Lynskey, another policeman and Éamonn Vaughan, to whom she had honored her promise. She had even been composed enough to give him a short interview on camera outside the museum. And to accept Jimbo's handsome apology for his earlier cynicism.

Then, she and Lynskey had come to his apartment directly from the museum: for once, he had been excused the briefing—or debriefing or whatever it was he normally had to do.

At first she had been reluctant to accompany him, feeling she would be better to go back to her own hotel, have a shower and make the necessary telephone calls. But, even as she was insisting, she was overtaken by lamb-like languor, which allowed Lynskey to persuade her to go with him. Once inside his apartment he had undressed her, quickly and efficiently, given her one of his shirts to wear as a nightdress and ordered her to bed. She had fallen asleep—within seconds, it seemed.

By what little available light there was, she saw that his tiny apartment was spartan. Apart from the bed, the room had a narrow floor-to-ceiling closet, a chest, which appeared to serve as a dressing table, one chair, on which her clothes had been neatly folded, and a single nightstand on her side of the bed, with a lamp, a telephone and an old-fashioned alarm clock with two bright silvery bells.

She realized that her hand ached and discovered that it was clenched into a fist and that she could not relax it. Lynskey's note remained speared between her fingernails and her palm, welded there when she had screamed to divert de Burgh's attention. Was this the reaction she had been expecting? Did she now have a paralysed hand?

"Are you awake?" He did not move.

"Yes."

"Would you like a cup of tea—sorry, coffee?"

"Sure." She wondered why they were whispering.

Behind her, she felt him slide out of bed and heard him pad toward the door. She eased a little into the warm space he had left.

"Will I put on the light?" He was back after five minutes or so, carrying two mugs.

"No, it's nice like this." She pushed her pillow up against the bedhead and leaned against it. He held out one of the mugs to her but as she tried to take it, she realized again that she could not open her hand.

"What's the matter with your hand, Sky?" He put down both mugs on the floor and got in beside her. "Show me." She let him take it and, after a brief examination, he leaned across her and switched on the bedside light. "It's bleeding. Sky, what happened?"

"I don't know. I can't open it—your note's in there."

He enclosed her hand in both of his and started to massage the inside of her wrist, just above the palm. Little by little, she sensed warmth, first in the heel, then creeping up her thumb. It was only when her nails finally unbedded that she felt the sting of the four small crescents of dried blood, like sickle moons, which lay along the center of the palm. The note was crushed and stained beyond legibility. "Don't worry about it." Gently, Lynskey prised it off.

"What did it say?

"It was nothing, forget it. Try to forget everything about this afternoon."

"I still have to write the piece. What I filed on the telephone was just a holding story."

"Yeah. How could I have been so silly?" He grinned. "Now do you want your coffee?"

They lay back together on their pillows. "Please tell me what was in the note, Fergus." Sky stared straight up at the ceiling.

She heard the smallest of hesitations, like a sigh on the intake, then: "The note would have said I love you."

"Would have?"

"Yeah, it was just a piece of paper. I thought it would distract you."

He loved her. Sky experienced no feeling of surprise, elation, or, for the first time when faced with this declaration, any panic or fear. "I think I love you too."

"You only think?" Another hesitation. Then he raised himself on an elbow.

"It doesn't come easy to me, you know."

He smiled, closed his eyes and lay back again, which was exactly the correct reaction. If he had pressed her she might have fled. The acknowledgment was fragile. The warm air of the room crept around the narrow bed and cocooned it in a shared intimacy such as she had experienced only once or twice in her life, and not for years.

She had nearly finished her coffee when the practical problems of a relationship with Lynskey rose to the surface of her sluggish brain. They might yet prove insurmountable.

"I love you, Sky." He turned his head toward her, pulled back a little so their eyes could focus on one another.

Sky smiled at his certainty. She could feel the smile beginning at the soles of her feet and traveling up the length of her body until it reached her face, and she thought she could never, ever wipe it away. "Would it be all right if I called the hospital?" She did not yet want to discuss the reasons for the smile. "I don't want Mom to see me on the early evening news."

"Go ahead." He smiled too, resumed his contemplation of the ceiling.

When she got through to Johanna, her grandmother was there, and Hermana, "and Buffy's coming in too for a spell. It's a real sorority dorm now, Sky, we're having a ball." As soon as Sky began to prepare her for what she might see on the TV, however, she was immediately disabused of the notion that this was news. "Fergus told us all about it.

You're a heroine, Sky, we're really, really proud of you, all of us."

As she heard the round robin of approval in the background, Sky looked over at Lynskey, who was calmly sipping his tea. "When did he call you?"

"Oh, ages ago, he's very proud of you too, Sky. You give him a big hug from all of us."

"When's Daniel Treacy's wake?" Sky thought it safer to change the subject. She had lost track of the days.

"Em . . ." her mother grew shifty.

"What's the matter, Mom? Is it over? Did something happen I should know about?"

"Look, Sky, your grandma would like to talk to you."

Sky heard whispering and, after a short pause, her grandmother was on the line. "What's all this about, Grandma?"

"Please don't take this amiss, Sky. We're just thinking about it and no decisions will be taken without your say-so. But your mother and I—that is all of us here, Buffy and Hermana too—had a thought. We were wondering how you would feel about all of us, not immediately, of course, for obvious reasons, temporarily taking on the care of Daniel's wife?"

The telephone was seized back before Sky could collect her wits. "What do you think, Sky?" Johanna's voice was as fresh as though she had been out picking daisies instead of cemented into a body cast in a hospital. "Sort of as a project. As your grandma says, not immediately, what with me in the hospital and poor Midge too. And you don't have to be involved, Sky. She has enough money coming to her that she could buy half of Butte. And your grandma says the house up in the foothills is lovely. Plenty of space up there—we can hire nurses until she gets on her feet again. But she has no one now, Sky. Only money. We'd all help. Freda Little Calf has a lot of experience in dealing with alcohol problems, you know she has—"

"Whoa, whoa, Mom." For Sky it was like turning back the clock. Nothing had happened in the last three weeks, no Lynskey, no Ireland, no guns or bullets or fantastical situations. She was back to square one with her mother.

And yet, suddenly, it was different. Suddenly she saw a gate opening on to a huge green field: she need not engage. "I think it's a great idea."

The astonished silence at the other end of the telephone

bore testimony to what had occurred between them. "Are you still there? Mom?"

"Are you sure you don't mind?"

"Why should I mind? Is Grandma going to stay there and help you?"

"No," her mother chuckled, "of course not, her life is in Ireland. But she'll stay long enough until we get the project up and running."

"You're amazing, Mom, do you know that? And I love you very, very much."

She hung up abruptly. It was then that the tears came. And came.

Lynskey held her.